Also by ADAM JOHNSON

EMPORIUM

PARASITES LIKE US

THE ORPHAN MASTER'S SON

RANDOM HOUSE | NEW YORK

THE

ORPHAN MASTER'S SON

A NOVEL

ADAM JOHNSON

Published in the United States by Random House,
an imprint of The Random House Publishing Group,
a division of Random House, Inc., New York.

RANDOM HOUSE and colophon are registered
trademarks of Random House, Inc.

LIBRARY OF CONGRESS CATALOGING-IN-PUBLICATION DATA
Johnson, Adam.
The orphan master's son : a novel / Adam Johnson.
p. cm.
ISBN 978-0-8129-9279-3
eBook ISBN 978-0-679-64399-9
1. Korea (North)—Fiction. I. Title.
PS3610.O3O76 2011
813'.6—dc22   2011013410

Printed in the United States of America on acid-free paper

www.atrandom.com

9 8 7 6 5

Book design by Barbara M. Bachman

FOR STEPHANIE—

my sun,

my moon,

my star and

satellite

CONTENTS

THE ORPHAN MASTER'S SON

CITIZENS, gather 'round your loudspeakers, for we bring important updates! In your kitchens, in your offices, on your factory floors—wherever your loudspeaker is located, turn up the volume!

In local news, our Dear Leader Kim Jong Il was seen offering on-the-spot guidance to the engineers deepening the Taedong River channel. While the Dear Leader lectured to the dredge operators, many doves were seen to spontaneously flock above him, hovering to provide our Reverend General some much needed shade on a hot day. Also to report is a request from Pyongyang's Minister of Public Safety, who asks that while pigeon-snaring season is in full swing, trip wires and snatch loops be placed out of the reach of our youngest comrades. And don't forget, citizens: the ban on stargazing is still in effect.

Later in the broadcast, we'll reveal the winning recipe for this month's cooking contest. Hundreds of recipes were entered, but only one can be declared the best way to prepare—Pumpkin Rind Soup! But first comes grave news from the East Sea, where American aggressors flirt with acts of all-out war after stopping and looting a North Korean fishing vessel. Once again, the Yankees have violated Korean waters to steal the precious contents of a sovereign ship, all the while accusing us of everything from banditry to kidnapping to cruelty to sharks. First off, it is the Americans and their puppets who are the pirates of the sea. Secondly, did an American woman not recently row around the entire world to defect to our great nation, a worker's paradise where citizens want for nothing? That alone should be proof enough that these persistent accusations of kidnapping are ludicrous.

But *cruelty to sharks*? This charge must be addressed. Known as the fisherman's friend, the shark has an ancient camaraderie with the Korean people. In the year 1592, did sharks not offer fish from their own mouths to help sustain Admiral Yi's sailors during the siege of Okpo Harbor? Have sharks not developed cancer-preventing powers in order to help their human friends live longer and healthier? Does our own Commander Ga, winner of the Golden Belt, not have a soothing bowl of shark-fin soup before each triumphant taekwondo match? And citizens, did you not see with your own eyes a movie entitled *A True Daughter of the Country,* right here in Pyongyang's own Moranbong Theater? Then certainly you remember the scene in which our national actress Sun Moon capsized in Inchon Bay while trying to prevent the American sneak attack. It was a scary moment for all of us as the sharks began to circle her, helpless amid the waves. But did the sharks not recognize Sun Moon's Korean modesty? Did they not smell the hot blood of her patriotism and lift her upon their fins to carry her safely to shore, where she could join the raging battle to repel the imperialist invaders?

By these deeds alone, citizens, you must know that the rumors swirling around Pyongyang—that Commander Ga and Sun Moon are anything less than utterly in love—are baseless lies! Baseless as the boarding of our innocent fishing vessels by foreign powers, baseless as the outlandish allegations of kidnapping leveled at us by the Japanese. Do the Japanese think we forget it is *they* who once enslaved our husbands and made comfort women of our wives? *Baseless* to think that any woman loves her husband more than Sun Moon. Did the citizens not behold how Sun Moon bestowed the Golden Belt upon her new husband, her cheeks flushed with modesty and love? Were you not assembled in Kim Il Sung Square to witness it firsthand?

What are you going to believe, citizens? Rumors and lies, or your very own eyes?

But let us return to the rest of today's programming, which includes a rebroadcast of Kim Il Sung's glorious speech of April Fifteenth, Juche 71, and a public-service announcement from the Minister of Procurement Comrade Buc on the topic of prolonging the life of compact fluorescent lightbulbs. But first, citizens, a treat: it is our pleasure to announce that Pyongyang has a new opera singer. The Dear Leader has dubbed her the Lovely Visitor. And here she is, to sing for your patriotic pleasure the arias from *Sea of Blood.* So return to your industrial lathes and vinalon looms, citizens, and double your output quotas as you listen to this Lovely Visitor sing the story of the greatest nation in the world, the Democratic People's Republic of Korea!

PART ONE

THE BIOGRAPHY OF JUN DO

JUN DO'S mother was a singer. That was all Jun Do's father, the Orphan Master, would say about her. The Orphan Master kept a photograph of a woman in his small room at Long Tomorrows. She was quite lovely—eyes large and sideways looking, lips pursed with an unspoken word. Since beautiful women in the provinces get shipped to Pyongyang, that's certainly what had happened to his mother. The real proof of this was the Orphan Master himself. At night, he'd drink, and from the barracks, the orphans would hear him weeping and lamenting, striking half-heard bargains with the woman in the photograph. Only Jun Do was allowed to comfort him, to finally take the bottle from his hands.

As the oldest boy at Long Tomorrows, Jun Do had responsibilities—portioning the food, assigning bunks, renaming the new boys from the list of the 114 Grand Martyrs of the Revolution. Even so, the Orphan Master was serious about showing no favoritism to his son, the only boy at Long Tomorrows who wasn't an orphan. When the rabbit warren was dirty, it was Jun Do who spent the night locked in it. When boys wet their bunks, it was Jun Do who chipped the frozen piss off the floor. Jun Do didn't brag to the other boys that he was the son of the Orphan Master, rather than some kid dropped off by parents on their way to a 9-27 camp. If someone wanted to figure it out, it was pretty obvious—Jun Do had been there before all of them, and the reason he'd never been adopted was because his father would never let someone take his only son. And it made sense that after his mother was stolen to Pyongyang, his father had applied for the one position that would allow him to both earn a living and watch over his son.

The surest evidence that the woman in the photo was Jun Do's mother was the unrelenting way the Orphan Master singled him out for punishment. It could only mean that in Jun Do's face, the Orphan Master saw the woman in the picture, a daily reminder of the eternal hurt he felt from losing her. Only a father in that kind of pain could take a boy's shoes in winter. Only a true father, flesh and bone, could burn a son with the smoking end of a coal shovel.

Occasionally, a factory would adopt a group of kids, and in the spring, men with Chinese accents would come to make their picks. Other than that, anyone who could feed the boys and provide a bottle for the Orphan Master could have them for the day. In summer they filled sandbags and in winter they used metal bars to break sheets of ice from the docks. On the machining floors, for bowls of cold *chap chai,* they would shovel the coils of oily metal that sprayed from the industrial lathes. The railyard fed them best, though, spicy *yukejang.* One time, shoveling out boxcars, they swept up a powder that looked like salt. It wasn't until they started sweating that they turned red, their hands and faces, their teeth. The train had been filled with chemicals for the paint factory. For weeks, they were red.

And then in the year Juche 85, the floods came. Three weeks of rain, yet the loudspeakers said nothing of terraces collapsing, earth dams giving, villages cascading into one another. The Army was busy trying to save the Sungli 58 factory from the rising water, so the Long Tomorrows boys were given ropes and long-handled gaffs to try to snare people from the Chongjin River before they were washed into the harbor. The water was a roil of timber, petroleum tanks, and latrine barrels. A tractor tire turned in the water, a Soviet refrigerator. They heard the deep booms of boxcars tumbling along the river bottom. The canopy of a troop carrier spun past, a screaming family clinging to it. Then a young woman rose from the water, mouth wide but silent, and the orphan called Bo Song gaffed her arm—right away he was jerked into the current. Bo Song had come to the orphanage a frail boy, and when they discovered he had no hearing, Jun Do gave him the name Un Bo Song, after the 37th Martyr of the Revolution, who'd famously put mud in his ears so he couldn't hear the bullets as he charged the Japanese.

Still, the boys shouted "Bo Song, Bo Song" as they ran the riverbanks, racing beside the patch of river where Bo Song should have been. They ran past the outfall pipes of the Unification Steelworks and along the muddy berms of the Ryongsong's leach ponds, but Bo Song was never seen again. The boys stopped at the harbor, its dark waters ropy with corpses, thousands of them in the throes of the waves, looking like curds of sticky millet that start to flop and toss when the pan heats.

Though they didn't know it, this was the beginning of the famine—first went the power, then the train service. When the shock-work whistles stopped blowing, Jun Do knew it was bad. One day the fishing fleet went out and didn't come back. With winter came blackfinger and the old people went to sleep. These were just the first months, long before the bark-eaters. The loudspeakers called the famine an Arduous March, but that voice was piped in from Pyongyang. Jun Do had never heard anyone in Chongjin call it that. What was happening to them didn't need a name—it was everything, every fingernail you chewed and swallowed, every lift of an eyelid, every trip to the latrine where you tried to shit out wads of balled sawdust. When all hope was gone, the Orphan Master burned the bunks, the boys sleeping around a pot stove that glowed on their last night. In the morning, he flagged down a Soviet Tsir, the military truck they called "the crow" because of its black canvas canopy on the back. There were only a dozen boys left, a perfect fit in the back of the crow. All orphans are destined for the Army eventually. But this was how Jun Do, at fourteen, became a tunnel soldier, trained in the art of zero-light combat.

And that's where Officer So found him, eight years later. The old man actually came underground to get a look at Jun Do, who'd spent an overnighter with his team inside a tunnel that went ten kilometers under the DMZ, almost to the suburbs of Seoul. When exiting a tunnel, they'd always walk out backward, to let their eyes adjust, and he almost ran into Officer So, whose shoulders and big rib cage spoke of a person who'd come of age in the good times, before the Chollima campaigns.

"Are you Pak Jun Do?" he asked.

When Jun Do turned, a circle of light glowed behind the man's close-cropped white hair. The skin on his face was darker than his scalp or jaw, making it look like the man had just shaved off a beard and thick, wild hair. "That's me," Jun Do said.

"That's a Martyr's name," Officer So said. "Is this an orphan detail?"

Jun Do nodded his head. "It is," he said. "But I'm not an orphan."

Officer So's eyes fell upon the red taekwondo badge on Jun Do's chest.

"Fair enough," Officer So said and tossed him a sack.

In it were blue jeans, a yellow shirt with a polo pony, and shoes called Nikes that Jun Do recognized from long ago, when the orphanage was used to welcome ferry-loads of Koreans who had been lured back from

Japan with promises of Party jobs and apartments in Pyongyang. The orphans would wave welcome banners and sing Party songs so that the Japanese Koreans would descend the gangway, despite the horrible state of Chongjin and the crows that were waiting to transport them all to *kwan li so* labor camps. It was like yesterday, watching those perfect boys with their new sneakers, finally coming home.

Jun Do held up the yellow shirt. "What am I supposed to do with this?" he asked.

"It's your new uniform," Officer So said. "You don't get seasick, do you?"

*

He didn't. They took a train to the eastern port of Cholhwang, where Officer So commandeered a fishing boat, the crew so frightened of their military guests that they wore their Kim Il Sung pins all the way across the sea to the coast of Japan. Upon the water, Jun Do saw small fish with wings and late morning fog so thick it took the words from your mouth. There were no loudspeakers blaring all day, and all the fishermen had portraits of their wives tattooed on their chests. The sea was spontaneous in a way he'd never seen before—it kept your body uncertain as to how you'd lean next, and yet you could become comfortable with that. The wind in the rigging seemed in communication with the waves shouldering the hull, and lying atop the wheelhouse under the stars at night, it seemed to Jun Do that this was a place a man could close his eyes and exhale.

Officer So had also brought along a man named Gil as their translator. Gil read Japanese novels on the deck and listened to headphones attached to a small cassette player. Only once did Jun Do try to speak to Gil, approaching him to ask what he was listening to. But before Jun Do could open his mouth, Gil stopped the player and said the word "Opera."

They were going to get someone—someone on a beach—and bring that someone home with them. That's all Officer So would say about their trip.

On the second day, darkness falling, they could see the distant lights of a town, but the Captain would take the boat no closer.

"This is Japan," he said. "I don't have charts for these waters."

"I'll tell you how close we get," Officer So said to the Captain, and with a fisherman sounding for the bottom, they made for the shore.

Jun Do got dressed, cinching the belt to keep the stiff jeans on.

"Are these the clothes of the last guy you kidnapped?" Jun Do asked.

Officer So said, "I haven't kidnapped anyone in years."

Jun Do felt his face muscles tighten, a sense of dread running through him.

"Relax," Officer So said. "I've done this a hundred times."

"Seriously?"

"Well, twenty-seven times."

Officer So had brought a little skiff along, and when they were close to the shore, he directed the fishermen to lower it. To the west, the sun was setting over North Korea, and it was cooling now, the wind shifting direction. The skiff was tiny, Jun Do thought, barely big enough for one person, let alone three and a struggling kidnap victim. With a pair of binoculars and a thermos, Officer So climbed down into the skiff. Gil followed. When Jun Do took his place next to Gil, black water lapped over the sides, and right away his shoes soaked through. He debated revealing that he couldn't swim.

Gil kept trying to get Jun Do to repeat phrases in Japanese. Good evening—*Konban wa.* Excuse me, I am lost—*Chotto sumimasen, michi ni mayoimashita.* Can you help me find my cat?—*Watashi no neko ga maigo ni narimashita?*

Officer So pointed their nose toward shore, the old man pushing the outboard motor, a tired Soviet Vpresna, way too hard. Turning north and running with the coast, the boat would lean shoreward as a swell lifted, then rock back toward open water as the wave set it down again.

Gil took the binoculars, but instead of training them on the beach, he studied the tall buildings, the way the downtown neon came to life.

"I tell you," Gil said. "There was no Arduous March in this place."

Jun Do and Officer So exchanged a look.

Officer So said to Gil, "Tell him what 'how are you' was again."

"*Ogenki desu ka,*" Gil said.

"*Ogenki desu ka,*" Jun Do repeated. "*Ogenki desu ka.*"

"Say it like 'How are you, my fellow citizen?' *Ogenki desu ka,*" Officer So said. "Not like how are you, I'm about to pluck you off this fucking beach."

Jun Do asked, "Is that what you call it, plucking?"

"A long time ago, that's what we called it." He put on a fake smile. "Just say it nice."

Jun Do said, "Why not send Gil? He's the one who speaks Japanese."

Officer So returned his eyes to the water. "You know why you're here."

Gil asked, "Why's he here?"

Officer So said, "Because he fights in the dark."

Gil turned to Jun Do. "You mean that's what you do, that's your career?" he asked.

"I lead an incursion team," Jun Do said. "Mostly we run in the dark, but yeah, there's fighting, too."

Gil said, "I thought my job was fucked up."

"What was your job?" Jun Do asked.

"Before I went to language school?" Gil asked. "Land mines."

"What, like defusing them?"

"I wish," Gil said.

They closed within a couple hundred meters of shore, then trolled along the beaches of Kagoshima Prefecture. The more the light faded, the more intricately Jun Do could see it reflected in the architecture of each wave that rolled them.

Gil lifted his hand. "There," he said. "There's somebody on the beach. A woman."

Officer So backed off the throttle and took the field glasses. He held them steady and fine-tuned them, his bushy white eyebrows lifting and falling as he focused. "No," he said, handing the binoculars back to Gil. "Look closer, it's two women. They're walking together."

Jun Do said, "I thought you were looking for a guy?"

"It doesn't matter," the old man said. "As long as the person's alone."

"What, we're supposed to grab just anybody?"

Officer So didn't answer. For a while, there was nothing but the sound of the Vpresna. Then Officer So said, "In my time, we had a whole division, a budget. I'm talking about a speedboat, a tranquilizing gun. We'd surveil, infiltrate, cherry-pick. We didn't pluck family types, and we never took children. I retired with a perfect record. Now look at me. I must be the only one left. I'll bet I'm the only one they could find who remembers this business."

Gil fixed on something on the beach. He wiped the lenses of the binoculars, but really it was too dark to see anything. He handed them to Jun Do. "What do you make out?" he asked.

When Jun Do lifted the binoculars, he could barely discern a male figure moving along the beach, near the water—he was just a lighter blur against a darker blur, really. Then some motion caught Jun Do's eye. An animal was racing down the beach toward the man—a dog it must've been, but it was big, the size of a wolf. The man did something and the dog ran away.

Jun Do turned to Officer So. "There's a man. He's got a dog with him."

Officer So sat up and put a hand on the outboard engine. "Is he alone?"

Jun Do nodded.

"Is the dog an akita?"

Jun Do didn't know his breeds. Once a week, the orphans had cleaned out a local dog farm. Dogs were filthy animals that would lunge for you at any opportunity—you could see where they'd attacked the posts of their pens, chewing through the wood with their fangs. That's all Jun Do needed to know about dogs.

Officer So said, "As long as the thing wags its tail. That's all you got to worry about."

Gil said, "The Japanese train their dogs to do little tricks. Say to the dog, Nice doggie, sit. *Yoshi yoshi. Osuwari kawaii desu ne.*"

Jun Do said, "Will you shut up with the Japanese?"

Jun Do wanted to ask if there was a plan, but Officer So simply turned them toward the shore. Back in Panmunjom, Jun Do was the leader of his tunnel squad, so he had a liquor ration and a weekly credit for one of the women. In three days, he had the quarterfinals of the KPA taekwondo tournament.

Jun Do's squad swept every tunnel under the DMZ once a month, and they worked without lights, which meant jogging for kilometers in complete darkness, using their red lights only when they reached a tunnel's end and needed to inspect its seals and trip wires. They worked as if they might encounter the South Koreans at any point, and except for the rainy season, when the tunnels were too muddy to use, they trained daily in zero-light hand to hand. It was said that the ROK soldiers had infrared and American night-vision goggles. The only weapon Jun Do's boys had was the dark.

When the waves got rough, and he felt panicky, Jun Do turned to Gil. "So what's this job that's worse than disarming land mines?"

"Mapping them," Gil said.

"What, with a sweeper?"

"Metal detectors don't work," Gil said. "The Americans use plastic mines now. We made maps of where they probably were, using psychology and terrain. When a path forces a step or tree roots direct your feet, that's where we assume a mine and mark it down. We'd spend all night in a minefield, risking our lives with every step, and for what? Come morning, the mines were still there, the enemy was still there."

Jun Do knew who got the worst jobs—tunnel recon, twelve-man submarines, mines, biochem—and he suddenly saw Gil differently. "So you're an orphan," he said.

Gil looked shocked. "Not at all. Are you?"

"No," Jun Do said. "Not me."

Jun Do's own unit was made up of orphans, though in Jun Do's case it was a mistake. The address on his KPA card had been Long Tomorrows, and that's what had condemned him. It was a glitch no one in North Korea seemed capable of fixing, and now, this was his fate. He'd spent his life with orphans, he understood their special plight, so he didn't hate them like most people did. He just wasn't one of them.

"And you're a translator now?" Jun Do asked him.

"You work the minefields long enough," Gil said, "and they reward you. They send you someplace cushy like language school."

Officer So laughed a bitter little laugh.

The white foam of the breakers was sweeping into the boat now.

"The shitty thing is," Gil said, "when I'm walking down the street, I'll think, *That's where I'd put a land mine.* Or I'll find myself not stepping on certain places, like door thresholds or in front of a urinal. I can't even go to a park anymore."

"A park?" Jun Do asked. He'd never seen a park.

"Enough," Officer So said. "It's time to get that language school a new Japanese teacher." He throttled back and the surf grew loud, the skiff turning sideways in the waves.

They could see the outline of a man on the beach watching them, but they were helpless now, just twenty meters from shore. When Jun Do felt the boat start to go over, he leaped out to steady it, and though it was only waist deep, he went down hard in the waves. The tide rolled him along the sandy bottom before he came up coughing.

The man on the beach didn't say anything. It was almost dark as Jun Do waded ashore.

Jun Do took a deep breath, then wiped the water from his hair.

"*Konban wa,*" he said to the stranger. "*Odenki kesu da.*"

"*Ogenki desu ka,*" Gil called from the boat.

"*Desu ka,*" Jun Do repeated.

The dog came running up with a yellow ball.

For a moment, the man didn't move. Then he took a step backward.

"Get him," Officer So shouted.

The man bolted, and Jun Do gave chase in wet jeans, his shoes caked with sand. The dog was big and white, bounding with excitement. The Japanese man ran straight down the beach, nearly invisible but for the dog moving from one side of him to the other. Jun Do ran for all he was worth. He focused only on the heartbeat-like thumps of feet padding ahead in the sand. Then he closed his eyes. In the tunnels, Jun Do had developed a sense of people he couldn't see. If they were out there, he could feel it, and if he could get within range, he could home in on them. His father, the Orphan Master, had always given him a sense that his mother was dead, but that wasn't true, she was alive and well, just out of range. And while he'd never heard news of what happened to the Orphan Master, Jun Do could feel that his father was no longer in this world. The key to fighting in the dark was no different: you had to perceive your opponent, sense him, and never use your imagination. The darkness inside your head is something your imagination fills with stories that have nothing to do with the real darkness around you.

From ahead came the body thud of someone falling in the dark, a sound Jun Do had heard a thousand times. Jun Do pulled up where the man was righting himself. His face was ghostly with a dusting of sand. They were huffing and puffing, their joined breath white in the dark.

The truth was that Jun Do never did that well in tournaments. When you fought in the dark, a jab only told your opponent where you were. In the dark, you had to punch as if you were punching through people. Maximum extension is what mattered—haymaker punches and great, whirling roundhouse kicks that took out whole swaths of space and were meant to cut people down. In a tournament, though, opponents could see moves like that coming from a mile away. They simply stepped aside. But a man on a beach at night, standing on the balls of his feet? Jun Do executed a spinning back kick to the head, and the stranger went down.

The dog was filled with energy—excitement perhaps, or frustration. It pawed at the sand near the unconscious man, then dropped its ball. Jun Do wanted to throw the ball, but he didn't dare get near those teeth. Its tail, Jun Do suddenly realized, wasn't wagging. Jun Do saw a glint in the dark, the man's glasses, it turned out. He put them on, and the fuzzy glow above the dunes turned into crisp points of light in people's windows. Instead of huge housing blocks, the Japanese lived in smaller, individual-sized barracks.

Jun Do pocketed the glasses, then took up the man's ankles and began pulling from behind. The dog was growling and giving short, aggressive barks. When Jun Do looked over his shoulder, the dog was growling in the man's face and using its paws to scratch his cheeks and forehead. Jun Do lowered his head and pulled. The first day in a tunnel is no problem, but when you wake on the second day from the darkness of a dream into true darkness, that's when your eyes must open. If you keep your eyes closed, your mind will show you all kinds of crazy movies, like a dog attacking you from behind. But with your eyes open, all you had to face was the nothingness of what you were really doing.

When finally Jun Do found the boat in the dark, he let the dead weight fall into its aluminum cross members. The man opened his eyes once and rolled them around, but there was no comprehension.

"What did you do to his face?" Gil asked.

"Where were you?" Jun Do asked. "That guy was heavy."

"I'm just the translator," Gil said.

Officer So clapped Jun Do on the back. "Not bad for an orphan," he said.

Jun Do wheeled on him. "I'm not a fucking orphan," he said. "And who the hell are you, saying you've done this a hundred times. We come out here with no plan, just me running someone down? You didn't even get out of the boat."

"I had to see what you were made of," Officer So said. "Next time we'll use our brains."

"There won't be any next time," Jun Do said.

Gil and Jun Do spun the boat to face the waves. They got battered while Officer So pull-started the motor. When the four of them were in and headed toward open water, Officer So said, "Look, it gets easier. Just don't think about it. I was full of shit when I said I'd kidnapped twenty-seven people. I never kept count. As they come just forget about them, one after another. Catch somebody with your hands, then let them go with your mind. Do the opposite of keeping count."

Even over the outboard, they could hear that dog on the beach. No matter how far out they got, its baying carried over the water, and Jun Do knew he'd hear that dog forever.

*

They stayed at a Songun base, not far from the port of Kinjye. It was surrounded by the earthen bunkers of surface-to-air missiles, and when the sun set, they could see the white rails of launchers glowing in the moonlight. Because they'd been to Japan now, they had to bunk apart from the regular KPA soldiers. The three were housed in the infirmary, a small room with six cots. The only sign it was an infirmary was a lone cabinet filled with blood-taking instruments and an old Chinese refrigerator with a red cross on its door.

They'd locked the Japanese man in one of the hot boxes in the drill yard, and Gil was out there now, practicing his Japanese through the slop hole in the door. Jun Do and Officer So leaned against the infirmary's window frame, sharing a cigarette as they watched Gil out there, sitting in the dirt, polishing his idioms with a man he'd helped kidnap. Officer So shook his head, like now he'd seen it all. There was one patient in the infirmary, a small soldier of about sixteen, bones knit from the famine. He lay on a cot, teeth chattering. Their cigarette smoke was giving him coughing fits. They moved his cot as far away as possible in the small room, but still he wouldn't shut up.

There was no doctor. The infirmary was just a place where sick soldiers were housed until it was clear they wouldn't recover. If the young soldier hadn't improved by morning, the MPs would hook up a blood line and drain four units from him. Jun Do had seen it before, and as far as he could tell, it was the best way to go. It only took a couple of minutes—first they got sleepy, then a little dreamy looking, and if there was a last little panic at the end, it didn't matter because they couldn't talk anymore, and finally, before lights out, they looked pleasantly confused, like a cricket with its feelers pulled off.

The camp generator shut down—slowly the lights dimmed, the fridge went quiet.

Officer So and Jun Do took to their cots.

There was a Japanese man. He took his dog for a walk. And then he was nowhere. For the people who knew him, he'd forever be nowhere. That's how Jun Do had thought of boys selected by the men with Chinese accents. They were here and then they were nowhere, taken like Bo Song to parts unknown. That's how he'd thought of most people—appearing in your life like foundlings on the doorstep, only to be swept away later as if by flood. But Bo Song hadn't gone nowhere—whether he sank down to the wolf eels or bloated and took the tide north to Vladivostok, he went somewhere. The Japanese man wasn't nowhere, either—he was in the hot box, right out there in the drill grounds. And Jun Do's mother, it now struck him—she was somewhere, at this very moment, in a certain apartment in the capital, perhaps, looking in a mirror, brushing her hair before bed.

For the first time in years, Jun Do closed his eyes and let himself recall her face. It was dangerous to dream up people like that. If you did, they'd soon be in the tunnel with you. That had happened many times when he remembered boys from Long Tomorrows. One slip and a boy was suddenly following you in the dark. He was saying things to you, asking why you weren't the one who succumbed to the cold, why you weren't the one who fell in the paint vat, and you'd get the feeling that at any moment, the toes of a front kick would cross your face.

But there she was, his mother. Lying there, listening to the shivering of the soldier, her voice came to him. "Arirang," she sang, her voice achy, at the edge of a whisper, coming from an unknown somewhere. Even those fucking orphans knew where their parents were.

Late in the night, Gil stumbled in. He opened the fridge, which was forbidden, and placed something inside. Then he flopped onto his cot. Gil slept with his arms and legs sprawled off the edges, and Jun Do could tell that as a child, Gil must've had a bed of his very own. In a moment, he was out.

Jun Do and Officer So stood in the dark and went to the fridge. When Officer So pulled its handle, it exhaled a faint, cool breath. In the back, behind stacks of square blood bags, Officer So fished out a half-full bottle of *shoju*. They closed the door quickly because the blood was bound for Pyongyang, and if it spoiled, there'd be hell to pay.

They took the bottle to the window. Far in the distance, dogs were barking in their warrens. On the horizon, above the SAM bunkers, there was a glow in the sky, moonlight reflecting off the ocean. Behind them, Gil began gassing in his sleep.

Officer So drank. "I don't think old Gil's used to a diet of millet cakes and sorghum soup."

"Who the hell is he?" Jun Do asked.

"Forget about him," Officer So said. "I don't know why Pyongyang started this business up again after all these years, but hopefully we'll be rid of him in a week. One mission, and if everything goes right, we'll never see that guy again."

Jun Do took a drink—his stomach clutching at the fruit, the alcohol.

"What's the mission?" he asked.

"First, another practice run," Officer So said. "Then we're going after a special someone. The Tokyo Opera spends its summers in Niigata. There's a soprano. Her name is Rumina."

The next drink of *shoju* went down smooth. "Opera?" Jun Do asked.

Officer So shrugged. "Some bigshot in Pyongyang probably heard a bootleg and had to have her."

"Gil said he survived a land-mine tour," Jun Do said. "For that, they sent him to language school. Is it true—does it work like that, do you get rewarded?"

"We're stuck with Gil, okay? But you don't listen to him. You listen to me."

Jun Do was quiet.

"Why, you got your heart set on something?" Officer So asked. "You even know what you'd want as a reward?"

Jun Do shook his head.

"Then don't worry about it."

Officer So walked to the corner and leaned over the latrine bucket. He braced himself against the wall and strained for a long time. Nothing happened.

"I pulled off a miracle or two in my day," he said. "I got rewarded. Now look at me." He shook his head. "The reward you want is this: don't become me."

Jun Do stared out the window at the hot box. "What's going to happen to him?"

"The dog man?" Officer So asked. "There are probably a couple of Pubyok on the train from Pyongyang right now to get him."

"Yeah, but what's going to *happen* to him?"

Officer So tried one last push to get some urine out.

"Don't ask stupid questions," he said through his teeth.

Jun Do thought of his mother on a train to Pyongyang. "For your reward, could you ask for a person?"

"What, a woman?" Officer So shook his *umkyoung* in frustration. "Yeah, you could ask for that." He came back and drank the rest of the bottle, saving only a swish in the bottom. This he poured, a dribble at a time, over the dying soldier's lips. Officer So clapped him good-bye on the chest, then he stuffed the empty bottle in the crook of the boy's sweat-soaked arm.

*

They commandeered a new fishing boat, made another crossing. Over the Tsushima Basin, they could hear the powerful clicks, like punches to the chest, of sperm whales hunting below, and nearing the island of Dogo, granite spires rose sudden from the sea, white up top from bird guano and orange below from great gatherings of starfish. Jun Do stared up toward the island's north promontory, volcanic black, limned in dwarf spruce. This was a world wrought for its own sake, without message or point, a landscape that would make no testimony for one great leader over another.

There was a famous resort on this island, and Officer So thought they could catch a tourist alone on the beach. But when they reached the lee of the island, there was an empty boat on the water, a black Avon inflatable, six-man, with a fifty-horse Honda outboard. They took the skiff over to investigate. The Avon was abandoned, not a soul upon the waters. They climbed aboard, and Officer So started the Honda engine. He shut it down. He pulled the gas can out of the skiff, and together they rolled it in the water—it filled quickly, going down ass-first with the weight of the Vpresna.

"Now we're a proper team," Officer So said as they admired their new boat.

That's when the diver surfaced.

Lifting his mask, the diver showed a look of uncertain wonder to discover three men in his boat. But he handed up a sack of abalone and took Gil's hand to help him aboard. The diver was larger than them, muscular in a wetsuit.

Officer So spoke to Gil, "Tell him our boat was damaged, that it sank."

Gil spoke to the diver, who gestured wildly and laughed.

"I know your boat sank," Gil translated back. "It almost landed on my head."

Then the diver noticed the fishing vessel in the distance. He cocked his head at it.

Gil clapped the diver on the back and said something to him. The diver stared hard into Gil's eyes and then panicked. Abalone divers, it turned out, carried a special kind of knife on their ankles, and Jun Do was a long time in subduing him. Finally, Jun Do took the diver's back and began to squeeze, the water wringing from his wetsuit as the scissors choke sank in.

When the knife was flying, Gil had jumped overboard.

"What the fuck did you say to him?" Jun Do demanded.

"The truth," Gil said, treading water.

Officer So had caught a pretty good gash in the forearm. He closed his eyes at the pain of it. "More practice," is all he could say.

*

They put the diver in the fishing boat's hold and continued to the mainland. That night, offshore from the town of Fukura, they put the Avon in the water. Next to Fukura's long fishing pier, a summer amusement park had set up, with lanterns strung and old people singing karaoke on a public stage. Here Jun Do and Gil and Officer So hovered beyond the beach break, waiting for the neon piping on the roller coaster to go dark, for the monkeyish organ music of the midway to fall silent. Finally, a solitary figure stood at the end of the pier. When they saw the red of a cigarette, they knew it was a man. Officer So started the engine.

They motored in on idle, the pier towering as they came astern it. Where its pilings entered the heavy surf, there was chaos, with some waves leaping straight up and others deflecting out perpendicular to shore.

"Use your Japanese," Officer So told Gil. "Tell him you lost your puppy or something. Get close. Then—over the rail. It's a long fall, and the water's cold. When he comes up, he'll be fighting to get in the boat."

Gil stepped out when they reached the beach. "I've got it," he said. "This one's mine."

"Oh, no," Officer So said. "You both go."

"Seriously," Gil said. "I think I can handle it."

"Out," Officer So said to Jun Do. "And wear those damn glasses."

The two of them crossed the tide line and came to a small square. Here were benches and a little plaza, a shuttered tea stand. There seemed to be no statue, and they could not tell what the square glorified. The trees were full with plums, so ripe the skins broke and juice ran in their hands. It seemed impossible, a thing not to be trusted. A grubby man was sleeping on a bench, and they marveled at it, a person sleeping any place he wished.

Gil stared at all the town houses around them. They looked traditional, with dark beams and ceramic roofs, but you could tell they were brand new.

"I want to open all these doors," he said. "Sit in their chairs, listen to their music."

Jun Do stared at him.

"You know," Gil said. "Just to see."

The tunnels always ended with a ladder leading up to a rabbit hole. Jun Do's men would vie to be the ones to slip out and wander South Korea for a while. They'd come back with stories of machines that handed out money and people who picked up dog shit and put it in bags. Jun Do never looked. He knew the televisions were huge and there was all the rice you could eat. Yet he wanted no part of it—he was scared that if he saw it with his own eyes, his entire life would mean nothing. Stealing turnips from an old man who'd gone blind from hunger? That would have been for nothing. Sending another boy instead of himself to clean vats at the paint factory? For nothing.

Jun Do threw away his half-eaten plum. "I've had better," he said.

On the pier, they walked planking stained from years of bait fishing. Ahead, at the end, they could see a face, lit from the blue glow of a mobile phone.

"Just get him over the rail," Jun Do said.

Gil took a breath. "Over the rail," he repeated.

There were empty bottles on the pier, cigarette butts. Jun Do was walking calmly forward, and he could feel Gil trying to copy this beside him. From below came the throaty bubble of an outboard idling. The figure ahead stopped speaking on the phone.

"*Dare?*" a voice called to them. "*Dare nano?*"

"Don't answer," Jun Do whispered.

"It's a woman's voice," Gil said.

"Don't answer," Jun Do said.

The hood of a coat was pulled back to reveal a young woman's face.

"I'm not made for this," Gil said.

"Stick to the plan."

Their footsteps seemed impossibly loud. It struck Jun Do that one day men had come for his mother like this, that he was now one of those men.

Then they were upon her. She was small under the coat. She opened her mouth, as if to scream, and Jun Do saw she had fine metal work all along her teeth. They gripped her arms and muscled her up on the rail.

"*Zenzen oyogenai'n desu*," she said, and though Jun Do could speak no Japanese, he knew it was a raw, imploring confession, like "I'm a virgin."

They threw her over the rail. She fell away silent, not a word or even the snatching of a breath. Jun Do saw something flash in her eyes, though—it wasn't fear or the senselessness of it. He could tell she was thinking of her parents and how they'd never know what became of her.

From below came a splash and the gunning of an outboard.

Jun Do couldn't shake that look in her eyes.

On the pier was her phone. He picked it up and put it to his ear. Gil tried to say something, but Jun Do silenced him. "Mayumi?" a woman's voice asked. "Mayumi?" Jun Do pushed some buttons to make it stop. When he leaned over the rail, the boat was rising and falling in the swells.

"Where is she?" Jun Do asked.

Officer So was staring into the water. "She went down," he said.

"What do you mean she went down?"

He lifted his hands. "She hit and then she was gone."

Jun Do turned to Gil. "What did she say?"

Gil said, "She said, *I can't swim.*"

"'I can't swim'?" Jun Do asked. "She said she couldn't swim and you didn't stop me?"

"Throwing her over, that was the plan. You said stick to it."

Jun Do looked into the black water again, deep here at the end of the pier. She was down there, that big coat like a sail in the current, her body rolling along the sandy floor.

The phone rang. It glowed blue and vibrated in Jun Do's hand. He and

Gil stared at it. Gil took the phone and listened, eyes wide. Jun Do could tell, even from here, that it was a woman's voice, a mother's. "Throw it away," Jun Do told him. "Just toss it."

Gil's eyes roamed as he listened. His hand was trembling. He nodded his head several times. When he said, "*Hai,*" Jun Do grabbed it. He jabbed his finger at the buttons. There, on its small screen, appeared a picture of a baby. He threw it into the sea.

Jun Do went to the rail. "How could you not keep count," he yelled down to Officer So. "How could you not keep count?"

*

That was the end of their practice. It was time to get the opera lady. Officer So was to cross the Sea of Japan on a fishing vessel, while Jun Do and Gil took the overnight ferry from Chongjin to Niigata. At midnight, with the singer in hand, they would meet Officer So on the beach. Simplicity, Officer So said, was the key to the plan.

Jun Do and Gil took the afternoon train north to Chongjin. At the station, families were sleeping under cargo platforms, waiting for darkness so they could make the journey to Sinuiju, which was just a swim across the Tumen River from China.

They made for the Port of Chongjin on foot, passing the Reunification Smelter, its great cranes rusted in place, the copper lines to its furnace long since pilfered for scrap. Apartment blocks stood empty, their ration outlet windows butcher-papered. There was no laundry hanging to dry, no onion smoke in the air. All the trees had been cut during the famine, and now, years later, the saplings were uniform in size, trunks ankle-thick, their clean stalks popping up in the oddest places—in rain barrels and storm drains, one tree bursting from an outhouse where a human skeleton had shit its indigestible seed.

Long Tomorrows, when they came to it, looked no bigger than the infirmary.

Jun Do shouldn't have pointed it out because Gil insisted they go in.

It was filled only with shadows. Everything had been stripped for fuel—even the doorframes had been burned. The roster of the 114 Grand Martyrs of the Revolution, painted on the wall, was the only thing left.

Gil didn't believe that Jun Do had named all the orphans.

"You really memorized all the Martyrs?" he asked. "What about number eleven?"

"That's Ha Shin," Jun Do said. "When he was captured, he cut out his own tongue so the Japanese could get no information from him. There was a boy here who wouldn't speak—I gave him that name."

Gil ran his finger down the list.

"Here you are," he said. "Martyr number seventy-six, Pak Jun Do. What's that guy's story?"

Jun Do touched the blackness on the floor where the stove had once been. "Even though he killed many Japanese soldiers," he said, "the revolutionaries in Pak Jun Do's unit didn't trust him because he was descended from an impure blood line. To prove his loyalty, he hanged himself."

Gil stared at him. "You gave yourself this name? Why?"

"He passed the ultimate loyalty test."

The Orphan Master's room, it turned out, was no bigger than a pallet. And of the portrait of the tormenting woman, Jun Do could find only a nail hole.

"Is this where you slept?" Gil asked. "In the Orphan Master's room?"

Jun Do showed him the nail hole. "Here's where the portrait of my mother hung."

Gil inspected it. "There was a nail here, all right," he said. "Tell me, if you lived with your father, how come you have an orphan's name?"

"He couldn't give me his name," Jun Do said, "or everyone would see the shame of how he was forced to raise his son. And he couldn't bear to give me another man's name, even a Martyr's. I had to do it."

Gil's expression was blank. "What about your mother?" he asked. "What was her name?"

They heard the horn of the *Mangyongbong-92* ferry in the distance.

Jun Do said, "Like putting a name to my problems would solve anything."

*

That night Jun Do stood in the dark stern of the ship, looking down into the turbulence of its wake. *Rumina,* he kept thinking. He didn't listen for her voice or let himself visualize her. He only wondered how she'd spend this last day if she knew he was coming.

It was late morning when they entered Bandai-jima Port—the customs houses displaying their international flags. Large shipping vessels, painted humanitarian blue, were being loaded with rice at their moorings. Jun Do and Gil had forged documents, and in polo shirts, jeans, and sneakers they descended the gangway into downtown Niigata. It was a Sunday.

Making their way to the auditorium, Jun Do saw a passenger jet crossing the sky, a big plume behind it. He gawked, neck craned—amazing. So amazing he decided to feign normalcy at everything, like the colored lights controlling the traffic or the way buses kneeled, oxenlike, to let old people board. Of course the parking meters could talk, and the doors of businesses opened as they passed. Of course there was no water barrel in the bathroom, no ladle.

The matinee was a medley of works the opera troupe would stage over the coming season, so all the singers took turns offering brief arias. Gil seemed to know the songs, humming along with them. Rumina—small, broad-shouldered—mounted the stage in a dress the color of graphite. Her eyes were dark under sharp bangs. Jun Do could tell she'd known sadness, yet she couldn't know that her greatest trials lay ahead, that this evening, when darkness fell, her life would become an opera, that Jun Do was the dark figure at the end of the first act who removes the heroine to a land of lament.

She sang in Italian and then German and then Japanese. When finally she sang in Korean, it came clear why Pyongyang had chosen her. The song was beautiful, her voice light now, singing of two lovers on a lake, and the song was not about the Dear Leader or defeating the imperialists or the pride of a North Korean factory. It was about a girl and a boy in a boat. The girl had a white *choson-ot,* the boy a soulful stare.

Rumina sang in Korean, and her dress was graphite, and she might as well have sung of a spider that spins white thread to capture her listeners. Jun Do and Gil wandered the streets of Niigata held by that thread, pretending they weren't about to abduct her from the nearby artists' village. A line kept ringing in Jun Do's mind about how in the middle of the water the lovers decide to row no further.

They walked the city in a trance, waiting for dark. Advertisements especially had an effect on Jun Do. There were no ads in North Korea, and here they were on buses and posters, across video screens. Immediate and imploring—couples clasping one another, a sad child—he asked Gil what each one said, but the answers pertained to car insurance and telephone rates. Through a window, they watched Korean women cut the toenails of Japanese women. For fun, they operated a vending machine and received a bag of orange food neither would taste.

Gil paused before a store that sold equipment for undersea exploration. In the window was a large bag made to stow dive gear. It was black and nylon, and the salesperson showed them how it would hold everything needed for an underwater adventure for two. They bought it.

They asked a man pushing a cart if they could borrow it, and he told them at the supermarket they could get their own. Inside the store, it was almost impossible to tell what most of the boxes and packages contained. The important stuff, like radish bushels and buckets of chestnuts, were nowhere to be seen. Gil purchased a roll of heavy tape and, from a section of toys for children, a little watercolor set in a tin. Gil at least had someone to buy a souvenir for.

Darkness fell, storefronts lit suddenly with red-and-blue neon, and the willows were eerily illuminated from below. Car headlights flashed in his eyes. Jun Do felt exposed, singled out. Where was the curfew? Why didn't the Japanese respect the dark like normal people?

They stood outside a bar, time yet to kill. Inside, people were laughing and talking.

Gil pulled out their yen. "No sense taking any back," he said.

Inside, he ordered whiskeys. Two women were at the bar as well, and Gil bought their drinks. They smiled and returned to their conversation. "Did you see their teeth?" Gil asked. "So white and perfect, like children's teeth." When Jun Do didn't agree, Gil said, "Relax, yeah? Loosen up."

"Easy for you," Jun Do said. "You don't have to overpower someone tonight. Then get her across town. And if we don't find Officer So on that beach—"

"Like that would be the worst thing," Gil said. "You don't see anyone around here plotting to escape to North Korea. You don't see them coming to pluck people off our beaches."

"That kind of talk doesn't help."

"Come, drink up," Gil said. "I'll get the singer into the bag tonight. You're not the only guy capable of beating a woman, you know. How hard can it be?"

"I'll handle the singer," Jun Do said. "You just keep it together."

"I can stuff a singer in a bag, okay?" Gil said. "I can push a shopping cart. You just drink up, you're probably never going to see Japan again."

Gil tried to speak to the Japanese women, but they smiled and ignored him. Then he bought a drink for the bartender. She came over and talked with him while she poured it. She was thin shouldered, but her shirt was tight and her hair was absolutely black. They drank together, and he said something to make her laugh. When she went to fill an order, Gil turned to Jun Do. "If you slept with one of these girls," Gil said, "you'd know it was because she wanted to, not like some military comfort girl trying to get nine stamps a day in her quota book or a factory gal getting married off by her housing council. Back home pretty girls never even raise their eyes to you. You can't even have a cup of tea without her father arranging a marriage."

Pretty girls? Jun Do thought. "The world thinks I'm an orphan, that's my curse," Jun Do told him. "But how did a Pyongyang boy like you end up doing such shitty jobs?"

Gil ordered more drinks, even though Jun Do had barely touched his. "Going to that orphanage really messed with your head," Gil said. "Just because I don't blow my nose in my hand anymore doesn't mean I'm not a country boy, from Myohsun. You should move on, too. In Japan, you can be anyone you want to be."

They heard a motorcycle pull up, and outside the window, they saw a man back it in line with a couple of other bikes. When he took the key from the ignition, he hid it under the lip of the gas tank. Gil and Jun Do glanced at one another.

Gil sipped his whiskey, swishing it around then tipping his head to delicately gargle.

"You don't drink like a country boy."

"You don't drink like an orphan."

"I'm not an orphan."

"Well, that's good," Gil said. "Because all the orphans in my land-mine unit knew how to do was take—your cigarettes, your socks, your *shoju*. Don't you hate it when someone takes your *shoju*? In my unit, they gobbled up everything around them, like a dog digests its pups, and for thanks, they left you the puny nuggets of their shit."

Jun Do gave the smile that puts people at ease in the moment before you strike them.

Gil went on. "But you're a decent guy. You're loyal like the guy in the martyr story. You don't need to tell yourself that your father was this and your mother was that. You can be anyone you want. Reinvent yourself for a night. Forget about that drunk and the nail hole in the wall."

Jun Do stood. He took a step back to get the right distance for a turn-buckle kick. He closed his eyes, he could feel the space, he could visualize the hip pivoting, the leg rising, the whip of the instep as it torqued around. Jun Do had dealt with this his whole life, the ways it was impossible for people from normal families to conceive of a man in so much hurt that he couldn't acknowledge his own son, that there was nothing worse than a mother leaving her children, though it happened all the time, that "take" was a word people used for those who had so little to give as to be immeasurable.

When Jun Do opened his eyes, Gil suddenly realized what was about to happen.

He fumbled his drink. "Whoa," he said. "My mistake, okay? I'm from a big family, I don't know anything about orphans. We should go, we've got things to do."

"Okay, then," Jun Do said. "Let's see how you treat those pretty ladies in Pyongyang."

*

Behind the auditorium was the artists' village—a series of cottages ringing a central hot spring. They could see the stream of water, still steaming hot, running from the bathhouse. Mineral white, it tumbled down bald, bleached rocks toward the sea.

They hid the cart, then Jun Do boosted Gil over the fence. When Gil came around to open the metal gate for Jun Do, Gil paused a moment and the two regarded one another through the bars before Gil lifted the latch and let Jun Do in.

Tiny cones of light illuminated the flagstone path to Rumina's bungalow. Above them, the dark green and white of magnolia blocked the stars. In the air was conifer and cedar, something of the ocean. Jun Do tore two strips of duct tape and hung them from Gil's sleeves.

"That way," Jun Do whispered, "they'll be ready to go."

Gil's eyes were thrilled and disbelieving.

"So, we're just going to storm in there?" he asked.

"I'll get the door open," Jun Do said. "Then you get that tape on her mouth."

Jun Do pried a large flagstone from the path and carried it to the door. He placed it against the knob and when he threw his hip into it, the door popped. Gil ran toward a woman, sitting up in bed, illuminated only by a television. Jun Do watched from the doorway as Gil got the tape across her mouth, but then in the sheets and the softness of the bed, the tide seemed to turn. He lost a clump of hair. Then she got his collar, which she used to off-balance him. Finally, he found her neck, and they went to the floor, where he worked his weight onto her, the pain making her feet curl. Jun Do stared long at those toes: the nails had been painted bright red.

At first, Jun Do had been thinking, *Grab her here, pressure her there,* but then a sick feeling rose in him. As the two rolled, Jun Do could see that she had wet herself, and the rawness of it, the brutality of what was happening, was newly clear to him. Gil was bringing her into submission, taping her wrists and ankles, and she was kneeling now, him laying out the bag and unzipping it. When he spread the opening for her, her eyes—wide and wet—failed, and her posture went woozy. Jun Do pulled off his glasses, and things were better with the blur.

Outside, he breathed deeply. He could hear Gil struggling to fold her up so she would fit in the bag. The stars over the ocean, fuzzy now, made him remember how free he'd felt on that first night crossing of the Sea of Japan, how at home he was on a fishing vessel. Back inside, he saw Gil had zipped the bag so that only Rumina's face showed, her nostrils flaring for oxygen. Gil stood over her, exhausted but smiling. He pressed the fabric of his pants against his groin so she could see the outline of his erection. When her eyes went wide, he pulled the zipper shut.

Quickly, they went through her possessions. Gil pocketed yen and a necklace of red and white stones. Jun Do didn't know what to grab. On a table were medicine bottles, cosmetics, a stack of family photos. When his eyes landed on the graphite dress, he pulled it from its hanger.

"What the fuck are you doing?" Gil asked.

"I don't know," Jun Do told him.

The cart, overburdened, made loud clacking sounds at every crease in the sidewalk. They didn't speak. Gil was scratched and his shirt was torn. It looked like he was wearing makeup that had smeared. A clear yellow fluid had risen through the scab where his hair was missing. When the cement sloped at the curbs, the wheels had a tendency to spin funny and spill the cart, the load dumping to the pavement.

Bundles of cardboard lined the streets. Dishwashers hosed down kitchen mats in the gutters. A bright, empty bus whooshed past. Near the park, a man walked a large white dog that stopped and eyed them. The bag would squirm awhile, then go still. At a corner, Gil told Jun Do to turn left, and there, down a steep hill and across a parking lot, was the beach.

"I'm going to watch our backs," Gil said.

The cart wanted free—Jun Do doubled his grip on the handle. "Okay," he answered.

From behind, Gil said, "I was out of line back there with that orphan talk. I don't know what it's like to have parents who are dead or who gave up. I was wrong, I see that now."

"No harm done," Jun Do said. "I'm not an orphan."

From behind, Gil said, "So tell me about the last time you saw your father."

The cart kept trying to break loose. Each time Jun Do had to lean back and skid his feet. "Well, there wasn't a going-away party or anything." The cart lurched forward and dragged Jun Do a couple of meters before he got his traction back. "I'd been there longer than anyone—I was never getting adopted, my father wasn't going to let anyone take his only son. Anyway, he came to me that night, we'd burned our bunks, so I was on the floor—Gil, help me here."

Suddenly the cart was racing. Jun Do tumbled as it came free of his grip and barreled downhill alone. "Gil," he yelled, watching it go. The cart got speed wobbles as it crossed the parking lot, and striking the far curb, the cart hopped high into the air, pitching the black bag out into the dark sand.

He turned but Gil was nowhere to be seen.

Jun Do ran out onto the sand, passing the bag and the odd way it had settled. Down at the waterline, he scanned the waves for Officer So, but there was nothing. He checked his pockets—he had no map, no watch, no light. Hands on knees, he couldn't catch his breath. Past him, billowing down the beach, came the graphite dress, filling and emptying in the wind, tumbling along the sand until it was taken by the night.

He found the bag, rolled it over. He unzipped it some, heat pouring out. He pulled the tape from her face, which was abraded with nylon burns. She spoke to him in Japanese.

"I don't understand," he said.

In Korean, she said, "Thank God you rescued me."

He studied her face. How raw and puffy it was.

"Some psychopath stuck me in here," she said. "Thank God you came along, I thought I was dead, and then you came to set me free."

Jun Do looked again for any sign of Gil, but he knew there wouldn't be.

"Thanks for getting me out of here," she said. "Really, thanks for setting me free."

Jun Do tested the strip of tape with his fingers, but it had lost much of its stickiness. A lock of her hair was fixed to the tape. He let it go in the wind.

"My God," she said. "You're one of them."

Sand blew into the bag, into her eyes.

"Believe me," he said. "I know what you're going through."

"You don't have to be a bad guy," she said. "There's goodness in you, I can see it. Let me go, and I'll sing for you. You won't believe how I can sing."

"Your song has been troubling me," he said. "The one about the boy who chooses to quit rowing in the middle of the lake."

"That was only an aria," she said. "From a whole opera, one filled with subplots and reversals and betrayals."

Jun Do leaned close now. "Does the boy stop because he has rescued the girl and on the far shore he will have to give her to his superiors? Or has the boy stolen the girl and therefore knows that punishment awaits?"

"It's a love story," she said.

"I understand that," he said. "But what is the answer? Could it be that he knows he's marked for a labor camp?"

She searched his face, as if *he* knew the answer.

"How does it end?" he asked. "What happens to them?"

"Let me out and I'll tell you," she said. "Open this bag and I'll sing you the ending."

Jun Do took the zipper and closed it. He spoke to the black nylon where her face had been. "Keep your eyes open," he said. "I know there's nothing to see, but whatever happens, don't shut them. Darkness and close quarters, they're not your enemy."

He dragged the bag to the waterline. The ocean, frothy cold, washed over his shoes as he scanned the waves for Officer So. When a wave reached high upon the sand and licked the bag, she screamed inside, and he had never heard such a shriek. From far up the beach, a light flashed at him. Officer So had heard her. He brought the black inflatable around, and Jun Do dragged the bag into the surf. Using the straps, the two of them rolled it into the boat.

"Where's Gil?" he asked.

"Gil's gone," Jun Do said. "He was right beside me, and then he wasn't."

They were knee-deep in waves, steadying the boat. The lights of the city were reflected in Officer So's eyes. "You know what happened to the other mission officers?" he asked. "There were four of us. Now there's only me. The others are in Prison 9—have you heard of that place, tunnel man? The whole prison's underground. It's a mine, and when you go in, you never see the sun again."

"Look, scaring me isn't going to change anything. I don't know where he is."

Officer So went on, "There's an iron gate at the minehead, and once you pass that, that's it—there are no guards inside, no doctors, no cafeteria, no toilets. You just dig in the dark, and when you get some ore, you drag it to the surface to trade through the bars for food and candles and pickaxes. Even the bodies don't come out."

"He could be anywhere," Jun Do said. "He speaks Japanese."

From the bag came Rumina's voice. "I can help you," she said. "I know Niigata like the lines on my palm. Let me out, and I swear I'll find him."

They ignored her.

"Who is this guy?" Jun Do asked.

"The spoiled kid of some minister," Officer So said. "That's what they tell me. His dad sent him here to toughen him up. You know—the hero's son's always the meekest."

Jun Do turned and considered the lights of Niigata.

Officer So put his hand on Jun Do's shoulder. "You're soldierly," he said. "When it comes time to dispense, you dispense." He removed the bag's nylon shoulder strap and made a slip loop at one end. "Gil's got a noose around our fucking necks. Now it's his turn."

*

Jun Do walked the warehouse district with a strange calm. The moon, such as it was, reflected the same in every puddle, and when a bus stopped for him, the driver took one look and asked for no fare. The bus was empty except for two old Korean men in back. They still wore their white paper short-order hats. Jun Do spoke to them, but they shook their heads.

Jun Do needed the motorcycle to stand a chance of finding Gil in this city. But if Gil had any brain at all, he and the bike were long gone. When Jun Do finally rounded the corner to the whiskey bar, the black motorcycle gleamed at the curb. He threw his leg over the seat, touched the handlebars. But when he felt under the lip of the tank, there was no key. He turned to the bar's front windows, and there through the glass was Gil, laughing with the bartender.

Jun Do took a seat beside Gil, who was intent on a watercolor in progress. He had the paint set open, and he dipped the brush in a shot glass of water tinctured purple-green. It was a landscape, with bamboo patches and paths cutting through a field of stones. Gil looked up at Jun Do, then wet his brush, swirling it in yellow to highlight the bamboo stalks.

Jun Do said to him, "You're so fucking stupid."

"You're the stupid one," Gil said. "You got the singer—who would come back for me?"

"I would," Jun Do told him. "Let's have the key."

The motorcycle key was sitting on the bar, and Gil slid it to him.

Gil twirled his finger in the air to signal another round. The bartender came over. She was wearing Rumina's necklace. Gil spoke to her, then peeled off half the yen and gave it to Jun Do.

"I told her this round's on you," Gil said.

The bartender poured three glasses of whiskey, then said something that made Gil laugh.

Jun Do asked, "What'd she say?"

"She said you look very strong, but too bad you're a pussy-man."

Jun Do looked at Gil.

Gil shrugged. "I maybe told her that you and I got in a fight, over a girl. I said that I was winning until you pulled out my hair."

Jun Do said, "You can still get out of this. We won't say anything, I swear. We'll just go back, and it'll be like you never ran."

"Does it look like I'm running?" Gil asked. "Besides, I can't leave my girlfriend."

Gil handed her the watercolor, and she tacked it on the wall to dry, next to another one of her looking radiant in the red-and-white necklace. Squinting from a distance, Jun Do suddenly understood that Gil had painted not a landscape but a lush, pastoral land-mine map.

"So you were in the minefields," he said.

"My mother sent me to the Mansudae to study painting," Gil said. "But Father decided the minefields would make a man of me, so he pulled some strings." Gil had to laugh at the idea of pulling a string to get posted on a suicide detail. "I found a way to make the maps, rather than do the mapping." As he spoke, he worked quickly on another watercolor, a woman, mouth wide, lit from below so her eye sockets were darkened. Right away it had the likeness of Rumina, though you couldn't tell whether she was singing with great intensity or screaming for her life.

"Tell her you'll have one last drink," Jun Do said and passed her all the yen.

"I'm really sorry about all this," Gil said. "I really am. But I'm not going anywhere. Consider the opera singer a gift, and send my regrets."

"Was it your father who wanted the singer, is that why we're here?"

Gil ignored him. He started painting a portrait of him and Jun Do together, each giving the thumbs-up sign. They wore garish, forced smiles, and Jun Do didn't want him to finish.

"Let's go," Jun Do said. "You don't want to be late for karaoke night at the Yanggakdo or whatever you elites do for fun."

Gil didn't move. He was emphasizing Jun Do's muscles, making them oversized, like an ape's. "It's true," Gil said. "I've tasted beef and ostrich. I've seen *Titanic* and I've been on the internet ten different times. And yeah, there's karaoke. Every week there's an empty table where a family used to sit but now they're gone, no mention of them, and the songs they used to sing are missing from the machine."

"I promise you," Jun Do said. "Come back, and no one will ever know."

"The question isn't whether or not I'll come with you," Gil said. "It's why you're not coming with me."

If Jun Do wanted to defect, he could have done it a dozen times. At the end of a tunnel, it was as easy as climbing the ladder and triggering a spring-loaded door.

"In this whole stupid country," Jun Do said, "the only thing that made sense to me were the Korean ladies on their knees cleaning the feet of the Japanese."

"I could take you to the South Korean embassy tomorrow. It's just a train ride. In six weeks you'd be in Seoul. You'd be very useful to them, a real prize."

"Your mother, your father," Jun Do said. "They'll get sent to the camps."

"Whether you're a good karaoke singer or bad, eventually your number comes up. It's only a matter of time."

"What about Officer So—will some fancy whiskey make you forget him digging in the dark of Prison 9?"

"He's the reason to leave," Gil said. "So you don't become him."

"Well, he sends his regards," Jun Do said and dropped the loop of nylon over Gil's head, pulling the slack so the strap was snug around his neck.

Gil downed his whiskey. "I'm just a person," he said. "I'm just a nobody who wants out."

The bartender saw the leash. Covering her mouth, she said, "*Homo janai.*"

"I guess I don't need to translate that," Gil said.

Jun Do gave the leash a tug and they both stood.

Gil closed his watercolor tin, then bowed to the bartender. "*Chousenjin ni turesarareru yo,*" he said to her. With her phone, she took a picture of the two of them, then poured herself a drink. She lifted it in Gil's honor before drinking.

"Fucking Japanese," Gil said. "You've got to love them. I said I was being kidnapped to North Korea, and look at her."

"Take a good, long look," Jun Do said and lifted the motorcycle key from the bar.

*

Past the shore break, they motored into swells sharpened by the wind—the black inflatable lifted, then dropped flat in the troughs. Everyone held the lifeline to steady themselves. Rumina sat in the nose, fresh tape around her hands. Officer So had draped his jacket around her—except for that, her body was bare and blue with cold.

Jun Do and Gil sat on opposite sides of the raft, but Gil wouldn't look at him. When they reached open water, Officer So backed off the engine enough that Jun Do could be heard.

"I gave Gil my word," he told Officer So. "I said we'd forget how he tried to run."

Rumina sat with the wind at her back, hair turbulent in her face. "Put him in the bag," she said.

Officer So had a grand laugh at that. "The opera lady's right," he said. "You caught a defector, my boy. He had a fucking gun to our heads. But he couldn't outsmart us. Start thinking of your reward," he said. "Start savoring it."

The idea of a reward, of finding his mother and delivering her from her fate in Pyongyang, now made him sick. In the tunnels, they would sometimes wander into a curtain of gas. You couldn't detect it—a headache would spike, and you'd see the darkness throb red. He felt that now with Rumina glaring at him. He suddenly wondered if she didn't mean him, that Jun Do should go in the bag. But he wasn't the one who beat her or folded her up. It wasn't his father who'd ordered her kidnapping. And what choice did he have, about anything? He couldn't help that he was from a town lacking in electricity and heat and fuel, where the factories were frozen in rust, where able-bodied men were either in labor camps or were listless with hunger. It wasn't his fault that all the boys in his care were numb with abandonment and hopeless at the prospect of being recruited as prison guards or conscripted into suicide squads.

The lead was still around Gil's neck. Out of pure joy, Officer So leaned over and yanked it hard, just to feel it cinch. "I'd roll you over the side," he said. "But I'd miss what they're going to do to you."

Gil winced from the pain. "Jun Do knows how to do it now," he said. "He'll replace you, and they'll send you to a camp so you never talk about this business."

"You don't know anything," Officer So said. "You're soft and weak. I fucking invented this game. I kidnapped Kim Jong Il's personal sushi chef. I plucked the Dear Leader's own doctor out of an Osaka hospital, in broad daylight, with these hands."

"You don't know how Pyongyang works," Gil said. "Once the other ministers see her, they'll all want their own opera singers."

A cold, white spray slapped them. It made Rumina inhale sharply, as if every little thing was trying to take her life. She turned to Jun Do, glaring again. She was about to say something, he could tell—a word was forming on her lips.

He unfolded his glasses, put them on—now he could see the bruising on her throat, the way her hands were fat and purple below the tape on her wrists. He saw a wedding ring, a birth-surgery scar. She wouldn't stop glaring at him. Her eyes—they could see the decisions he'd made. They could tell it was Jun Do who'd picked which orphans ate first and which were left with watery spoonfuls. They recognized that it was he who assigned the bunks next to the stove and the ones in the hall where blackfinger lurked. He'd picked the boys who got blinded by the arc furnace. He'd chosen the boys who were at the chemical plant when it made the sky go yellow. He'd sent Ha Shin, the boy who wouldn't speak, who wouldn't say no, to clean the vats at the paint factory. It was Jun Do who put the gaff in Bo Song's hands.

"What choice did I have?" Jun Do asked her. He really needed to know, just as he had to know what happened to the boy and the girl at the end of the aria.

She raised her foot and showed Jun Do her toenails, the red paint vibrant against the platinum dark. She spoke a word, then drove her foot into his face.

The blood, it was dark. It trickled down his shirt, last worn by the man they'd plucked from the beach. Her big toenail had cut along his gums, but it was okay, he felt better, he knew the word now, the word that had been upon her lips. He didn't need to speak Japanese to understand the word "die." It was the ending to the opera, too, he was sure of it. That's what happened to the boy and the girl on the boat. It wasn't a sad story, really. It was one of love—the boy and the girl at least knew each other's fates, and they'd never be alone.

THERE WERE many kidnappings to come—years of them, in fact. There was the old woman they came upon in a tidal pool on Nishino Island. Her pants were rolled up and she peered into a camera mounted on three wooden legs. Her hair was gray and wild and she went without protest, in exchange for Jun Do's portrait. There was the Japanese climatologist they discovered on an iceberg in the Tsugaru Strait. They plucked his scientific equipment and red kayak, too. There was a rice farmer, a jetty engineer, and a woman who said she'd come to the beach to drown herself.

Then the kidnappings ended, as suddenly as they'd begun. Jun Do was assigned to language school, to spend a year learning English. He asked the control officer in Kyongsong if the new post was a reward for stopping a minister's son from defecting. The officer took Jun Do's old military uniform, his liquor ration card and coupon book for prostitutes. When the officer saw the book was nearly full, he smiled. *Sure,* he said.

Majon-ni, in the Onjin Mountains, was colder than Chongjin had ever been. Jun Do was grateful for the blue headphones he wore all day, as they drowned out the endless tank exercises of the Ninth Mechanized, which was stationed there. The school officials had no interest in teaching Jun Do to speak English. He simply had to transcribe it, learning vocabulary and grammar over the headphones and, key by clacking key, parroting it back on his manual typewriter. *I would like to purchase a puppy,* the woman's voice would say over the headphones, and this Jun Do would tap out. At least near the end, the school got a human teacher, a rather sad man, prone to depression, that Pyongyang had acquired from Africa. The man spoke no Korean, and he spent the classes asking the students grand, unanswerable questions, which greatly increased their command of the interrogative mode.

For four seasons, Jun Do managed to avoid poisonous snakes,

self-criticism sessions, and tetanus, which struck soldiers nearly every week. It would start innocently enough—a barbed-wire puncture, a cut from the rim of a ration tin—but soon came fevers, tremors, and finally, a coiling of the musculature that left the body too twisted and rigid for a casket. Jun Do's reward for these achievements was a listening post in the East Sea, aboard the fishing vessel *Junma*. His quarters were down in the *Junma*'s aft hold, a steel room big enough for a table, a chair, a typewriter, and a stack of receivers that had been pilfered from downed American planes in the war. The hold was lit only by the green glow of the listening equipment, which was reflected in the sheen of fish water that seeped under the bulkheads and constantly slicked the floor. Even after three months aboard the ship, Jun Do couldn't stop visualizing what was on the other side of those metal walls: chambers of tightly packed fish sucking their last breath in the refrigerated dark.

They'd been in international waters for several days now, their North Korean flag lowered so as not to invite trouble. First they chased deep-running mackerel and then schools of jittery bonito that surfaced in brief patches of sun. Now they were after sharks. All night the *Junma* had long-lined for them at the edge of the trench, and at daybreak, Jun Do could hear above him the grinding of the winch and the slapping of sharks as they cleared the water and struck the hull.

From sunset to sunrise, Jun Do monitored the usual transmissions: fishing captains mostly, the ferry from Uichi to Vladivostok, even the nightly check-in of two American women rowing around the world—one rowed all night, the other all day, ruining the crew's theory that they'd made their way to the East Sea for the purpose of having girl sex.

Hidden inside the *Junma*'s rigging and booms was a strong array antenna, and above the helm was a directional antenna that could turn 360 degrees. The U.S. and Japan and South Korea all encrypted their military transmissions, which sounded only like squeals and bleats. But how much squeal and where and when seemed really important to Pyongyang. As long as he documented that, he could listen to whatever he liked.

It was clear the crew didn't like having him aboard. He had an orphan's name, and all night he clacked away on his typewriter down there in the dark. It was as if having a person aboard whose job it was to perceive and record threats made the crew, young men from the port of Kinjye, sniff the air for danger as well. And then there was the Captain. He had reason to be wary, and each time Jun Do made him change course to track down an unusual signal, it was all he could do to contain his anger at the ill luck of having a listening officer posted to his fishing ship. Only when Jun Do started relating to the crew the updates of the two American girls rowing around the world did they begin to warm to him.

When Jun Do had filled out his daily requisition of military soundings, he roamed the spectrum. The lepers sent out broadcasts, as did the blind, and the families of inmates imprisoned in Manila who broadcast news into the prisons—all day the families would line up to speak of report cards, baby teeth, and new job prospects. There was Dr. Rendezvous, a Brit who broadcast his erotic "dreams" every day, along with the coordinates of where his sailboat would be anchored next. There was a station in Okinawa that broadcast portraits of families that U.S. servicemen refused to claim. Once a day, the Chinese broadcast prisoner confessions, and it didn't matter that the confessions were forced, false, and in a language he didn't understand—Jun Do could barely make it through them. And then came that girl who rowed in the dark. Each night she paused to relay her coordinates, how her body was performing, and the atmospheric conditions. Often she noted things—the outlines of birds migrating at night, a whale shark seining for krill off her bow. She had, she said, a growing ability to dream while she rowed.

What was it about English speakers that allowed them to talk into transmitters as if the sky were a diary? If Koreans spoke this way, maybe they'd make more sense to Jun Do. Maybe he'd understand why some people accepted their fates while others didn't. He might know why people sometimes scoured all the orphanages looking for one particular child when any child would do, when there were perfectly good children everywhere. He'd know why all the fishermen on the *Junma* had their wives' portraits tattooed on their chests, while he was a man who wore headphones in the dark of a fish hold on a boat that was twenty-seven days at sea a month.

Not that he envied those who rowed in the daylight. The light, the sky, the water, they were all things you looked *through* during the day. At night, they were things you looked *into*. You looked *into* the stars, you looked *into* dark rollers and the surprising platinum flash of their caps. No one ever stared at the tip of a cigarette in the daylight hours, and with the sun in the sky, who would ever post a "watch"? At night on the *Junma*, there was acuity, quietude, pause. There was a look in the crew members' eyes that was both faraway and inward. Presumably there was another English linguist out there on a similar fishing boat, pointlessly listening to broadcasts from sunrise to sunset. It was certainly another lowly transcriber like himself. He'd heard that the language school where they taught you to *speak* English was in Pyongyang and was filled with *yangbans,* kids of the elite who were in the military as a prerequisite to the Party and then a life as a diplomat. Jun Do could just imagine their patriotic names and fancy Chinese clothes as they spent their days in the capital practicing dialogs about ordering coffee and buying overseas medicines.

Above, another shark flopped onto the deck, and Jun Do decided to call it a night. As he was turning off his instruments, he heard the ghost broadcast: once a week or so, an English transmission came through that was powerful and brief, just a couple of minutes before it was gone. Tonight the speakers had American and Russian accents, and as usual, the broadcast was from the middle of a conversation. The two spoke about a trajectory and a docking maneuver and fuel. Last week, there'd been a Japanese speaker with them. Jun Do manned the crank that slowly turned the directional antenna, but no matter where he aimed it, the signal strength was the same, which was impossible. How could a signal come from everywhere?

Just like that, the broadcast seemed to end, but Jun Do grabbed his UHF receiver and a handheld parabolic, and headed above decks. The ship was an old Soviet steel-hulled vessel, made for cold water, and its sharp, tall bow made it plunge deep into waves and leap the troughs.

He held the rail and pointed the dish into the morning haze, sweeping the horizon. He picked up some chatter from container-vessel pilots and toward Japan he got all the craft advisories crosscut with a VHF Christian broadcast. There was blood on the deck, and Jun Do's military boots left drunk-looking tracks all the way to the stern, where the only transmissions were the squawks and barks of U.S. naval encryption. He did a quick sweep of the sky, dialing in a Taiwan Air pilot who lamented the approach of DPRK airspace. But there was nothing, the signal was gone.

"Anything I should know about?" the Captain asked.

"Steady as she goes," Jun Do told the Captain.

The Captain nodded toward the directional antenna atop the helm, which was made to look like a loudspeaker. "That one's a little more subtle," he said. There was an agreement that Jun Do wouldn't do anything foolish, like bringing spying equipment on deck. The Captain was older. He'd been a heavy man, but he'd done some time aboard a Russian penal vessel and that had leaned him so that now his skin hung loose. You could tell he'd once been an intense captain, giving clear-eyed commands, even if they were to fish in waters contested by Russia. And you could tell he'd been an intense prisoner, laboring carefully and without complaint under intense scrutiny. And now, it seemed, he was both.

The Captain lit a cigarette, offered one to Jun Do, then returned to tallying sharks, using a hand counter to click off each one the Machinist winched aboard. The sharks had been hanging from lead lines in open water so they were in a low-oxygen stupor when they breached the water and slammed against the hull before being boomed up. On deck, they moved slowly, nosing around like blind puppies, their mouths opening and closing as if there were something they were trying to say. The job of the Second Mate, because he was young and new to the ship, was to retrieve the hooks, while the First Mate, in seven quick cuts, dorsal to anal, took the fins and then rolled the shark back into the water, where, unable to maneuver, it could race nowhere but down, disappearing into the blackness, leaving only a thin contrail of blood behind.

Jun Do leaned over the side and watched one descend, following it down with his parabolic. The water crossing the shark's gills would revive its mind and perceptions. They were above the trench now, almost four kilometers deep, perhaps a half hour of free fall, and through his headphones, the background hiss of the abyss sounded more like the creeping, spooky crackle of pressure death. There was nothing to hear down there—all the subs communicated with ultralow-frequency bursts. Still, he pointed his parabolic toward the waves and slowly panned from bow to stern. The ghost broadcast had to come from somewhere. How could it seem to come from every direction if it didn't come from below? He could feel the eyes of the crew.

"You find something down there?" the Machinist asked.

"Actually," Jun Do said, "I lost something."

Come first light, Jun Do slept, while the crew—Pilot, Machinist, First Mate, Second Mate, and Captain alike—spent the day crating the shark fins in layers of salt and ice. The Chinese paid in hard currency, and they were very particular about their fins.

Jun Do woke before dinner, which was breakfast time for him. He had reports to type before darkness fell. There had been a fire on the *Junma* which took the galley, the head, and half of the bunks, leaving only the tin plates, a black mirror, and a toilet that had cracked in two from the heat. But the stove still worked, and it was summer, so everyone sat on the hatches to eat, where it was possible for the men to view a rare sunset. On the horizon was a carrier group from the American fleet, ships so large they didn't look as if they could move, let alone float. It looked like an island chain, so fixed and ancient as to have its own people and language and gods.

On the longline, they'd caught a grouper, whose cheeks they ate raw on the spot, and a turtle, unusual to hook. The turtle would take a day to stew, but the fish they baked whole and pulled off the bone with their fingers. A squid had also snagged on the line, but the Captain wouldn't abide them on board. He had lectured them many times on the squid. He considered the octopus the most intelligent animal in the ocean, the squid the most savage.

They took off their shirts and smoked, even as the sun fell. The *Junma* was pilotless, cantering in the waves, buoys rolling loose on the deck, and even the cables and booms glowed orange in the oven-colored light. The life of a fisherman was good—there were no endless factory quotas to fill, and on a ship there was no loudspeaker blaring government reports all day. There was food. And even though they were leery about having a listening officer on board, it meant that the *Junma* got all the fuel coupons it needed, and if Jun Do directed the ship in a way that lowered the catch, everyone got extra ration cards.

"So, Third Mate," the Pilot said. "How are our girls?"

That's what they called Jun Do sometimes, the Third Mate, as a joke.

"They're nearing Hokkaido," Jun Do told them. "At least they were last night. They're rowing thirty kilometers a day."

"Are they still naked?" the Machinist asked.

"Only the girl who rows in the dark," said Jun Do.

"To row around the world," the Second Mate said. "Only a sexy woman would do that. It's so pointless and arrogant. Only sexy Americans would think the world was something to defeat." The Second Mate couldn't have been more than twenty. On his chest, the tattoo of his wife was new, and it was clear she was a beauty.

"Who said they were sexy?" Jun Do asked, though he pictured them that way, too.

"I know this," the Second Mate said. "A sexy girl thinks she can do anything. Trust me, I deal with it every day."

"If your wife is so hot," the Machinist asked, "how come they didn't sweep her up to be a hostess in Pyongyang?"

"It's easy," the Second Mate said. "Her father didn't want her ending up as a barmaid or a whore in Pyongyang, so he pulled some strings and got her assigned to the fish factory. A beautiful girl like that, and along comes me."

"I'll believe it when I see it," the First Mate said. "There's a reason she doesn't come to see you off."

"Give it time," the Second Mate said. "She's still coping. I'll show her the light."

"Hokkaido," the Pilot said. "The ice up there is worse in the summer. The shelves break up, currents chum it. It's the ice you don't see, that's what gets you."

The Captain spoke. Shirtless, you could see all his Russian tattoos. They looked heavy in the sideways light, as if they were what had pulled his skin loose. "The winters up there," he said, "everything freezes. The piss in your prick and the fish gore in your beard. You try to set a knife down and you can't let go of it. Once, we were on the cutting floor when the ship hit a growler. It shook the whole boat, knocked us down into the guts. From the floor, we watched that ice roll down the side of the ship, knuckling big dents in the hull."

Jun Do looked at the Captain's chest. The tattoo of his wife was blurred and faded to a watercolor. When the Captain's ship didn't return one day, his wife had been given a replacement husband, and now the Captain was alone. Plus, they'd added the years he was in prison to his service debt to the state, so there'd be no retirement now. "The cold can squeeze a ship," the Captain suddenly said, "contract the whole thing, the metal doorframes, the locks, trapping you down in the waste tanks, and nobody, nobody's coming with buckets of hot water to get you out."

The Captain didn't throw a look or anything, but Jun Do wondered if the prison talk was aimed at him, for bringing his listening equipment on deck, for raising the specter that it could all happen again.

*

When darkness fell and the others went below, Jun Do offered the Second Mate three packs of cigarettes to climb atop the helm and shinny the pole upon which the loudspeaker was mounted.

"I'll do it," the Second Mate said. "But instead of cigarettes, I want to listen to the rowers."

The boy was always asking Jun Do what cities like Seoul and Tokyo were like, and he wouldn't believe that Jun Do had never been to Pyongyang. The kid wasn't a fast climber, but he was curious about how the radios worked, and that was half of it. Jun Do had him practice pulling the cotter pin so that the directional antenna could be lifted and pointed toward the water.

Afterward, they sat on the winch house, which was still warm, and smoked. The wind was loud in their ears. It made their cigarettes flare. There wasn't another light on the water, and the horizon line separated the absolute black of the water from the milk dark of the star-choked sky. A couple of satellites traversed above, and to the north, tracers of shooting stars.

"Those girls in the boat," the Second Mate said. "You think they're married?"

"I don't know," Jun Do said. "What's it matter?"

"What's it take to row around the world, a couple years? Even if they don't have husbands, what about everyone else, the people they left behind? Don't those girls give a shit about anybody?"

Jun Do picked some tobacco off his tongue and looked at the boy, who had his hands behind his head as he squinted at the stars. It was a good question—*What about the people left behind?*—but an odd one for the Second Mate to ask. "Earlier tonight," Jun Do said, "you were all for sexy rowers. They do something to piss you off?"

"I'm just wondering what got into them, to just take off and paddle around the world?"

"Wouldn't you, if you could?"

"That's my point, you can't. Who could pull it off—all those waves and ice, in that tiny boat? Someone should have stopped them. Someone should have taken that stupid idea out of their heads."

The kid sounded new to whatever heavy thinking was going on in his brain. Jun Do decided to talk him down a bit. "They already made it half-way," he pointed out. "Plus, they have to be some pretty serious athletes. They're trained for this, it's probably what they love. And when you say boat, you can't be thinking of this bucket. Those are American girls, their craft is hi-tech, with comforts and electronics—you can't be picturing them like Party officials' wives rowing a tin can around."

The Second Mate wasn't quite listening. "And what if you do make it around the world—how do you wait in line for your dormitory toilet again, knowing that you've been to America? Maybe the millet tasted better in some other country and the loudspeakers weren't so tinny. Suddenly it's *your* tap water that smells not so good—then what do you do?"

Jun Do didn't answer him.

The moon was coming up. Above, they could see a jet rising out of Japan—slowly it began its great veer away from North Korean airspace.

After a while, the Second Mate said, "The sharks will probably get them." He flicked his cigarette away. "So, what's this all about, pointing the antenna and all? What's down there?"

Jun Do wasn't sure how to answer. "A voice."

"In the ocean? What is it, what's it say?"

"There are American voices and an English-speaking Russian. Once a Japanese guy. They talk about docking and maneuvering. Stuff like that."

"No offense, but that sounds like the conspiracy talk the old widows are always trading in my housing block."

It did sound a little paranoid when the Second Mate said it out loud. But the truth was the idea of conspiracy appealed to Jun Do. That people were in communication, that things had a design, that there was intention, significance, and purpose in what people did—he needed to believe this. Normal people, he understood, had no need for such thinking. The girl who rowed during the day had the horizon of where she came from, and when she turned to look, the horizon of where she was headed. But the girl who rowed in the dark had only the splash and pull of each stroke and the belief that they'd all add up to get her home.

Jun Do looked at his watch. "It's about time for the night rower to broadcast," he said. "Or maybe it's the daytime girl you want?"

The Second Mate suddenly bristled. "What kind of a question is that? What's it matter which one? I don't want either of them. My wife is the most beautiful woman in her housing block. When I look into her eyes, I know exactly what she's thinking. I know what she's going to say before she says it. That's the definition of love, ask any old-timer."

The Second Mate smoked another cigarette and then tossed it in the sea. "Say the Russians and Americans are at the bottom of the ocean—what makes you think they're up to no good?"

Jun Do was thinking about all the popular definitions of love, that it was a pair of bare hands clasping an ember to keep it alive, that it was a pearl that shines forever, even in the belly of the eel that eats the oyster, that love was a bear that feeds you honey from its claws. Jun Do visualized those girls: alternating in labor and solitude, that moment when the oar-locks were handed off.

Jun Do pointed to the water. "The Americans and Russians are down there, and they're up to something, I know it. You ever hear of someone launching a submarine in the name of peace and fucking brotherhood?"

The Second Mate leaned back on the winch house, the sky vast above them. "No," he said, "I suppose not."

The Captain came out of the pilothouse and told the Second Mate he had shit buckets to clean. Jun Do offered the Captain a smoke, but when the boy had gone below, the Captain refused it. "Don't put ideas in his head," he said, and walked deliberately across the dark gangway to the high-riding bow of the *Junma*. A large vessel was creeping by, its deck carpeted with new cars. As it passed, likely headed from South Korea to California, the moonlight flashed in rapid succession off a thousand new windshields.

*

A couple of nights later, the *Junma*'s holds were full, and she was headed west for home. Jun Do was smoking with the Captain and the Pilot when they saw the red light flash on and off in the pilothouse. The wind was from the north, pacing them, so the deck was calm, making it seem like they were standing still. The light flashed on and off again. "You going to get that?" the Pilot asked the Captain.

The Captain pulled the cigarette out of his mouth and looked at it. "What's the point?"

"What's the point?" the Pilot asked.

"Yeah, what's the point? It's shit for us either way."

Finally, the Captain stood, straightened his jacket. His time in Russia had cured him of alcohol, yet he walked to the pilothouse as if for the harsh inevitability of a drink, rather than a radio call from the maritime minister in Chongjin. "That guy's only got so much," the Pilot said, and when the red light went off, they knew the Captain had answered the call. Not that he had a choice. The *Junma* was never out of range. The Russians who'd owned the *Junma* had outfitted it with a radio taken from a submarine—its long antenna was meant to transmit from below the surface, and it had a 20-volt wet-cell battery to power it.

Jun Do watched the Captain silhouetted in the pilothouse and tried to imagine what he might be saying into the radio by the way he pushed his hat back and rubbed his eyes. Jun Do, in his hold, only received. He'd never transmitted in his life. He was secretly building a transmitter on shore, and the closer he got to completion, the more nervous he became over what he'd say into it.

When the Captain returned, he sat at the break in the rail where the winch swung over, his legs hanging free over the side. He took off his hat, a filthy thing he only sometimes wore, and set it aside. Jun Do studied the brass crest with the sickle and hammer embossed over a compass face and a harpoon. They didn't even make hats like that anymore.

"So," the Pilot said. "What do they want?"

"Shrimp," the Captain said. "Live shrimp."

"In these waters?" the Pilot asked. "This time of year?" He shook his head. "No way, can't be done."

Jun Do asked, "Why don't they just buy some shrimp?"

"I asked them that," the Captain said. "The shrimp must be North Korean, they said."

A request like that could only come from the top, perhaps the very top. They'd heard cold-water shrimp were in big demand in Pyongyang. It was a new fashion there to eat them while they were still alive.

"What should we do?" the Pilot asked.

"What to do," the Captain said. "What to do."

"Well, there's nothing to do," Jun Do said. "We were ordered to get shrimp, so we must get shrimp, right?"

The Captain didn't say anything, he leaned back on the deck with his feet over the side and closed his eyes. "She was a believer, you know," the Captain said. "My wife. She thought socialism was the only thing that would make us strong again. There would be a difficult period, she always said, some sacrifices. And then things would be better. I didn't think I would miss that, you know. I didn't realize how much I needed someone to keep telling me *why.*"

"Why?" the Pilot asked. "Because other people depend on you. Everybody here needs you. Imagine if the Second Mate didn't have you to ask stupid questions to all day."

The Captain waved him off. "The Russians gave me four years," he said. "Four years on a fish-gutting ship, forever at sea, never once did we go to port. I got the Russians to let my crew go. They were young, village boys mostly. But next time? I doubt it."

"We'll just go out for shrimp," the Pilot said, "and if we don't get any, we don't get any."

The Captain didn't say anything to that plan. "The trawlers were always coming," he said. "They'd be out for weeks and then show up to transfer their catch to our prison ship. You never knew what it would be. You'd be down on the gutting floor, and you'd hear the engines of a trawler coming astern and then the hydraulic gates opening up and sometimes we'd even stand on our saw tables because down the chute, like a wave, would come thousands of fish—yellowtail, cod, snapper, even little sardines—and suddenly you were hip deep in them, and you'd fire up your pneumatic saws because nobody was getting out until you'd gutted your way out. Sometimes the fish were hoarfrosted from six weeks in a hold and sometimes they'd been caught that morning and still had the slime of life on them.

"Toward afternoon, they'd sluice the drains, and thousands of liters of guts would purge into the sea. We'd always go up top to watch that. Out of nowhere, clouds of seabirds would appear and then the topfish and sharks—believe me, a real frenzy. And then from below would rise the squid, huge ones from the Arctic, their albino color like milk in the water. When they got agitated, their flesh turned red and white, red and white, and when they struck, to stun their victims, they lanterned up, flashing bright as you could imagine. It was like watching underwater lightning to see them attack.

"One day, two trawlers decided to catch those squid. One set a drop net that hung deep in the water. The bottom of this net was tethered to the other trawler, which acted like a tug. The squid slowly surfaced, a hundred kilos some of them, and when they started to flash, the net was towed beneath them and buttoned up.

"We all watched from the deck. We cheered, if you can believe that. Then we went back to work as if hundreds of squid, electric with anger, weren't about to come down that chute and swamp the lot of us. Send down a thousand sharks, please—they don't have ten arms and black beaks. Sharks don't get angry or have giant eyes or suckers with hooks on them. God, the sound of the squid tumbling down the chute, the jets of ink, their beaks against the stainless steel, the colors of them, flashing. There was this little guy on board, Vietnamese, I'll never forget him. A nice guy for sure, kind of green, much like our young Second Mate, and I sort of took him under my wing. He was a kid, didn't know anything about anything yet. And his wrists, if you'd seen them. They were no bigger than this."

Jun Do heard the story as if it were being broadcast from some far-off, unknown place. Real stories like this, human ones, could get you sent to prison, and it didn't matter what they were about. It didn't matter if the story was about an old woman or a squid attack—if it diverted emotion from the Dear Leader, it was dangerous. Jun Do needed his typewriter, he needed to get this down, this was the whole reason he listened in the dark.

"What was his name?" he asked the Captain.

"The thing is," the Captain said, "the Russians aren't the ones who took her from me. All the Russians wanted was four years. After four years they let me go. But here, it never ends. Here, there is no limit to anything."

"What's that mean?" the Pilot asked.

"It means wheel her around," the Captain told him. "We're heading north again."

The Pilot said, "You're not going to do anything stupid, are you?"

"What I'm going to do is get us some shrimp."

Jun Do asked him, "Were you shrimping when the Russians got you?"

But the Captain had closed his eyes.

"Vu," he said. "The boy's name was Vu."

*

The next night, the moon was strong, and they were far north, on the shoals of Juljuksan, a disputed island chain of volcanic reefs. All day, the

Captain had told Jun Do to listen for anything—"anything or anybody, anywhere near us"—but as they approached the southernmost atoll, the Captain ordered everything turned off so that all the batteries could power the spotlights.

Soon, they could hear patches of open break, and seeing the white water froth against the invisibility of black pumice was unnerving. Even the moon didn't help when you couldn't see the rocks. The Captain was with the Pilot at the wheel, while the First Mate was in the bow with the big spotlight. Using handhelds, the Second Mate was to starboard and Jun Do was to port, everyone lighting up the water in an effort to gauge the depth. Holds full, the *Junma* was low in the water and slow to respond, so the Machinist was with the engine in case power was needed fast.

There was a single channel that wound through fields of frozen lava that even the tide was at pains to crawl over, and soon the tide began drawing them fast and almost sideways through the trough, the dark glitter of bottom whirring by in Jun Do's light.

The Captain seemed revived, with a wild, nothing-to-lose smile on his face. "The Russians call this chute the foxtrot," he said.

Out there in the tide, Jun Do saw a vessel. He called to the First Mate, and together, they lit it up. It was a patrol boat, broken up, on its side upon an oyster bar. There were no markings left, and it had been upon the rocks for some time. The antenna was small and spiraled, so he figured there was no radio worth salvaging.

"Bet they cracked up someplace else and the tide brung her here," the Captain said.

Jun Do wasn't so sure about that. The Pilot said nothing.

"Look for her lifeboat," the Captain told them.

The Second Mate was upset to be on the wrong side of the ship. "To see if there were survivors?" he asked.

"You just man that light," the Pilot told him.

"Anything?" the Captain asked.

The First Mate shook his head no.

Jun Do saw the red of a fire extinguisher strapped to the boat's stern, and much as he wished the *Junma* had an extinguisher, he kept his mouth shut and with a whoosh, they flashed past the wreck and it was gone.

"I suppose no lifeboat's worth sinking for," the Captain lamented.

They'd used buckets to put out the fire on the *Junma*, so the moment of abandoning ship, the moment in which it would have been revealed to the Second Mate that they had no lifeboat, never came.

The Second Mate asked, "What's the deal with their lifeboat?"

"You just man that light," the Pilot told him.

They cleared the offshore break, and as if cut from a tether, the *Junma* settled into calmer water. The craggy ass of the island was above them, and in its lee, finally, was a large lagoon that the outer currents kept in motion. Here was where the shrimp might congregate. They killed the lights, and then the engine, and entered the lagoon on inertia. Soon, they were slowly backpedaling with the circular tide. The current was constant and calm and rising, and even when the hull touched sand, no one seemed to worry.

Below raked obsidian bluffs was a steep, glassy black beach whose glint looked sharp enough to bleed your feet. In the sand, dwarfed, gnarled trees had anchored themselves, and in the blue light, you could see that the wind had curled even their needles. Upon the water, the moon revealed clumps of detritus swept in from the straits.

The Machinist extended the outriggers, then dipped the nets, soaking them so they'd submerge during skim runs. The mates secured the lines and the blocks, then raised the nets to see if any shrimp had turned up. Out in the green nylon webbing, a few shrimp bounced toward the trap, but there was something else out there, too.

They spilled the nets, and on the deck, amid the flipping and phosphorescing of a few dozen shrimp, were a couple of athletic shoes. They didn't match.

"These are American shoes," the Machinist said.

Jun Do read the word written on the shoe. "Nike," he said.

The Second Mate grabbed one.

Jun Do could read the look in his eye. "Don't worry," Jun Do said. "The rowers are far from here."

"Read the label," the Second Mate said. "Is it a woman's shoe?"

The Captain came over and examined a shoe. He smelled it, and then bent the sole to see how much water squished out. "Don't bother," the Captain said. "The thing's never even been worn." He told the Pilot to turn on the floodlights, which revealed hundreds of shoes bobbing out in the jade-gray water. Thousands, maybe.

The Pilot scanned the waters. "I hope there's no shipping container swirling 'round this bathtub with us," he said, "waiting to take our bottom out."

The Captain turned to Jun Do. "You pick up any distress calls?"

Jun Do said, "You know the policy on that."

The Second Mate asked, "What's the policy on distress calls?"

"I know the policy," the Captain said. "I'm just trying to find out if there are a bunch of vessels headed our way in response to a call."

"I didn't hear anything," Jun Do said. "But people don't cry on the radio anymore. They have emergency beacons now, things that automatically transmit GPS coordinates up to satellites. I can't pick up any of that. The Pilot's right—a shipping container probably fell off a deck and washed up here."

"Don't we answer distress calls?" the Second Mate asked.

"Not with him on board," the Captain said and handed Jun Do a shoe. "Okay, gentlemen, let's get those nets back in the water. It's going to be a long night."

Jun Do found a general broadcast station, loud and clear out of Vladivostok, and played it through a speaker on deck. It was Strauss. They started skimming the black water, and there was little time to marvel at the American shoes that began to pile atop the hatches.

While the crew seined for shoes above, Jun Do donned his headphones. There were lots of squawks and barks out there, and that would make someone, somewhere, happy. He'd missed the Chinese confessions just after sundown, which was for the best, as the voices always sounded hopelessly sad, and therefore guilty, to him. He did catch the Okinawan families making appeals to fathers listening on their ships, but it was hard to feel too bad for kids who had mothers and siblings. Plus the "adopt us" good cheer was enough to make a person sick. When the Russian families broadcast nothing but good cheer for their inmate fathers, it was to give the men strength. But trying to plead a parent into returning? Who would fall for that? Who would want to be around such a desperate, pathetic kid?

Jun Do fell asleep at his station, a rarity. He woke to the voice of the girl who rowed in the dark. She'd been rowing in the nude, she said, and under a sky that was "black and frilled, like a carnation stemmed in ink." She'd had a vision that humans would one day return to the oceans, growing flippers and blowholes, that humanity would become one again in the oceans, and there'd be no intolerance or war. Poor girl, take a day off, he thought, and decided not to give the Second Mate that update.

*

In the morning, the *Junma* was headed south again, the seine net full and swinging wildly with its lightweight purse of shoes. There were hundreds of shoes across the deck, the First and Second Mates stringing them together by general design. These garlands hung from all the cleats to dry in the sun. It was clear they'd found only a few matches. Still, even without sleep, they seemed to be in high spirits.

The First Mate found a pair, blue and white, and stowed them under his bunk. The Pilot was marveling over a size fifteen, over what manner of human would take that size, and the Machinist had created a tall pile of shoes he intended for his wife to try. The silvers and reds, the flashy accents and reflective strips, the whitest of whites, they were pure gold, these shoes: they equaled food, gifts, bribes, and favors. The feeling of them on, as though you weren't wearing anything on your feet. The shoes made the crew's socks look positively lousy, and their legs looked mottled and sun-worn amid such undiluted color. The Second Mate sifted through every shoe until he found a pair of what he called his "America shoes." They were both women's shoes. One was red and white, the other blue. He threw his own shoes overboard, then he traversed the deck with a different Nike on each foot.

Ahead, a large cloud bank had formed to the east, with a vortex of seabirds working the leading edge of it. It was an upwelling, with cold water from deep in the trench rising to the surface and condensing the air. This was the deep water that sperm whales hunted and six-gill sharks called home. Surfacing in that upwell would be black jellyfish, squid, and deepwater shrimp, white and blind. Those shrimp, it was said, with their large, occluded eyes, were taken still wriggling and peppered with caviar by the Dear Leader himself.

The Captain grabbed his binoculars and surveyed the site. Then he rang the bell, and the mates sprang up in their new shoes.

"Come on, lads," the Captain said, "we'll be heroes of the revolution."

The Captain took to rigging the nets himself, while Jun Do helped the Machinist fashion a live well from two rain barrels and a ballast pump. But entering the upwell proved trickier than they'd thought. What seemed like a mist at first became a cloud bank several kilometers deep. The waves came at odd angles, so it was hard to keep your balance, and fast-moving islets of fog raced along the wavecaps, making quick-flashing forests and meadows of visibility.

The first take was successful. The shrimp were clear in the water, white when the net was raised, then clear again when they were pitching with the slosh of the live well, their long antennas unfurling and retracting. When the Captain ordered the nets out again, the birds had vanished, and the Pilot began motoring through the fog to find them.

It wasn't possible from the water to sense which bearing they took, but the mates groomed the nets, and leaned with the waves. There was a sudden thrashing upon the surface. "The tuna have found them," the Captain called, and the First Mate sent the nets again into the water. The Pilot cranked the wheel and began a "circle in" while the drag of the nets nearly keeled her over. Two waves converged, double-troughing the *Junma*, sending loose shoes tumbling into the water, yet the catch held fast, and when the Machinist winched the haul into the air, there was a great flashing in the trap, as if they'd gone trolling for chandeliers. Then the shrimp in the tank, as if by some means of secret communication, began to phosphoresce in sympathy.

Everyone was needed at the live well to land the catch, which might swing in any direction once over the deck. The Machinist was operating the winch, but at the last moment the Captain shouted for him to hold fast, the net oscillating wildly. At the gunwale the Captain stared into the fog. Everyone else paused as well, staring at what they weren't sure, unsettled by such stillness amid the bucking of the ship and the gyration of the catch. The Captain signaled the Pilot to sound the horn, and they all attended the gloom for a response.

"Go below," the Captain told Jun Do, "and tell me what you hear."

But it was too late. A moment later, the fog flashing clear, the steady bow of an American frigate was visible. The *Junma* pitched for all it was worth, but there was barely any motion from the American ship, whose rail was lined with men holding binoculars. Then, an inflatable boarding craft was upon them, and the Americans were throwing lines. Here were the men who wore size fifteen shoes.

For the first few minutes, the Americans were all business, following a procedure that involved the crisp leveling and lifting of their black rifles. They made their way through the pilothouse and galley into the quarters below. From the deck, you could hear them move through the ship, shout-ing "clear-clear-clear" the whole way.

With them was a South Korean Navy officer who stayed up top while the Americans secured the ship. The ROK officer was crisp in his white uniform, and his name was Pak. His helmet was white with black and light-blue bands, rimmed in polished silver. He demanded a manifest and registration of ship's origin and the Captain's license, none of which they had. Where was their flag, Pak wanted to know, and why hadn't they an-swered when hailed?

The shrimp swung in the net. The Captain told the First Mate to dump it in the live well.

"No," Pak said. He pointed at Jun Do. "That one will do it."

Jun Do looked to the Captain. The Captain nodded. Jun Do went to the net and tried to steady it against the motion of the ship. Though he'd seen it done many times, he'd never actually dumped a haul. He found the release for the trap. He tried to time the swing of the net over the live well, thinking the catch would burst out, but when he pulled the cord, the shrimp came out in a stream that poured into the barrel, and swing-ing away dumped all along the deck, the gutterboards, and, finally, his boots.

"You didn't look like a fisherman," Pak said. "Look at your skin, look at your hands. Take off your shirt," he demanded.

"I give the orders around here," the Captain said.

"Take off your shirt, you spy, or I'll have the Americans take it off for you."

It only took a couple of buttons for Pak to see that Jun Do's chest was without a tattoo.

"I'm not married," Jun Do said.

"You're not married," Pak repeated.

"He said he's not married," the Captain said.

"The North Koreans would never let you out on the water if you weren't married. Who would there be to throw in prison if you defected?"

"Look," the Pilot said. "We're fishermen and we're headed back to port. That's the whole story."

Pak turned to the Second Mate. "What's his name?" he asked, indicat-ing Jun Do.

The Second Mate didn't say anything. He looked at the Captain.

"Don't look at him," Pak said, and stepped closer. "What's his position?"

"His position?"

"On the ship," Pak said. "Okay, what's your position?"

"Second mate."

"Okay, Second Mate," Pak said. He pointed at Jun Do. "This nameless guy here. What's his position?"

The Second Mate said, "The third mate."

Pak started laughing. "Oh, yes, the third mate. That's great, that's a good one. I'm going to write a spy novel and call it *The Third Mate*. You lousy spies, you make me sick. These are free nations you're spying on, democracies you're trying to undermine."

Some of the Americans came up top. They had black smudges on their faces and shoulders from squeezing through tight, half-burned passages. Security sweep over, their rifles were on their backs, and they were relaxed and joking. It was surprising how young they were, this huge battleship in the hands of kids. Only now did they seem to notice all the shoes. One sailor picked up a shoe. "Damn," he said. "These are the new Air Jordans— you can't even get these in Okinawa."

"That's evidence," Pak said. "These guys are all spies, and pirates and bandits, and we're going to arrest them all."

The sailor with the shoe looked at the fishermen with admiration. He said, "Smokey, smokey?" and offered them all a cigarette. Only Jun Do took him up on it, a Marlboro, very rich. His lighter was emblazoned with a smiling cruise missile whose wing was a flexed biceps. "My man," the sailor said. "North Koreans gettin' all bandity."

Two other sailors were shaking their heads at the condition of the ship, especially the way the bolts for the lifelines had rusted out. "Spies?" one of them asked. "They don't even have radar. They're using a fucking compass. There are no charts in the chart room. They're dead reckoning this bitch around."

"You don't know how devious these North Koreas are," Pak countered. "Their whole society is based on deception. You wait, we'll tear this boat apart, and you'll know I'm right." He bent down and opened the hatch to the forward hold. Inside were thousands of small mackerel, mouths open from being frozen alive.

Jun Do understood suddenly that they'd laugh at his equipment if they found it, that they'd tear it out and drag it into the bright lights and laugh at how he had it all rigged. And then he'd never hear an erotic tale from Dr. Rendezvous again, he wouldn't know if the Russian prisoners got paroled, it would be an eternal mystery if his rowers made it home, and he had had enough of eternal mysteries.

A sailor came out of the pilot house wearing the DPRK flag as a cape.

"Motherfucker," another sailor accosted him. "How the fuck did you end up with that? You are the sorriest sailor in the Navy, and I will be taking that from you."

Another sailor came up from below. His name tag read, "Lieutenant Jervis," and he had a clipboard. "Do you have any life vests?" he asked the crew.

Jervis tried to mime a vest, but the crew of the *Junma* shook their heads no. Jervis checked a box on his list. "How about a flare gun?" he asked and mimed shooting in the air.

"Never," the Captain said. "No guns on my ship."

Jervis turned to Pak. "Are you a translator or what?" he asked.

"I'm an intelligence officer," he answered.

"Would you just fucking translate for once?"

"Didn't you hear me, they're spies!"

"Spies?" Jervis asked. "Their ship is half-burned. They don't even have a shitter on this thing. Just ask them if they've got a fire extinguisher."

Jun Do's eyes lit up.

"Look," Pak said, "that one completely understood you. They probably all speak English."

Jervis mimed a fire extinguisher, sound effects and all.

The Machinist clasped his hands as if in prayer.

Even though he had a radio, Jervis yelled up to the ship, "We need a fire extinguisher."

There was some discussion up there. Then came the response: "Is there a fire?"

"Jesus," Jervis yelled. "Just send one down."

Pak said, "They'll just sell it on the black market. They're bandits, a whole nation of them."

When Jun Do saw a red fire extinguisher descend from that battleship on a rope, he suddenly understood that the Americans were going to let them go. He'd barely spoken English before, it had never been part of his training, but he sounded out, "Life raft."

Jervis looked at him. "You don't have a life raft?"

Jun Do shook his head no.

"And send down an inflatable," Jervis yelled up to the ship.

Pak was at the edge of losing it. He took his helmet off and ran his fingers along the surface of his flattop. "Isn't it obvious why they're not allowed to have a raft?"

"I got to hand it to you," Jervis said to Pak. "I think you're right about that one understanding English."

In the pilothouse, some sailors were screwing around with the radio. You could hear them in there transmitting messages. One picked up the handset and said, "This is a person-to-person message to Kim Jong Il from Tom John-son. We have intercepted your primping boat, but can't locate your hairspray, jumpsuit, or elevator shoes, over."

The Captain had been expecting a lifeboat, so when down the rope came a yellow bundle no bigger than a twenty-kilogram rice sack, he was confused. Jervis showed him the red deployment handle and mimed with large arms how it would expand.

All the Americans had little cameras, and when one started taking pictures, the rest of them did, too, of the piles of Nikes, of the brown sink where the crew shaved, of the turtle shell drying in the sun, of the notch the Machinist cut in the rail so he could crap into the sea. One sailor got ahold of the Captain's calendar of the actress Sun Moon, depicting movie stills from her latest films. They were laughing about how North Korean pinup girls wore full-length dresses, but the Captain was having none of it: he went over and snatched it back. Then one of the sailors came out of the pilothouse with the ship's framed portrait of Kim Jong Il. He'd managed to pry it off the wall, and he was holding it up.

"Get a load of this," he said. "It's the man himself."

The crew of the *Junma* stood graven.

Pak was instantly in motion. "No, no, no," he said. "This is very serious. You must put that back."

The sailor wasn't giving up the portrait. "You said they were spies, right? Finders fucking keepers, right, Lieutenant?"

Lieutenant Jervis tried to defuse things. "Let the boys have a couple tokens," he said.

"But this is nothing to joke about," Pak said. "People go to prison over this. In North Korea, this could mean death."

Another sailor came out of the pilothouse, and he'd gotten loose the portrait of Kim Il Sung. "I got his brother," he announced.

Pak held out his hands. "Wait," he said. "You don't understand. You could be sending these men to their graves. They need to be detained and questioned, not condemned."

"Look what I got," another sailor said. He came out of the pilothouse wearing the Captain's hat, and in two short steps, the Second Mate had drawn his sharking knife and put it to the sailor's throat.

A half-dozen rifles were unslung, and they made a nearly instantaneous *click*. Above, on the deck of the frigate, all the sailors with their cups of coffee froze. In the quiet was the familiar clank of the rigging, and water sloshing out of the live well. Jun Do could feel how the waves rebuffed from the frigate's bow double-rocked the *Junma*.

Very calmly, the Captain called to the Second Mate. "It's just a hat, son."

The Second Mate answered the Captain, though he didn't unlock eyes with the sailor. "You can't go around the world doing whatever you want. There are rules and the rules have to be followed. You can't just up and steal people's hats."

Jun Do said to him, "Let's just let the sailor go."

"I know where the line is," the Second Mate said. "I'm not crossing it—they are. Someone has to stop them, someone has to take those ideas out of their heads."

Jervis had his sidearm out. "Pak," he said. "Please translate that this man is about to get shot."

Jun Do stepped forward. The Second Mate's eyes were cold and flashing with uncertainty, and the sailor looked to him for help. Jun Do carefully took the hat off the sailor's head, then put a hand on the Second Mate's shoulder. The Second Mate said, "A guy has to be stopped before he does something stupid," then took a step back and tossed his knife into the sea.

Rifles high, the sailors cast an eye toward Jervis. He approached Jun Do. "Obliged for helping your man stand down," he said, and with a handshake, slipped Jun Do his officer's card. "If you're ever in the free world," he said, then gave the *Junma* a last, long look. "There's nothing here," he added. "Let's have a controlled withdrawal, gentlemen."

And then in what was almost a ballet—rifle down, retreat, shift, replace, rifle up—the eight Americans left the *Junma* so that seven rifles were pointed at the crew at all times, and yet, in a brief series of silent moments, the deck was clear and the boarding craft was away.

Right away, the Pilot was at the helm to bring the *Junma* about, and already the fog was stealing the edges of the frigate's gray hull. Jun Do half closed his eyes, trying to peer inside it, imagining its communications deck and the equipment there, how it could perceive anything, how it had power to apprehend everything that was uttered in the world. He looked at the card in his hand. It wasn't a frigate at all, but an interceptor, the USS *Fortitude,* and his boots, he realized, were crawling with shrimp.

*

Even though their fuel was low, the Captain ordered a heading of due west, and the crew hoped he was making for the safety of North Korean waters, rather than a shallow cove in which to scuttle the disgraced *Junma.* They were running with the waves at a good clip, and with land in sight it was strange not to have a flag clapping above. The Pilot at the helm kept looking at the two white squares on the wall where their leaders' portraits had been.

Jun Do, exhausted in the middle of the day, swept the shrimp he'd spilled into the gutter troughs and out into the water, returning them to whatever world had made them. But it was fake work, this sweeping, as it was fake work that the mates were about with the live well, just as the wrench the Machinist held was a prop. The Captain was circumnavigating the deck, growing angrier, judging by the way he muttered to himself, and while no one wanted to be near him when he was like this, no one wanted to take an eye off him, either.

The Captain passed Jun Do again. The old man's skin was red, the black of his tattoos practically shouting. "Three months," he said. "Three months on this boat, and you can't even pretend to be a fisherman? You've watched us empty a seine purse on this deck a hundred times—don't you eat off the same plates as us and shit in the same bucket?"

They watched the Captain walk to the bow, and when he came back, the mates stopped pretending to work, and the Pilot stepped out of the helm.

"You camp down there with your headphones on, tuning your dials and clacking all night on your typewriter. When you came aboard, they said you knew taekwondo, they said you could kill. I thought that when the time came you would be strong. But what kind of intelligence officer are you—you can't even pretend to be an ignorant peasant like the rest of us."

"I'm not in intelligence," Jun Do said. "I'm just a guy they sent to language school."

But the Captain wasn't listening. "What the Second Mate did was stupid, but he took action, he was defending us, not putting us in jeopardy. But you, you froze, and now it may be over for us."

The First Mate tried to say something, but the Captain glared at him. "You could have said you were a reporter, doing a story on humble fishermen. You could have said you were from Kim Il Sung University, that you were studying shrimp. That officer wasn't trying to be your friend. He doesn't care about you at all." The Captain pointed toward the shore. "And they're even worse," he said. "People don't mean anything to them, anything at all."

Jun Do stared, without affect, into the Captain's eyes.

"Do you understand?"

Jun Do nodded.

"Then say it."

"People don't mean anything to them," Jun Do said.

"That's right," the Captain said. "They only care about the story we're going to tell, and that story will be useful to them or it won't. When they ask you what happened to our flag and portraits, what story are you going to tell them?"

"I don't know," Jun Do told him.

The Captain turned to the Machinist.

The Machinist said, "There was another fire, this time in the helm, and the portraits, unfortunately, burned. We could light the fire, and when it looked burned enough, put it out with the extinguisher. We'd want the ship to still be smoking when we entered the harbor."

"Good, good," the Captain said. He asked the Machinist what his role would be.

"I burned my hands trying to save their portraits."

"And how did the fire start?" the Captain asked.

"Cheap Chinese fuel," the Second Mate said.

"Good," the Captain said.

"Tainted South Korean fuel," the First Mate said.

"Even better," the Captain said.

The Pilot said, "And I burned my hair off trying to save the flag."

"And you, Third Mate," the Captain asked. "What was your role in the fire?"

Jun Do thought about it. "Um," he said. "I poured buckets of water?"

The Captain looked at him with disgust. He picked up a shoe and regarded its colors—green and yellow, with the diamond of the nation of Brazil. "There's no way we'll be able to explain these," he said and threw it overboard. He picked up another, white with a silver swoosh. This, too, he tossed overboard. "Some humble fishermen were out in the bountiful North Korean waters, adding with their efforts to the riches of the most democratic nation in the world. Though they were tired, and though they'd far exceeded their revolutionary quotas, they knew the birthday of the Great Leader Kim Il Sung was nearing, and that dignitaries from all over the world would be visiting to pay their respects."

The First Mate retrieved the pair of shoes he'd saved. With a deep, painful breath, he threw them into the sea. He said, "What could they do, these humble fishermen, to show their respect for the great leader? They decided to harvest some delicious North Korean shrimp, the envy of the world."

The Pilot kicked a shoe into the sea. "In praise of the Great Leader, the shrimp leaped willingly from the ocean into the fishermen's nets."

The Machinist began pushing whole stacks of shoes overboard. "Hiding in the fog like cowards were the Americans," he said, "in a giant ship bought with the blood money of capitalism."

The Second Mate closed his eyes for a moment. He removed his shoes, and now he had none. The look in his eyes said that the wrongest thing that had ever happened was happening right now. And then the shoes slipped from his hand and into the water. He pretended to look at the horizon so that no one would see his face.

The Captain turned to Jun Do. "In this story of naked imperial aggression, what role did you play, citizen?"

"I was witness to it all," Jun Do said. "The young Second Mate is too humble to speak of his own bravery, but I saw it, I saw all of it—how the Americans boarded in a surprise attack, how an ROK officer led the Americans around like dogs on a chain. I saw them insult our country and parade in our flag, but when they touched the portraits of our Leaders, lightning fast, the Second Mate, in the spirit of true self-sacrifice, drew his knife and took on the entire platoon of American pigs. Within moments, the Americans were retreating for their lives, such was the bravery and revolutionary zeal of the Mate."

The Captain came and clapped Jun Do on the back. With that, all of the Nikes went into the sea, leaving a slick of shoes behind. What had taken all night to gather went over in a few minutes. Then the Captain called for the extinguisher.

The Machinist brought it to the edge of the ship, and everyone watched as it went into the water. Nose first, a flash of red, and it was barreling for the deeps. Then it was time for the life raft, which they balanced on the rail. They took one last look at it, beyond yellow in the afternoon light, and when the First Mate went to push it over, the Captain stopped him. "Wait," the Captain said and took a moment to gather his resolve. "At least let's see how it works." He pulled the red handle, and as promised, it deployed with a burst before it even hit the water. It was so new and clean, double-ringed under a foul-weather canopy, big enough for all of them. A little red light flashed on top, and together they watched as their rescue boat sailed off without them.

*

Jun Do slept until they made port in Kinjye that afternoon. The crew all donned their red Party pins. Waiting for them at the dock was a large group—several soldiers, the maritime minister from Chongjin, some local Party officials, and a reporter from the regional office of *Rodong Sinmun*. They'd all heard about the insulting American radio transmissions, though the last thing they were going to do was brave the American fleet to rescue the *Junma*.

Jun Do told his story, and when the reporter asked his name, Jun Do said it didn't matter, as he was only a humble citizen of the greatest nation in the world. The reporter liked that. There was an older gentleman at the dock whom Jun Do hadn't noticed at first. He wore a gray suit and had a flattop of short white hair. His hands, though, were unforgettable—they'd been broken and had mishealed. Really, they looked as if they'd been drawn into the *Junma*'s winch. When it was all over, the older man and the reporter led the Second Mate off to confirm the story and get more quotes.

With dark, Jun Do made his way down the fish-cart paths that led to the new cannery. The old cannery had had a bad batch of tins and many citizens were lost to botulism. The problem proved impossible to locate, so they built a new cannery next to the old one. He passed the fishing boats, and the *Junma* at her tether, men in button-down shirts already unloading her. Whenever bureaucrats in Chongjin were caught being less than supremely obedient, they'd have to make a pilgrimage down to Wonsan or Kinjye to serve a couple of weeks doing revolutionary labor, like hand-hauling fish night and day.

Jun Do lived in the Canning Master's house, a large, beautiful dwelling that no one else wished to occupy because of what had happened to the Canning Master and his family. Jun Do inhabited only one room, the kitchen, which had all that he needed: a light, a window, a table, the stove, and a cot he'd set up. It was only a couple of days a month that he was ashore, and if there were ghosts, they didn't seem to bother him.

Spread across the table was the transmitter he'd been building. If he broadcast in short bursts, the way the Americans did from the bottom of the sea, he might be able to use it undetected. But the closer it came to completion, the slower he worked, because what in the world would he have to broadcast about? Would he speak of the soldier who said, "Smokey, smokey?" Perhaps he'd tell the world about the look on the Captain's face as they motored south past the wide, empty beaches of Wonsan, which is where all the bureaucrats in Pyongyang are told they will go when they enter the paradise of retirement.

Jun Do made a cup of tea in the kitchen, and he shaved for the first time in three weeks. Out the window, he watched the men unloading the *Junma* in the dark, men who were certainly praying for the moment the power went out, and they could retreat to their bunks. First he shaved the lather from around his mouth, and then instead of finishing his tea, he sipped Chinese whiskey as he drew the razor, the sound like a blade through sharkskin. There'd been a certain thrill to telling the reporter the tall tale, and it was amazing how the Captain was right: the reporter didn't even want his name.

Later in the night, after the power was out and the moon had set, Jun Do went on his roof in the absolute darkness and felt his way to the stove flue. He hoped to rig an antenna that would extend from the flue with the pull of a rope. Tonight, he was just running the cable, and even that had to be done under cover of total dark. He could hear the ocean out there, feel the offshoreness of it in the air on his face. And yet, when he sat on the pitch, he could make out none of it. He'd seen the sea in the daylight, been upon it countless times, but what if he hadn't? What might a person think was out there in the unfathomably grand darkness that lay ahead? The finless sharks, at least, had seen what was below the ocean, and their consolation was that they knew toward what they were descending.

At dawn, the shock-work whistles sounded, usually Jun Do's signal to go to bed. The loudspeaker came on and began blaring the morning announcements.

"Greetings, citizens!" it began.

There was a knock at the door, and when Jun Do answered, he found the Second Mate. The young man was quite drunk, and he'd been in a vicious fight.

"Did you hear the news?" the Second Mate asked. "They made me a Hero of the Eternal Revolution—that comes with all the medals and a hero's pension when I retire."

The Second Mate's ear was torn, and they needed to get the Captain to give his mouth some stitches. The swelling on the boy's face was general, with a few bright, isolated knots. Pinned on his chest was a medal, the Crimson Star. "Got any snake liquor?" he asked.

"How about we step down to beer?" Jun Do responded before popping the caps off two bottles of Ryoksong.

"I like that about you—always ready to drink in the morning. What's that toast? *The longer the night, the shorter the morning.*"

When the Second Mate drank from his bottle, Jun Do could see there were no marks on his knuckles. He said, "Looks like you made some new friends last night."

"Let me tell you," the Second Mate said. "Acts of heroism are easy—becoming a hero is a bitch."

"Let's drink to acts of heroism, then."

"And their spoils," the Second Mate added. "Speaking of which, you have got to check out my wife—wait till you get a load of how beautiful she is."

"I look forward to it," Jun Do told him.

"No, no, no," the Second Mate said. He went to the window and pointed to a woman standing alone in the fish-cart lane. "Look at her," he said. "Isn't she something? Tell me she's not something."

Jun Do peered through the window. The girl had wet, wide-set eyes. Jun Do knew the look on her face: as if she desperately wanted to be adopted, but not by the parents who were visiting that day.

"Tell me she's not outrageous," the Second Mate said. "Show me the more beautiful woman."

"There's no denying it," Jun Do said. "You know she's welcome to come in."

"Sorry," the Second Mate said, and plopped back in his chair. "She won't set foot in this place. She's afraid of ghosts. Next year, I'll probably put a baby in her—then her breasts will swell with milk. I can tell her to come closer if you want a better look. Maybe I'll have her sing. You'll fall out the window when you hear that."

Jun Do took a pull from his beer. "Have her sing the one about true heroes refusing all rewards."

"You've got a screwed-up sense of humor," the Second Mate said, holding the cold beer bottle against his ribs. "You know the children of heroes get to go to red-tier schools? Maybe I'll have a whole brood and live in a house like this. Maybe I'll live in this very one."

"You're welcome to it," Jun Do told him. "But it doesn't look like your wife would join you."

"Oh, she's a child," he said. "She'll do anything I say. Seriously, I'll call her in here. You'll see, I can make her do anything."

"And what about you, you're not afraid of ghosts?" Jun Do asked.

The Second Mate looked around, newly appraising the house. "I wouldn't want to put too much thought into how things ended for the Canning Master's kids," he said. "Where did it happen?"

"Upstairs."

"In the bathroom?"

"There's a nursery."

The Second Mate leaned his head back and looked at the ceiling. And then he closed his eyes. For a moment, Jun Do thought he was asleep. Then the Second Mate spoke up. "Kids," he said. "That's what it's all about, right? That's what they say."

"That's what they say," Jun Do said. "But people do things to survive, and then after they survive, they can't live with what they've done."

The Second Mate had been a babe in the '90s, so to him, these years after the famine must have been ones of glorious plenitude. He took a long drink of beer. "If everyone who had it shitty and bit the dust became a fart," he said, "the world would stink to the treetops, you know what I mean?"

"I suppose."

"So I don't believe in ghosts, okay? Someone's canary dies, and they hear a tweet in the dark, and they think, *Oh, it's the ghost of my bird.* But if you ask me, a ghost is just the opposite. It's something you can feel, that you know is there, but you can't get a fix on. Like the captain of the *Kwan Li.* The doctors ended up having to amputate. I don't know if you heard that or not."

"I didn't," Jun Do told him.

"When he woke in the hospital, he asked, *Where's my arm,* and the doctors said, *Sorry, but we had to amputate,* and the captain says, *I know my arm is gone, where is it,* but they won't tell him. He can feel it, he says, making a fist without him. In the tub, he can feel the hot water with his missing arm. But where is it—in the trash or burned? He knows it's out there, he can literally feel it, but he's got no powers."

"To me," Jun Do said, "what everybody gets wrong about ghosts is the notion that they're dead. In my experience, ghosts are made up only of the living, people you know are out there but are forever out of range."

"Like the Captain's wife?"

"Like the Captain's wife."

"I never even met her," the Second Mate said. "But I see her face on the Captain, and it's hard not to wonder where she is and who she's with and does she still think about the Captain."

Jun Do lifted his beer and drank in honor of this insight.

"Or maybe your Americans at the bottom of the ocean," the Second Mate said. "You hear them down there tinkering around, you know they're important, but they're just beyond your reach. It only makes sense, you know, it's right in line with your profile."

"My profile? What's my profile?"

"Oh, it's nothing," the Second Mate said. "Just something the Captain talked about once."

"Yeah?"

"He only said that you were an orphan, that they were always after things they couldn't have."

"Really? You sure he didn't say it was because orphans try to steal other people's lives?"

"Don't get upset. The Captain just said I shouldn't be too friendly with you."

"Or that when they die, orphans like to take other people with them? Or that there's always a reason someone becomes an orphan? There are all kinds of things people say about orphans, you know."

The Second Mate put his hand up. "Look," he said. "The Captain just told me that nobody had ever taught you loyalty."

"Like you know anything about it. And if you have any interest in facts, I'm not even an orphan."

"He said you'd say that. He wasn't trying to be mean," the Second Mate said. "He just said that the military weeds out all the orphans and puts them through special training that makes them not have feelings when bad things happen to other people."

Through the window, the sun was starting to glow in the rigging of the fishing fleet. And the young woman outside stepped aside every time a two-wheeled, fish-hauling cart came by.

Jun Do said, "How about you tell me what you're doing here?"

"I told you," he said. "I wanted to show you my wife—she's very beautiful, don't you think?"

Jun Do just looked at him.

The Second Mate went on, "Of course she is. She's like a magnet, you know, you can't resist her beauty. My tattoo doesn't do her justice. And we practically have a family already. I'm a hero now, of course, and it's pretty much a lock that I'll make Captain someday. I'm just saying, I'm a guy who's got a lot to lose." The Second Mate paused, choosing his words. "But you, you got no one. You're on a cot in the kitchen of a monster's house." The woman outside made a gesture of beckoning, but the Second Mate waved her off. "If you'd just punched that American in the face," he said, "you'd be in Seoul by now, you'd be free. That's what I don't get. If a guy has no strings, what's stopping him?"

How to tell the Second Mate that the only way to shake your ghosts was to find them, and that the only place Jun Do could do that was right here. How to explain the recurring dream that he's listening to his radio, that he's getting the remnants of important messages, from his mother, from other boys in his orphanage. The messages are hard to dial in, and he's awoken before with his hand on the bunk post, as if it were his UHF fine tuner. Sometimes the messages are from people who are relaying messages from other people who have spoken to people who have seen his mother. His mother wants to get urgent messages to him. She wants to tell him where she is, she wants to tell him why, she keeps repeating her name, over and over, though he can't quite make it out. How to explain that in Seoul, he knows, the messages would stop.

"Come," Jun Do said. "We should get you to the Captain for some stitches."

"Are you kidding? I'm a hero. I get to go to the hospital now."

*

When the *Junma* left port again, they had new portraits of the Great and Dear Leaders Kim Il Sung and Kim Jong Il. They had a new galley table, and they also had a new commode, for it was not right for a hero to shit in a bucket, though heroes of North Korea have endured far worse and done so without complaint. They also had a new DPRK flag, which they lowered eleven kilometers from shore.

The Captain was in high spirits. On deck was a new locker, and with a foot upon it, he called the crew together. From the locker, he first produced a hand grenade. "This," he said, "I have been given in the event the Americans return. I am to drop it in the aft hold and scuttle our dear ship the *Junma*."

Jun Do's eyes went wide. "Why not drop it in the engine room?"

The Machinist gave him a *screw you* look.

The Captain then threw the grenade into the sea, where it made not so much as a *zip* as it went under the surface. To Jun Do, he said, "Don't worry, I would have knocked first." The Captain kicked open the locker to reveal an inflatable life raft, clearly taken out of an old Soviet passenger jet. It had once been orange, but was now faded to a dull peach, and next to its red handle was an ominous warning against smoking during deployment. "After the grenade goes off, and our beloved vessel slips below the waves, I have been ordered to deploy *this,* lest we lose the life of our resident hero. I don't have to tell you the trust that has been placed in us to receive such a gift."

The Second Mate stepped forward, almost as if he was afraid of the thing, to inspect the Cyrillic writing. "It's bigger than the other one," he said.

"A whole planeload of people could fit in that raft," the Machinist told him. "Or the greatness of one hero."

"Yeah," the First Mate said. "I for one would be honored to tread water next to a raft that contained a true Hero of the Eternal Revolution."

But the Captain wasn't done. "And I figure it is time to make the Third Mate an official member of our crew." He withdrew from his pocket a folded piece of waxed paper. Within this were nine fine sewing needles, cauterized together. The tips of the needles were blackened from many tattooings. "I'm no Russian," he told Jun Do, "but you'll see I became pretty handy at this. And here we don't even have to worry about the ink freezing."

In the galley, they reclined Jun Do upon the table and had him take off his shirt. When the Pilot saw Jun Do's naked chest, he said, "Ah, a virgin," and everyone laughed.

"Look," Jun Do said, "I'm not so sure about this. I'm not even married."

"Relax," the Captain said. "I'm going to give you the most beautiful wife in the world."

While the Pilot and the First Mate flipped through the calendar of the actress Sun Moon, the Captain sprinkled his powdered ink into a spoon and mixed it with drops of water until it was just wetter than paste. The calendar had hung for a long time in the pilothouse, but Jun Do had never really given it much attention because it reeked of the patriotism that came over the loudspeakers. He'd only ever glimpsed a couple of movies in his life, and those were Chinese war movies his unit was shown during bad weather days in the military. Certainly there'd been posters around for Sun Moon's movies, but they must not have seemed to apply to him. Now, watching the First Mate and Pilot flip through the movie posters, discussing which one had the best image and expression for a tattoo, he was jealous of the way they recalled famous scenes and lines of North Korea's national actress. He noted a depth and sadness in Sun Moon's eyes, the faint lines around them bespeaking a resoluteness in the face of loss, and it took everything in him to suppress the memory of Rumina. And then the idea of a portrait, of any person, placed over your heart, forever, seemed irresistible. How was it that we didn't walk around with every person who mattered tattooed on us forever? And then Jun Do remembered that he had no one that mattered to him, which was why his tattoo would be of an actress he'd never seen, taken from a calendar at the helm of a fishing boat.

"If she's such a famous actress," Jun Do said, "then everyone in North Korea will recognize her and know she's not my wife."

"The tattoo," the Captain said, "is for the Americans and South Koreans. To them, it will simply be a female face."

"Honestly," Jun Do said. "I don't even know why you guys do this, what's the point of tattooing your wife's face on your chest?"

The Second Mate said, "Because you're a fisherman, that's why."

"So they can identify your body," the Pilot said.

The quiet Machinist said, "So that whenever you think of her, there she is."

"Oh, that sounds noble," the First Mate said. "But it's to give the wives peace of mind. They think no other woman will sleep with a man who has such a tattoo, but there are ways of course, there are girls."

"There is only one reason," the Captain said. "It's because it places her in your heart forever."

Jun Do thought about that. A childish question came to him, one that marked him as someone who had never known any kind of love. "Are you placing Sun Moon in my heart forever?" he asked.

"Oh, our young Third Mate," the Captain said, smiling to the others. "She's an actress. When you see her movies, that's not really her. Those are just characters she plays."

Jun Do said, "I haven't seen her movies."

"There you go, then," the Captain said. "There's nothing to worry about."

"What kind of name is Sun Moon?" Jun Do asked.

"I guess she's a celebrity," the Captain said. "Maybe all the *yangbans* in Pyongyang have strange names."

They selected an image from *Tyrants Asunder*. It was a head shot, and instead of staring duty-bound toward a distant imperialist army or looking up to Mount Paektu for guidance, Sun Moon here regarded the viewer with a reverence for all they would have lost together by the time the final movie credits rolled.

The Pilot held the calendar steady, and the Captain began with her eyes. He had a good technique—he'd draw the needles backward, teasing them in and out of the skin with the kind of shimmy you use to cinch a bosun's knot. That way the pain was less, and the needle tips went in at an angle, anchoring the ink. The Captain used a wet rag to wash away stray ink and blood.

As he worked, the Captain wondered aloud to himself. "What should the Third Mate know of his new wife?" he mused. "Her beauty is obvious. She is from Pyongyang, a place none of us will ever see. She was discovered by the Dear Leader himself and cast in *A True Daughter of the Country,* the first North Korean movie. How old was she then?"

"Sixteen," the First Mate said.

"That sounds about right," the Pilot said. "How old are you?" he asked the Second Mate.

"Twenty."

"Twenty," the Pilot said. "That movie was made the year you were born."

The roll of the ship seemed not to bother the Captain at all. "She was the darling of the Dear Leader, and she was the only actress. No one else could star in a movie, and this went on for years. Also, despite her beauty, or because of it, the Dear Leader would not allow her to marry, so that all of her roles were only roles, as she did not know herself of love."

"But then came Commander Ga," said the Machinist.

"Then came Commander Ga," the Captain repeated in the absent way of someone lost in fine details. "Yes, he is the reason you don't have to worry about Sun Moon being placed too deeply in your heart."

Jun Do had heard of Commander Ga—he was practically preached in the military as a man who'd led six assassination missions into South Korea, won the Golden Belt in taekwondo, and purged the Army of all the homosexuals.

The Second Mate said, "Commander Ga even fought a bear."

"I'm not so sure about that part," the Captain said, outlining the subtle contours of Sun Moon's neck. "When Commander Ga went to Japan and beat Kimura, everyone knew that upon his return to Pyongyang, he would name his prize. The Dear Leader made him Minister of Prison Mines, which is a coveted position, as there is no work to be done. But Commander Ga demanded possession of the actress Sun Moon. Time passed, there was trouble in the capital. Finally, the Dear Leader bitterly relented. The couple married, had two children, and now Sun Moon is remote and melancholy and alone."

Everyone went quiet when the Captain said this, and Jun Do suddenly felt for her.

The Second Mate threw him a pained look. "Is that true?" he asked. "Do you know that's how she ended up?"

"That's how all wives end up," the Captain said.

*

Late that night, Jun Do's chest hurt, and he yearned to hear from the girl who rowed in the dark. The Captain had told him that seawater would keep the tattoo from getting septic, but Jun Do wouldn't take the chance of going up top for a bucket and missing her. More and more, he felt as if he was the only one in the world who understood her. It was Jun Do's curse to be nocturnal in a nation without power at night, but it was his duty, too, like picking up a pair of oars at sunset or letting the loudspeakers fill your head as you sleep. Even the crew thought of her as rowing toward dawn, as if dawn was a metaphor for something transcendent or utopian. Jun Do understood that she was rowing *until* dawn, when with weariness and fulfillment she could pack it in for sleep. It was deep into the night when he finally found her signal, faint from traveling so far from the north.

"The guidance system is broken," she said. "It keeps saying the wrong things. We're not where it says we are, we can't be. Something's out on the water, but we can't see it."

The line went quiet, and Jun Do reached to fine-tune the signal.

Then she was back. "Does this work?" she asked. "Is it working? There's a ship out there, a ship without lights. We shot it with a flare. The red streak bounced off the hull. Is anyone out there, can anyone rescue us?"

Who was attacking her? he wondered. What pirate would attack a woman who wished nothing more than to make her way through the dark? Jun Do heard a pop over the line—was it the pop of gunfire?—and parading through his head came all the reasons it was impossible to rescue her: that she was too far north, that the Americans would find her, that they didn't even have maps of those waters. All true, but of course the real reason was him. Jun Do was why they couldn't chart a course to rescue her. He reached forward and turned off the receiver, the green afterimage of its dials lingering in his eyes. He felt the sudden static of cool air when he removed his headphones. Up on deck, he scanned the horizon, looking for the lone red arc of her emergency flare.

"Lose something?" the Captain asked. He was just a voice from the helm.

Jun Do turned to see the tip of his glowing cigarette.

"Yeah," Jun Do said. "I think I did."

The Captain didn't leave the pilothouse. "That boy's pretty messed up right now," he said. "The last thing he needs is some craziness from you."

Using a lanyard, Jun Do fished a bucket of water from the sea and poured it on his chest. He felt the pain as a memory, something from long ago. He looked upon the sea some more. The black waves would rise and clap, and in the troughs between them, you could imagine anything was out there. *Someone will save you,* he thought. *If you just hold tight long enough, someone's bound to.*

*

The crew put down longlines all day, and when Jun Do woke at sunset, they were bringing aboard the first sharks. Now that they'd been boarded by Americans, the Captain was no longer afraid of being boarded by Americans. He asked that Jun Do channel the broadcasts through a speaker on the deck. It would be late, Jun Do warned them, before the naked rower checked in, if that's what they were hoping for.

The night was clear, with regular rollers from the northeast, and the deck lights penetrated far into the water, showing the red eyeshine of creatures just a little too deep to make out. Jun Do used the array antenna, and rolled the crew through the whole spectrum, from the ultralow booms of sub-to-sub communications to the barking of transponders guiding jet autopilots through the night. He let them listen to the interference caused when the radar of distant vessels swept through them. At the top of the dial was the shrill rattle of a braille book broadcaster, and out there at the very peak was the trancelike hiss of solar radiation in the Van Allen belts. The Captain was more interested in the drunk Russians singing while they operated an offshore drilling platform. He muttered every fourth or fifth line, and if they gave him a minute, he said, he'd name the song.

The first three sharks they brought aboard had been eaten by a larger shark, and nothing remained below the gills. Jun Do found a woman in Jakarta who read English sonnets into a shortwave, and he approximated them as the Captain and mates examined the bite radius and peered through the sharks' empty heads. He played for them two men in unknown countries who were attempting to solve a mathematical problem over a ham radio, but it proved very difficult to translate. For a while, Jun Do would stare toward the northerly horizon, then he would force himself not to stare. They listened to planes and ships and the strange echoes that came from the curve of the earth. Jun Do tried to explain concepts like FedEx, and the men debated whether a parcel could really be sent between any two humans on earth in twenty-four hours.

The Second Mate kept asking about the naked rower.

"I bet her nipples are like icicles," he said. "And her thighs must be white with goose pimples."

"We won't hear from her until dawn," Jun Do said. "No use talking about it till then."

The Machinist said, "You need to look out for those big American legs."

"Rowers have strong backs," the First Mate said. "I bet she could tear a mackerel in half."

"Tear me in half, please," the Second Mate said. "Wait till she finds out I'm a hero. I could be an ambassador, we could make some peace."

The Captain said, "And wait till she finds out you like women's shoes."

"I bet she wears men's shoes," the Pilot said.

"Cold on the outside and warm on the inside," the Second Mate said. "That's the only way."

Jun Do turned to him. "You want to shut up about it already?"

The novelty of radio surveillance suddenly wore off. The radio played on, but the crewmen worked in silence, nothing but the winches, the flapping of ventral fins, and the sound of knives. The First Mate was rolling a shark to cut its anal fin when a flap opened, and from it was ejected, viscous and yolk-covered, a satchel of shark pups, most of them still breathing from sacs. These the Captain kicked in the water, and then called for a break. Rather than sink, they lay flat on the surface, floating with the ship, their half-formed eyes bulging this way and that.

The men smoked Konsol cigarettes, and up on the hatches felt the wind on their faces. They never stared toward North Korea in moments like these—always it was east, toward Japan, or even farther out into the limitless Pacific.

Despite the tension, a feeling came over Jun Do that he sometimes got as a boy after working in the orphanage's fields or whatever factory they'd been taken to that day. The feeling came when, with his group of boys, he'd been working hard, and though there was still heavy lifting to be done, the end was near, and soon there would be a group dinner of millet and cabbage and maybe melon-skin soup. Then sleep, communal, a hundred boys bunked four tiers deep, all their common exhaustion articulated as a singularity. It was nothing short of belonging, a feeling that wasn't particularly profound or intense, it was just the best he tended to get. He'd spent most of his life since trying to be alone, but there were moments aboard the *Junma* where he felt *a part,* and that came with a satisfaction that wasn't located inside, but among.

The scanners were rolling through the frequencies, playing short selections of each, and it was the Second Mate who first cocked his head at the tenor of something he'd heard before. "It's them," he said. "It's the ghost Americans." He slipped off his boots and began to climb barefoot up the pilothouse. "They're down there again," he said. "But this time we've got them."

The Captain shut down the winch motor so they could hear better. "What are they saying?" he asked.

Jun Do ran to the receiver and isolated the broadcast, fine-tuning it even though the reception was strong. "Queen to knight four," Jun Do said. "It's the Americans. There's one with a Russian accent, another one sounds Japanese." All of the Americans were laughing, clear as a bell over the speaker. Jun Do translated. "Look out, Commander," he said. "Dmitri always goes for the rook."

The Captain went to the rail and stared into the water. He squinted and shook his head. "But that's the trench," he said. "Nothing can go that deep."

The First Mate joined him. "You heard them. They're playing chess down there."

Jun Do craned his neck to the Second Mate, who had shinnied up the pole and was working on unhooking the directional. "Careful of the cable," he called, then checked his watch: almost two minutes in. Then he thought he heard some Korean interference over the broadcast, some voice talking about experiments or something. Jun Do raced to narrow the reception and squelch out the other transmission, but he couldn't get rid of it. If it wasn't interference . . . he tried to keep his mind from thinking that a Korean was down there, too.

"What are the Americans saying?" the Captain asked.

Jun Do stopped to translate, "The stupid pawns keep floating away."

The Captain looked back into the water. "What are they doing down there?"

Then the Second Mate got the directional off the pole, and the crew went silent as he aimed it into the deeps. Quietly, they waited as he slowly swept the antenna across the water, hoping to pinpoint the source of the transmission, but they heard nothing.

"Something's wrong," Jun Do told him. "It must have come unplugged."

Then Jun Do saw a hand pointing into the sky. It was the Captain's, and it was aimed at a point of light racing through the stars. "Up there, son," the Captain said, and as the Second Mate lifted the directional and lined it up with the arc of light, there was a squeal of feedback and suddenly it sounded like the American, the Russian, and the Japanese voices were right there on the ship with them.

Jun Do said, "The Russian just said, *That's checkmate,* and the American is saying, *Bullshit, the pieces floated away, that's grounds for a new game,* and now the Russian is telling the American, *Come on, give up the board. We might have time for a rematch of Moscow versus Seoul before the next orbit.*"

They watched the Second Mate track the point of light to the horizon, and when the light went around the curve of the earth, the broadcast vanished. The crew kept staring at the Second Mate, and the Second Mate kept staring at the sky. Finally, he looked down at them. "They're in space together," he said. "They're supposed to be our enemies, but they're up there laughing and screwing around." He lowered the directional and looked at Jun Do. "You were wrong," he said. "You were wrong—they are doing it for peace and fucking brotherhood."

*

Jun Do woke in the dark. He rose on his arms to sit on his bunk, silent, listening—for what? The frost of his breath was something he could feel occupying the space before him. There was just enough light to see water sheen on the floor as it shifted with the movement of the ship. Fish oil that seeped through the bulkhead seams, normally a black gloss down the rivets, was stiff and milk-colored with the cold. Of the shadows in his small room, Jun Do had the impression that one of them was a person, perfectly still, hardly breathing. For a while, he held his breath, too.

Near dawn, Jun Do woke again. He heard a faint hissing sound. He turned in his sleep toward the hull, so that he could imagine through the steel the open water at its darkest just before sunrise. He put his forehead to the metal, listening, and through his skin, he felt the thump of something nudging the side of the ship.

Up top, the wind clipped cold across the deck. It made Jun Do squint. The pilothouse was empty. Then Jun Do saw a mass off the stern, something sprawling and gray-yellow in the waves. He stared at it a moment before it made sense, before he understood it was the life raft from the Russian jetliner. Where it was tethered to the ship, several tins of food were stacked. Jun Do kneeled and held the rope in disbelief.

The Second Mate popped his head from the raft to grab the last tins.

"Aak," he said at the sight of Jun Do. He took a deep breath, composed himself. "Hand me those tins," he said.

Jun Do passed them down. "I saw a man defect once," he told the Second Mate. "And I saw what happened to him after he was brought back."

"You want in, you're in," the Second Mate said. "No one will find us. The current is southerly here. No one's going to bring us back."

"What about your wife?"

"She's made up her mind, and nothing's going to change it," he said. "Now hand me the rope."

"What about the Captain, the rest of us?"

The Second Mate reached up and untied the rope himself. He pushed off. Floating free, he said, "We're the ones at the bottom of the ocean. You helped me see that."

*

In the morning, the light was flat and bright and when the crew went on deck to do their laundry, they found the Second Mate gone. They stood next to the empty locker, trying to scan the horizon, but the light off the wavecaps was like looking into a thousand mirrors. The Captain had the Machinist inventory the cabin, but in the end little was missing but the raft. As to the Second Mate's course, the Pilot shrugged and pointed east, toward the sun. So they stood there, looking and not looking at what had come to pass.

"His poor wife," the Machinist said.

"They'll send her to a camp for sure," the First Mate said.

"They could send us all away," the Machinist said. "Our wives, our kids."

"Look," Jun Do said. "We'll say he fell overboard. A rogue wave came and washed him away."

The Captain had been silent until now. "On our first trip with a life raft?"

"We'll say the wave washed the raft overboard." Jun Do pointed at the nets and buoys. "We'll throw that stuff over, too."

The Captain pulled off his hat and his shirt, and these he tossed aside and he didn't look where they landed. He sat down in the middle of the deck and put his head in his hands. It was only then that real fear seemed to inhabit the men. "I can't live like that again," he said. "I haven't got another four years to give."

The Pilot said, "It wasn't a rogue wave, but the wake from a South Korean container vessel. They nearly swamped us."

The First Mate said, "Let's run her aground near Wonsan and swim for it. Then, you know, the Second Mate just didn't make it. We'll make for a beach filled with retirees, and there will be plenty of witnesses."

"There are no retirees," the Captain said. "It's just what they tell you to keep you going."

Jun Do said, "We could go looking for him."

"Suit yourself," the Captain said.

Jun Do shielded his eyes and looked again upon the waves. "Do you think he can survive out there? Do you think he can make it?"

The First Mate joined him. "His poor fucking wife."

"Without either the raft or the man, we're screwed," the Captain said. "With both gone, they'll never believe us." There were fish scales on the deck, dry and flashing in the light. The Captain ran a couple around with a finger. "If the *Junma* goes down, and we go down with her," he said, "the mates' wives get pensions, the Machinist's wife gets a pension, the Pilot's wife gets a pension. They all live."

"They live with replacement husbands," the First Mate said. "What about my kids and some stranger raising them?"

"They live," the Captain said. "They stay out of the camps."

"The Americans were mad," Jun Do said. "They came back and they took him."

"What's that?" the Captain asked. He shielded his eyes and looked up at Jun Do.

"They wanted revenge," he said. "And they came back to get the guy that had outfought them. They boarded us again, and they kidnapped the Second Mate."

The Captain lay back on the deck in a strange position. He looked as if he'd fallen from the rigging and was in that moment where you don't move, where you're only trying to assess if anything's broken. He said, "If Pyongyang really thinks a citizen has been kidnapped by the Americans, they'll never let up. They'll ride it forever, and eventually the truth will come to light. Plus, there's no proof the Americans came back—the only thing that saved us last time was those idiots fooling with the radio."

From his pocket, Jun Do produced the card that Jervis had left him, embossed with the seal of the U.S. Navy. He gave it to the Captain. "Maybe the Americans wanted Pyongyang to know exactly who had come and kicked some ass. In fact, it was the exact same guys—we all got a good look at them. We could tell almost the same story."

The Machinist said, "We were longlining when the Americans came aboard. They caught us by surprise. They grabbed the Second Mate and mocked him for a while, and then they threw him to the sharks."

"Yeah," the First Mate said. "We threw the raft down to him, but the sharks tore it up with their teeth."

"Yeah," the Pilot said. "The Americans just stood there with their guns, laughing while our comrade died."

The Captain studied the card. He reached for a hand, and they helped him up. There was that wild light in his eyes. "And then one of us," he said, "without regard for his own safety, jumped into the shark-filled sea to save the Second Mate. This crewman suffered ferocious bite wounds, but he didn't care because he only thought about saving the Second Mate, a hero of the Democratic People's Republic of Korea. But it was too late—half eaten, the Second Mate slipped below the waves. His last words were of praise for the Dear Leader, and it was only in the nick of time that we pulled the other crew member, bleeding and half dead, back aboard the *Junma*."

Things suddenly got quiet.

The Captain told the Machinist to start the winch. "We'll need a fresh shark," he said.

The Captain came to Jun Do and cupped the back of his neck, pulling him close in a tender way until they were almost forehead to forehead. No one had ever done that to Jun Do before, and it felt like there was no one else in the world. The Captain said, "It's not just because you're the one who put all the stupid ideas in the Second Mate's head. Or that you're the one with the actress tattooed on your chest instead of a real woman, at home depending on you. It's not because you're the one who's had military training in pain. It's because no one ever taught you about family and sacrifice and doing whatever it takes to protect your own."

The Captain's eyes were open and calm and so close to Jun Do's that it felt they were communicating in some pure, wordless way. The hand on the back of his neck was solid, and Jun Do found himself nodding.

The Captain said, "You never had anyone to guide you, but I'm here, and I'm telling you this is the right thing to do. These people are your family, and I know you'd do anything for them. All that's left is the proof."

The shark had been hanging on the line all night and was stupid with death. When it came out of the water, its eyes were white, and on deck, it opened and closed its mouth less as if trying to take in oxygen than as if trying to expel whatever was slowly killing it.

The Captain told the Pilot to get a firm grip on Jun Do's arm, but no, Jun Do said, he would hold it out himself. The Mate and Machinist hefted the shark, which was not quite two meters, tip to tail.

Jun Do took a deep breath and turned to the Captain. "Sharks and guns and revenge," he said. "I know I thought it up, but this isn't a story that anyone could really believe."

"You're right," the Captain said. "But it's a story they can use."

*

After they radioed for help, a shore patrol boat escorted them to Kinjye, where many people had gathered at the fish-hauling ramp. There were a couple of representatives from the Ministry of Information and a pair of reporters from *Rodong Sinmun* and there were some local security guys you'd never meet unless you drank. Steam poured from the new cannery, which meant they were in a sterilization cycle, so the workers sat on downturned buckets, waiting for a glimpse of the man who had fought the sharks. Even the urchins and cripple kids had come to eye the scene warily through the glass of the live tanks, making their faces look large and distorted as schools of *aji* swam by.

A doctor approached Jun Do with a unit of blood. The doctor searched for a vein in the wounded arm, but Jun Do stopped him. "If you put the blood in this arm, won't it all leak out?"

"Look, I only treat heroes," the doctor said. "So I know my way around blood. And where it's leaking from is exactly where it should go." Then he ran the line into a vein behind the knuckle, taping it off and handing the bag to Jun Do to hold high with his good arm. The doctor unwrapped the bloody T-shirt, and there was no denying the wound. The shark's teeth, like flakes of milk-glass, had gone all the way, and when the troughs of flesh were irrigated, visible at the base of each of them was the white slick of arm bone.

To the reporter and minister, Jun Do gave a brief summary of his encounter with American aggression. They didn't ask many questions. It was corroboration they seemed interested in. Suddenly, before him was the older man with the flattop and busted hands who had taken away the Second Mate. He wore the same gray suit and up close Jun Do could see his eyelids were very heavy, making it look as if he was resting his eyes while he spoke.

"I'll need to confirm the details of your story," he said, and flashed a silver badge that bore the name of no agency. There was only an image of a thick block wall, floating above the ground.

Jun Do was led down a path, his good arm holding the blood bag, the other in a sling. Ahead was the Captain, who was speaking with the wife of the Second Mate. They stood next to a pile of bricks, and she was not weeping. She eyed the old man and then Jun Do, then she turned to the Captain, who put an arm around her to console her. Jun Do looked back to the commotion at the dock, his mates gesturing large as they recounted the story, but they suddenly seemed very far away.

The old man took him to the abandoned cannery. All that was left of the high-ceilinged factory were the giant steam chambers, the lonely gas manifolds, and the rusty tracks embedded in the cement floor. Shafts of light came down through holes in the roof, and here was a folding table and two chairs.

On the table was a thermos. The old man sat and slowly unscrewed its raspy lid with hands that worked as if through heavy mittens. Again he seemed to rest his eyes by closing them, but he was just old.

"So are you an inspector or something?" Jun Do asked.

"What is the answer to that?" the old man mused. "I was very reckless in the war. And after we won, I was still ready for anything." He leaned forward into the light, and Jun Do could see there were many scars in his short gray hair. "I would have called myself an inspector back then."

Jun Do decided to play it safe. "It was great men like you who won the war and drove out the imperial aggressors."

The old man poured tea into the lid of the thermos, but he did not drink it—he just held the steaming cup in both hands, slowly turning it. "It's a sad story, this young fisherman friend of yours. The funny thing is that he really was a hero. I confirmed the story myself. He really did fight off armed Americans with only a fishing knife. Crazy stuff like that gains you respect but loses friends. I know all about it. Perhaps that's what happened between the crew and the young mate."

Jun Do said, "The Second Mate didn't ask for the Americans to come back. He wasn't looking for trouble, let alone death. You did hear how he was eaten alive by sharks, right?"

The old man didn't say anything.

"Shouldn't you have a pencil or some paper or something?"

"We picked up your friend in a raft this morning. This was even before you radioed in about your so-called attack. He had plenty of cigarettes, but he had fumbled his matches and they were wet. They said your friend had been crying over what he'd done, that he couldn't stop."

Jun Do's mind turned on that. That poor, stupid boy, he thought. Jun Do had thought the two of them were in this together, but now he understood he was alone, and all he had was the story.

"I wish that lie you just told were true," Jun Do said, "because then the Second Mate would be alive, then he wouldn't have died in front of all of us. Then the Captain wouldn't have to tell his wife that she'll never see him again."

"He'll never be seen again, you can count on that," the old man said. Again it looked like he'd gone to sleep. "Don't you want to know the reasons he defected? I believe he mentioned your name."

"The Second Mate was a friend and a hero," Jun Do said. "You should maybe show some respect for the dead."

The old man stood. "What I should maybe do is confirm *your* story," he said, and the first assault that followed was brief and frontal—several snapping blows to the face, and with one arm hurt and the other holding the blood bag, there was nothing for Jun Do to do but take it.

"Tell me whose idea it was," the old man said. He struck Jun Do once on each collarbone. "Why didn't you launch him farther south, closer to the DMZ?" Jun Do was somehow trapped in the chair, and two chopping blows to the floater ribs anchored him for good. "Why didn't more of you defect? Or were you casting him away?" In quick succession, pain flashed in his neck, nose, and ear, and then his eyes didn't seem to work right.

"The Americans came back," Jun Do said. "They were blaring music. They wore street clothes, including shoes with silver swooshes. One of them threatened to burn the ship. He had a lighter with a cruise missile on it. They had made fun of us because we didn't have a toilet but now they made fun of us because we did."

The old man punched Jun Do directly in the breastplate, and in the fire of his new tattoo, he felt Sun Moon's face as a burning outline over his heart. The old man stopped to pour more tea, but he did not drink. He just warmed his hands around the cup. Jun Do now understood how it would go. In the military, his pain mentor was Kimsan. The whole first week, they sat at a table, not unlike this one, and contemplated a candle burning between them. There was the flame, small and hot at its tip. There was the glow, warm on their faces. Then there was the darkness beyond the glow. *Never let pain push you into the darkness,* Kimsan said. *There you are nobody and you are alone. Once you turn from the flame, it is over.*

The old man began again, this time asking not about the Second Mate in the raft, but the Second Mate on the *Junma,* about how many sharks, how high the seas, whether the American rifles were on safety. The old man was pacing himself, dealing long, slow strings of measured blows, to the cheeks and mouth and ears, switching to the soft body when his hands seemed to hurt. *In the candle's flame, the fingertip hurts, though the whole rest of the body is in the warm glow of its light. Keep the pain in the fingertip and your body in the glow.* Jun Do put up his partitions—a strike to the shoulder must hurt only the shoulder and he mentally cordoned that off from the rest of the body. And when the strikes came to the face, Jun Do would adjust his head as the strike was delivered, so no two landed in the same place. *Keep the flame on the fingers, keep the fingers in motion, let the rest of you relax in the glow.*

A wince of pain crossed the old man's face and he stopped to stretch his back. Bending this way and that, he said, "There's a lot of big talk about the war. Practically everyone was named a hero. Even trees have been named heroes. It's true. Everyone in my division is a war hero, except for the new guys, of course. Maybe your friend became a hero, and you didn't like that. Maybe you wanted to be one, too."

Jun Do tried to stay in the glow, but he was having trouble focusing. He kept wondering when the next punch was coming.

"If you ask me," the old man said, "heroes are unstable and unpredictable. They get the job done, but damned if they're not difficult to work with. Trust me, I know," he said, and pointed to a long scar down his arm. "In my division, all the new guys are college types."

When the glint returned to the old man's eyes, he grabbed the back of Jun Do's neck to brace himself. Then came a series of dull blows to Jun Do's stomach. "Who threw him in the water?" he asked and delivered one to the sternum. "What were his last words?" One, two, three, they came. "Why don't you know what the Captain was doing?" The fists pushed the air from his lungs. "Why didn't you radio for help?" Then the old man answered all his own questions: "Because the Americans never came. Because you got tired of that crazy punk and you killed him and threw him overboard. You're all going to the camps, you know that, it's already been decided. So you might as well just tell me."

The old man broke off. He paced for a moment, one hand inside the other, eyes shut with what seemed like relief. Then Jun Do heard Kimsan's voice, as if he were very close, right in the room. *You are the flame,* Kimsan said. *The old man keeps touching the hot flame of you with only his hands.* Kimsan would tell him to also hit with his elbows and forearms and feet and knees, *but only his hands touch your flame, and look how it burns him.*

"I can't say I was thinking," Jun Do said. "But when I jumped, the saltwater on my new tattoo made me panic. The sharks would baby bite, muzzling you before they went for meat, and the Americans were laughing with all their white teeth and those two things became one in my head."

The old man came back in frustration. "No," he said. "These are all lies." Then he went to work again. As the blows came, he told Jun Do everything that was wrong with the story, how they were jealous of the mate's new hero status, how Jun Do couldn't remember people's clothes, how . . . *the flame is tiny. It would take all day to burn the whole surface of your body. You must stay in the glow. You must never go into the darkness, for there you are alone, and people don't come back.* Kimsan said this was the most difficult lesson for Jun Do, because that's what he'd done as a boy, gone into the darkness. That was the lesson his parents had taught him, whoever they were. If you go into the darkness, if you turn off like that, you could do anything—you could clean tanks at the Pangu paint factory until your head throbbed and you coughed pink mist and the sky above turned yellow. You could good-naturedly smile when other kids got adopted by smelters and meat factories, and when you were crouched in the darkness, you could say "Lucky you" and "So long" when men with Chinese accents came.

It was difficult to tell how long the old man had been working on him. All his sentences ran together to make one sentence that didn't make sense. Jun Do was there, in the water, he could see the Second Mate. "I was trying to grab the Second Mate," Jun Do said, "but his body would pop and jag and shift, and I knew what they were doing to him, I knew what was happening below the surface. In my hands he didn't weigh anything, it was like trying to rescue a seat cushion, that's all that was left of him, but still I couldn't do it."

When Jun Do had cordoned off the pounding in his eyes, and the hot blood in his nose, when he'd stopped the split in his lips and the sting in his ears from coming inside, when he'd blocked his arms and torso and shoulders from feeling, when that was all blocked off, there was only the inside of him, and what he discovered was a little boy in there who was stupidly smiling, who had no idea what was happening to the man outside. And suddenly the story was true, it had been beaten into him, and he began crying because the Second Mate had died and there was nothing he could do about it. He could suddenly see him in the dark water, the whole scene lit by the red glow of a single flare.

"My friend," Jun Do said, the tears streaming down his face, "I couldn't save him. He was alone and the water was dark. I couldn't even save a piece of him. I looked in his eyes, and he didn't know where he was. He was calling for help, saying, *I think I need a rescue,* his voice calm and eerie, and then my leg was going over the side and I was in the water."

The old man paused. He stood there with his hands held high, like a surgeon. They were covered with spit and mucus and blood.

Jun Do kept going. "*It's dark, I don't know where I am,* he said. *I'm here,* I told him, *listen to the sound of my voice.* He asked, *Are you out there?* I put my hand on his face, which was cold and white. *I can't be where I think I am,* he said. *A ship is out there—I can't see its lights.* That was the last thing he said."

"*I can't see its lights*? Why would he say that?" When Jun Do said nothing, the old man asked, "But you did try to rescue him, didn't you? Isn't that when you got bit? And the Americans, you said their guns were on you, right?"

The blood bag in Jun Do's hand weighed a thousand kilos, and it was all he could do to keep it aloft. When he managed to focus his eye he saw that the bag was empty. He looked at the old man. "What?" he asked.

"Earlier you said his last words were *All praise Kim Jong Il, Dear Leader of the Democratic People's Republic of Korea*? You admit that's a lie."

The candle had gone out. The flame, the glow, the darkness—they were all suddenly gone and now there was nothing. Kimsan never talked about what to do after the pain.

"Don't you see? It's all a lie," Jun Do said. "Why didn't I radio for help? Why didn't I get the crew to mount a real rescue? If the whole crew worked together, we could've saved him. I should have begged the crew, I should have gotten on my knees. But I didn't do anything. I just got wet. The only thing I felt was the sting of my tattoo."

The old man took the other chair. He poured fresh tea, and this time he drank it. "No one else got wet," he said. "You don't see anyone else with a shark bite." He looked around the building as if wondering for the first time what kind of place this was. "I'm going to retire soon," he said. "Soon all the old-timers will be gone. I don't know what's going to happen to this country."

"What will become of her?" Jun Do asked.

"The Second Mate's wife? Don't worry, we'll find someone good. We'll find someone worthy of his memory."

From his pack, the old man shook out a cigarette and with some struggle, lit it. The brand was Chollima, the kind they smoked in Pyongyang. "Looks like your ship is a regular hero factory," he said.

Jun Do kept trying to drop the blood bag, but his hand wouldn't let go. A person could learn to turn an arm off, so you didn't feel anything that happened to it, but how did you turn it back on?

"I'm certifying you," the old man said. "Your story checks out."

Jun Do turned to him. "What story are you talking about?"

"What story?" the old man asked. "You're a hero now."

The old man offered Jun Do a cigarette, but Jun Do couldn't take it.

"But the facts," Jun Do said. "They don't add up. Where are the answers?"

"There's no such thing as facts. In my world, all the answers you need to know come from here." He pointed at himself, and Jun Do couldn't tell if the old man indicated his heart, his gut, or his balls.

"But where are they?" Jun Do asked. He could see the girl rower shooting flares his way, he could feel the Mate's cold cheek as the sharks pulled him under. "Will we ever find them?"

JUN DO dreamed of sharks biting him, of the actress Sun Moon blinking and squinting, the way Rumina had when the sand was in her eyes. He dreamed of the Second Mate drifting farther and farther into that harsh light. A stab of pain would arrive, and was he awake or asleep? His eyes roamed the insides of lids swollen shut. The endless smell of fish. Shock-work whistles signaled dawn, and he knew night had arrived when the hum of a little fridge went off with the power.

All his joints felt locked up, and taking too deep a breath was like opening the furnace slats of pain. When his good arm could finally reach over to inspect the bad arm, he could feel fat horsefly hairs, the coarse thread of surgical stitching. He had a half memory of the Captain helping him up the stairs of the community housing block where the Second Mate lived with his wife.

The loudspeaker—*Citizens!*—took care of him during the day. Afternoons, she came from the cannery, the faint scent of machine oil still on her hands. The little teapot would rattle and whistle and she would hum along with *The March of Kim Jong Il*, which signaled the end of the news. Then her hands, ice cold with alcohol, would disinfect his wounds. Those hands rolled him left and right to change the sheets and empty his bladder, and he was sure he could feel in her fingers the trace of her wedding ring.

Soon, the swelling had gone down, and now it was gunk sealing his eyes shut, rather than inflammation. She was there with a hot cloth to steam them open. "There he is," she said when his vision was finally back. "The man who loves Sun Moon."

Jun Do lifted his head. He was on a pallet on the floor, naked under a light yellow sheet. He recognized the louvered windows of the housing block. The room was strung with little perch, drying on wires like laundry.

She said, "My father believed that if his daughter married a fisherman, she'd never starve."

And into focus came the Second Mate's wife.

"What floor are we on?" he asked.

"The tenth."

"How'd you get me up here?"

"It wasn't so bad. The way my husband described you, I thought you'd be a lot bigger." She ran the hot cloth over his chest, and he tried not to wince. "Your poor actress, her face is black and blue. It makes her look old, like her time has passed. Have you seen her movies?"

Shaking his head no made his neck hurt.

"Me either," she said. "Not in this dumpy town. The only movie I ever saw was a foreign film, a love story." She immersed the cloth in hot water again, then soaked the ridges of all his scars. "It was about a ship that hits an iceberg and everybody dies."

She climbed onto the pallet next to him. With both arms, she muscled him over and onto his side. She held a jar to him and maneuvered it until his *umkyoung* was inside. "Come on," she said, then gave him a couple claps on the back to get him going. His body pulsed in pain, and then the stream began. When he was done, she lifted the jar to the light. The fluid was cloudy and rust-colored. "Getting better," she announced. "Soon you'll be walking down the hall to the tenth-floor toilet like a big boy."

Jun Do tried to roll onto his back by himself, but he couldn't, so he just lay there, curled on his side. On the wall, beneath the portraits of the Dear and Great Leaders, was a little shelf with the Second Mate's "America" shoes on them. Jun Do tried to figure out how the Second Mate had gotten them home, when the whole crew had seen them go into the water. Tacked large on the wall was the main chart from the *Junma*. It showed the entire Korean Sea, and it was the chart by which all the other charts onboard were referenced. They'd thought it burned with the others in the fire. On it were pushpins marking every fishing ground they'd visited, and in pencil were traced the coordinates of several northerly positions.

"Is that the course of the rowers?" Jun Do asked her.

"The rowers?" she asked. "This is a map of all the places he'd been. The red pins are cities he'd heard about. He was always talking about the places he'd take me."

She looked into Jun Do's eyes.

"What?" he asked.

"Did he really do it? Did he really pull a knife on American commandos, or is that some bullshit story you guys cooked up?"

"Why would you listen to me?"

"Because you're an intelligence officer," she said. "Because you don't give a shit about anybody around this backwater. When your mission's done, you'll go back to Pyongyang and never think about fishermen again."

"And what's my mission?"

"There's going to be a war at the bottom of the ocean," she said. "Maybe my husband shouldn't have told me, but he did."

"Don't fool yourself," he said. "I'm just a radio guy. And yes, your husband took on the U.S. Navy with a knife."

She shook her head with muted admiration.

"He had so many crazy plans," she said. "Hearing that makes me think if he'd have lived, he might have really gone through with one."

She ladled sweetened rice water into Jun Do's mouth, then rolled him back, covering him with a sheet again. The room was getting dark, and soon the power would fail.

"Look, I've got to go out," she said. "If you have an emergency, give a yell, and the floor official will come. She's at the door if someone so much as farts in here."

She took a sponge bath by the door, where he couldn't see her. He could only hear the faint sound of the cloth on her skin and the sound of water as it dripped from her body to the pan she crouched in. He wondered if it was the same cloth she'd used on him.

Before she left, she stood over him in a dress that bore the wrinkles of having been hand-wrung and hung to dry. Though he beheld her through the oceany vision of newly opened eyes, it was clear she was a true beauty—tall and square-shouldered, yet cloaked in a soft layer of baby fat. Her eyes were large and unpredictable and black bobbed hair framed a round face. She had an English dictionary in her hand. "I've seen some people get hurt at the cannery," she said. "You're going to be all right." Then, in English, she added, "Sweet dreams."

*

In the morning, he woke with a start—a dream ending with a flash of pain. The sheet smelled of cigarettes and sweat, and he knew that she'd slept next to him. Beside the pallet was a jar filled with urine that looked tinctured with iodine. At least it was clear. He reached to touch the jar—it was cold. When he managed to sit up, there was no sign of her.

The light was amplified by the sea, filling the room. He pulled off his sheet. Bright bruising fanned his chest, and there were pressure cuts on the ribs. His stitches were crusty, and after smelling them, he knew they'd have to be expressed. The loudspeaker greeted him—"Citizens, today it is announced that a delegation is to visit America to confront some of the problems facing our two fearsome nations." Then the broadcast went on in the usual formula: evidence of the worldwide admiration for North Korea, an example of Kim Jong Il's divine wisdom, a new method to help citizens avoid starvation, and, finally, warnings to civilians from various ministries.

A draft through the window set the dried fish swaying on their lines, the cartilage of their fins the color of lantern paper. From the roof came a series of yips and howls, and the constant clicking of nails on cement. For the first time in days, he felt a pang of hunger.

Then the door opened and, breathing hard, the Second Mate's wife came in.

She was carrying a suitcase and two five-liter jugs of water. She was sweating, but there was a weird smile on her face.

"What do you think of my new suitcase?" she asked. "I had to barter for it."

"What did you barter?"

"Don't be an ass," she said. "Can you believe I didn't own a suitcase?"

"I guess you never went anywhere."

"I guess I never went anywhere," she said to herself.

She ladled some rice water into a plastic cup for him.

He took a drink and asked her, "Are there dogs on the roof?"

"That's life on the top floor," she said. "Broken elevator, leaky roof, toilet vents. I don't even notice the dogs anymore. The housing council's breeding them. You should hear them on Sundays."

"What are they breeding them for? Wait—what happens on Sundays?"

"The guys at the karaoke bar say that dogs are illegal in Pyongyang."

"That's what they say."

"Civilization," she said.

"Aren't they going to start missing you at the cannery?"

She didn't answer. Instead, she knelt down and began rifling the pockets of the suitcase, looking for any evidence of its previous owner.

Jun Do said, "They're going to give you a criticism session."

"I'm not going back to the cannery," she said.

"Not ever?"

"No," she said. "I'm going to Pyongyang."

"You're going to Pyongyang."

"That's right," she said. In a fold of the suitcase's lining, she found some expired travel passes, stamped by every checkpoint between Kaesong and Chongjin. "Typically it takes a couple weeks, but I don't know, I got a feeling it could happen any day."

"What could happen?"

"Them finding my replacement husband."

"And you think he's in Pyongyang?"

"I'm a hero's wife," she said.

"A hero's widow, you mean."

"Don't say that word," she said. "I hate the sound of it."

Jun Do finished his rice water, and slowly, slowly lay back down.

"Look," she said, "it's horrible what happened to my husband. I can't even think about it. Seriously, whenever my mind goes there, something inside me just turns away. But we were only married a few months, and he was on a boat with you almost the whole time."

It had taken a lot out of him to sit up, and when his head touched the pallet, the comfort of yielding to exhaustion overtook the discomfort of recovery. Almost everything on him hurt, yet a feeling of well-being came over his body, as if he'd been working hard all day with his mates. He closed his eyes and felt the hum of it. When he opened them again, it was afternoon. Jun Do had a feeling that what had awakened him was the sound of her closing the door as she left. He rolled some, so he could see the corner of the room. There was the pan that she used to wash herself. He wished he could reach it, to check if the water was still warm.

Come twilight, the Captain stopped by. He lit a couple of candles and sat in a chair. Looking up at him, Jun Do could see he'd brought a bag. "Look here, son," the Captain said, and from the bag produced a slab of tuna and two Ryoksong beers. "It's time to get your health back."

The Captain opened the bottles and sectioned the tuna raw with his bosun's knife. "To heroes," the Captain said, and, halfheartedly, they both drank. The tuna, though, was exactly what Jun Do needed. The fat of the sea, he savored it against the roof of his mouth.

"The catch was good?" Jun Do asked.

"The waters were lively," the Captain said. "It wasn't the same without you or the Second Mate, of course. We got a couple hands to help out from the *Kwan Li*. You heard their captain ended up losing his arm, right?"

Jun Do nodded.

The Captain shook his head. "You know, I'm real sorry about how they worked you over. I wanted to warn you, but it wouldn't have made much difference."

"Well, it's over," Jun Do said.

"The hard part's over, and you took it well, no one else could've done what you did. Now comes the reward part," the Captain said. "They're going to give you some time to heal up, figure out exactly how things will work, and then they're going to want to show you off. A hero who risked his life at gunpoint to save another hero who'd been fed to the sharks by Americans? Come on, you're going to be a big story. They're going to get some use out of you. After that thing with the Canning Master and then the captain of the *Kwan Li,* they need some good news. Anything you want, you'll be able to name it."

"I've already been to language school," Jun Do said, then added, "You think it's possible, I mean with the currents and all, that he could make it back?"

"We all love that boy," the Captain said. "And mistakes were made, but he can't come back. He's not part of the story anymore. That's not how the story goes now. You've got to get your head straight about that. The girl, she's doing okay with this, right?"

But before Jun Do could answer, the Captain noticed the chart on the wall. The room was dim, and he stood with his candle. "What the hell," he said. He started tearing out pins and dropping them to the floor. "A week he's been gone, and still that kid is tormenting me." He pulled the chart free. "Look," the Captain said, "there's something you should know. Before, when we thought the Second Mate hadn't taken anything with him, we really hadn't looked close enough. We didn't think to check down in the hold, where your equipment was."

"What are you saying?"

"One of your radios is gone. He took a radio with him."

"Was it the black one?" Jun Do asked. "Or the one with the silver handles?"

"The one with the green dials," the Captain said. "Is that going to be a problem? Is this going to hurt us?"

Jun Do could see it so clearly now, the Second Mate out on the raft in the dark with nothing but a battery, the green glow of a radio, and cigarettes without matches.

"That radio's pretty basic," Jun Do said. "We can scrounge another one."

"That's the spirit," the Captain said. He put on a smile. "Here, here, I'm being an idiot, have some more tuna. And the girl, what do you think of her? I talked to her, you know. She has quite a high impression of you. What can I get you, is there anything you need?"

The beer was running right through Jun Do. "That jar over there," he said. "Can you hand it to me."

"Sure, sure," the Captain said, but when he picked it up, he eyed it with great suspicion. He looked like he was going to smell it, but then he just passed it along.

Jun Do rolled to his side and brought the jar under the sheet with him. Then the only sound in the room was the sound of urine filling the jar in fits and spurts.

The Captain talked over the sound. "Well, you're going to have to do some thinking. You're a hero now, and they're going to ask you what you want. How about it, is there anything you'd pick?"

When he was done, Jun Do opened his eyes. Then he carefully handed the jar to the Captain. "The only thing I'd like," Jun Do said, "is to stay on the *Junma*. I feel comfortable there."

"Of course you do," the Captain said. "Your equipment's there."

"And there's power at night."

"And there's power at night," the Captain said. "Consider it done. You now live on the *Junma*. It's the least I can do. But what is it you really want, something only the officials can give you?"

Jun Do hesitated. He took a pull of beer and tried to think of one thing that North Korea could give him that would make his life better.

The Captain sensed his hesitation and started describing others who'd done great deeds and the prizes they'd asked for, "like the guys in Yongbyon who put out the fire at the power plant—one of them got a car, it was in the paper. Another guy wanted his own telephone—done, no questions, they ran a wire to his apartment. When you're a hero, that's how it works."

"I'd have to think about it," Jun Do said. "You caught me a little off guard. I'm not so good off the top of my head."

"See, I knew that," said the Captain. "I knew that about you because we're family. You're the kind of guy who doesn't want anything for himself. You're a guy who doesn't need much, but when it comes to other people, the sky's the limit. You showed it the other day, you really proved it, and now you're acting like family. I went to jail for my crew, you know. I'm no hero, but I took four years so my boys could go home. That's how I showed it."

The Captain was looking agitated, worried even. He was still holding the jar of urine, and Jun Do wanted to tell him to put it down. The Captain moved to the edge of his chair, like maybe he was going to come down to the pallet.

"Maybe it's just 'cause I'm old," the Captain said. "I mean, other people have problems. A lot of people have it worse off than me, but I just can't live without her, I just can't do it. It's where my mind goes, it always goes back to that, and I'm not mad or resentful about how it happened, I just need my wife, I've got to have her back. And see, you can do that, you're in a position to make that happen. Very soon, you're going to be able to say the word, and anything can happen."

Jun Do tried to speak, but the Captain cut him off. "She's old—I know what you're thinking. I'm old, too, but age doesn't have anything to do with it. In fact, it only seems to get worse with each year. Who would have thought it would get worse? Nobody tells you that, nobody ever talks about that part." The Captain heard some dogs moving across the roof, and he looked up at the ceiling. He set down the jar and stood. "We would be strangers for a while," he said. "After I got her back, there would be things she couldn't talk about, I know that. But a kind of discovery would begin, I'm sure of it. And then what we had would return."

The Captain took up his chart. "Don't say anything," he said. "Don't say anything at all. Just think about it, that's all I ask." Then, in the candlelight, the Captain rolled the chart tight with two hands. It was a gesture Jun Do had seen him make a thousand times. It meant that a bearing had been chosen, the men had been tasked, and whether full nets or empty lay ahead, a decision was made, events set in motion.

*

From below in the courtyard came a whoop, followed by a sound that might have been a laugh or a cry, and Jun Do somehow knew that at the center of these drunk people was the Second Mate's wife. From above came the clicking nails of dogs standing to take an interest, and he followed the sounds as they moved to the edge of the roof. Even on the tenth floor, the windows managed to capture the sounds, and from all over the housing block came the squeaks of people cranking their louvered windows open to see which citizen was up to no good.

Jun Do pulled himself up and by pushing a chair like a walker, he made his way to the window. There was just a sliver of moon, and in the courtyard far below, he located several people by their sharp laughs, though he could make out only the black sheen of them. He could picture the luster of her hair, though, the glow of her neck and shoulders.

The town of Kinjye was dark—the bread collective, the magistrate, the school, the ration station. Even the karaoke bar's generator was silent, its blue neon light gone blank. Wind whistled through the old cannery and heat waves emanated off the steaming chambers of the new. There was the outline of the Canning Master's house and in the harbor was only a single light—the Captain reading late aboard the *Junma*. Beyond that, the dark sea. Jun Do heard a sniffing sound and looked up to the roof overhang to see two paws and a cocked puppy's face looking down at him.

He'd lit a candle and was in a chair, covered with a sheet, when she came in, unsteady through the door. She'd been crying.

"Assholes," she said and lit a cigarette.

"Come back," a voice yelled from the courtyard below. "We were only joking."

She went to the window and threw a fish down at them.

She turned to Jun Do. "What are you looking at?" From a chest of drawers, she grabbed some of her husband's clothes. "Put a shirt on, would you?" she said and threw a white undershirt at him.

The shirt was small and smelled sharp, like the Second Mate. It was murder to get his arms through. "Maybe the karaoke bar isn't the place for you," he said.

"Assholes," she said and smoked in the other chair, looking up as if there was something she was trying to figure out. "All night long they were toasting my husband the hero." She ran a hand through her hair. "I must have had ten plum wines. Then they started picking sad songs on the karaoke machine. By the time I sang 'Pochonbo' I was practically a wreck. Then they were all fighting to *take my mind off it.*"

"Why would you spend time with those guys?"

"I need them," she said. "My new husband's going to be picked soon. I have to make a good impression on people. They need to know I can sing. This is my chance."

"Those guys are local bureaucrats. They're nobodies."

She grabbed her stomach in discomfort. "I am so tired of getting fish parasites and then having to eat chlorine pills. Smell me, I reek of it. Can you believe my father did this to me? How can I get to Pyongyang when I smell like fish and chlorine?"

"Look," Jun Do said, "I know it seems like a raw deal, but your father must have known the options. Certainly, he picked the one that was best for you." It felt low and ugly to pass along the line that he'd fed so many times to the other boys—*You don't know what they were going through, your parents wouldn't have put you in an orphanage if it wasn't their best option, maybe their only one.*

"A couple times a year these guys would come to town. They'd line up all the girls, and the pretty ones, they just"—she leaned her head back and blew smoke—"disappeared. My father had a connection, he always got wind of it, and I'd stay home sick that day. Then he sends me down the coast to this place. But what's the point, you know? Why be safe, why survive if you're going to gut fish for fifty years?"

"What are those girls now?" Jun Do asked. "Barmaids, room cleaners, *worse*? You think doing that for fifty years is any better?"

"If that's how it works, just say so. If that's what happens to them, tell me."

"I have no way of knowing. I've never been to the capital."

"Then don't call them whores, then," she said. "Those girls were my friends." She gave him an angry look. "What kind of spy are you, anyway?"

"I'm just a radio guy."

"Why don't I believe you? Why don't you have a real name? All I know about you is that my husband, who had the maturity of a thirteen-year-old, worshipped you. That's why he fiddled with your radios. That's why he nearly burned the ship up reading your dictionaries by candlelight in the toilet."

"Wait," he said. "The Machinist said it was the wiring."

"Suit yourself."

"He started the fire?"

"You want to know the other things he didn't tell you about?"

"I would have taught him some English. All he had to do was ask. What did he want it for?"

"Oh, he was full of ridiculous plans."

"To get out?"

"He said the key was a big distraction. He said the Canning Master had the right idea—make a scene so gruesome that nobody wants to go near it. Then you slip away."

"But the Canning Master's family, they didn't slip away."

"No," she said. "They didn't."

"And after the distraction, what was the plan?"

She shrugged. "I never really wanted out," she said. "He wanted the outside world. For me, it's Pyongyang. I finally got him to see that."

All the exertion had exhausted Jun Do. He pulled the yellow sheet tighter around his waist, but really, he wanted to lie down.

"You look tired," she said. "Are you ready for your jar?"

"I think I am," he said.

She got the jar, but when he reached for it, she didn't let go. The two of them held it, and the candlelight made her eyes look bottomless.

"Beauty means nothing here," she said. "It's only how many fish you can process. No one cares that I can sing except the boys who want to take my mind off it. But Pyongyang, that's where the theater is, the opera, television, the movies. Only in Pyongyang will I matter. For all his faults, that's something my husband was trying to give me."

Jun Do took a deep breath. When he used the jar, the night would be over, and he didn't want that because when she blew out the candle the room would be as dark as the sea and the Second Mate upon it.

"I wish I had my radio," he said.

"You've got a radio?" she asked. "Where is it?"

He nodded toward the window, and the Canning Master's house beyond. "It's in my kitchen," he said.

*

Jun Do slept all night, then woke in the morning, so turned around was his system now. All of the fish that had been strung through the room were gone, and sitting on the chair was his radio, the loose parts in a plastic bowl. When the news came on, he could feel the entire housing block hum with two hundred loudspeakers. He stared at the place on the wall where the chart had been while he was informed of the coming negotiations in America, of the Dear Leader's inspection of a cement factory in Sinpo, of the news that North Korea had defeated the Libyan badminton team in straight sets, and finally, a reminder that it is illegal to eat swallows, as they control insect populations that feed on rice seedlings.

Jun Do stood awkwardly and scrounged a piece of brown paper. Then he pulled on the blood-soaked pants he'd been wearing four days ago, when it all happened. Outside, at the end of the hall, was the line for the tenth-floor toilet. With all the adults at the cannery, the line was made up of old women and children, each waiting with scraps of paper in their hands. When it was his turn, though, Jun Do saw the wastebasket was filled instead with wadded pages of *Rodong Sinmun,* which was illegal to tear, let alone wipe your ass with.

He was in there a long time. Finally, he scooped two ladles of water into the toilet, and when he was leaving, an old lady in line stopped him. "You're the one who lives in the Canning Master's house," she said.

"That's right," Jun Do told her.

"They should burn that place," she said.

The apartment door was open when he returned. Inside Jun Do found the old man who'd interrogated him. He held the pair of Nikes in his hands. "What the hell is on your roof?" he asked.

"Dogs," Jun Do told him.

"Filthy animals. You know they're illegal in Pyongyang. That's the way it should be. Besides, I'll take pork any day." He held up the Nikes. "What are these?"

"They're some kind of American shoes," Jun Do told him. "We found them in our nets one night."

"You don't say. What are they for?"

It was hard to believe an interrogator from Pyongyang had never seen nice athletic shoes. Still, Jun Do said, "They're for exercise, I think."

"I've heard that," the old man said. "That Americans do pointless labor for fun." He pointed at the radio. "And what about this?" he said.

"That's work-related," Jun Do said. "I'm fixing it."

"Turn it on."

"It's not all put together." Jun Do pointed at the bowl of parts. "Even if it was, there's no antenna."

The old man put the shoes back and walked to the window. The sun was high but still rising, and the angle made the water, despite its depth, shimmer light blue.

"Look at that," he said. "I could stare at that forever."

"It's quite a lovely sea, sir," Jun Do said.

"If a guy walked down to that dock and cast a line in," the old man said, "would he catch a fish?"

The place to catch a fish was a little to the south, where the canning factory's waste pipes pumped fish sludge into the sea, but Jun Do said, "Yeah, I think he might."

"And up north, in Wonsan," the old man said. "They have beaches there, no?"

"I've never visited," Jun Do told him. "But you can see the sand from our ship."

"Here," the old guy said. "I brought you this." He handed Jun Do a crimson velvet case. "It's your medal for heroism. I'd pin it on you, but I can tell you're not a medal guy. I like that about you."

Jun Do didn't open the case.

The old interrogator looked again out the window. "To survive in this world, you got to be many times a coward but at least once a hero." Here he laughed. "At least, that's what a guy told me one time when I was beating the shit out of him."

"I just want to get back on my boat," Jun Do said.

The old interrogator took a look at Jun Do. "I think that saltwater made your shirt shrink," he said. He tugged Jun Do's sleeve up to look at the scars, which were red-lipped and wept at the corners.

Jun Do pulled his arm back.

"Easy, there, tiger. There'll be plenty of time to fish. First, we've got to show those Americans. They've got to get theirs. I hear a plan's in motion.

So we've got to get you presentable. Right now, it looks like the sharks won."

"This is all some kind of test, isn't it?"

The old interrogator smiled. "What do you mean?"

"Asking about Wonsan like some kind of fool when everybody knows no one retires there. Everyone knows that's just a place for military leaders to vacation. Why not just say what you want from me?"

A flash of uncertainty crossed the old interrogator's face. It shifted slightly to measurement and then settled into a smile. "Hey," he said. "I'm the one who's supposed to be rattling you." He laughed. "Seriously, though, we're both legally heroes. We're on the same team. Our mission is to stick it to the Americans who did this to you. First, though, I need to know if you've got some kind of beef with the Captain. We can't be having any surprises."

"What are you talking about?" Jun Do asked. "Never, not at all."

He looked out the window. Half the fleet was out, but the *Junma* had its nets spread across the docks, drying them for a mend.

"Okay, then, forget I said anything. If you didn't say anything to piss him off, I believe you."

"The Captain's my family," Jun Do said. "If you've got something to say about him then you'd better say it."

"It's nothing. The Captain just came to me and asked if I could put you on another boat."

Jun Do stared at him in disbelief.

"The Captain said he's tired of heroes, that he only has so much time left, and he just wants to do his job and fish. I wouldn't sweat it—the Captain, he's a capable man, a real solid hand, but you get old, you lose your flexibility. I've seen it many times."

Jun Do sat down in a chair. "It's because of his wife," he said. "That's got to be it. That's something you guys did to him, giving his wife away."

"I doubt that's how it worked. I'm not familiar with the case, but she was an old woman, right? Not too many replacement husbands are clamoring for an old woman. The Captain went to jail, and she left him. That sounds pretty likely. As the Dear Leader says, *The simplest answer is usually the right one.*"

"And the Second Mate's wife. Are you handling that case?"

"She's a pretty girl, she'll do well. You don't have to worry about her. She won't be living underneath dogs anymore, that's for sure."

"What will happen to her?"

"I think there's a warden in Sinpo who's high on the list, and down in Chongwang there's a retired Party official making some noise to get his hands on her."

"I thought girls like her got sent to Pyongyang."

The old man cocked his head. "She's no virgin," he finally said. "Plus, she's twenty now, and headstrong. Most of the girls who go to Pyongyang are seventeen—all they know is how to listen. But what do you care? You don't want her for yourself, do you?"

"No," Jun Do said. "Not at all."

"'Cause that's suddenly not so heroic. If you want a girl, we can get you a girl. But the wife of a fallen comrade, that's discouraged."

"I'm not saying that's what I want," Jun Do said. "But I'm a hero. I've got rights."

"Privileges," the old man said. "You get some privileges."

✳

All day he worked on the radio. The light was good at the window ledge. There he used the flattened end of a wire as a jeweler's screwdriver and melted fine strands of solder with a candle flame. There, too, he could keep an eye on the harbor to observe the Captain pacing the decks.

Toward twilight, she returned. She was in high spirits, radiant.

"I see some of you still works," she said.

"I couldn't stay in bed without any fish to look at. They were my mobile."

"Some impression that would make," she said. "Showing up in Pyongyang with a suitcase full of fish." Then she pulled back her hair to reveal a new pair of earrings made from thin tails of gold. "Not a bad trade, huh? I'll have to wear my hair up so people can see them."

She went to the radio. "Does it work?"

"Yeah," he said. "Yeah, I rigged an antenna. We should set it up on the roof, though, before the power goes out."

She grabbed the pair of Nikes.

"Okay," she said. "But there's something I've got to do first."

They took the stairs, carefully, down to the sixth floor. They passed apartments ringing with family arguments, but most were eerily silent. The walls here were painted with slogans to the Dear and Great Leaders, accompanied by depictions of children singing from the songbooks of the revolution and peasant farmers pausing at their rich harvests, sickles high, to gaze into the pure light of everlasting wisdom.

The Second Mate's wife knocked on a door, waited a moment, then went inside. The windows were covered with ration paper, and the room smelled of the crotch rot that would spread through the DMZ tunnels. Here they found a man sitting in a plastic dining chair, a bandaged foot elevated on a stool. From the shape of the bandages, you could tell there was no room for toes. He wore overalls from the canning factory, and his name patch said "Team Leader Gun." Gun's eyes lit when he saw the shoes. He beckoned for them, then turned them in his hands, smelled them.

"Can you get more of these?" he asked her.

"Maybe," she said. She saw a box on a table, about the size of a funeral cake. "Is this it?"

"Yes," he said, marveling at the Nikes. Then he pointed at her box. "That wasn't easy to get, you know—it's straight from the South."

Without looking inside, she put the box under her arm.

"What does your friend want?" Gun asked her.

Jun Do looked around the room, at the cases of strange Chinese liquor and the bins of old clothing, at the dangling wires where a loudspeaker should have been. There was a birdcage, jammed full with rabbits. He answered for himself. "I don't need anything."

"Ah, but I asked what you want," Gun said, smiling for the first time. "Come, accept a gift. I think I have a belt that will fit you." He strained for a plastic bag on the floor that was filled with used belts.

"Don't bother," Jun Do told him.

The Second Mate's wife saw a pair of shoes she liked. They were black and almost new. While she tried them on, Jun Do looked at all the crates of merchandise. There were Russian cigarettes and baggies of pills with handwritten labels and a dish filled with sunglasses. There was a stack of family cooking pans, their handles pointing in different directions, and they seemed almost tragic to him.

On a small bookshelf, he found his English dictionaries, and he looked over his old notes in the margins, noting all the idioms he'd once found impossible, like "dry run" and "close but no cigar." Rummaging further, he found the badger-hair shaving brush that had belonged to the Captain. Jun Do didn't blame the Second Mate for pilfering things, even personal things, but when Jun Do turned to observe the Second Mate's wife regard the black shoes in a mirror, it suddenly mattered whether it was she or her husband who'd sold them here.

"Okay," she said. "I want them."

"They look good," Gun said. "That leather is Japanese, you know, the best. You bring me another pair of Nikes, and we'll trade."

"No," she said. "The Nikes are far too valuable. When I get another pair, we'll see what you have that's equal."

"When you get another pair, you will bring them to me. Agreed."

"Agreed," she said.

"Good," he said. "You take those shoes, and then you can owe me one."

"I'll owe you one," she said.

"Don't do it," Jun Do told her.

"I'm not afraid," she said.

"Good," Gun told her. "When the time comes that you can be of service, I will come for you, and then we will be even."

Box under her arm, they turned to go. On a small table, though, something caught Jun Do's eye. He picked it up. It was a stationmaster's watch on a little chain. The Orphan Master had had such a watch, and with it he ran their entire lives, from dawn to lights-out, as he farmed the boys out to clean septic tanks or to be sent down shafts on bare ropes to drain oil sumps. Every moment went by that watch, and he'd never tell the boys the time, but they learned by his facial expressions how things would go until he next checked it.

"Take the watch," Gun said. "I got it from an old man who said it ran perfectly for a lifetime."

Jun Do set down the watch. When they'd left and the door closed behind them, he asked, "What happened to him?"

"He hurt his foot last year, from a steam line under pressure, something like that."

"Last year?"

"The wound won't close, that's what the foreman says."

"You shouldn't have made that deal with him," Jun Do said.

"When he comes to collect," she told him, "I'll be long gone."

Jun Do looked at her. In this moment he felt truly sad for her. He thought of the men who were lobbying for her, the warden in Sinpo and the old Party boss in Chongwang, men who were right now preparing their homes for her arrival. Had they been shown a photo of her, told some kind of story, or had they only heard over their loudspeakers the tragic news that a hero had been lost to the sharks, leaving a beautiful young wife behind?

Winding the stairwell to the roof, they pushed through the metal door into darkness and stars. The adult dogs were free and skittish, their eyes locating them. In the center of the roof, there was a screened-in shed to keep insects off the sides of dog—rubbed with coarse salt and crushed green peppercorns—hanging to cure in the ocean air.

"It's beautiful up here," he said.

"Sometimes I come up here to think," she said. They looked far out onto the water. "What's it like out there?" she asked.

"When you're out of sight of shore," he said, "you could be anybody, from anywhere. It's like you have no past. Out there, everything is spontaneous, every lick of water that kicks up, every bird that drops in from nowhere. Over the airwaves, people say things you'd never imagine. Here, nothing is spontaneous."

"I can't wait to hear that radio," she said. "Can you get the pop stations from Seoul?"

"It's not that kind of radio," he said and jammed the antenna through the mesh of the puppy warren, the little dogs scurrying in terror.

"I don't get it."

Jun Do tossed the cable off the overhang, where they could retrieve it from the window below. "This radio doesn't receive broadcasts," he said. "It transmits them."

"What's the point of that?"

"We have a message to send."

Inside the apartment, his fingers worked quickly to hook up the antenna cable and a small microphone. "I had a dream," he told her. "I know it doesn't make any sense, but I dreamed your husband had a radio, that he was on a raft, heading into shimmering water, bright like a thousand mirrors."

"Okay," she said.

Jun Do turned the radio on and they both stared at the sodium-yellow glow of its power meter. He set it to 63 megahertz, then squeezed the breaker bar: "Third Mate to Second Mate, Third Mate to Second Mate, over." Jun Do repeated this, knowing that, just as he couldn't hear, the

Second Mate couldn't respond. Finally, he said, "My friend, I know you're out there and you mustn't despair." Jun Do could've explained how to unbraid a single strand of copper from the battery leads, then connect the strand to both poles so it would heat up enough to light a cigarette. Jun Do could have told the Second Mate how to make a compass from the magnet in the radio's windings, or how surrounding the capacitors is a foil he could flash as a signal mirror.

But the survival skills the Second Mate needed concerned enduring solitude and tolerating the unknown, topics about which Jun Do had some practice. "Sleep during the day," Jun Do told him. "At night your thoughts will come clear. We have looked at the stars together—chart them each night. If they are in the right places, you're doing fine. Use your imagination only on the future, never on the present or the past. Do not try to picture people's faces—you will despair if they don't come clear. If you are visited by people from far away, don't think of them as ghosts. Treat them as family, ask them questions, be a good host.

"You will need a purpose," he told the Second Mate. "The Captain's purpose was to get us home safe. Your purpose will be to stay strong so that you can rescue the girl who rows in the dark. She is in trouble and needs help. You're the only one out there who can help her. Scan the horizons at night, look for lights and flares. You must save her for me.

"I'm sorry that I let you down. It was my job to look out for you. I was supposed to save you, and I failed. You were the real hero. When the Americans came, you saved us all, and when you needed us, we weren't there for you. Somehow, one day, I'll make things right."

Jun Do stopped broadcasting, and the needle on the meter went flat.

The Second Mate's wife just looked at him. "That must have been one sad dream. Because that was the saddest message one person ever sent another." When Jun Do nodded, she said, "Who was the girl who rows in the dark?"

"I don't know," he said. "She was just in the dream."

He handed the microphone to her.

"I think you should say something to him," he said.

She didn't take it. "This is about your dream, not mine. What would I say?" she asked. "What would I tell him?"

"What would you have told him if you knew you'd never see him again?" he asked. "Or you don't have to say anything. He told me how much he loved your singing."

Jun Do went to his knees, turned, and rolled onto the pallet. On his back, he took several large breaths. When he tried to pull the shirt off, he found he couldn't.

"Don't listen," she told him.

He put his fingers in his ears, the same inside feeling as wearing head-phones, and watched her lips move. She spoke only for a little bit, her eyes pointed toward the windows, and when he realized she was singing, he opened his ears and welcomed the sound, a children's lullaby:

> *The cat's in the cradle, the baby's in the tree.*
> *The birds up above all click their beaks.*
> *Papa's in the tunnel, preparing for the storm,*
> *Here comes mama, her hands are worn.*
> *She holds out her apron for the baby to see.*
> *The baby full of trust lets go the tree.*

Her voice was simple and pure. Everyone knew their lullabies, but how did he know his? Had someone ever sung them to him, from before he could remember?

When she was done, she turned off the radio. The lights would go off soon, so she lit a candle. She came to his side, and there was something new in her eyes. "I needed that," she said. "I didn't know I needed that." She took a deep breath. "I feel like something's been lifted."

"That was beautiful," he said. "I recognized that lullaby."

"Of course you did," she said. "Everyone knows it." She put her hand on the box. "I've been carrying this around, and not once have you asked what it is."

"So show me," he said.

"Close your eyes," she told him.

He did. First came the unzipping of her canning-line jumpsuit, and then he heard the whole process, the opening of the box, the shuffle of stiff satin, the shush as she stepped into it and drew it up her legs, and then the whisper as it spun on her body, the shimmy of a final position, and then her arms, almost without sound, entering the sleeves.

"You can open your eyes now," she told him, but he did not want to.

Eyes closed, he could see her skin in long flashes, in the comfortable man-ner of someone unobserved. She was trusting him, completely, and he wished for anything but to have that end.

She kneeled beside him again, and when he did open his eyes, he saw she was in a shimmering yellow dress.

"This is the kind they wear in the West," she said.

"You're beautiful," he told her.

"Let's get that shirt off."

She slid a leg over his waist, the hem of her dress enveloping his mid-section. Straddling him, she pulled his arms till he was sitting up, then taking hold of his shirt, she let the gravity of his return peel it off.

"I can see those earrings from here," he said.

"Maybe I don't need to cut my hair, then."

He looked up at her. The yellow of her dress shined in the black of her hair.

She asked him, "How come you never married?"

"Bad *songbun*."

"Oh," she said. "Were your parents denounced?"

"No," he answered. "People think I'm an orphan."

"That will do it," she said, then hesitated. "Sorry, that sounded bad, the way I said that."

What was there to say? Jun Do shrugged at her.

She said, "You said my husband's purpose was to save the girl who rowed in your dreams."

"I just told him that to keep him strong and focused," Jun Do said. "The mission is always to stay alive."

"My husband isn't alive, is he? You'd tell me, right?"

"Yes, I'd tell you," Jun Do said. "But no, he's not alive."

She looked in his eyes.

"My lullaby, could everybody hear that broadcast?"

"Anyone on the East Sea."

"What about Pyongyang, could they hear it there?"

"No," he said. "That's too far, there's mountains. The signal travels far-ther over water."

"But anyone who was listening," she said.

"Ships, navigation stations, naval craft, they all heard. And I'm sure he heard you, too."

"In this dream of yours?"

"In my dream, yes," Jun Do said. "The dream of him floating away, the bright lights, his radio. It's as real as the sharks rising out of the dark water, as the teeth in my arm. I know one is real and one's a dream, but I keep forgetting which is which, they're both so true. I can't tell anymore. I don't know which one."

"Choose the beautiful story, with the bright lights, the one where he can hear us," she told him. "That's the true one. Not the scary story, not the sharks."

"But isn't it more scary to be utterly alone upon the waters, completely cut off from everyone, no friends, no family, no direction, nothing but a radio for solace?"

She touched the side of his face. "That's your story," she said. "You're trying to tell me your story, aren't you?"

Jun Do stared at her.

"Oh, you poor boy," she said. "You poor little boy. It doesn't have to be that way. Come in off the water, things can be different. You don't need a radio, I'm right here. You don't have to choose the alone."

She leaned in close and kissed him tenderly on the forehead and once on each cheek. She sat up and regarded him. She stroked his hand. When she leaned in again, moving as if to kiss him, she paused, staring at his chest.

"What is it?" he asked.

"It's stupid," she said. She covered her mouth.

"No it isn't. Tell me."

"I'm just used to looking down at my husband and seeing my face over his heart. I've never known anything different."

*

When the shock-work whistles blew in the morning, and the housing block was a hive of loudspeakers, they went onto the roof to remove the antenna. The morning sun was flat and brilliant upon the waters, yet lacking the heat to revive the flies or the stink of dog waste. The dogs, which seemed to snap and herd one another all day, were cowered in a single, sleeping mass in the crisp morning air, their coats white with dew.

The Second Mate's wife walked to the edge of the roof and sat with her legs swinging over the edge. Jun Do joined her, but the sight of the court-yard ten stories below made him close his eyes a moment.

"I won't be able to use mourning as an excuse much longer," she said. "At work, they'll hold a criticism session about me and reinstate my quota."

Below, a steady procession of workers in their jumpsuits crossed the courtyard, traversing the fish-cart paths and passing the Canning Master's house for the gates of the fish-processing factory.

"They never look up," she said. "I sit out here all the time and watch them. Not one has ever looked up and caught me."

Jun Do found the courage to gaze down upon them, and it was noth-ing like looking into the depths of the ocean. A hundred feet of air or sea alike would kill you, but the water would shuttle you, slowly, to a new realm.

Toward the sea, the sun was now hard to look at, so many flashes off the water. If it reminded her of Jun Do's dream about her husband, she didn't show it. The *Junma* could now be discerned from the other helms in the harbor, its peculiar bow-to-stern pitch from even the slightest wake of a passing vessel. Its nets were back aboard and it would be upon the water again soon. By shielding his eyes and squinting, Jun Do could make out a figure at the rail, looking down into the water. Only the Captain would stare into the water like that.

Below in the courtyard, a black Mercedes pulled up. It drove very slowly over the small, rutted fish-cart path and came to a stop in the grass of the courtyard. Two men in blue suits got out.

"I can't believe it," she said. "It's happening."

The men below shielded their eyes and gave the building a once-over. At the sound of their car doors slamming shut, the dogs stood and shook the wet from their fur. She turned to Jun Do. "It's really happening." Then she made for the metal door of the stair shaft.

The first thing she did was pull on her yellow dress, and this time there was no asking Jun Do to close his eyes. She moved frantically through the one-room apartment, throwing things in her suitcase.

"I can't believe they're here already," she said. She looked around the room, the expression on her face suggesting that everything she needed was eluding her. "I'm not ready. I didn't get a chance to cut my hair. I'm not even close to being ready."

"I care about what happens to you," Jun Do told her. "And I can't let them do this to you."

She was pulling items from a chest of drawers. "That's sweet," she said. "You're sweet, too, but this is my destiny, I have to go."

"We've got to get you out of here," Jun Do told her. "Maybe we can get you to your father. He'll know what to do."

"Are you insane?" she asked. "He's how I got stuck here."

For some reason, she handed him a stack of clothes.

"There's something I should have told you," he said.

"About what?"

"The old interrogator. He described the guys they picked out for you."

"What guys?"

"Your replacement husbands."

She stopped packing. "There's more than one?"

"One's a warden in Sinpo. The other guy's old, a Party official down in Chongwang. The interrogator didn't know which one was going to get you."

She cocked her head in confusion. "There's got to be some kind of mistake."

"Let's just get you out of here," he said. "It'll buy you some time till they come back."

"No," she said, her eyes fixing on him. "You can do something about this, you're a hero, you have powers. They can't say no to you."

"I don't think so," Jun Do said. "I don't think it works like that, not really."

"Tell them to go away, tell them you're marrying me."

There was a knock at the door.

She grabbed his arm. "Tell them you're marrying me," she said.

He studied her face, vulnerable—he'd never seen her like this.

"You don't want to marry me," he told her.

"You're a hero," she said. "And I'm a hero's wife. You just need to come to me." She took the hem of her skirt and held it out like an apron. "You're the baby in the tree, and you just need to trust me."

He went to the door, but paused before opening it.

"You talked about my husband's purpose," she said. "What about yours? What if your purpose is me?"

"I don't know if I have a purpose," he told her. "But you know yours—it's Pyongyang, not a radio man in Kinjye. Don't underestimate yourself—you'll survive."

"Survive like you?" she asked.

He didn't say anything.

"You know what you are?" she said. "You're a survivor who has nothing to live for."

"What would you rather, that I die for something I cared about?"

"That's what my husband did," she said.

The door was forced open. It was the two men from below. They didn't look happy about all those stairs. "Pak Jun Do?" one asked, and when Jun Do nodded, the man said, "You'll need to come with us."

The other one asked, "Have you got a suit?"

THE MEN in suits drove Jun Do along the cannery tracks before following a military road that wound up and out of the hills above Kinjye. Jun Do turned and watched everything recede in glimpses through the rear window. Through cuts in the road, he could see boats bobbing blue in the harbor and ceramic tiles flashing from the Canning Master's roof. He saw for a moment the town's red spire honoring April Fifteenth. The town looked suddenly like one of the happy villages they paint on the side of ration buildings. Going over the hill, there was only a plume of steam rising high from the cannery, a last sliver of ocean, and then he could see nothing. Real life was back again—a new work detail had been assigned, and Jun Do had no illusions about what kind of business it might entail. He turned to the men in suits. They were talking about a co-worker who was sick. They speculated on whether or not the sick man had a stockpile of food, and who would get his apartment if he died.

The Mercedes had windshield-wiper blades, something you never saw, and the radio was factory, capable of picking up broadcasts from South Korea and Voice of America. Breaking that law alone could get you sent to a mining camp, unless you happened to be above the law. While the men spoke, Jun Do observed that their teeth had been fixed with gold, something possible only in Pyongyang. Yes, the hero thought, this might be his ugliest assignment yet.

The two men drove Jun Do inland to a deserted air base. Some of the hangars had been converted into hothouses, and in the meadows surrounding the runway, Jun Do could see broken-down cargo planes had been pushed off the blacktop. They lay this way and that in the grass, their fuselages now serving as ostrich warrens—the birds' small heads watched him pass through clouded cockpit windows. They came to a small airliner, engines running. Descending its steps came two men in blue suits. One was older and quite small—like a grandfather wearing the dress clothes of his grandson. The old man took a look at Jun Do, then turned to the man next to him.

"Where's his suit?" the old man asked. "Comrade Buc, I told you he must have a suit."

Comrade Buc was young and lean, with round glasses. His Kim Il Sung pin was perfectly placed. But he had a deep vertical scar above his right eye. It had mishealed so that his eyebrow was broken into two pieces that didn't quite line up.

"You heard Dr. Song," he told the drivers. "The man must have a suit."

Comrade Buc ushered the smaller driver to Jun Do, where he compared their shoulders. Then he had the taller driver stand back-to-back with Jun Do. When Jun Do felt the other man's shoulder blades, it began to really sink in, that he probably wouldn't be upon the sea again, that he'd never know what would become of the Second Mate's wife, beyond the image of the hem of her yellow dress being fingered by an old warden from Sinpo. He thought of all the broadcasts he'd miss, of lives continuing beyond him. His whole life, he'd been assigned to work details without warning or explanation. There'd never been any point in asking questions or speculating on why—it never changed the work that had to be done. But then again, he'd never had anything to lose before.

To the taller driver, Dr. Song said, "Come, come, off with it."

The driver began to shed the jacket. "This suit's from Shenyang," he complained.

Comrade Buc was having none of it. "You got that in Hamhung, and you know it."

The driver loosened the shirt buttons and then the cuffs, and when he had it off, Jun Do offered in return the Second Mate's work shirt.

"I don't want your lousy shirt," the driver said.

Before Jun Do could don the new shirt, Dr. Song said, "Not so fast. Let's have a look at that shark bite of yours." Dr. Song lowered his glasses and leaned in close. He touched the wound very delicately, and rotated Jun Do's arm to examine the stitches.

In the sunlight, Jun Do could see the redness around the sutures, the way the seams wept.

"Very convincing," Dr. Song said.

"Convincing?" Jun Do asked. "I nearly died from that."

"The timing is perfect," Comrade Buc said. "Those stitches will have to come out soon. Will you have one of their doctors do it, or would it speak louder if we pulled them ourselves?"

"What kind of a doctor are you?" Jun Do asked.

Dr. Song didn't answer. His watery eyes were fixed on the tattoo on Jun Do's chest.

"I see our hero is a patron of the cinema," Dr. Song said. With a finger, he rapped Jun Do on the arm as a sign to get dressed, then asked him, "Did you know Sun Moon is Comrade Buc's girlfriend?"

Comrade Buc smiled, indulging the old man. "She's my neighbor," he corrected.

"In Pyongyang?" Jun Do asked. Immediately, he knew the question marked him as a rube. To cover his ignorance, he said, "Then you know her husband Commander Ga?"

Dr. Song and Comrade Buc went silent.

Jun Do went on, "He was the winner of the Golden Belt in taekwondo. They said he rid the military of homosexuals."

Gone was the playful light in Dr. Song's eyes. Comrade Buc looked away.

The driver removed a comb and a pack of cigarettes from his pockets, passed the suit jacket to Jun Do, and began unbuttoning his pants.

"Enough of Commander Ga's exploits," Dr. Song said.

"Yes," said Comrade Buc. "Let's see how that jacket fits."

Jun Do slid into the jacket. He had no way of knowing if it fit or not. The driver, in his underwear, handed over his pants, and then the last item, a silk tie. Jun Do studied it, running his eyes along the fat and skinny ends.

"Look," the driver said, lighting a cigarette and breathing out smoke. "He doesn't even know how to tie it."

Dr. Song took the tie. "Come, I will show you the nuances of Western neckwear," he said, then asked Comrade Buc, "Should we employ the Windsor knot or the half Windsor?"

"Four square," Buc said. "That's what the young men are wearing now."

Together, they ushered Jun Do up the stairs. From the top step, Comrade Buc turned to the driver. "File a requisition form with your regional allocations clerk," he said. "That'll put you in line for a new suit."

Jun Do looked back to his old clothes on the ground, soon to be scattered among ostrich warrens by the jet wash.

*

Inside the cabin, gold-framed portraits of the Dear Leader and Great Leader were paired on the bulkheads. The plane smelled of cigarettes and dirty dishes. Jun Do could tell that dogs had been aboard. He scanned the rows and rows of empty seats but saw no sign of animals. Up front sat a lone man in a black suit and high-brimmed military hat. He was being attended by a stewardess of perfect complexion. Toward the rear of the plane, a half-dozen young men were engrossed in paperwork. One of them employed a computer that folded open and closed. Thrown across a few seats, Jun Do spotted a yellow emergency life raft with a red inflation handle and instructions in Russian. Jun Do placed his hand on it—the sea, the sun, a tin of meat. So many days upon the water.

Comrade Buc approached. "Afraid of flying?" he asked.

"I don't know," Jun Do said.

The engines began to ramp, and the plane wandered toward the far end of the runway.

"I'm in charge of procurement," Comrade Buc said. "This plane's taken me all over the world—to Minsk for fresh caviar, to France for brandy straight from the caves. So don't worry about it going down."

"What am I doing here?" Jun Do asked.

"Come," Comrade Buc said. "Dr. Song wants you to meet the Minister."

Jun Do nodded and they approached the front of the plane, where Dr. Song was speaking to the Minister. "Refer to him only as Minister," Comrade Buc whispered. "And never speak to him directly, only through Dr. Song."

"Minister," Dr. Song said. "Here is Pak Jun Do, a bona fide hero of the Democratic People's Republic, no?"

The Minister shook his head dismissively. His face was stippled with gray whiskers and hanging clumps of brow obscured his eyes.

"Certainly, Minister," Dr. Song continued. "You can tell the boy is strong and handsome, yes?"

The Minister conceded this with a nod.

Dr. Song said, "We will all spend more time together soon, perhaps?"

The Minister shrugged and gave a look that said maybe, maybe not.

That was the extent of their discussion.

Walking away, Jun Do asked, "What's he a minister of?"

"Petroleum and tire pressure," Dr. Song said, and laughed. "He's my driver. But don't worry, that man's seen just about all there is to see in this world. He's strong. His only job is to say nothing on this trip, and to enact the *yes, no,* and *perhaps* at the end of my questions. You caught that, yes, the way I guided his response? This will keep the Americans occupied while we work our magic."

"Americans?" Jun Do asked.

"Didn't those drivers tell you anything?" Dr. Song asked.

The plane pivoted at the end of the runway and began to accelerate. Jun Do braced himself in the aisle.

Comrade Buc said, "I do not think our hero has flown before."

"Is this true, have you not flown?" Dr. Song asked. "We must get you a seat, then, we're about to take wing."

With mandarin formality, Dr. Song ushered them into seats. "Here is the safety belt," he said to Jun Do. "A hero may wear one or not, as he wishes. I am old and have no need for safety, but Comrade Buc, you must apply the belt. You are young, you have a wife and children."

"Only because of your great concern," Comrade Buc said, and fastened the belt.

The Ilyushin rose into the western wind, then banked north so that the coast was to starboard. Jun Do could see the shadow of the plane shuddering on the water and, beyond, the blue expanse of the sea. He did not see the water upon which he fished the seasons with the Captain of the *Junma,* but instead the currents that took him on missions to Japan, every one of them a struggle. The worst part was always the long trip back, listening to the abductees down in the hold, yelling, banging around as they struggled to get free of their ropes. He looked around the cabin, imagined a kidnap victim strapped into one of these seats. He imagined dragging away an American, then spending sixteen hours with him inside this plane.

"I think you've got the wrong man for your job," Jun Do volunteered. "My file perhaps suggests I'm an expert kidnapper, and it's true, I led a lot of missions, and only a couple of the targets died on my watch. But I'm not that man anymore. These hands, they tune radio dials now. They no longer know how to do what you want them to do."

"So forthright and earnest," Dr. Song said. "Don't you think, Comrade Buc?"

Comrade Buc said, "You chose well, Dr. Song. The Americans will swoon for such sincerity."

Dr. Song turned to Jun Do. "Young man," he said. "On this mission, it is your words, not your fists, that you will employ."

Comrade Buc said, "Dr. Song is headed to Texas to lay some groundwork for future talks."

"These are the talks before the talks," Dr. Song said. "Nothing formal, no delegation, no pictures, no security men—we are merely opening a channel."

"Talks about what?" Jun Do asked.

"The subject doesn't matter," Dr. Song said. "Only the posture. The Yankees want a few things from us. We want things as well—high among them is that they halt the boarding of our fishing vessels. You know we use fishing boats for many important tasks. When the moment is right, you will tell the story of your friend being thrown to the sharks by the U.S. Navy. The Americans are very civil. A story like that will have an impact on them, especially the wives."

The stewardess brought Dr. Song a glass of juice and ignored Jun Do and Comrade Buc. "She is a beauty, yes?" Dr. Song asked. "They comb the entire nation to find them. Young men, all you care about is pleasure, I know, I know. You can't lie to me. I bet you're salivating to meet a CIA agent. Well, I can assure you they don't all look like the beautiful seductresses in the movies."

"I've never seen a movie," Jun Do said.

"You've never seen a movie?" Dr. Song asked.

"Not a whole one," Jun Do said.

"Oh, you'll have those American ladies eating out of your hand. Wait till they see that wound, Jun Do. Wait till they hear your story!"

"But my story," Jun Do said. "It's so improbable. I hardly believe it myself."

To Comrade Buc, Dr. Song said, "Please, my friend. Will you bring us the tiger?"

When Buc was gone, Dr. Song turned to Jun Do. "Where we are from," he said, "stories are factual. If a farmer is declared a music virtuoso by the state, everyone had better start calling him maestro. And secretly, he'd be wise to start practicing the piano. For us, the story is more important than the person. If a man and his story are in conflict, it is the man who must change." Here, Dr. Song took a sip of juice, and the finger he lifted trembled slightly. "But in America, people's stories change all the time. In America, it is the man who matters. Perhaps they will believe your story and perhaps not, but you, Jun Do, they will believe *you*."

Dr. Song called the stewardess over. "This man is a hero of the Democratic People's Republic of Korea, and he must have juice." After she raced to get it, he said, "See?" Shaking his head, he said, "But you try explaining all this to the central bunker." Here Dr. Song pointed downward, and Jun Do knew he was indicating the Dear Leader Kim Jong Il himself.

Comrade Buc returned with an ice chest. This he handed to Jun Do. "The tiger," he said.

Inside was a slab of meat wrapped in a dirty plastic bag. Sprigs of grass clung to the meat, which was warm to the touch.

Jun Do said, "Perhaps some ice would be called for."

Dr. Song smiled. "Oh," he said. "The Americans, I can see their faces now."

"Tiger! Imagine their response." Comrade Buc was laughing. "I would love to," he said in English, "but I had tiger for lunch."

"Looks delicious," Dr. Song said. "Too bad I'm on a leopard-only diet."

Comrade Buc said, "Wait till the Minister gets in on the act."

"The Minister would like to cook it personally, yes?" Dr. Song said. "The Minister insists all the Americans must partake, yes?"

Jun Do looked at the cooler, which bore a red cross. He'd seen a cooler like it before—it was the kind they used to get the blood to Pyongyang.

"Two things about the Americans," Dr. Song said. "First, their minds are fast, and they puzzle over everything. You must give them a riddle to redirect those minds. So we offer them the Minister. Second, they must have moral superiority. They don't know how to negotiate without it. Always their talks open with human rights, personal freedoms, and so on. But the tiger changes all that. Their horror at the notion that we would casually eat an endangered species will immediately put them on high ground. Then we can get down to business."

In English, Comrade Buc said, "Here, Senator, let me pass you the platter."

"Yes, Senator," Dr. Song said. "You must have seconds."

They laughed until they saw Jun Do's face. "You do understand," Dr. Song said, "that in this cooler is only cow flank. The tiger part is only a story. That's what we're really serving them, a story."

"But what if they eat it?" Jun Do asked. "If they believe it is tiger, yet out of a wish not to offend, they eat it and feel morally degraded, won't they take it out on you in the talks?"

Comrade Buc turned in anticipation of Dr. Song's response.

"If the Americans use their senses and keep their heads level," Dr. Song said, "then no tiger story will fool them. They will taste that this is cow. But if the Americans are just toying with us, if they don't plan on seeking the facts and negotiating seriously, then they will taste tiger."

"You think if they believe the tiger story," Jun Do said, "then they'll believe my story."

Dr. Song shrugged. "Yours will certainly be the tougher meat to chew," he said.

One of the young men on Comrade Buc's procurement team came forward with three identical watches. Comrade Buc took them. "One for the Minister," he said, and handed the others to Dr. Song and Jun Do. "They're set to Texas time. Everybody gets the same one. It sends a message to the Americans about Korean equality and solidarity."

"What about you?" Jun Do asked. "Where's your watch?"

Comrade Buc said, "Oh, I've got no business in Texas."

"Sadly, Comrade Buc won't be joining us," Dr. Song said. "He has another mission."

Comrade Buc stood. "Yes, I should go prepare my team."

The stewardess passed by with hot towels and handed one to Dr. Song.

"What do I have to do?" Comrade Buc said after she'd left.

"She cannot help it," Dr. Song said. "Women naturally respond to the allure of an older gentleman. It is a fact that only an older man can truly please a woman."

Comrade Buc laughed. "I thought you always said only a small-statured man can please a woman."

Dr. Song defended himself. "I'm hardly small-statured. I have the exact dimensions of the Dear Leader, even my shoe size."

"It's true," Comrade Buc said. "I procure for the Dear Leader. They are two of a kind."

*

Jun Do took a window seat as they flew north over Sakhalin, Kamchatka, and the Sea of Okhotsk, where the Captain had been imprisoned, somewhere down there in the blue. They outran the sunset by flying north, into perpetual summer light. They stopped at the Russian Air Force base in Anadyr to refuel, and all the old pilots came out to marvel at the sight of an Ilyushin Il-62, which they concluded was forty-seven years old. They ran their hands along the belly of the plane and talked about all the problems that were corrected in later versions, and everyone had a hair-raising story about flying them before the remnants of the fleet were shipped to Africa in the late '80s. The tower operator came forward, a large man, and Jun Do could see the places he'd once had frostbite. The tower operator said even the Ilyushin's replacements—the early Antonovs and Tupolevs—were rare these days. "I heard the last Ilyushin Il-62 went down in Angola in the year 1999," he added.

Dr. Song broke into Russian. "It is lamentable," he said, "that the once great nation that created this fine aircraft is no longer able to do so."

Comrade Buc added, "Please know that news of your country's complete collapse was met with sadness in our nation."

"Yes," Dr. Song said. "Your nation and ours were once the world's twin beacons of communism. Sadly, we now bear that burden alone."

Comrade Buc opened a suitcase of new U.S. hundred-dollar bills to pay for the fuel, but the tower operator shook his head no.

"Euros," he said.

Indignant, Dr. Song said, "I am personal friends with the mayor of Vladivostok."

"Euros," said the tower operator.

Comrade Buc had another suitcase, it turned out, this one filled with European money.

As they were departing, Dr. Song told the pilots to make a statement. They rolled the engines hard during takeoff, rattling the airframe in a tremendous display of ascent.

The Aleutians, the international date line, and nine thousand meters up, the crisp outlines of container vessels against a stippled, green-white sea. The Captain had told Jun Do that off the east coast of Japan the ocean was nine thousand meters deep, and now he understood what that meant.

Witnessing the vastness of the Pacific—how impossibly monumental that you could row across it!—he understood how rare his radio contacts had been.

Where was the arm of the captain of the *Kwan Li*? Jun Do suddenly wondered. In whose hands were his old dictionaries right now, and what person shaved this morning with the Captain's brush? In what tunnel was his team now running, and what had become of the old woman they'd kidnapped, the one who said she would go willingly if she could take his picture? What could the look on his face have been, and what story did the Niigata bartender tell of the night she drank with kidnappers? The Second Mate's wife suddenly came to him in her canning-line jumpsuit, her skin glistening with fish oil, her hair wild from steam, and that rustling yellow dress enveloped him, took him deep into sleep.

Somewhere over Canada, Dr. Song gathered everyone for a protocol briefing on the subject of Americans. He spoke to the Minister and Jun Do, as well as Comrade Buc's team of six. The copilot and stewardess eavesdropped. Dr. Song prefaced everything with a preamble on the evils of capitalism and a recounting of American war crimes against subjugated peoples. Then he began by tackling the concept of Jesus Christ, examining the special case of the American Negro, and listing the reasons Mexicans defected to the United States. Next, he explained why affluent Americans drove their own cars and spoke to their servants as equals.

One young man asked how to behave should he encounter a homosexual.

"Point out that this is a new experience for you," Dr. Song said, "as there are no such individuals where you are from. Then treat him as you would any visiting Juche scholar from foreign lands like Burma or Ukraine or Cuba."

Dr. Song then got practical. He said it was okay to wear shoes indoors. Women were free to smoke in America and should not be confronted. Disciplining other people's children in America was not okay. He drew for them on a piece of paper the shape of a football. With great discomfort, Dr. Song touched on American standards of personal hygiene, and then he delivered a mini-lecture on the subject of smiling. He concluded with dogs, noting how Americans were very sentimental, with a particular softness toward canines. You must never hurt a dog in America, he said. They are considered part of the family and are given names, just like people.

Dogs also have their own beds and toys and doctors and houses, which should not be referred to as warrens.

When they finally began their descent, Comrade Buc sought out Jun Do.

"About Dr. Song," he said. "He's had a long and famous career, but in Pyongyang, you're only as safe as your last success."

"Safe?" Jun Do asked. "Safe from what?"

Comrade Buc touched the watch that Jun Do now wore. "You just help him succeed."

"What about you, why aren't you coming with us?"

"Me?" Comrade Buc asked. "I've got twenty-four hours to get to Los Angeles, buy three hundred thousand dollars' worth of DVDs, and then get back. Is it true you've never seen a movie?"

"I'm not a rube or anything. I just never had the opportunity."

"Now's your chance," Comrade Buc said. "Dr. Song has requested a movie about sopranos."

"I'd have no way of playing a DVD," Jun Do told him.

"You'd find a way," Comrade Buc said.

"What about Sun Moon? I'd see a movie starring her."

"They don't sell our films in America."

"Is it true that she's sad?"

"Sun Moon?" Comrade Buc nodded. "Her husband Commander Ga and the Dear Leader are rivals. Commander Ga is too famous to punish, so it is his wife who gets no more movie roles. We hear her next door. She plays the *gayageum* all day, teaching that sad, wandering sound to her children."

Jun Do could see her fingers pluck the strings, each note striking, flaring, and losing timbre like a match that burns to smoke.

"Last chance for an American movie," Comrade Buc said. "They're the only real reason to learn English."

Jun Do tried to gauge the nature of the offer. In Comrade Buc's eyes, Jun Do saw a look he knew well from childhood, the look of a boy who thought the next day would be better. Those boys never lasted. Still, Jun Do liked them the most.

"Okay," he said. "Which one's the best?"

"*Casablanca*," Comrade Buc said. "They say that one is the greatest."

"*Casablanca*," Jun Do said. "I'll take that one."

*

It was morning when they landed at Dyess Air Force Base south of Abilene, Texas.

Jun Do's nocturnal schedule served him now on the other side of the world. He was awake and alert—through the Ilyushin's yellowed window, he could see that two older cars had pulled onto the blacktop to meet them. There were three Americans in hats out there, two men and a woman. When the Ilyushin rested its engines, they rolled up a metal stairway.

"In twenty-four hours," Dr. Song said as a farewell to Comrade Buc.

Comrade Buc executed a quick bow, and then opened the door.

The air was dry. It smelled of hot metal and withered cornstalks. Fighter jets, a row of them, were parked at a shimmering distance—they were things Jun Do had only seen in inspirational murals.

At the bottom of the stairs, their three hosts were waiting. Standing in the center was the Senator, who was perhaps older than Dr. Song, yet tall and tan in blue pants and an embroidered shirt. Jun Do could see a molded medical device filling the Senator's ear. If Dr. Song was sixty, the Senator must have had a decade on him.

Tommy was the Senator's friend, a black man, much the same age, though leaner, with hair that had gone white and a face more deeply creased. And then there was Wanda. She was young, thick-bodied, and had a yellow ponytail sticking out the back of a ball cap that read "Blackwater." She wore a red cowgirl shirt with silver snaps.

"Minister," the Senator said.

"Senator," the Minister said, and there were general greetings all around.

"Come," the Senator said. "We've got a little side trip planned."

The Senator directed the Minister toward an old American car. When the Minister moved to open the driver's-side door, the Senator gently directed him to the other side.

Tommy indicated a white convertible whose chrome lettering proclaimed "Mustang."

"I must travel with them," Dr. Song said.

"They're in a Thunderbird," Wanda said. "It only seats two."

"But they don't speak the same language," Dr. Song said.

Tommy said, "Half a Texas don't speak the same language."

The Mustang, top down, followed the Thunderbird out onto a county road. Jun Do rode in the backseat with Dr. Song. Tommy drove.

Wanda lifted her head into the wind, moving her face back and forth, enjoying it. Far ahead and far behind, Jun Do could make out the black of security vehicles. The side of the road glimmered with broken glass. Why would a country be strewn with razor-sharp glass? To Jun Do, it seemed like some tragedy had taken place every step of the way. And where were all the people? A barbed-wire fence paced them, making it feel as if they were in a normal control-permit zone. But rather than concrete poles with insulators for the electricity, the posts were made from gnarled, bleached branches that looked like broken limbs or old bones, as if something had died to build every five meters of that fence.

"This is quite a special car," Dr. Song said.

"It's the Senator's," Tommy said. "We've been friends since our Army days." Tommy's arm was hanging outside the car in the wind. He slapped the metal twice. "I had known war in Vietnam," he said. "And I had known Jesus, but it wasn't till I borrowed this Mustang, with rolled-and-tucked backseats, that I knew Mary McParsons and took my first breath as a man."

Wanda laughed.

Dr. Song shifted uncomfortably on the leather.

Jun Do could see on the face of Dr. Song the great insult that had been done him to be informed he was sitting where Tommy had once had intercourse.

"Oh," Tommy went on, "I cringe when I think of the guy I used to be. Thank God I ain't still him. I married that woman, by the way. I did that right, rest her soul."

Dr. Song observed a political sign bearing the image of the Senator and an American flag. "There is an election coming, no?" he asked.

"That's right," Tommy said. "The Senator's got a primary in August."

"We are lucky, Jun Do," Dr. Song said, "to witness American democracy in action."

Jun Do tried to think of how Comrade Buc would respond. "Most exciting," Jun Do said.

Dr. Song asked, "Will the Senator retain his representative position?"

"It's pretty much a sure thing," Tommy said.

"A sure thing?" Dr. Song asked. "That doesn't sound very democratic."

Jun Do said, "That's not how we were taught democracy works."

"Tell me," Dr. Song said to Tommy. "What will be the voter turnout?"

Tommy looked at them in the rearview mirror. "Of registered voters? For a primary, that would be about forty percent."

"Forty percent?" Dr. Song exclaimed. "Voter turnout in the Democratic People's Republic of Korea is ninety-nine percent—the most democratic nation in the world! Still, the United States needn't feel shame. Your country can still be a beacon for countries with lower turnouts, like Burundi, Paraguay, and Chechnya."

"Ninety-nine-percent turnout?" Tommy marveled. "With democracy like that, I'm sure you'll soon be over a hundred."

Wanda laughed, but then she looked back, caught Jun Do's eye, and offered him a smile that was sly-eyed, seeming to include him in the humor.

Tommy looked at them in the rearview mirror. "You don't actually believe that 'most democratic nation' business, do you? You know the truth about where you're from, right?"

Wanda said, "Don't ask them questions like that. The wrong answer could get them in trouble back home."

Tommy said, "Tell me you at least know the South won the war. Please know that much."

"But you're wrong, my dear Thomas," Dr. Song said. "I believe it was the Confederacy that lost the war. It was the North that prevailed."

Wanda smiled at Tommy. "He got you on that one," she said.

Tommy laughed. "He sure did."

They pulled off the road at a cowboy emporium. The parking lot was empty save for the Thunderbird and a black car parked to the side. Inside, several salespersons were waiting to outfit the visitors in Western attire. Dr. Song translated to the Minister that cowboy boots were gifts from the Senator and he could have any pair he wished. The Minister was fascinated by the exotic boots and tried on pairs made from lizard, ostrich, and shark. Finally he decided on snake, and the staff began seeking out pairs in his size.

Dr. Song conferred briefly with the Minister, then announced, "The Minister must make a defecate."

The Americans clearly wished to laugh, but didn't dare.

The Minister was gone a long time. Jun Do found a pair of black boots that spoke to him, but in the end he set them aside. He then went through many pairs of women's boots before he found some he thought would fit the Second Mate's wife. They were yellow and stiff, with fancy stitching around the toe.

Dr. Song was offered smaller and smaller sizes, until finally a pair of simple black boots fit him in a boy's size. To help save face, Jun Do turned to Dr. Song. "Is it true," he said loudly, "that you take the exact shoe size as the Dear Leader Kim Jong Il?"

Everyone watched as Dr. Song took a pleasant stroll in his boots, dress shoes in his hands. He stopped before a mannequin in cowboy clothes. "Observe, Jun Do," he said. "Instead of their most beautiful women, the Americans employ artificial people to display the clothes."

"Most ingenious," Jun Do said.

"Perhaps," Wanda said, "our most beautiful women are otherwise engaged."

Dr. Song bowed at the truth of this. "Of course," he said. "How short-sighted of me."

On the wall, mounted behind a piece of glass, was an ax. "Look," Dr. Song said. "The Americans are always prepared for a sudden outbreak of violence."

The Senator glanced at his watch, and Jun Do could tell he'd had enough of this game.

The Minister returned and was handed a pair of boots. Each scale of the snakeskin seemed to catch the light. Clearly pleased, the Minister took a few steps in them like a gunslinger.

"Have you seen this movie *High Noon*?" Dr. Song asked them. "It is the Minister's favorite."

And suddenly the Senator was smiling again.

Dr. Song spoke to the Minister. "They fit perfectly, no?" he asked.

The Minister looked sadly down at his new boots. He shook his head.

The Senator snapped his fingers. "Let's get some more boots over here," he told the sales clerks.

"I'm sorry," Dr. Song said. He sat to remove his own boots. "But the Minister believes it would be an insult to the Dear Leader to receive the gift of new boots when the Dear Leader himself received none."

Jun Do returned the boots he'd chosen for the Second Mate's wife. It was a fantasy idea, anyway, he knew. The Minister, too, sat to pull off his boots.

"This can be easily fixed," the Senator said. "Of course we can send a pair of boots to Mr. Kim. We know he takes the same size as Dr. Song here. We'll just get an extra pair."

Dr. Song laced his dress shoes back on.

"The only insult," Dr. Song said, "would be for a humble diplomat such as myself to wear shoes fit for the most revered leader of the greatest nation on earth."

Wanda's eyes passed back and forth upon this scene. Her gaze landed on Jun Do, and he knew it was him that she was puzzling over.

They left without boots.

*

The ranch had been prepared to give the Koreans a taste of Texas life. They crossed a cattle grate to enter the property, then switched to pickup trucks. Again the Senator traveled with the Minister, while the rest of the group followed in a four-door work truck. They took a road of sand and shale, and they passed through wind-bent bushes and gnarled trees that looked burned and split, with even their tall branches twisted to the ground. There was a field of spiked plants, their shark claws aglow. Each was alone in the way it groped from the rocky earth, looking to Jun Do like gestures from those buried underneath.

During the ride to the ranch, the Americans seemed to ignore the Koreans, making comments about cattle that Jun Do could find no sign of, and then slipping into a shorthand of their own that Jun Do could make no sense of.

"Blackwater," Tommy said to Wanda. "They your new outfit?"

They were heading toward a stand of trees from which blew white, vinalon-like fibers.

"Blackwater?"

"That's what your hat says."

"It's just a free hat," she said. "Right now I think I'm working for a civilian subsidiary of a government contractor to the military. No use trying to keep it straight. I've got three Homeland passes, and I've never set foot in the place."

"Headed back to Baghdad?" he asked.

She looked across the Texas hardpan. "Friday," she said.

The sun was direct when they climbed down from the big truck. Jun Do's dress shoes filled with sand. A table had been set up with a barrel cooler of lemonade, and three gift baskets, each wrapped in cellophane. The baskets contained a cowboy hat, a pint of bourbon, a carton of American Spirit cigarettes, some beef jerky, a water bottle, sunscreen, a red kerchief, and a pair of calfskin gloves.

"My wife's doing," the Senator said.

The Senator invited them to retrieve the hats and gloves from their gift baskets. A motorized saw and weed cutter had been set out, and the Koreans donned safety goggles to cut brush. Dr. Song's eyes, through the plastic, were seething with indignity.

Tommy pull-started the weed cutter and handed it to the Minister, who seemed to take a strange pleasure in moving the blade back and forth through the dead brambles.

When it was Dr. Song's turn, he said, "It seems I, too, have the pleasure." He positioned his goggles, then raced the engine through brush and stubble before stalling the blade in the sand.

"I fear I have little aptitude for groundskeeping," Dr. Song said to the Senator. "But, as the Great Leader Kim Il Sung prescribes, *Ask not what the Democratic People's Republic of Korea can do for you; ask what you can do for the Democratic People's Republic of Korea.*"

The Senator sucked air through his teeth.

Tommy said, "Isn't he also the great leader who regretted that his citizens had but one life to give for their country?"

"Okay," the Senator said. "Let's try our hand at fishing."

Poles had been laid out at a stock pond fed by well pumps. The sun was relentless, and in his dark suit, Dr. Song looked unsteady. The Senator took two folding chairs from the bed of his truck, and he and Dr. Song sat in the shade of a tree. Though he fanned himself with the hat as the Senator did, Dr. Song did not loosen his tie.

Tommy spoke low and respectfully to the Minister. Jun Do translated.

"Cast beyond the trunk of that fallen tree," Tommy suggested. "Jiggle the tip of the pole to make your lure dance as you reel in."

Wanda approached Jun Do with two glasses of lemonade.

"I have once been fishing with cables of electricity," the Minister said. "Very effective."

It was the first time the Minister had spoken all day. Jun Do could think of no way to soften this statement. Finally, he translated it to Tommy as, "The Minister believes victory is at hand."

Jun Do took the lemonade from Wanda, who had an eyebrow raised in suspicion. It let Jun Do know that she was no clear-complexioned stewardess offering drinks to powerful men.

It took the Minister a few casts to get the knack of it, Tommy pantomiming advice.

"Here," she said to Jun Do. "Here's my contribution to your gift basket." She handed him a tiny LED flashlight. "They give 'em away at the trade shows," she said. "I use them all the time."

"You work in the dark?" he asked.

"Bunkers," she said. "That's my specialty. I analyze fortified bunkers. I'm Wanda, by the way. I didn't get to introduce myself."

"Pak Jun Do," he said, taking her hand. "How do you know the Senator?"

"He visited Baghdad, and I gave him a tour of Saddam's Saladin Complex. A very impressive structure. High-speed rail tunnels, triple-filtered air, nuke resistant. Once you see someone's bunker, you know everything about him. You get news of the war?"

"Constantly," Jun Do told her. He clicked the light on and cupped his hand over the beam to measure its brightness. "The Americans use lights in tunnel combat?"

"How could you not use lights?" she asked.

"Doesn't your army have goggles that see in the dark?"

"Honestly," she said, "I don't think Americans have done that kind of fighting since Vietnam. My uncle was one of them, a tunnel rat. These days, if there was a situation underground, they'd send a bot."

"A bot?"

"You know, a robot, remote controlled," she said. "They've got some beauties."

The Minister's pole bent as a fish ran with the lure. The Minister kicked his shoes off and stepped ankle-deep into the water. It put up a tremendous struggle, the pole moving this way and that, and Jun Do thought there must be a more placid variety of fish to stock a pond with. The Minister's shirt was soaked with sweat when he finally reeled the fish close. Tommy landed it, a fat, white thing. Tommy removed the hook, and then held it high, for everyone to see, a finger in its gaping mouth to demonstrate the jaws. Then Tommy released the fish back into the pond.

"My fish!" the Minister shouted. He took a step forward in anger.

"Minister," Dr. Song called and rushed over. He placed his hands on the Minister's shoulders, which were rising and falling. "Minister," Dr. Song said more softly.

"Why don't we move right along to target practice," the Senator suggested.

They walked a short pace through the desert. Dr. Song had a difficult time taking the uneven terrain in his dress shoes, though he would accept no help.

The Minister spoke, and Jun Do translated: "The Minister has heard that Texas is home to a most poisonous snake. He desires to shoot one, so that he might see if it is more powerful than our country's dreaded rock mamushi."

"In the middle of the day," the Senator said, "rattlesnakes are down in their holes, where it's cool. In the morning, that's when they're out and about."

Jun Do relayed this to the Minister, who said, "Tell the American Senator to have his black helper pour water down the snake's hole, and I will shoot the specimen when it emerges."

Hearing the answer, the Senator smiled, shook his head. "The problem is the rattlesnake's protected."

Jun Do translated, yet the Minister was confused. "Protected from what?" he wanted to know.

Jun Do asked the Senator, "From what is the snake protected?"

"From the people," the Senator said. "The law protects them."

This was found most humorous by the Minister, that a vicious, man-killing snake would be protected from its victims.

They came to a shooting bench with several Wild West revolvers lined up. Various cans had been placed at a distance as a shooting gallery. The .45 caliber revolvers were heavy and worn and, the Senator assured them, had all revoked the lives of men. His great-grandfather had been a sheriff in this county, and these pistols had been taken as evidence in murder cases.

Dr. Song declined to shoot. "I do not trust my hands," he said, and sat in the shade.

The Senator said that his shooting days were behind him, too.

Tommy began loading the weapons. "We got plenty of pistols," he told Wanda. "You going to give us a demonstration?"

She was refastening her ponytail. "Who, me?" she asked. "I don't think so. The Senator would be mad if I embarrassed our guests."

The Minister, however, was in his element. He set about wielding the pistols as if he'd spent his days smoking and conversing and firing at things propped in the distance by his servants, rather than parked at a curb reading the daily *Rodong Sinmun,* waiting for his boss Dr. Song to finish with his meetings.

"Korea," Dr. Song said, "is a land of mountains. Gunshots bring swift responses from the canyon walls. Here, the bang goes off into the distance, never to return."

Jun Do agreed. It was a truly lonesome thing to have such a commotion be swallowed by the landscape, to have the sound of fire make no echo.

The Minister was surprisingly accurate, and soon he was feigning quick draws and attempting trick shots as Tommy reloaded for him. They all watched the Minister go through boxes of ammo, firing with two hands, a cigarette in his lips, the cans popping and leaping. Today, *he* was the minister, people drove *him* around, *he* pulled the trigger.

The Minister turned to them. He addressed them in English. "The Good," he said, blowing smoke from the barrel, "the Bad, and the Ugly."

*

The ranch house was single-level and half hidden by trees, deceptively sprawling. A nearby corral contained picnic tables and a "chuckwagon" grill, where several people were lined up for lunch. The cicadas were active, and Jun Do could smell the cooking coals. A midday breeze stirred, heading for anvil clouds too distant to promise rain. Free-roaming dogs leaped in and out of the corral's fencing. At one point the dogs noticed something moving in a distant bush. They stood at attention, bristling. Walking past, the Senator said, "Hunt," and at the command, the dogs raced off to flush a group of small birds that ran quickly through the brush.

When the dogs returned, the Senator gave them treats from his pocket, and Jun Do understood that in communism, you'd threaten a dog into compliance, while in capitalism, obedience is obtained through bribes.

The food line favored no rank or privilege—standing together were the Senator, the ranch hands, the house servants, the security agents in their black suits, the wives of Texas officials. While the Minister took a seat at a picnic table and was brought his food by the Senator's wife, Dr. Song and Jun Do lined up with plates made from paper. The young man next to Jun Do and Dr. Song introduced himself as a PhD candidate from the university. He was writing a dissertation on the North Korean nuclear program. He leaned in close and said, quietly, "You know the South won the war, right?"

They were served beef ribs, corn grilled in the husk, marinated tomatoes, and a scoop of macaroni. Dr. Song and Jun Do made their way to where the Minister ate with the Senator and his wife. Dogs followed them.

Dr. Song sat with them. "Please, join us," he said to Jun Do. "There is plenty of room, no?"

"I'm sorry," Jun Do told them. "I'm sure you have important matters to discuss."

He sat alone at a wooden picnic table that had been vandalized with people's initials. The meat was both sweet and spicy, the tomatoes tangy, but the corn and noodles were made most foul by butter and cheese, substances he knew only from dialogs they'd heard recited over tapes in his language school. *I would like to buy some cheese. Please pass the butter.*

A large bird circled above. He didn't know its variety.

Wanda joined him. She was licking a white plastic spoon.

"Jesus," she said. "Don't miss out on the pecan pie."

He had just finished eating a rib and his hands were covered with sauce.

She nodded to the end of the table, where a dog sat patiently, staring. Its eyes were cloudy blue, and its coat was marbled gray and brindle. How could a dog, obviously well fed, capture the exact look of an orphan boy, relegated to the end of the line?

"Go ahead," Wanda said. "Why not?"

He threw the bone, which was snapped from the air.

"That's a Catahoula dog," she said. "A gift from the governor of Louisiana for helping out after the hurricane."

Jun Do lifted another rib. He couldn't stop eating them, even when it felt as if the meat was backing up in his throat.

"Who are all these people?" he asked.

Wanda looked around. "A couple think-tankers, some NGO folk, various lookey-loos. The North Koreans don't visit every day, you know."

"What about you?" he asked. "Are you a think-tanker or a lookey-loo?"

"I'm the shadowy intelligence figure," she said.

Jun Do stared at her.

She smiled. "Come on, do I look shadowy?" she asked. "I'm an open-source gal. I'm all about sharing. You can ask me anything you want."

Tommy crossed the corral holding a cup of iced tea, coming from wherever he'd stored the poles and pistols. Jun Do watched Tommy line up and get served, offering a bow of the head when he was handed his plate.

Jun Do said to Wanda, "You're looking at me like maybe I never saw a black person before."

Wanda shrugged. "It's possible."

"I met the U.S. Navy before," Jun Do said. "Lots of those guys are black. And my English teacher was from Angola. The only black man in the DPRK. He said it wasn't so lonely as long as he gave us all African accents."

Wanda said, "I heard a story that in the '70s an American soldier crossed the DMZ, a boy from North Carolina who was drunk or something. The North Koreans made him a language teacher, but had to stop after he taught all the agents to talk like crackers."

Jun Do didn't know what she meant by "cracker." "I never heard that story," he said. "And I'm not an agent, if that's what you're suggesting."

Wanda watched him dig into another rib. "I'm surprised you didn't take me up on my offer to answer any question," she said. "I'd have bet you'd ask me if I spoke Korean."

"Do you?" he asked.

"No," she said. "But I can tell when someone's muddling a translation. That's why I figure you're here as something other than a lowly interpreter."

Dr. Song and the Minister stood at their picnic table. Dr. Song announced, "The Minister wishes to present gifts to the Senator and his wife. For the Senator, *The Selected Works of Kim Jong Il*." Here, Dr. Song produced the bound, eleven-volume set.

A Mexican woman walked by with a tray full of food. "EBay," she said to Wanda.

"Oh, Pilar," Wanda called after her. "You're bad."

The Senator accepted the gift with a smile. "Are they signed?" he asked.

Dr. Song's face showed a flash of uncertainty. He conferred with the Minister. Jun Do couldn't hear them, but their words were flashing back and forth. Then Dr. Song smiled. "The Dear Leader Kim Jong Il would be happy to inscribe the books in person should the Senator visit as our guest in Pyongyang."

In return, the Senator gave the Minister an iPod loaded with country music.

Dr. Song then began to speak publicly of the beauty and graciousness of the Senator's wife, while the Minister prepared to offer her the cooler.

The smell of that meat returned to Jun Do's nose. He set the rib aside and looked away.

"What?" Wanda asked him. "What's in that cooler?"

This seemed like a turning point somehow, that Dr. Song's ruses up till now were all in fun, but the tiger ploy was of a different sort—one sniff and the Americans would know that the meat was foul, that some ugly game was being played, and everything would be different.

"I need to know," Jun Do asked her. "Were you serious?"

"Of course," she said. "Serious about what?"

He took her hand. With a pen, he wrote across her palm the name of the Second Mate.

"I need to know if he made it," Jun Do said. "Did he get out?"

Using her phone, Wanda took a picture of her hand. She typed a message using both her thumbs and then pressed *Send.* "Let's find out," she said.

Dr. Song finished his tribute to the loveliness of the Senator's wife, and the Minister handed her the cooler. "From the citizens of the Democratic People's Republic of Korea," he said. "Fresh tiger meat, taken recently from a majestic beast culled from the peaks of Mount Paektu. You can't imagine how white was his fur. The Minister desires that we all feast of it tonight, yes?"

The Minister nodded with pride.

Dr. Song adopted a wily smile. "And remember," he said to the Senator's wife, "when you eat of the tiger, you become like the tiger."

People stopped eating to witness the Senator's wife's reaction to this, but she said nothing. The clouds were thicker now, and the air smelled of rain that probably wouldn't arrive. The Senator removed the cooler from the table. "Let me see if I can take charge of that," he said with a business-like smile. "Tiger sounds like a man's business."

The Senator's wife turned her attention to a dog at her side; she cupped its ears with both hands and spoke sweetly to it.

The gift ceremony seemed to have slipped from Dr. Song's hands. He was at a loss as to what had gone wrong. He came over to Jun Do. "How are you holding up, son?" he asked. "It's the arm, it's hurting quite badly, I can tell, yes?"

Jun Do rotated his shoulder a couple of times. "Yes, but I'll be okay, Dr. Song. I'll manage."

Dr. Song looked frantic. "No, no need, son. I knew this time would come. There's no bravery lost in seeking medical attention." He looked to Wanda. "You wouldn't have a knife or some scissors we could use?"

Wanda looked to Jun Do. "Is your arm hurt?" she asked. When he nodded, Wanda called the Senator's wife over, and for the first time, Jun Do took true notice of her—a lean woman with shoulder-length white hair and pale, pearled eyes. "I think our friend here is hurt," Wanda told her.

To the Senator's wife, Dr. Song asked, "Is it possible to get some alcohol and a knife? It's no emergency. We simply have some stitches to remove."

"Are you a doctor doctor?" the Senator's wife asked.

"No," Dr. Song said.

She turned to Jun Do. "Where are you hurt?" she asked him. "I used to practice medicine."

"It's nothing," Dr. Song said. "We probably should have removed the stitches before we left."

She turned to Dr. Song, glaring. Her lack of patience for him blazed until he looked away. She brought out a pair of glasses and placed them on the end of her nose. "Show me," she said to Jun Do. He removed his suit coat, and then his shirt. He offered his arm for the Senator's wife to examine. She lifted her head to employ the lenses. The eyelets of the sutures were red and inflamed. When she pressed her thumb, they wept.

"Yes," she said. "These must come out. Come, I have a good light in the kitchen."

*

Soon the Senator's wife and Wanda had him shirtless, sitting on the kitchen counter. The kitchen was bright yellow, the walls papered with blue checked print and sunflowers. Pinned to the refrigerator by magnets were many snapshots of children, but also groups of young people, arms thrown around each other. One photo depicted the Senator in an orange astronaut's suit, space helmet tucked under his arm.

The Senator's wife scrubbed her hands under steaming sink water. Wanda did, too, in case she was needed. The woman Wanda called Pilar came into the kitchen carrying the cooler of tiger meat. She said something in Spanish when she saw Jun Do shirtless, and she said something else in Spanish when she saw his wound.

The Senator's wife scrubbed well past her elbows. Without looking from her work, she said, "Jun Do, this is Pilar, our family's special helper."

"I'm the maid," Pilar said. "John Doe? Isn't that the name you give a missing person?"

"It's Pak Jun Do," Jun Do said, then he pronounced it slowly. "*Jhun Doh.*"

Pilar looked at the cooler, studying the way someone had attempted to scrape away the Red Cross insignia. "My nephew Manny drives a truck that moves organs and eyes and things between hospitals," she said, "He uses a cooler just like this."

The Senator's wife popped on latex gloves. "Actually," she said, "I don't think a John Doe is a missing person. I think it's when you have the person, just not his identity."

Wanda blew into her latex gloves. "A John Doe has an exact identity," she said, and considered the patient. "It's just yet to be discovered."

The Senator's wife poured hydrogen peroxide up and down his arm, massaging it into the wounds. "This will loosen the sutures," she said.

For a moment, there was only the hiss of his arm foaming white. It didn't hurt, exactly—it felt like ants, maybe, swarming in and out of him.

Wanda said, "Are you all right being treated by a female doctor?"

Jun Do nodded. "Most of the doctors in Korea are women," he said. "Though I've never seen one."

"A woman doctor?" Wanda asked.

"Or any doctor?" the Senator's wife asked.

"Any doctor," he said.

"Not even in the military, for a physical?" the Senator's wife asked.

"I guess I've never been sick," he said.

"Who patched you up?"

"A friend," Jun Do said.

"A friend?"

"A guy I work with."

While the wound foamed, the Senator's wife lifted his arms, spread them wide, then brought them forward, her eyes following invisible lines on his body. He watched as she noted the burns on the undersides of his arms—candle marks from his pain training. She touched the ridges of the scars with her fingertips. "A bad place to get burned," she said. "The skin is quite sensitive here." She ran her hand across his chest to the collarbone. "This knitting," she said. "That's a fresh break to the clavicle." She brought his hands up, as though she were going to kiss a ring—instead, she studied the alignment of his finger bones. "Do you want me to look you over? Do you have any complaints?"

He wasn't as muscular as when he'd been in the military, but his physique was strong, and he could feel the women looking at him.

"No," he said. "It's just these stitches. They itch like crazy."

"We'll get those out in no time," she said. "Can I ask what happened?"

"It's a story I'd rather not tell," he said. "But it was a shark that did it."

"*Madre de Dios,*" Pilar said.

Wanda was standing next to the Senator's wife. She held open a white first-aid kit the size of a briefcase. "You mean the kind with the fins, that live in the ocean?" Wanda asked.

"I lost a lot of blood," he said.

They just stared at him.

"My friend wasn't so lucky," he added.

"I understand," the Senator's wife said. "Take a deep breath."

Jun Do inhaled.

"Really deep," she said. "Lift your shoulders."

He took a breath, deep as he could. It came with a wince.

The Senator's wife nodded. "Your eleventh rib," she said. "Still healing. Seriously, you want a full checkup, now's your chance."

Did she sniff his breath? Jun Do had the feeling there were things she was noting but no longer pointing out. "No, ma'am," he told her.

Wanda found a pair of tweezers and some finger scissors with pointed, baby blades. He had nine lacerations total, each one laced shut, and the Senator's wife started with the longest one, along the peak of his biceps.

Pilar pointed at his chest. "Who's she?"

Jun Do looked down. He didn't know what to say. "That's my wife," he said.

"Very beautiful," Pilar said.

"She is beautiful," Wanda said. "It's a beautiful tattoo, too. Do you mind if I take a pic?"

Jun Do had only had his photograph taken that one time, by the old Japanese woman with the wooden camera, and he never saw the picture that came of it. But it haunted him, what she must have seen. Still, he didn't know how to say no.

"Great," Wanda said, and with a small camera, she snapped a picture of his chest, then his injured arm, and finally she lifted the camera to his face and there was a flash in his eyes.

Pilar asked, "Is she a translator, too?"

"My wife's an actress," he said.

"What's her name?" Wanda asked.

"Her name?" Jun Do asked. "Her name is Sun Moon."

The name was beautiful, he noticed, and it felt good in his mouth and to say aloud, the name of his wife, to these three women. *Sun Moon.*

"What is this stuff?" the Senator's wife asked. She held up a strand of suturing she'd removed. It was variously clear, yellow, and rust-colored.

"It's fishing line," he said.

"I guess if you'd caught tetanus, we'd already know by now," she said. "In med school, they taught us never to use monofilament, but I can't for the life of me remember why."

"What are you going to bring her?" Wanda asked. "As a souvenir of your trip to Texas?"

Jun Do shook his head. "What do you suggest?"

Distractedly, the Senator's wife asked, "What's she like?"

"She likes traditional dresses. Her yellow one is my favorite. She wears her hair back to show off her gold earrings. She likes to sing karaoke. She likes movies."

"No," Wanda said. "What's she like, her personality?"

Jun Do took a moment. "She needs lots of attention," he said, then paused, unsure how to proceed. "She is not free with her love. Her father was afraid that men would take advantage of her beauty, that they would be drawn to her for the wrong reasons, so when she was sixteen, he got her a job in a fish factory, where no men from Pyongyang would find her. That experience shaped her, made her strive for what she wanted. Still, she found a husband who is domineering. They say he can be a real asshole. And she is trapped by the state. She cannot choose her own movie roles. Except for karaoke, she can only sing the songs they tell her to sing. I suppose what matters is that, despite her success and stardom, her beauty and her children, Sun Moon is a sad woman. She is unaccountably alone. She plays the *gayageum* all day, plucking notes that are lonesome and forlorn."

There was a pause, and Jun Do realized all three women were staring at him.

"You're not an asshole husband," Wanda said. "I know the look of one."

The Senator's wife stopped tugging sutures, and wholly without guile, appraised his eyes. She looked at the tattoo on Jun Do's chest. She asked, "Is there a way I could talk to her? I feel that if I could just speak to her, I would be able to help." On the counter was a phone, one with a loopy cord that connected the handset to the base. "Can you get her on the line?" she asked.

"There are few phones," Jun Do said.

Pilar opened her cell phone. "I have international minutes," she said.

Wanda said, "I don't think North Korea works like that."

The Senator's wife nodded and finished removing the stitches in silence. When she was done, she irrigated the wounds again, then stripped off her gloves.

Jun Do pulled on the driver's shirt he'd been wearing for two days. His arm felt as thick and raw as the day of the bite. As for the tie, he held it in his hand as the Senator's wife did his buttons—her fingers strong and measured as they coaxed each button through its eye.

"Was the Senator an astronaut?" he asked her.

"He trained as one," the Senator's wife said. "But he never got the call."

"Do you know the satellite?" he asked. "The one that orbits with people from many nations aboard?"

"The Space Station?" Wanda asked.

"Yes," Jun Do said. "That must be it. Tell me, is it built for peace and brotherhood?"

The ladies looked at each other. "Yes," the Senator's wife said. "I suppose it is."

The Senator's wife rummaged through kitchen drawers until she found a few doctors' samples of antibiotics. She slipped two foil packets into his shirt pocket. "For later, if you get sick," she said. "Take them if you have a fever. Can you tell the difference between a bacterial and a viral infection?"

He nodded.

"No," Wanda said to the Senator's wife. "I don't think he can."

The Senator's wife said, "If you have a fever and are bringing up green or brown mucus, then take three of these a day until they're gone." She popped the first capsule out of the foil and handed it to him. "We'll start a cycle now, just in case."

Wanda poured him a glass of water, but after he'd popped the pill in his mouth and chewed it up, he said, "No thanks, I'm not thirsty."

"Bless your heart," the Senator's wife said.

Pilar opened the cooler. "Ay," she said and quickly closed it. "What I'm supposed to do with this? Tonight is Tex-Mex."

"My word," the Senator's wife said, shaking her head. "Tiger."

"I don't know," Wanda said. "I kind of want to try it."

"Did you smell it?" Pilar asked.

"Wanda," the Senator's wife said. "We could all go to hell for what's in that cooler."

Jun Do jumped off the counter. With one hand, he began tucking in his shirt.

"If my wife were here," he said, "she'd tell me to throw it out and replace it with flank steak. She'd say you can't taste the difference, anyway, and now everyone eats, and no one loses face. At dinner, I'd talk about how great it was, how it was the best meat I'd ever had, and that would make her smile."

Pilar looked to the Senator's wife. "Tiger tacos?"

The Senator's wife tried the words in her mouth. "Tiger tacos."

*

"Pak Jun Do, what's called for now is rest," the Senator's wife said. "I'm going to show you to your room," she added with a quiet fierceness, as if she were transgressing somehow by being alone with him. The house had many hallways, lined with more family photos, these framed in wood and metal. The door to the room where he would sleep was slightly open, and when they swung it wide, a dog leaped off the bed. The Senator's wife didn't seem concerned. The bed was covered with a quilt, and by pulling it taut, she removed the dog's impression.

"My grandmother was quite the quilter," she said, then looked into Jun Do's eyes. "That's where you make a blanket out of scraps from your life. It doesn't take money, and the blanket tells a story." Then she showed Jun Do how to read the quilt. "There was a mill in Odessa that printed panels of Bible stories on its flour sacks. The panels were like church windows—they let people see the story. This piece of lace is from the window of the house Grandmother left when she was married at fifteen. This panel is Exodus and here is Christ Wandering, both from flour sacks. The black velvet is from the hem of her mother's funeral dress. She died not long after my grandmother came to Texas, and the family sent her this black swatch. This starts a sad time in her life—a patch of baby blanket from a lost child, a swatch of a graduation gown she purchased but never got to wear, the faded cotton of her husband's uniform. But look here, see the colors and fabrics of a new wedding, of children and prosperity? And of course the last panel is the Garden. Much loss and uncertainty she had to endure before she could sew that ending to her own story. If I could have reached your wife Sun Moon, that's what I would have spoken to her about."

On the bedside table was a Bible. She brought it to him. "Wanda's right—you're not an a-hole husband," she said. "I can tell you care about your wife. I'm just a woman she never met on the other side of the world, but could you give her this for me? These words always bring me solace. Scripture will always be there, no matter what doors are closed to her."

Jun Do held the book, felt its soft cover.

"I could read some with you," she said. "Do you know of Christ?"

Jun Do nodded. "I've been briefed on him."

A pain came to the corners of her eyes, then she nodded in acceptance.

He handed back the book. "I'm sorry," Jun Do told her. "This book is forbidden where I come from. Possessing it comes with a high penalty."

"You don't know how it sorrows me to hear that," she said, then went to the door, where a white guayabera hung. "Hot water on that arm, you hear? And wear this shirt tonight."

When she left, the dog leaped back onto the bed.

He pulled off his dress shirt and looked around the guest room. It was filled with memorabilia of the Senator—photos of him with proud people, plaques of gold and bronze. There was a small writing desk, and here a phone rested atop a white book. Jun Do lifted the phone's receiver, listened to its solid tone. He took up the book underneath it, leafed through its pages. Inside were thousands of names. It took him a while to understand that everyone in central Texas was listed here, with their full names and addresses. He couldn't believe that you could look up anyone and seek them out, that all you had to do to prove you weren't an orphan was to open a book and point to your parents. It was unfathomable that a permanent link existed to mothers and fathers and lost mates, that they were forever fixed in type. He flipped through the pages. Donaldson, Jimenez, Smith—all it took was a book, a little book could save you a lifetime of uncertainty and guesswork. Suddenly he hated his small, backward homeland, a land of mysteries and ghosts and mistaken identities. He tore a page from the back of the book and wrote across the top: Alive and Well in North Korea. Below this he wrote the names of all the people he'd helped kidnap. Next to Mayumi Nota, the girl from the pier, he placed a star of exception.

In the bathroom, there was a basket filled with new razors and miniature tubes of toothpaste and individually wrapped soaps. He didn't touch them. Instead, he stared in the mirror, seeing himself the way the Senator's wife had seen him. He touched his lacerations, his broken clavicle, the burn marks, the eleventh rib. Then he touched the face of Sun Moon, the beautiful woman in this halo of wounds.

He went to the toilet and stared into its mouth. It came in a moment, the meat, three heaves of it, and then he was empty. His skin had gone tight, and he felt weak.

In the shower, he made the water hot. He stood there, steeping his wound in the spray, like fire on his arm. When he closed his eyes, it was like being nursed by the Second Mate's wife again, back when his eyes were still swollen shut and she was just the smell of a woman, the sounds a woman made, and he had a fever and he didn't know where he was and he had to imagine the face of the woman who would save him.

*

Toward twilight, Jun Do dressed in his white guayabera shirt, with its stiff collar and fancy stitching. Through the window, he could see Dr. Song and the Minister exit a shiny black mobile home where they had been holding talks with the Senator all afternoon. The dog stood and came to the edge of the bed. There was a harness around its neck. It was kind of a sad thing, a dog without a warren. A band started playing somewhere, perhaps Spanish voices. When Jun Do turned to go out into the night, the dog followed.

The hallway was lined with photographs of the Senator's family, always smiling. To move toward the kitchen was like going back in time, the graduation photos becoming sports photos, and then there were scouting clubs, pigtails, birthday parties, and finally the pictures were of babies. Was this what a family was, how it grew—straight as the children's teeth? Sure, there was an arm in a sling and over time the grandparents disappeared from the photos. The occasions changed, as did the dogs. But this was a family, start to finish, without wars or famines or political prisons, without a stranger coming to town to drown your daughter.

Outside, the air was dry and cool and smelled of cactus ribs and aluminum stock tanks. The stars wavered as Texas gave off the last of its heat. Jun Do followed the sounds of Mexican singers and a whirring blender to the corral, where the men wore white shirts and the women were wrapped in colorful shawls. There was a tripod of fire, illuminating the sheen of people's faces. It was a thrilling idea—setting wood ablaze just so people could mingle and enjoy one another's company in the dark. By the flickering light, the Senator played his fiddle and sang a song called "The Yellow Rose of Texas."

Wanda walked by holding so many limes she had to press them against her chest. When Jun Do stopped, the dog stopped, its coat in the firelight orange and black. "Okay, dog," Jun Do said, and stiffly patted its head like an American would.

Wanda juiced limes with a wooden baton as Pilar upturned bottles of liquor into the blender. Wanda jazzed its button in time with the music, then Pilar filled a line of yellow plastic cups with great flair. Wanda brought him a drink when she saw him.

He stared at the salt on the rim. "What's this?" he asked.

"Go ahead," she said. "Be a sport. You know what Saddam had in the deepest room of his bunker? I'm talking below the hardened war rooms and command centers. He had an Xbox video game, with only one controller."

He gave her a look of incomprehension.

"Everybody needs to have fun," she said.

Jun Do drank from the cup—tart and dry, it tasted like thirst itself.

"I looked into your friend," Wanda said. "The Japanese and South Koreans don't have anybody who fits the bill. If he crossed the Yalu into China, then who knows. And maybe he's not going by his real name. Give it time, he might turn up. Sometimes they make their way to Thailand."

Jun Do unfolded his piece of paper and handed it to Wanda. "Can you pass along this message for me?"

"'Alive and Well in North Korea,'" she read. "What is this?"

"It's a list of Japanese kidnap victims."

"Those kidnappings all made the news," Wanda said. "Anyone could have made this list. It doesn't prove anything."

"Prove?" Jun Do asked. "I'm not trying to prove anything. I'm trying to tell you what no one else can—that none of these people were lost, that they all survived their kidnappings and that they are alive and well. Not knowing, that's the worst. That list isn't for you—it's a message from me to those families, for their peace of mind. It's all I have to give them."

"They're all alive and well," she said. "Except for the one with the star?"

Jun Do made himself speak her name. "Mayumi," he said.

She sipped her drink and looked at him sideways. "Do you speak Japanese?"

"Enough," he said. "*Watashi no neko ga maigo ni narimashita?*"

"What's that mean?"

"Can you help me find my kitty-cat?"

Wanda gave him a look, then slid the paper into her back pocket.

*

It wasn't until dinner that Jun Do got a good look at Dr. Song. Jun Do tried to guess how the talks had gone by the way Dr. Song poured margaritas for the ladies and nodded in approval at the spiciness of the salsa. The table was round and seated eight, with Pilar swooping in to add and remove dishes. She named everything on the lazy Susan at the center of the table, including flautas, mole, rellenos, and fix-it-yourself tacos: there was a tortilla warmer and dishes of cilantro, onion, diced tomatoes, shredded cabbage, Mexican cream, black beans, and tiger.

When Dr. Song tasted his tiger, a look of pure glee crossed his face.

"Tell me this isn't the best tiger you've had," he said. "Tell me American tiger can measure up. Is the Korean tiger not fresher, more vital?"

Pilar brought another platter of meat. "*Bueno,*" she said. "Too bad there is no Mexican tiger."

"You've outdone yourself, Pilar," the Senator's wife said. "Your best Tex-Mex yet."

Dr. Song eyed them both with suspicion.

The Minister held up his taco. In English, he said, "Yes."

Tommy ate his taco and nodded in approval. "The best meat I ever had," he said, "was with me and some buddies on leave. We raved and raved about the dinner, eating until we were stuffed. We spoke so highly they brought out the chef, who said he would make us some to go, that it was no problem because he had another dog out back."

"Oh, Tommy," the Senator's wife said.

"I was with a tribal militia once," Wanda said. "They prepared a feast of fetal pigs, boiled in goat's milk. That's the most tender meat ever."

"Enough," the Senator's wife said. "Another topic, please."

The Senator said, "Anything but politics."

"There is something I must know," Jun Do said. "When I was upon the waters, in the Sea of Japan, we followed the broadcasts of two American girls. I never knew what became of them."

"The rowers," Wanda said.

"What an awful story," the Senator's wife said. "Such a waste."

The Senator turned to Tommy. "They found the boat, right?"

"They found the boat but no girls," Tommy said. "Wanda, you get any backchannel on what really went down?"

Wanda was leaning over her plate to eat, a stream of taco juice running down her hand. "I hear the boat was partly burned," she said with her mouth full. "They found the blood of one girl but nothing of the other. A murder-suicide, perhaps."

"It was the girl who rowed in the dark," Jun Do said. "She used a flare gun."

The table went silent.

"She rowed with her eyes closed," Jun Do said. "That was her problem. That's how she got off course."

Tommy asked, "Why would you ask what happened to those girls if you already knew?"

"I didn't know what happened," Jun Do said. "I only knew how."

"Tell us what happened to you," the Senator's wife asked Jun Do. "You said you've spent some time on the water. How did you come by such a wound?"

"It is too soon," Dr. Song cautioned them. "The wound is still fresh. This story is as difficult to hear as it is for my friend to tell." He turned to Jun Do. "Another time, yes."

"It's okay," Jun Do said, "I can tell it," and he proceeded to recount their encounter with the Americans in great detail, how the *Junma* was boarded, the way the soldiers moved with their rifles and how they became blackened with soot. He explained the shoes that he had found, and how they littered the decks, and Jun Do described how the soldiers smoked and sorted through the shoes after the boat was declared clear, how they began stealing souvenirs, including the most sacred portraits of the Dear and Great Leaders, and how a knife was then drawn and the Americans were forced to retreat. He mentioned the fire extinguisher. He told them how officers on the American ship drank coffee and watched. He described the cruise missile that flexed its biceps on a sailor's lighter.

The Senator said, "But how'd you get hurt, son?"

"They came back," Jun Do said.

"Why would they come back?" Tommy asked. "They'd already cleared your vessel."

"What were you doing on a fishing vessel in the first place?" the Senator asked.

"Clearly," Dr. Song said with some force, "the Americans were ashamed that a single North Korean, armed only with a knife, made cowardly an entire armed American unit."

Jun Do took a drink of water. "All I know," he said, "is that it was first light, the sun to the starboard. The American ship came out of the brightness, and suddenly we were boarded. The Second Mate was on deck with the Pilot and the Captain. It was laundry day, so they were boiling seawater. There was screaming. I went up top with the Machinist and the First Mate. The man from before, Lieutenant Jervis, had the Second Mate at the rail. They were shouting at him about the knife."

"Wait a minute," the Senator said. "How do you know this sailor's name?"

"Because he gave me his card," Jun Do said. "He wanted us to know who had settled the score." Jun Do passed the business card to Wanda, who read the name "Lieutenant Harlan Jervis."

Tommy stepped forward and took the card. "The *Fortitude,* Fifth Fleet," he said to the Senator. "That must be one of Woody McParkland's boats."

The Senator said, "Woody wouldn't tolerate any bad apples in his out-fit."

The Senator's wife lifted her hand. "What happened next?" she asked.

Jun Do said, "Then he was thrown to the sharks, and I jumped in to save him."

Tommy said, "But where did all the sharks come from?"

"The *Junma* is a fishing boat," Jun Do explained. "Sharks were always following us."

"So there was just a swirl of sharks?" Tommy asked.

"Did the boy know what was happening to him?" the Senator asked.

Tommy asked, "Did Lieutenant Jervis say anything?"

"Well, there weren't many sharks at first," Jun Do said.

The Senator asked, "Did this Jervis fellow throw the boy in himself, with his own hands?"

"Or did he order one of his sailors to do it?" Tommy asked.

The Minister placed his hands flat on the table. "Story," he declared in English, "true."

"No," the Senator's wife said.

Jun Do turned to her, her old-lady eyes pale and cloudy.

"No," she said. "I understand that during wartime, no side has a mo-nopoly on the unspeakable. And I am not naive enough to think that the engines of the righteous aren't powered by the fuel of injustice. But these are our finest boys, under our best command, flying the colors of this na-tion. So, no sir, you are wrong. No sailor of ours ever did such an act. I know this. I know this for a fact."

She rose from the table.

Jun Do rose, too.

"I apologize for disturbing you," he said. "I shouldn't have told the story. But you must believe that I have looked into the eyes of sharks, seen them stupid with death. When you're near them, an arm's length away, their eyes flick white. They'll turn sideways and lift their heads when they want a better look before they bite you. I didn't feel the teeth in my flesh, but it was icy and electric when they hit bone. The blood, I could smell it in the water. I know the feeling of seeing a boy right in front of you, and he is about to be gone. You suddenly understand you'll never see him again. I've heard the last gibberish a person says. When a person slips into the water, right in front of you, the disbelief of it, that never leaves you. And the artifacts people leave behind, a shaving brush, a pair of shoes, how dumb they seem—you can handle them in your fingers, stare at them all you want, they don't mean anything without the person." Jun Do was shaking, now. "I've held the widow, *his widow,* with these arms as she sang nursery rhymes to him, wherever he was."

*

Later, Jun Do was in his room. He was looking up all the Korean names in Texas, the hundreds of Kims and Lees, and he was almost to Paks and Parks when the dog on his bed suddenly stood.

Wanda was at the door—she knocked lightly twice, then opened.

"I drive a Volvo," she said from the threshold. "It's a hand-me-down from my dad. When I was a kid, he worked security at the port. He always had a maritime scanner going, so he could know if a captain was in trouble. I have one, too, and I turn it on when I can't sleep."

Jun Do just stared at her. The dog lay down again.

"I found out some things about you," Wanda said. "Like who you really are." She shrugged. "I thought it only fair to share a few things about me."

"Whatever your file says about me," Jun Do told her, "it's wrong. I don't hurt people anymore. That's the last thing I want to do." How did she have a file on him anyway, he wondered, when Pyongyang couldn't even get his info right.

"I put your wife Sun Moon into the computer, and you popped right up, Commander Ga." She studied him for a reaction, and when he gave none, she said, "Minister of Prison Mines, holder of the Golden Belt in taekwondo, champion against Kimura in Japan, father of two, winner of the Crimson Star for unnamed acts of heroism, and so on. There were no current photos, so I hope you don't mind me uploading the pictures I took."

Jun Do closed the phone book.

"You've made a mistake," he said. "And you must never call me that in front of the others."

"Commander Ga," Wanda said, like she was savoring the name. She held up her phone. "There's an app that predicts the orbit of the Space Station," she said. "It will be passing over Texas in eight minutes."

He followed her outside, to the edge of the desert. The Milky Way reeled above them, the smell of creosote and dry granite sweeping down from the mountains. When a coyote called, the dog moved between them, its tail twitching with excitement, the three of them waiting for another coyote to respond.

"Tommy," Jun Do said. "He's the one who speaks Korean, right?"

"Yes," Wanda said. "The Navy stationed him there for ten years."

They cupped their hands and stared at the sky, scanning for the arc of the satellite.

"I don't understand any of this," Wanda said. "What's the Minister of Prison Mines doing here in Texas? Who's the other man claiming to be a minister?"

"None of this is his fault. He just does what he's told. You've got to understand—where he's from, if they say you're an orphan, then you're an orphan. If they tell you to go down a hole, well, you're suddenly a guy who goes down holes. If they tell you to hurt people, then it begins."

"Hurt people?"

"I mean if they tell him to go to Texas to tell a story, suddenly he's nobody but that."

"I believe you," she said. "I'm trying to understand."

Wanda was the first to spot the International Space Station, diamond bright and racing across the sky. Jun Do tracked it, as amazed as when the Captain first indicated it above the sea.

"You're not looking to defect, are you?" she asked. "If you were looking to defect, that would cause a lot of problems, trust me. It could be done, mind you. I'm not saying it's impossible."

"Dr. Song, the Minister," Jun Do said. "You know what would happen to them. I could never do that to them."

"Of course," she said.

Far in the distance, too many kilometers away to gauge, a lightning storm clung to the horizon. Still, its flashes were enough to silhouette closer mountain ranges and give hints of others even farther yet. The strobe of one bolt gave them a glimpse of a dark owl, caught mid-flight, as it silently hunted through the tall, needley trees.

Wanda turned to him. "Do you feel free?" she asked. She cocked her head. "Do you know what free feels like?"

How to explain his country to her, he wondered. How to explain that leaving its confines to sail upon the Sea of Japan—that was being free. Or that as a boy, sneaking from the smelter floor for an hour to run with other boys in the slag heaps, even though there were guards everywhere, *because* there were guards everywhere—that was the purest freedom. How to make someone understand that the scorch-water they made from the rice burned to the bottom of the pot tasted better than any Texas lemonade?

"Are there labor camps here?" he asked.

"No," she said.

"Mandatory marriages, forced-criticism sessions, loudspeakers?"

She shook her head.

"Then I'm not sure I could ever feel free here," he said.

"What am I supposed to do with that?" Wanda asked. She seemed almost mad at him. "That doesn't help me understand anything."

"When you're in my country," he said, "everything makes simple, clear sense. It's the most straightforward place on earth."

She looked out toward the desert.

Jun Do said, "Your father was a tunnel rat, yes?"

"It was my uncle," she said.

"Okay, your uncle. Most people walking around—they don't think about being alive. But when your uncle was about to enter an enemy tunnel, I bet he was thinking about nothing but that. And when he made it out, he probably felt more alive than we'll ever feel, the most alive in the world, and that until the next tunnel, nothing could touch him, he was invincible. You ask him if he felt more alive here or over there."

"I know what you're saying and all," Wanda said. "When I was a kid, he was always telling hair-raisers about the tunnels, like it was no big deal. But when he visits Dad's now, and you get up in the middle of the night for a glass of water, there he is, wide awake in the kitchen, just standing there, staring into the sink. That's not invincible. That's not wishing you were back in Vietnam where you felt alive. That's wishing you'd never even seen the place. Think about what that does to your freedom metaphor."

Jun Do gave a look of sad recognition. "I know this dream your uncle has," he said. "The one that woke him and made him walk to the kitchen."

"Trust me," she said. "You don't know my uncle."

Jun Do nodded. "Fair enough," he said.

She stared at him, almost vexed again.

"Okay," she said. "Go on and tell it."

"I'm just trying to help you understand him."

"Tell it," she said.

"When a tunnel would collapse," Jun Do said.

"In the prison mines?"

"That's right," he said. "When a tunnel would collapse, in a mine, we'd have to go dig men out. Their eyeballs would be flat and caked. And their mouths—they were always wide open and filled with dirt. That's what you couldn't stand to look at, a throat packed like that, the tongue grubbed and brown. It was our greatest fear, ending up with everyone standing around in a circle, staring at the panic of your last moment. So your uncle, when you find him at the sink late at night, it means he's had the dream where you breathe the dirt. In the dream, everything's dark. You're holding your breath, holding it, and when you can't hold it anymore, when you're about to breathe the dirt—that's when you wake, gasping. I have to wash my face after that dream. For a while I do nothing but breathe, but it seems like I'll never get my air back."

Wanda studied him a moment.

She said, "I'm going to give you something, okay?"

She handed him a small camera that fit in his palm. He'd seen one like it in Japan.

"Take my picture," she said. "Just point it and press the button."

He held the camera up in the dark. There was a little screen upon which he could barely see her outline. Then there was a flash.

Wanda reached in her pocket, and removed a bright red cell phone. When she held it up, the picture he'd taken of her was on its screen. "These were made for Iraq," she said. "I give them to locals, people who are friendly. When they think I need to see something, they take a picture of it. The picture goes to a satellite, then only to me. The camera has no memory, so it doesn't store the pictures. No one could ever find out what you took a picture of or where it went."

"What do you want me to take a picture of?"

"Nothing," she said. "Anything. It's up to you. If there's ever something you'd like to show me, that would help me understand your country, just push this button."

He looked around, as if trying to decide what in this dark world he would photograph.

"Don't be scared of it," she said and leaned in close to him. "Reach out and take our picture," she told him.

He could feel her shouldering into him, her arm around his back.

He took the picture, then looked at it on the screen.

"Was I supposed to smile?" he asked, handing it to her.

She looked at the picture. "How intimate," she said, and laughed. "You could loosen up a bit, yeah. A smile wouldn't hurt."

"'Intimate,'" he said. "I don't know this word."

"You know, close," she said. "When two people share everything, when there are no secrets between them."

He looked at the picture. "Intimate," he said.

*

That night, in his sleep, Jun Do heard the orphan Bo Song. Because he had no hearing, Bo Song was one of the loudest boys when he tried to speak, and in his sleep he was even worse, clamoring on through the night in the slaw of his deaf-talk. Jun Do gave him a bunk in the hall, where the cold stupefied most boys—there'd be some teeth chattering for a while, and then silence. But not Bo Song—it only made him talk louder in his sleep. Tonight, Jun Do could hear him, whimpering, whining, and in this dream, Jun Do somehow began to understand the deaf boy. His stray sounds started to form words, and though Jun Do couldn't quite make the words into sentences, he knew that Bo Song was trying to tell him the truth about something. There was a grand and terrible truth, and just as the orphan's words started to make sense, just as the deaf boy was finally making himself heard, Jun Do woke.

He opened his eyes to see the muzzle of the dog, who'd crept up to share the pillow with him. Jun Do could see that behind the eyelid, the dog's eye was rolling and twitching with each whimper of its own bad dream. Reaching out, Jun Do stroked the dog's fur, calming it, and the whines and whimpers ceased.

Jun Do pulled on pants and his new white shirt. Barefoot, he made his way to Dr. Song's room, which was empty, save for a packed travel suitcase waiting at the foot of the bed.

The kitchen was empty, as was the dining room.

Out in the corral was where Jun Do found him, sitting at a wooden picnic table. There was a midnight wind. Clouds flashed across a newly risen moon. Dr. Song had changed back into a suit and a tie.

"The CIA woman came to see me," Jun Do said.

Dr. Song didn't respond. He was staring at the fire pit—its coals still gave off warmth, and when the wind eddied away fresh ashes, the pit throbbed pink.

"You know what she asked me?" Jun Do said. "She asked if I felt free."

On the table was Dr. Song's cowboy hat, his hand keeping it from blowing away.

"And what did you tell our spunky American gal?" he asked.

"The truth," Jun Do said.

Dr. Song nodded.

His face seemed puffy somehow, his eyes almost drooped shut with age.

"Was it a success?" Jun Do asked. "Did you get what you came for, whatever it was that you needed?"

"Did I get what I needed?" Dr. Song asked himself. "I have a car and a driver and an apartment on Moranbong Hill. My wife, when I had her, was love itself. I have seen the white nights in Moscow and toured the Forbidden City. I have lectured at Kim Il Sung University. I have raced a Jet Ski with the Dear Leader in a cold mountain lake, and I have witnessed ten thousand women tumble in unison at the Arirang Festival. Now I have tasted Texas barbecue."

That kind of talk gave Jun Do the willies.

"Is there something you need to tell me, Dr. Song?" he asked.

Dr. Song fingered the crest of his hat. "I have outlasted everyone," he said. "My colleagues, my friends, I have seen them sent to farm communes and mining camps, and some just went away. So many predicaments we faced. Every fix, every pickle. Yet here I am, old Dr. Song." He gave Jun Do a fatherly pat on the leg. "Not bad for a war orphan."

Jun Do still felt a bit like he was in the dream, that he was being told something important in a language almost understood. He looked over to see his dog had followed him out and was now watching from a distance, its coat seeming to change pattern with shifts in the wind.

"At this moment," Dr. Song said, "the sun is high over Pyongyang—still, we must try to get some sleep." He stood and placed the hat upon his head. Walking stiffly away, he added, "In the movies about Texas, they call it shut-eye."

*

In the morning, there were no big good-byes. Pilar filled a basket with muffins and fruit for their plane trip, and everyone gathered out front where the Senator and Tommy had pulled up the Thunderbird and the Mustang. Dr. Song translated the Minister's farewell wishes, which were really invitations for them all to visit him soon in Pyongyang, especially Pilar, who would be hard-pressed to return from a worker's paradise if she did.

To all, Dr. Song offered only a bow.

Jun Do approached Wanda. She wore a jogging top, so he could see the power of her chest and shoulders. Her hair, for the first time, was down, framing her face.

"Happy trails to you," he said to her. "That's a Texas good-bye, no?"

"Yes," she said, smiling. "Do you know the response? It's 'Until we meet again.'"

The Senator's wife held a puppy, her fingertips moving through the soft folds of its skin.

She considered Jun Do for a long moment.

He said, "Thank you for tending to my wound."

"I've taken an oath," she said. "To assist all in medical need."

"I know you don't believe my story," he said.

"I believe you come from a land of suffering," she said. Her voice was measured and resonant, the way she'd spoken when she'd talked about the Bible. "I also believe your wife is a good woman, one that only needs a friend. Everyone tells me I'm not allowed to be that friend to her." She kissed the puppy, then held it out to Jun Do. "So this is the best I can do."

"A heartfelt gesture," Dr. Song said, smiling. "Unfortunately, canines are not legal in Pyongyang."

She pressed the dog into Jun Do's hands. "Don't listen to him, or his rules," she said. "Think of your wife. Find a way."

Jun Do accepted the dog.

"The Catahoula is bred to herd," she said. "So when that puppy's mad at you, he'll bite at your heels. And when he wants to show his love, he'll bite at your heels."

"We have a plane to catch," Dr. Song said.

"We call him Brando," the Senator's wife said. "But you can name him whatever you like."

"Brando?"

"Yes," she said. "See this mark on his haunch? That's where a brand would go."

"A brand?"

"A brand's a permanent mark that says something's yours."

"Like a tattoo?"

She nodded. "Like your tattoo."

"Then Brando it is."

The Minister began walking toward the Thunderbird, but the Senator stopped him.

"No," the Senator said. He pointed at Jun Do. "Him."

Jun Do looked to Wanda, who gave a nodding shrug. Tommy had his arms crossed and wore a satisfied smile.

Jun Do took a seat in the coupe. The Senator joined him, their shoulders almost touching, and slowly they began moving down the gravel road.

"We thought the talkative one was manipulating the dumb one," the Senator said. He shook his head. "Turns out you were the one all along. Is there any end to you people? And controlling him with yeses and nos at the end of sentences. How dumb do you think we are? I know you've got the backward-nation card to play and the I'll-get-thrown-in-a-gulag excuse. But coming all this way to pretend to be a nobody? Why tell that cockamamie shark story? And what the hell does a minister of prison mines do, exactly?"

The Senator's accent was getting stronger as he spoke, and though Jun Do couldn't catch all the words, he knew exactly what the Senator was saying.

"I can explain," Jun Do said.

"Oh, I'm listening," the Senator told him.

"It's true," Jun Do said. "The Minister is not really a minister."

"So who is he?"

"Dr. Song's driver."

The Senator laughed in disbelief. "Christ a'mighty," he said. "Did you even consider playing level with us? You don't want us to board your fishing boats, that's something to talk about. We sit down in the same room. We suggest that you maybe don't use fishing boats to smuggle Taepodong missile parts, counterfeit currency, heroin, and so on. Then we reach an agreement. Instead I'm wasting my time talking to the chumps, while you were what, getting a gander?"

"Suppose you had dealt with me," Jun Do said, even though he had no idea what he was talking about. "What is it you would have wanted?"

"What would I want?" the Senator asked. "I never heard what you had to offer, exactly. We'd want something solid, something you can mount above the mantel. And it would have to be precious. Everyone would have to know it cost your leader dearly."

"For something like that, you'd give us what we wanted?"

"The boats? Sure we could lay off them, but why? Every damn one of them is freighted with mayhem and compassed toward trouble. But the Dear Leader's toy?" A whistle came from the Senator's teeth. "That's a different prospect. To hand that thing back, we might as well take a piss on the Prime Minister of Japan's peach tree."

"But you admit," Jun Do said, "that it belongs to the Dear Leader, that you're holding his property?"

"The talks are over," the Senator said. "They happened yesterday, and they went nowhere."

The Senator then took his foot off the gas pedal.

"There is, however, one more issue, Commander," the Senator said as they drifted to the side of the road. "And it has nothing to do with the negotiations or whatever games y'all are playing."

The Mustang pulled beside them. From its passenger seat, her hand hanging out the window, Wanda spoke to the Senator. "You boys all right?" she asked.

"Just getting a few things straight," the Senator said. "Don't wait for us—we'll be right along."

Wanda slapped her hand on the side of the Mustang, and Tommy drove on. Jun Do caught a glimpse of Dr. Song in the backseat, but he couldn't tell if the old man's eyes were crinkled in fear or narrowed by betrayal.

"Here's the thing," the Senator said, and his eyes were locked into Jun

Do's. "Wanda says you've done some deeds, that there's blood on your file. I invited you into my house. You slept in my bed, walked amongst my people, a killer. They tell me life isn't worth much where you're from, but all these people you met here, they mean an awful lot to me. I've dealt with killers before. In fact, I'll only deal with you next time. But such dealings don't take place unawares, such people don't sit down to dinner with your wife, unbeknownst. So, Commander Ga, you can give a message direct to the Dear Leader, and this is on my letterhead. You tell him this kind of business is not appreciated. You tell him no boat is safe now. You tell him he'll never see his precious toy again—he can kiss it good-bye."

*

The Ilyushin was littered with fast-food wrappers and empty Tecate beer cans. Two black motorcycles blocked the aisle in first class, and most of the seats were taken up by the nine thousand DVDs Comrade Buc's team had purchased in Los Angeles. Comrade Buc himself looked as though he hadn't slept. He was camped out in the back of the plane where his boys were watching movies on fold-up computers.

Dr. Song meditated alone on the plane for some time, and he didn't stir until they were far from Texas. He came to Jun Do. "You have a wife?" Dr. Song asked.

"A wife?"

"The Senator's wife, she said the dog was for your wife. Is this true, have you a wife?"

"No," Jun Do said. "I lied to explain the tattoo on my chest."

Dr. Song nodded. "And the Senator, he figured out our ruse with the Minister, and he felt he could only put his faith in you. This is why you rode with him?"

"Yes," Jun Do said. "Though the Senator said it was Wanda who figured it out."

"Of course," he said. "And concerning the Senator, what was the nature of your conversation?"

"He said that he disapproved of our tactics, that the boarding of fishing boats would continue, and that we would never see our precious toy again. That's the message he wanted me to deliver."

"To whom?"

"To the Dear Leader."

"To the Dear Leader, you?" Dr. Song asked. "Why should he think you had his ear?"

"How should I know?" Jun Do asked. "He must have thought I was someone I'm not."

"Yes, yes, that's a useful tactic," Dr. Song said. "We cultivated that."

"I didn't do anything wrong," Jun Do said. "I don't even know what toy he was talking about."

"Fair enough," Dr. Song said. He took Jun Do's shoulder and squeezed it in a good-natured way. "I suppose it doesn't matter now. You know what radiation is?"

Jun Do nodded.

"The Japanese invented an instrument called a background radiation detector. They pointed it at the sky, to study something about space. When the Dear Leader heard of this device, he asked his scientists if such a thing could be attached to an airplane. He wanted to fly over our mountains and use it to find uranium deep underground. His scientists were unanimous. So the Dear Leader sent a team to the Kitami Observatory in Hokkaido."

"They stole it?"

Dr. Song got a wild look on his face. "The thing's the size of a Mercedes," he said. "We sent a fishing boat to pick it up, but along came the Yankees." Here, Dr. Song laughed. "Perhaps it was the same crew who fed you to the sharks."

Dr. Song woke the Minister, and together, the three concocted a story to mitigate their failure. Dr. Song believed that they should depict their talks as a complete success until, as they were about to agree on the deal, a higher power interceded via a phone call. "It will be assumed this is the American President, and Pyongyang's anger will be redirected from us to a meddlesome, vexing figure."

Together, they practiced timelines, rehearsed key moments, and repeated significant American phrases. The phone was brown. It sat on a tall stool. It rang three times. The Senator only spoke four words into it, "Yes . . . certainly . . . of course."

The trip back seemed to take twice as long. Jun Do fed the puppy a half-eaten breakfast burrito. Then it disappeared under all those seats and proved impossible to find. When darkness came, he could see the red and green lights of other, distant jetliners. Once everyone was asleep, and there was no life on the plane but the pilots smoking in the glow of their instruments, Comrade Buc sought him out.

"Here's your DVD," he said. "The best movie ever made."

Jun Do turned the case in the faint light. "Thanks," he said, but then he asked, "Is this a story of triumph or of failure?"

Comrade Buc shrugged. "They say it's about love," he said. "But I don't watch black-and-white films." Then he looked more closely at Jun Do. "Hey, look, your trip wasn't a failure, if that's what you're thinking."

He pointed into the dark cabin, where Dr. Song was asleep, puppy in his lap.

"Don't you worry about Dr. Song," Comrade Buc said. "That guy's a survivor. During the war, he got an American tank crew to adopt him. He helped the GIs read the road signs and negotiate with civilians. They gave him tins of food, and he spent the whole war in the safety of a turret. That's what he could do when he was only seven."

"Are you telling me this to reassure me, or yourself?" Jun Do asked.

Comrade Buc seemed not to hear this. He shook his head and smiled. "How the hell am I going to get these fucking motorcycles off the plane?"

In darkness, they set down on the uninhabited island of Kraznatov to refuel. There were no landing lights, so the pilots dead-reckoned the approach and then lined up by the purple glow of the moonlit strip. Two thousand kilometers from the nearest land, the station had been built to service Soviet sub-hunting planes. In the shed that held the pump batteries was a coffee can. Here, Comrade Buc placed a sheaf of hundred-dollar bills, then helped the pilots with the heavy Jet A-1 hoses.

While Dr. Song slept on the plane, Jun Do and Comrade Buc smoked in the crackling wind. The island was nothing more than three fuel tanks and a strip surrounded by rocks glazed white with bird guano and littered with chips of multicolored plastic and beached drift nets. Comrade Buc's scar glowed in the moonlight.

"Nobody's ever safe," Comrade Buc said, and gone was his jovial sidekick tone. Behind them, the old Ilyushin's wings drooped and groaned as they took on their payload of fuel. "But if I thought someone on this plane was headed to the camps," he added, turning to Jun Do to make sure he was being heard, "I'd smash his head on these rocks myself."

The pilots pulled the blocks and spun the plane, nose into the wind. They cycled the engines, but before lifting over the dark, choppy water, they opened the bilge, slopping out all the plane's sewage in a midnight streak down the runway.

They crossed China in darkness, and with dawn, they flew above the train tracks leading south from Shenyang, following them all the way to Pyongyang. The airport was north of the city, so Jun Do could get no good look at the fabled capital, with its May Day Stadium, Mansudae Mausoleum, and flaming-red Tower of Juche. Ties were straightened, the trash picked up, and, finally, Comrade Buc brought Jun Do the puppy, which his men had crawled the length of the cabin to capture.

But Jun Do wouldn't take the dog. "It's a gift for Sun Moon," he said. "Will you get it to her for me?"

Jun Do could see the questions moving through Comrade Buc's eyes, but he voiced none of them. Instead, Comrade Buc offered a simple nod.

The landing gear was lowered, and on approach, the goats on the runway somehow knew the moment to wander away. But touching down, Dr. Song saw the vehicles that were waiting to meet the plane, and he turned, panic on his face.

"Forget everything," he called to the Minister and Jun Do. "The plan must completely change."

"What is it?" Jun Do asked. He looked at the Minister, whose eyes showed fear.

"There's no time," Dr. Song said. "The Americans never intended to return what they stole from us. You got that? That's the new story."

They huddled in the galley, bracing themselves as the pilots leaned hard on the brakes.

"The new story is this," Dr. Song said. "The Americans had an elaborate plan to humiliate us. They made us do groundskeeping and cut the Senator's weeds, yes?"

"That's right," Jun Do said. "We had to eat outside, with our bare hands, surrounded by dogs."

The Minister said, "There was no band or red carpet to greet us. And they drove us around in obsolete cars."

"We were shown nice shoes at a store, but then they were put away," Jun Do said. "At dinner, they made us wear peasant shirts."

The Minister said, "I had to share my bed with a dog!"

"Good, good," Dr. Song said. He had a desperate smile on his face, but his eyes sparkled with the challenge. "This will speak to the Dear Leader. This might save our skins."

*

The vehicles on the runway were Soviet Tsirs, three of them. The crows were all manufactured in Chongjin, at the Sungli 58 factory, so Jun Do had seen thousands of them. They were used to move troops and cargo, and they had hauled many an orphan. In the rainy season, a Tsir was the only thing that could move at all.

Dr. Song refused to look at the crows or their drivers smoking together on the running boards. He smiled broadly and greeted the two men who were there to debrief them. But the Minister, grim faced, couldn't stop staring, at the tall truck tires, the drum fuel tanks. Jun Do suddenly understood that if someone were to be transported from Pyongyang to a prison camp, only a crow could get you over the bad mountain roads.

Jun Do could see the giant portrait of the Great Leader Kim Il Sung atop the airport terminal. But the two debriefers led them in a different direction—past a group of women in jumpsuits who faced a pile of shovels as they did their morning calisthenics and past a plane whose fuselage lay on the ground, blowtorched into four sections. Old men seated on buckets were stripping the copper wire from it.

They came to an empty hangar, voluminous inside. Potholes in the cement floor were pooled with muddy water. There were several mechanics' bays filled with tools, lifts, and workbenches, and Dr. Song, the Minister, and Jun Do were each placed in one, just out of sight of one another.

Jun Do sat at a table with the debriefers, who began going through his things.

"Tell us about your trip," one said. "And don't leave anything out."

There was a hooded typewriter on the table, but they made no move to use it.

At first, Jun Do only mentioned the things they'd agreed upon—the indignities of dogs, the paper plates, of eating under the hot sun. As he spoke, the two men opened his bourbon and, drinking, both approved. They divided his cigarettes right in front of him. They seemed especially fond of the little flashlight, and they interrupted him to make sure he wasn't hiding another. They tasted his beef jerky, tried on his calfskin gloves.

"Start again," the other one told him. "And say it all."

He kept listing the humiliations—how there was no band at the airport, no red carpet, how Tommy had left his spoor in the backseat. Like animals, they had been made to eat with their bare hands. He tried to remember how many bullets had been fired from the old guns. He described the old cars. Did he mention the dog in his bed? Could he have a glass of water? No time, they said, soon this would be over.

One debriefer turned the DVD in his hand. "Is this high definition?" he asked.

The other debriefer waved him off. "Forget it," he said. "That movie's black-and-white."

They snapped several pictures with the camera, but could find no way to view them.

"It's broken," Jun Do said.

"And these?" they asked, holding up the antibiotics.

"Female pills," Jun Do told them.

"You'll have to give us your story," one of them said. "We'll need to get all of it down. We're going to be right back, but while we're gone, you should practice. We'll be listening, we'll be able to hear everything you say."

"Start to finish," the other man said.

"Where do I start?" Jun Do asked him. Did the story of his trip to Texas begin when the car came for him or when he was declared a hero or when the Second Mate drifted off into the waves? And finish? He had a horrible feeling that this story was nowhere near finished.

"Practice," the debriefer said.

Together, they left the repair bay, and then he could hear the muffled echoes of the Minister now telling his story. "A car came for me," Jun Do said aloud. "It was morning. The ships in the harbor were drying their nets. The car was a Mercedes, four-door, with two men driving. It had windshield wipers and a factory radio . . ."

He spoke to the rafters. Up there, he could see birds bobbing their heads as they looked down upon him. The more detailed he made his story, the more strange and unbelievable it seemed to him. Had Wanda really served him iced lemonade? Had the dog actually brought him a rib bone after his shower?

When the debriefers returned, Jun Do had only recited his story to the part about first opening the cooler of tiger meat on the plane. One of them was listening to the Minister's iPod, and the other one looked upset. For some reason, Jun Do's mouth went back to the script. "There was a dog on the bed," he said. "We were forced to cut brush, the seat had been spoored."

"You sure you don't have one of these?" one asked, holding up the iPod.

"Maybe he's hiding it."

"Is that true? Are you hiding it?"

"The cars were ancient," Jun Do said. "The guns dangerously old."

The first story kept coming back into his mind, and he became paranoid that he might accidentally say that the phone had rung four times and the Senator had said three words into it. Then he remembered that was wrong, the phone had rung three times, and the Senator had spoken four words, and then Jun Do tried to clear his mind because that was wrong, the phone never rang, the American President didn't call at all.

"Hey, snap out of it," one of the debriefers said. "We asked the old man where his camera was, and he said he didn't know what we were talking about. You all got the same gloves and cigarettes and everything."

"There's nothing else," Jun Do said. "You've got everything I own."

"We'll see what the third guys says."

They handed him a piece of paper and a pen.

"It's time to get it down," they said, and left the bay again.

Jun Do picked up the pen. "A car came for me," he wrote, but the pen barely had any ink in it. He decided to skip to when they were already in Texas. He shook the pen and added, "And took me to a boot store." He knew the pen only had one more sentence in it. By pressing hard he scratched out, "Here my humiliations began."

Jun Do lifted the paper and read his two-sentence story. Dr. Song had said that what mattered in North Korea was not the man but his story—what did it mean, then, when his story was nothing, just a suggestion of a life?

One of the crow drivers entered the hangar. He came to Jun Do, asked him, "You the guy I'm taking?"

"Taking where?" Jun Do asked.

A debriefer came over. "What's the problem?" he asked.

"My headlights are shot," the driver said. "I have to go now or I'll never make it."

The debriefer turned to Jun Do. "Look, your story checks out," he said. "You're free to go."

Jun Do lifted the paper. "This is all I got," he said. "The pen ran out of ink."

The debriefer said, "All that matters is that you got something. We sent your actual paperwork in already. This is just a personal statement. I don't know why they make us get them."

"Do I need to sign it?"

"Couldn't hurt," the debriefer said. "Yes, let's make it official. Here, use my pen."

He handed Jun Do the pen Dr. Song had been given from the mayor of Vladivostok.

The pen wrote beautifully—he hadn't signed his name since language school.

"Better take him now," the debriefer told the driver. "Or he'll be here all day. The one old guy asked for extra paper." He gave the driver a pack of American Spirit cigarettes, then asked the driver if he had the medics with him.

"Yeah, they're in the truck," the driver said.

The debriefer handed Jun Do his DVD of *Casablanca* and his camera and his pills. He led Jun Do to the hangar door. "These guys are headed east," he told Jun Do. "And you're going to catch a ride with them. Those medics are on a mission of mercy, they're true heroes of the people, those guys, the hospitals in the capital need them like you can't believe. So if they need help, you help them, I don't want to hear later that you were being lazy or selfish—you got that?"

Jun Do nodded. At the door, though, he looked back. He couldn't see Dr. Song or the Minister, the way they were tucked back in the repair bays, but he could hear Dr. Song's voice, clear and precise. "It was a most fascinating journey," Dr. Song was saying. "Never to be repeated."

*

Nine hours in the back of a crow. The washboard road rattled his guts, the engine vibrated so much he couldn't tell where his flesh ended and the wooden bench began. When he tried to move, to piss through the slats to the dirt road below, his muscles wouldn't answer. His tailbone had gone from numb to fire to dumb. Dust filled the canopy, gravel shot up through the transaxles, and his life returned to enduring.

Also in the back of the truck were two men. They sat on either side of a large white cooler, and they wore no insignia or uniform. They were particularly dead-eyed, and of all the shit jobs on earth, Jun Do thought, these guys had it the worst. Still, he tried to make small talk.

"So, are you guys medics?" he asked them.

The truck hit a rock. The lid of the cooler lifted, and a wave of pink ice water sloshed out.

He tried again, "The guy at the airport said you two were real heroes of the people."

They wouldn't look at him. The poor bastards, Jun Do thought. He'd choose a land-mine crew before being tasked out to a blood-harvesting detail. He only hoped they'd get him east to Kinjye before they made a stop to practice their trade, and he distracted himself by thinking of the gentle motion of the *Junma,* of cigarettes and small talk with the Captain, of the moment he turned the dials and his radios came to life.

They breezed through all the checkpoints. How the soldiers manning them could tell that a blood team was on board, Jun Do couldn't figure, but he wouldn't want to stop their truck either. Jun Do noticed for the first time that spinning in eddies of wind through the floorboards were the shells of hard-boiled eggs, a dozen of them, perhaps. This was too many eggs for a single person to eat, and nobody would share their eggs with a stranger, so it must have been a family. Through the back of the truck, Jun Do watched crop-security towers flash past, a local cadre in each with an old rifle to guard the corn terraces from the farmers who tended them. He saw dump trucks filled with peasants on their way to help with construction projects. And the roads were lined with conscripts bearing huge rocks on their shoulders to shore up washed-out sections. Yet this was happy work compared with the camps. He thought of whole families being carried off together to such destinations. If children had sat where he sat, if old people had occupied this bench, then absolutely no one was safe—one day a truck like this might come for him, too. The cast-off eggshells spun like tops in the wind. There was something carefree and whimsical about their movement. When the shells drifted near Jun Do's feet, he stomped them.

It was late afternoon when the truck descended into a river valley. On the near shore was a large encampment—thousands of people living in mud and squalor to be close to their loved ones on the other side. Across the bridge, everything changed. Through a flap in the black canvas, Jun Do could see harmonica-style barracks, hundreds of them, housing thousands of people, and soon the stink of distilling soy was in the air. The truck passed a crowd of small boys stripping the bark from a stack of yew branches. They had only their teeth to start the cut, their nails to peel back a flap, and their little biceps to then rip the branch clean. Normally, a sight like this would reassure him, make him feel comfortable. But Jun Do had seen no living boy so sinewy, and they moved faster than the Long Tomorrows orphans ever had.

The gates were a simple affair: there was one man to throw a large electrical switch while another wheeled back an electrified section of fencing. The medics removed old surgical gloves from their pockets, ones that had clearly been used many times, and pulled them on. They parked by a dark wooden building. The medics jumped out and told Jun Do to carry the cooler. But he didn't move. His legs were filled with static, and he sat there, watching a woman rolling a tire past the back of the truck. Both of her legs were missing below the knee. She had a pair of work boots that she'd fashioned to wear backward, so that her short stumps went into the boots' toe boxes while her knees were planted in the heels. The boots were laced up tight, and she was surprisingly nimble in them, swinging her short legs in circles in pursuit of the tire.

One of the medics picked up a handful of dirt and threw it in Jun Do's face. His eyes filled with grit and welled over. He wanted to kick that punk's head off. But this was not the place to make a mistake or do anything stupid. Besides, it was all he could do to swing his legs off the back of the truck and keep his balance while he hefted the cooler. No, it was best to get this over with and get out of here.

He followed the medics into a processing center, where there were dozens of infirmary cots filled with people who seemed on both sides of the edge of death. Listless and murmuring, they were like the fish at the bottom of the hold, offering no more than one last twitch of a gill when the knife came down. He saw the inward gaze of a heavy fever, the yellow-green skin of organ failure, and wounds that lacked only blood to keep bleeding. Spookiest of all, he couldn't tell the men from the women.

Jun Do dropped the cooler on a table. His eyes were on fire, and trying to wipe them clean with his shirt only made them burn more. He had no choice. Opening the cooler, he used the blood-laced ice water to splash the dirt from his eyes. There was a guard in the room, sitting on a crate and leaning against the wall. He threw his cigarette away to accept an American Spirit cigarette from the medics. Jun Do came up to get a cigarette, too.

A medic turned to the guard. "Who is this guy?" he asked, indicating Jun Do.

The guard inhaled deep on his fancy cigarette. "Someone important enough to arrive on a Sunday," he said.

"They're my cigarettes," Jun Do said, and the medic reluctantly gave him one.

The smoke was rich and smooth, and it was worth a little eye sting. An old woman entered the room. She was thin and bent and wore strips of cloth wrapped around her hands. She had a large camera on a wooden tripod that looked exactly like the one the Japanese photographer was using when they kidnapped her.

"There she is," the guard said. "Time to get to work."

The medics began tearing strips of tape in preparation.

He was about to witness the darkest of trades, but the cigarette calmed him.

Just then, something caught his eye. He looked up to the blank wall above the doorway. It was completely empty—there was simply nothing there. He pulled the camera from his pocket. And while the guard and the medics were discussing the merits of various tobacco brands, Jun Do snapped a picture of the empty white wall. *Understand that, Wanda,* he thought. Never in his life had he been in a room without portraits of Kim Il Sung and Kim Jong Il above the door. Not in the lowliest orphanage, not in the oldest train car, not even in the burned-out shitter of the *Junma.* Never had he been in a place that did not merit the gaze of the Dear and Great Leaders' constant concern. The place he was in, he knew now, was below mattering—it didn't even exist.

While he was pocketing his camera, he caught the old woman staring at him. Her eyes were like those of the Senator's wife—he felt she was seeing something he didn't even know about himself.

One of the medics yelled at Jun Do to grab a crate from the corner, where there was a stack of them. Jun Do took a crate and met the medic at the bedside of a woman who had her jaw tied shut with strips of cloth that circled her head. One medic began unlacing her shoes, which were just rotten tire treads wrapped with wire. The other began unwrapping tubing and intravenous lines, all precious medical supplies.

Jun Do touched the woman's skin, which was cool.

"I think we're too late," he told them.

The medics ignored him. They each ran a line into a vein in the tops of her feet, then attached two empty blood bags. The old photographer appeared with her camera. She called to the guard for the woman's name, and when he told her, the photographer wrote it on a gray slate and placed it on the woman's chest. Then the photographer unwound the strips of cloth from the woman's head. When the photographer removed the woman's cap, most of her hair came off with it, lining it with a black swirl.

"Here," the photographer said, slipping the cap to Jun Do. "Take it."

The cap looked heavy with ground-in grease. Jun Do hesitated.

"Do you know who I am?" the old photographer asked. "I'm Mongnan. I take the pictures of all who arrive and depart from this place." She shook the cap insistently. "It's wool. You'll need it."

Jun Do pocketed the cap as a way to shut her up, to stop her and her crazy talk.

When Mongnan took the woman's picture, the flash awakened her for a moment. She reached from the cot to Jun Do's wrist and clenched it. In her eyes was a very clear desire to take him with her. The medics yelled at Jun Do to lift the head of the cot. When he did so, they kicked the crate underneath, and soon the four blood bags were filling nicely.

Jun Do said to the medics, "We'd better work fast. It's getting dark, and that driver said he doesn't have headlights."

The medics ignored him.

The next person was a teenager, his chest cool and pale blue. His eyes were drawn, so that they turned with labor, in increments. One of his arms hung off the cot, outstretched to the rough-hewn floorboards.

"What's your name?" Mongnan asked him.

His mouth kept making a motion as though he was trying to wet his lips before speaking, but the words never came.

Soft and tender, with the voice of a mother, she whispered to the dying boy.

"Close your eyes," she said, and when he did she snapped the photo.

The medics used the strips of medical tape to secure the blood lines, and the process repeated itself. Jun Do lifted the cot and slid the next crate under it, the boy's head gently lolled, and then Jun Do was left carrying the warm bags to the cooler. The life of the boy, the true life of him, had literally drained warm into these bags that Jun Do held, and it was like the boy was still alive in the bags until Jun Do personally snuffed him by dropping them into the ice water. For some reason, he expected the warm bags of blood to float, but they sank to the bottom.

Mongnan whispered to Jun Do, "Find a pair of boots."

Jun Do gave her a wary look but did as he was told.

There was only one man with boots that might fit. The uppers had been patched many times, but the soles were from a pair of military boots. In his sleep, the man made a croaking noise, as if bubbles kept rising up his throat to pop in his mouth.

"Get them," Mongnan said.

Jun Do began unlacing the boots. They wouldn't make him put on a pair of work boots unless they had another ugly task in store for him—he could only hope it wasn't burying all these fucking people.

While Jun Do was wriggling the man's boots off, he woke. "Water," he said, before he could even open his eyes. Jun Do froze, hoping the man wouldn't come to. But the guy found his focus. "Are you a doctor?" the man asked. "An ore cart tipped over—I can't feel my legs."

"I'm just helping out," Jun Do said, and it was true, when the boots slipped off, the man seemed not to notice. The man wore no socks. Several of his toes were blackened and broken, and some were missing, with the remaining stubs leaking a tea-colored juice.

"Are my legs okay?" the man asked. "I can't feel them."

Jun Do took the boots and backed away, back to where Mongnan had her camera set up.

Jun Do shook the boots and clapped them together, but no toes fell out. Jun Do lifted each boot and peeled back its tongue in an effort to peer as deep inside as he could—but he could see nothing. He hoped the missing toes had fallen off someplace else.

Mongnan raised the tripod to Jun Do's height. She handed him a little gray slate and a chalk stone. "Write your name and date of birth."

Pak Jun Do, he wrote, for the second time in one day.

"My birth date is unknown," he told her.

He felt like a child when he lifted the slate to his chin, like a little boy. He thought, *Why is she taking my picture?* but he didn't ask this.

Mongnan pressed a button and when the flash went off, everything seemed different. He was on the other side of the bright light now, and that's where all the bloodless people on cots were—on the other side of her flash.

The medics yelled at him to lift a cot.

"Ignore them," she said. "When they're done, they're going to sleep in the truck, and in the morning, they're going home. You, we've got to take care of you before it's too dark."

Mongnan called to the guard for the barracks number of Pak Jun Do. When he told her, she wrote it on the back of his hand. "We don't usually get people on Sundays," she said. "You're kind of on your own. First thing is to find your barracks. You need to get some sleep. Tomorrow's Monday— the guards are hell on Monday."

"I've got to go," he said. "I don't have time to bury anybody."

She lifted his hand and showed him the barracks number written across the back of his knuckles. "Hey," she said. "This is you now. You're in my camera. Those are now your boots."

She started walking him toward a door. Over his shoulder, he looked for the pictures of Kim Jong Il and Kim Il Sung. A flash of panic struck him. Where were they when he needed them?

"Hey," one of the medics said. "We're not done with him."

"Go," Mongnan said. "I'll handle this."

"Find your barracks," she said. "Before it's too dark. "

"But then. What do I do then?"

"Do what everyone else does," she said, and pulled from her pocket a milky white ball of corn kernels. This she gave to him. "If people eat fast, you eat fast. If they drop their eyes when someone comes around, so do you. If they denounce a prisoner, you chime in."

When Jun Do opened the door, boots in hand, he looked out onto the dark camp, rising in every direction into the icy canyons of a huge mountain range, its peaks still visible in the last of the setting sun. He could see the glowing mouths of the mineheads and the torchy flicker of workers moving within. Ore carts pushed forth from them under human power, strobing from security lights that reflected off the slag ponds. Everywhere, cooking fires cast an orange glow upon the harmonica houses, and the acrid smoke of green firewood made him cough. He didn't know where this prison was. He didn't even know its name.

"Don't let anyone see you use that camera," Mongnan told him. "I'll come find you in a couple days."

He closed his eyes. It seemed he could make out the plaintive groans of roofing metal in the evening wind, of nails squeaking in the grip of contracting wood, of human bones stiffening and hardening on thirty thousand bunks. He could hear the slow swivel of searchlight tripods and he could make out the hum of electricity charging perimeter wires and the icy crackle of ceramic insulators on their poles. And soon he would be in the center of it, in the belly of the ship once again, but this time, there would be no surface, no hatch, just the slow endless pitch of everything to come.

Mongnan indicated the boots in his hand. "They'll try to get those from you. Can you fight?"

"Yeah," he said.

"Then put them on," she told him.

The way you dig into a boot for old sticky toes is the way you spring a trapdoor in a DMZ tunnel or pull a stranger off a beach in Japan: you just take that breath and go. Closing his eyes, Jun Do breathed deeply and reached inside the dank boots, sweeping his fingers back and forth, feeling all the way in. Finally, he turned his wrist so he could scrape out the depths, and he removed what he had to remove. It left a scowl on his face.

He turned to the medics, to the guard, to the doomed half-dead.

"I was a model citizen," he told them. "I was a hero of the state," he added, and then stepped through the door in his new boots, out into a matterless place, and from this point forward nothing further is known of the citizen named Pak Jun Do.

PART TWO

THE CONFESSIONS OF COMMANDER GA

ONE YEAR LATER

WE WERE finalizing a month-long interrogation of a professor from Kaesong when a rumor spread through the building that Commander Ga had been apprehended and was here, in custody, in our own Division 42. Right away, we sent the interns, Q-Kee and Jujack, upstairs to processing to see if this was true. Certainly we were dying to get our eyes on Commander Ga, especially after all the stories that had been flying around Pyongyang lately. Could it be the same Commander Ga who'd won the Golden Belt, who'd bested Kimura in Japan, who'd rid the military of homosexuals and then married our nation's actress?

But our work with the professor was at a critical stage and couldn't be abandoned for a little celebrity gawking. The professor's was a textbook case, really: he had been accused of counterrevolutionary teachings, specifically using an illegal radio to play South Korean pop songs to his students. It was a silly charge, probably just the work of a rival at his university. Such things are hard to prove one way or another. Most people in North Korea work in pairs, so there is always a co-worker ready to give evidence or denounce his partner. Not so with a professor, whose classroom is his own domain. It would've been easy to get the professor to confess, but that's not us, we don't work that way. You see, Division 42 is really two divisions.

Our rival interrogation team is the Pubyok, named after the "floating wall" defenders that saved Pyongyang from invaders in 1136. There are only a dozen or so Pubyok left, old men with silver crewcuts who walk in a row like a wall and truly believe they can float, stealthy as ghosts, from one citizen to the next, interrogating them as a wind interrogates the leaves. They are constantly breaking their hands, on the principle that the bones grow back stronger, knitting in extra layers. It is a terrible thing to see, old men, out of nowhere, cracking their hands on doorjambs or the rims of fire barrels. The Pubyok all gather 'round when one is about to break a hand, and the rest of us, the thinking, principled remainder of Division 42, have to look away. *Junbi,* they say, almost softly, then count *hana, dul, set* and shout *Sijak!* Then there's the weirdly dead sound of a hand striking the edge of a car door. The Pubyok believe that all subjects arriving at Division 42 should be met with brutality right away—senseless, extended, old-fashioned hurt.

And then there is my team—correction: *our* team, for it truly is a group effort. We have no need for a nickname, and sharp minds are our only interrogation tools. The Pubyok experienced either the war or its aftermath when they were young, and their ways are understandable. We pay respect to them, but interrogation is a science now, and long-term, consistent results are what matter. Thuggery has its place, we concede, but it should come tactically, at specific moments, over a long relationship. And pain—that towering white flower—can only be used once the way we apply it, complete, enduring, transformational pain, without cloak or guise. And since everyone on our team is a graduate of Kim Il Sung University, we have a soft spot for old professors, even our sad candidate from a regional college down in Kaesong.

In an interrogation bay, we reclined our professor into one of the Q & A chairs, which are amazingly comfortable. We have a contractor in Syria who makes them for us—they're similar to dental chairs, with baby-blue leather and arm- and headrests. There's a machine next to the chair, though, that makes people nervous. It's called an autopilot. I suppose that's our only other tool.

"I thought you had all you needed to know," the professor said. "I answered the questions."

"You were wonderful," we told him. "Absolutely."

Then we showed him the biography we'd made of his life. At 212 pages, it was the product of dozens of hours of interviews. It contained all of him, from his earliest memories—Party education, defining personal moments, achievements and failures, affairs with students, and so on, a complete documentation of his existence, right to his arrival at Division 42. He flipped through the book, impressed. We use a binding machine, the kind that seals the spines of doctoral dissertations, and it gives the biographies a real professional look. The Pubyok simply beat you until you confess to using a radio, whether there's a radio or not. Our team discovers an entire life, with all its subtleties and motivations, and then crafts it into a single, original volume that contains the person himself. When you have a subject's biography, there is nothing between the citizen and the state. That's harmony, that's the idea our nation is founded upon. Sure, some of our subject's stories are sweeping and take months to record, but if there's one commodity we have no shortage of in North Korea, it's forever.

We hooked the professor up to the autopilot, and he looked quite surprised when the pain delivery began. The expression on his face conveyed a desperation to determine what we wanted from him, and how he could give it, but the biography was complete, there were no more questions. The professor watched in horror as I reached across his body to his shirt pocket, where I removed a gold pen clipped there—such an object can concentrate the electrical current, setting the clothes on fire. The professor's eyes—they understood now that he was no longer a professor, that he would never have need of a pen again. It wasn't long ago, when we were young, that people like the professor, probably with a handful of his students, would be shot in the soccer stadium on a Monday morning before work. While we were in college, the big trend was to throw them all into the prison mines, where life expectancy is six months. And of course now organ harvesting is where so many of our subjects meet their end.

It's true that when the mines open their maw for more workers, everyone must go, we have no say over that. But people like the professor, we believe, have an entire life of happiness and labor to offer our nation. So we ramp up the pain to inconceivable levels, a shifting, muscular river of pain. Pain of this nature creates a rift in the identity—the person who makes it to the far shore will have little resemblance to the professor who now begins the crossing. In a few weeks, he will be a contributing member of a rural farm collective, and perhaps we can even find a widow to comfort him. There's no way around it: to get a new life, you've got to trade in your old one.

For now, it was our little professor's alone time. We set the autopilot, which monitors all of a subject's vitals and brings the pain in modulated waves, and then we closed the soundproof door and made for the library. We'd see the professor again this afternoon, pupils dilated, teeth chattering, and help him step into his street clothes for the big trip to the countryside.

Our library, of course, is really just a storeroom, but each time our team delivers a new biography, I like to do it with some ceremony. Again, my apologies for using that regrettable pronoun "I." I try not to bring it to work with me. Shelves line the walls, floor to ceiling, and fill the room in freestanding rows. In a society where it is the collective that matters, we're the only people who make the individuals count. No matter what happens to our subjects after we interrogate them, we still have them here. We've saved them all. The irony of course is that the average citizen, the average interrogator walking the street, for instance, never gets his story told. Nobody asks him his favorite Sun Moon movie, nobody wants to know does he prefer millet cakes or millet porridge. No, in a cruel twist, it's only enemies of the state that get this kind of star treatment.

With a little fanfare, we placed the professor's biography on the shelf, right next to the girl dancer from last week. She had us all weeping as she described how her little brother lost his eyes, and when the moment came to apply the autopilot to her, the pain made her limbs rise and sweep the air in rhythmic, graceful gestures, as if she were telling her story one last time through movement. You can see that "interrogation" isn't even the right word for what we do—it's a clumsy holdover from the Pubyok era. When the last Pubyok finally retires, we will lobby to have our name changed to Division of Citizen Biographies.

Our interns, Q-Kee and Jujack, returned out of breath.

"A team of Pubyok are there," Q-Kee said.

"They got to Commander Ga first," Jujack added.

We raced upstairs. When we got to the holding room, Sarge and some of his guys were just leaving. Sarge was the leader of the Pubyok, and there was no love lost between us. His forehead was prominent, and even in his seventies, he had the body of an ape. Sarge was what we called him. I never knew his real name.

He stood in the doorway, rubbing one hand in the other.

"Impersonating a national hero," Sarge said, shaking his head. "What's our nation coming to? Is there any honor left at all?"

There were some marks on Sarge's face, and as he spoke blood trickled from his nose.

Q-Kee touched her own nose. "Looks like Commander Ga got the best of you guys."

That girl Q-Kee—what cheek!

"It's not Commander Ga," Sarge said. "But, yeah, he had a nifty little trick he pulled on us. We're sending him down to the sump tonight. We'll show him some tricks of our own."

"But what about his biography?" we asked.

"Didn't you hear me?" Sarge asked. "It's not Commander Ga. The guy's an imposter."

"Then you won't mind if our team tries its hand. We're only after the truth."

"The truth isn't in your silly books," Sarge said. "It's something you can see in a man's eyes. You can feel it here, in your heart."

Personally, I felt bad for Sarge. He was an old man, of large stature. To have that kind of size meant you'd eaten meat as a child, something that would most likely come from collaborating with the Japanese. Whether he'd cozied up to the Japs or not, everyone he'd met, over his whole life, probably suspected he had.

"But yeah, the guy's all yours," Sarge said. "After all, what are we without honor?" he added, but he said the word "we" in a way that didn't include us. He started to walk away, but then turned back. "Don't let him near the light switch," he warned.

Inside, we found Commander Ga in a chair. The Pubyok had done a number on him, and he certainly didn't look like the kind of guy who'd led assassination missions into the South to silence loudmouth defectors. He looked us over, trying to decide whether we meant to beat him as well, though he didn't seem inclined to offer any defense if we did.

His busted lips looked pitiful, and his reddened ears were filling with fluid from being slapped with the soles of dress shoes. We could see old frostbite marks on his fingers, and his shirt had been torn off, revealing a tattoo on his chest of the actress Sun Moon. We shook our heads. Poor Sun Moon. There was also a large scar on his arm, though the rumors that Commander Ga had wrestled a bear were just that, rumors. In his rucksack, we found only a pair of black cowboy boots, a single can of peaches, and a bright red cell phone, battery dead.

"We're here for your story," we told him.

His face was still ringing from Pubyok fists.

"I hope you like happy endings," he said.

We helped him to an interrogation bay and into his own Q & A chair. We gave him aspirin and a cup of water, and soon he was asleep.

We scribbled off a quick note that said, "Is not Commander Ga." This we placed in a vacuum tube and, with a whoosh, sent it deep into the bunker complex below us, where all the decisions were made. How deep the bunker went and who exactly was down there, we didn't know. The deeper the better was how I felt. I mean we felt.

Before we'd even turned to go, the vacuum tube had raced back and dropped into our hopper. When we opened it, the note inside read simply, "Is Commander Ga."

It was only at the very end of the day, when we were about to hang up our smocks, that we returned to him. The swelling had started on the face of Commander Ga, or whoever he was, though there was something peaceful about his sleep. We noticed that his hands rested on his stomach, and they seemed to be typing, as if he were transcribing the dream he was having. We stared at his fingers awhile but could make no sense of what he might be writing.

"We're not the ones who hurt you," we said when we woke him. "That was the work of another party. Answer a simple question for us, and we'll get you a room, a comfortable bed."

Commander Ga nodded. There were so many questions we were dying to ask him.

But then our intern Q-Kee suddenly spoke up. "What did you do with the actress's body?" she blurted out. "Where did you hide it?"

We took Q-Kee by the shoulder and led her out of the interrogation bay. She was the first female intern in the history of Division 42, and boy, was she a firebrand. The Pubyok were beside themselves that a woman was in the building, but to have a modern, forward-thinking interrogation division, a female interrogator was going to be essential.

"Start slow," we told Q-Kee. "We're building a relationship here. We don't want to put him on the defensive. If we earn his trust, he'll practically write his story for us."

"Who cares about the biography?" she asked. "Once we find out the location of the dead actress and her kids, they'll shoot him in the street. End of story."

"Character is destiny," we told her, reminding her of the famous quote from Kim Il Sung. "That means that once we discover the inside of a subject, what makes him tick, we not only know everything he's done but everything he will do."

Back in the interrogation bay, Q-Kee reluctantly asked a more appropriate question.

"How did you first meet the actress Sun Moon?" she asked.

Commander Ga closed his eyes. "So cold," he said. "She was on the side of the infirmary. The infirmary was white. The snow fell heavily, it blocked my view of her. The battleship burned. They used the infirmary because it was white. Inside, people moaned. The water was on fire."

"He's worthless," Q-Kee muttered.

She was right. It had been a long day. Up top, on ground level, the rust-colored light of afternoon would be stretching long now through downtown Pyongyang. It was time to call it quits and get home before the power went out.

"Wait," Jujack said. "Just give us something, Commander Ga."

The subject seemed to like being called Commander Ga.

Jujack went on, "Just tell us what you were dreaming about. Then we'll take you to a room."

"I was driving a car," Commander Ga said. "An American car."

"Yes," Jujack said. "Keep going. Have you really driven an American car?"

Jujack was one fine intern—he was the first minister's boy who'd ever been worth a damn.

"I have," Commander Ga said.

"Why not start there, why not tell us about driving an American car?"

Slowly, he began to speak. "It's nighttime," he said. "My hand shifts through the gears. The streetlights are off, electric buses are crammed with third-shift factory workers, silently racing down Chollima Street and Reunification Boulevard. Sun Moon is in the car with me. I don't know Pyongyang. *Left,* she says. *Right.* We are driving to her house, across the river, on the heights of Mount Taesong. In the dream, I believe that this night will be different, that when we arrive home she will finally let me touch her. She is wearing a platinum *choson-ot,* shimmery as crushed diamonds. On the streets, people in black pajamas dart into our path, people carrying bundles and groceries and extra work to take home, but I do not slow. I am Commander Ga in the dream. My whole life, I've been steered by others, I've been the one trying to escape from their paths. But Commander Ga, he is a man who steps on the gas."

"In the dream, have you just become Commander Ga?" we asked him.

But he kept going, as if he didn't hear us. "We cut through Mansu Park, mist from the river. In the woods, families are stealing chestnuts from the trees—the children running through the branches, kicking the nuts down to parents who crack them open between rocks. Once you spotted a yellow or blue bucket, they all came into focus—once your eyes adjusted they were everywhere, families risking prison to steal nuts from public parks. *Are they playing some kind of game?* Sun Moon asked me. *They are so amusing, up in the trees in their white bedclothes. Or maybe it's athletics they're performing. You know, gymnastics. It's such a treat, this kind of surprise. What a fine movie it would make—a family of circus performers who practice in the trees of a public park at night. They must practice in secret because a rival circus family is always stealing their tricks. Can't you just picture this movie,* she asked me, *up on the screen?* The moment was so perfect. I would've driven off the bridge and killed us both to make that moment last forever, such was my love for Sun Moon, a woman who was so pure, she didn't know what starving people looked like."

The five of us stood there in awe of the story. Commander Ga had certainly earned his sedative. I gave Q-Kee a look that said, *Now do you understand the subtle art of interrogation?*

You shouldn't be in this business if you don't find your subjects endlessly interesting. If all you want to do is rough them up. We determined that Ga was the type to tend his own wounds, so we locked him in a room with some disinfectant and a bandage. Then we traded our smocks for vinalon coats and discussed his case as we reclined on the steep escalators that led down into the Pyongyang Metro. Notice how our subject's identity shift is near total—the imposter even dreams he is Commander Ga. Notice, too, how he began his story as a love story might open, with beauty and an insight that combined pity with the need to protect. He does not start his story by admitting where he really got this American car. He does not mention that they are driving home from a party, hosted by Kim Jong Il, where Ga was assaulted for the amusement of the guests. It slips his mind that he has somehow disposed of the husband of this woman he "loves."

Yes, we know a few of the facts of Ga's story, the outside of it, if you will. The rumors had been swirling around the capital for weeks. It was the inside we'd have to discover. I could already tell this would be the biggest, most important biography we'd ever write. I could already picture the cover of Commander Ga's biography. I could imagine the subject's true name, whatever that would turn out to be, embossed on the spine. Mentally, I had already finished that book. I was already placing that book on a shelf and turning out the lights and then closing the door to a room where the dust snowed through the darkness at a rate of three millimeters per decade.

The library is a sacred place to us. No visitors are allowed, and once a book is closed, it never gets opened. Oh, sure, sometimes the boys from Propaganda will nose around for a feel-good story to play to the citizens over the loudspeakers, but we're story takers, not storytellers. We're a far cry from the old veterans who spin weepers to passersby in front of the Respect for Elders Retirement Home on Moranbong Street.

The Kwangbok station, with its beautiful mural of Lake Samji, is my stop. The city is filled with wood smoke when I emerge from the subway into my Pottongang neighborhood. An old woman is grilling green-onion tails on the sidewalk, and I catch the traffic girl switching her blue sunglasses for an amber-tinted nighttime pair. On the streets, I barter the professor's gold pen for cucumbers, a kilo of U.N. rice, and some sesame paste. Apartment lights come to life above us as we bargain, and you can see that no one lives above the ninth floor of their apartment buildings. The elevators never work, and if they do, the power's bound to go out when you're between floors and trap you in a shaft. My building's called the Glory of Mount Paektu, and I'm the sole occupant of the twenty-second floor, a height that makes sure my elderly parents never go out unattended. It doesn't take as long as you'd think to climb the stairs—a person can get used to anything.

Inside, I'm assaulted by the evening propaganda broadcasts coming over the apartment's hardwired loudspeaker. There's one in every apartment and factory floor in Pyongyang, everywhere but where I work, as it was deemed the loudspeakers would give our subjects too much orienting information, like date and time, too much normalcy. When subjects come to us, they need to learn that the world of before no longer exists.

I cook my parents dinner. When they taste the food, they praise Kim Jong Il for its flavor, and when I ask after their day, they say it certainly wasn't as hard as the day of the Dear Leader Kim Jong Il, who carries the fate of a people on his back. Their eyesight failed at the same time, and they have become paranoid that there might be someone around they can't perceive, ready to report them for anything they say. They listen to the loudspeaker all day, hail me as *citizen!* when I get home, and are careful to never reveal a personal feeling, lest it get them denounced by a stranger they can't quite lay their eyes on. That's why our biographies are important—instead of keeping things from your government by living a life of secrecy, they're a model of how to share everything. I like to think I'm part of a different tomorrow in that regard.

I finish my bowl on the balcony. I look down upon the rooftops of smaller buildings, which have all been covered with grass as part of the Grass into Meat Campaign. All the goats on the roof across the street are bleating because dusk is when the eagle owls come down from the mountains to hunt. Yes, I thought, Ga's would be quite a story to tell: an unknown man impersonates a famous one. He is now in possession of Sun Moon. He is now close to the Dear Leader. And when an American delegation comes to Pyongyang, this unknown man uses the distraction to slay the beautiful woman, at his own peril. He doesn't even try to get away with it. Now that's a biography.

I've attempted to write my own, just as a means of better understanding the subjects I ask to do so. The result is a catalog more banal than anything that comes from the guests of Division 42. My biography was filled with a thousand insignificances—the way the city fountains only turn on the couple of times a year when the capital has a foreign visitor, or how, despite the fact that cell phones are illegal and I've never seen a single person using one, the city's main cellular tower is in my neighborhood, just across the Pottong Bridge, a grand tower painted green and trimmed in fake branches. Or the time I came home to find an entire platoon of KPA soldiers sitting on the sidewalk outside Glory of Mount Paektu, sharpening their bayonets on the cement curb. Was it a message to me, to someone? A coincidence?

As an experiment, the biography was a failure—where was the *me* in it, where was *I?*—and of course it was hard to get past the feeling that if I finished it, something bad would happen to me. The real truth was that I couldn't stand the pronoun "I." Even at home, in the privacy of my own notepad, I have difficulty writing that word.

As I sipped the cucumber juice at the bottom of my rice bowl, I watched the last light play like a flickering fire on the walls of a housing block across the river. We write our subject biographies in the third person, to maintain our objectivity. It might be easier if I wrote my own biography that way, as though the story wasn't about me but about an intrepid interrogator. But then I'd have to use my name, which is against the rules. And what's the point of telling a personal story if you're only referred to as "The Interrogator"? Who wants to read a book called *The Biographer*? No, you want to read a book with someone's name on it. You want to read a book called *The Man Who Killed Sun Moon*.

In the distance, the light reflecting off the water flashed and danced against the housing block, and I had a sudden idea.

"I forgot something at work," I told my parents and then locked them in.

I took the subway across town, back to Division 42, but it was too late—the power went out when we were deep in the tunnel. By the light of matchbooks, we all poured out of the electric train cars and filed along the dark tracks to the Rakwan station, where the escalator was now a ramp of stairs, to climb the hundred meters to the surface. It was full dark when I made it to the street, and the sensation of emerging from one darkness to another was one I didn't like—it felt like I was in Commander Ga's dream, with flashes of black and buses cruising like sharks in the dark. I almost let myself imagine there was an American car out there, moving just beyond my perception, following me.

When I woke Commander Ga, his fingers were transcribing his dream again, but this time in a slow and slurred manner. We North Koreans do know how to make a world-class sedative.

"When you said you met Sun Moon," I said, "you mentioned she was on the side of a building, right?"

Commander Ga only nodded.

"They were projecting a movie on the wall of a building, yes? So you first met her through a film."

"A film," Commander Ga said.

"And they picked the infirmary because its walls were white, which means you were outside when you saw the movie. And the snow was heavy because you were high in the mountains."

Commander Ga closed his eyes.

"And the burning ships, this was her movie *Tyrants Asunder*?"

Commander Ga was fading, but I wasn't going to stop.

"And the people moaning in the infirmary, they were moaning because this was a prison, wasn't it?" I asked him. "You were a prisoner, weren't you?"

I didn't need an answer. And of course, what better place to meet the real Commander Ga, the Minister of Prison Mines, than in a prison mine? So he'd met them both there, husband and wife.

I pulled Commander Ga's sheets high enough to cover his tattoo. I was already starting to think of him as Commander Ga. When we finally discovered his real identity, it was going to be a shame, for Q-Kee was right—they'd shoot him in the street. You don't kill a minister and then escape from prison and then kill the minister's family and still get to become a peasant in a rural farm collective. I studied the man before me. "What did the real Commander Ga do to you?" I asked him. His hands raised above the sheets and he began typing on his stomach. "What could the Minister have done that was so bad you killed him and then went after his wife and kids?"

As he typed, I stared at his eyes, and his pupils weren't moving behind the lids. He wasn't transcribing what he saw in his dream. Perhaps it was what he heard that he'd been trained to record. "Good night, Commander Ga," I said, and watched as his hands typed four words, and then paused, waiting for more.

I took a sedative myself and then left Commander Ga to sleep through the night. Ideally, the sedative wouldn't take effect until after I'd made it across town. If things worked out just right, it would kick in after the twenty-second flight of stairs.

COMMANDER GA tried to forget about the interrogator, though Ga could smell the cucumber on his breath long after the man had swallowed his pill and walked out the door. Speaking of Sun Moon had put fresh images of her in Ga's mind, and that's what Ga cared about. He could practically see the movie they'd been talking about. *A True Daughter of the Country.* That was the name of the movie, not *Tyrants Asunder.* Sun Moon had played a woman from the southern island of Cheju who leaves her family and journeys north to battle the imperialists at Inchon. Cheju, he learned, was famous for its women abalone divers, and the movie opens with three sisters on a raft. Opaque waves capped with pumice-colored foam lift and drop the women. A wave the color of charcoal rolls into the frame, blotting the women from view until it passes, while brutal clouds scrape the volcanic shore. The oldest sister is Sun Moon. She splashes water on her limbs, to prepare herself for the cold, and adjusts her mask as her sisters speak of village gossip. Then Sun Moon hefts a rock, breathes deeply, and rolls backward off the raft into water so dark it should be night. The sisters switch their talk to the war and their sick mother and their fears that Sun Moon will abandon them. They lie back on the raft in a moment filmed from the mast above, and the sisters speak of village life again, of their neighbors' crushes and spats, but they have gone somber and it is clear that what they are not talking about is the war and how, if they do not go to it, it will come to them.

He'd watched this movie with the others, projected onto the side of the prison infirmary, the only building that was painted white. It was Kim Jong Il's birthday, February 16, their one day off work a year. The inmates sat on upended pieces of firewood that they'd beaten free of ice, and this was his first look at her, a woman luminous with beauty who plunges into darkness and simply won't seem to return. The sisters speak on and on, the waves build and break, the patients in the infirmary weakly moan as their blood-collection bags fill, and still Sun Moon will not surface. He wrings his hands at the loss of her, all the prisoners do, and even though she eventually surfaces, they all know that for the rest of the movie she will have that power over them.

It was that night, he now remembered, that Mongnan saved his life for the second time. It was very cold, the coldest he'd ever been, for work was what kept them warm all day, and watching a movie in the snow had allowed his body temperature to dangerously fall.

Mongnan appeared at his bunk, touching his chest and his feet to gauge his aliveness.

"Come," she said. "We must move quickly."

His limbs barely functioned as he followed the old woman. Others in their bunks stirred as they passed, but none sat up, as there was so little time for sleep. Together, they raced for a corner of the prison yard that was normally brightly lit and watched by a two-man guard tower. "The bulb to the main searchlight has burned out," Mongnan whispered to him as they ran. "It will take them a while to get another, but we must be quick." In the dark, they crouched, picking up all the moths that had fallen dead before the lamp had died. "Fill your mouth," she said. "Your stomach doesn't care." He did as he was told and soon he was chewing a wad of them—their furry abdomens drying his mouth, despite the goop that burst from them and a sharp aspirin taste from some chemical on their wings. His stomach hadn't been filled since Texas. He and Mongnan fled in the dark with handfuls of moths—wings slightly singed but ready to keep them alive another week.

GOOD MORNING, CITIZENS! In your housing blocks, on your factory floors, gather 'round your loudspeakers for today's news: the North Korean table-tennis team has just defeated its Somali counterpart in straight sets! Also, President Robert Mugabe sends his well wishes on this, the anniversary of the founding of the Workers' Party of Korea. Don't forget, it is improper to sit on the escalators leading into the subways. The Minister of Defense reminds us that the deepest subways in the world are for your civil-defense safety, should the Americans sneak-attack again. No sitting! And kelp-harvesting season will soon be upon us! Time to sterilize your jars and cans. And, finally, it is once again our privilege to crown the year's Best North Korean Story. Last year's tale of sorrow at the hands of South Korean missionaries was a one-hundred-percent success. This year's promises to be even more grand—it is a true story of love and sorrow, of faith and endurance, and of the Dear Leader's unending dedication to even the lowliest citizen of this great nation. Sadly, there is tragedy. Yet there is redemption, too! And taekwondo! Stay close to your loudspeakers, citizens, for each daily installment.

THE NEXT MORNING, my head was foggy from the sedative. Still, I raced to Division 42, where we checked on Commander Ga. As is the law of beatings, the real hurt came the day after. Rather ingeniously, he had stitched up the cut over his eye, but by what means he'd improvised a needle and thread we couldn't tell. We would have to discover his method so that we could ask him about it.

We took Commander Ga to the cafeteria, a place we thought would seem less threatening. Most people believe that harm won't come to them in a public space. We had the interns fetch Ga some breakfast. Jujack fixed a bowl of *bi bim bop*, while Q-Kee heated a kettle for *cha*. None of us liked the name "Q-Kee." It went against the professionalism we were trying to project at Division 42, something sorely missing with Pubyok wandering around in forty-year-old suits from Hamhung and *bulgogi*-stained ties. But since the new opera diva started going by her initials, all the young women were doing it. Pyongyang can be so trendy that way. Q-Kee countered our complaints with the fact that we wouldn't reveal our names, and she was unmoved when we explained that the policy was a holdover from the war, when subjects were seen as possible spies rather than citizens who had lost their revolutionary zeal and gone astray. She didn't buy it, and neither did we. How could you build a reputation in an environment where the only people who got names were the interns and the sad old retirees who clamber in to relive the glory days?

While Commander Ga ate his breakfast, Q-Kee engaged him in some small talk.

"Which *kwans* do you think have a shot at the Golden Belt this year?" she asked.

Commander Ga simply wolfed his food. We'd never met someone who'd made it out of a mining prison before, but one look at how he ate told us all we needed to know about the conditions at Prison 33. Imagine stepping from a place like that into Commander Ga's beautiful house on Mount Taesong. His view of Pyongyang is suddenly yours, his famed rice-wine collection is suddenly yours, and then there is his wife.

Q-Kee tried again. "One of the girls in the fifty-five-kilo division just qualified using the *dwi chagi ga*," she said. This was Ga's signature move. He'd personally modified the *dwi chagi* so that now its execution required turning your back to the opponent to lure him in. Ga either knew nothing of taekwondo or he didn't take the bait. Of course this wasn't the real Commander Ga, so he should have no real knowledge of Golden Belt–level martial arts. The questioning was a necessary step in determining the degree to which he actually believed he was Commander Ga.

Ga horsed down the last swallow, wiped his mouth, and pushed the bowl away.

"You'll never find them," he said to us. "I don't care what happens to me, so don't bother trying to make me tell you."

His voice was stern, and interrogators aren't used to being spoken to that way. Some of the Pubyok at another table caught wind of this tone and came over.

Commander Ga pulled the teapot to him. Instead of pouring a cup, he opened the pot and removed the steaming teabag. This he placed on the cut over his eye. He squinted at the pain, and tears of hot tea ran down his cheek. "You said you wanted my story," he told us. "I'll give it to you, everything but the fates of the woman and her kids. But first, I need something."

One of the Pubyok pulled off a shoe and advanced upon Ga.

"Stop," I called. "Let him finish."

The Pubyok hesitated, shoe high.

Ga paid this threat no mind. Was this a result of his pain training? Was he accustomed to beatings? Some people simply feel better after a beating—beatings are often good cures for guilt and self-loathing. Was he suffering from these?

In a calmer voice, we told the Pubyok, "He's ours. Sarge gave his word."

The Pubyok backed down, but they joined us at our table, four of them, with their teapot. Of course they drink *pu-erh,* and they stink of it all day long.

"What is this thing you need?" we asked him.

Commander Ga said, "I need the answer to a question."

The Pubyok were beside themselves. Never in their lives had they heard such talk from a subject. The team looked my way. "Sir," Q-Kee said. "This is the wrong road to go down."

Jujack said, "With all due respect, sir. We should give this guy a sniff of the towering white flower."

I put my hand up. "Enough," I said. "Our subject will tell us how he first met Commander Ga, and when he is finished we will answer one question, any question he wishes."

The old-timers looked on with seething disbelief. They leaned on their hard, ropy forearms, their knotted hands and bent fingers and misgrown fingernails squeezed tight with restraint.

Commander Ga said, "I met Commander Ga twice. The first time was in the spring—I heard he would be visiting the prison on the eve of his arrival."

"Start there," we told him.

"Shortly after I entered Prison 33," he said, "Mongnan started a rumor that one of the new inmates was an undercover agent from the Ministry of Prison Mines, sent there to catch guards who were killing inmates for fun and thus lowering the production quotas. It worked, I suppose—they said fewer inmates were maimed for the sport of it. But the guards thumping on you—when winter came, that was the least of your worries."

"What did the guards call you?" we asked him.

"There are no names," he said. "I made it through winter, but afterward I was different. I can't make you understand what the winter was like, what that did to me. When the thaw came, I didn't care about anything. I would leer at the guards like they were orphans. I kept acting out at self-criticism sessions. Instead of confessing that I could have pushed one more ore cart or mined an extra ton, I would berate my hands for not listening to my mouth or blame my right foot for not following my left. Winter had changed me—I was someone else now. The cold, there are no words for it."

"For the love of Juche," the old Pubyok said. He still had his shoe on the table. "If we were interrogating this idiot, there'd already be a funeral team on its way to retrieve that glorious, glorious actress and her poor tots."

"This isn't even Commander Ga," we reminded him.

"Then why are we listening to him whimper about prison?" He turned to Commander Ga. "You think those mountains are cold? Imagine them with Yankee snipers and B-29 strikes. Imagine those hills without a camp cook to serve you hot cabbage soup every day. Imagine there's no comfortable infirmary cot where they painlessly put you out of your misery."

Nobody ever dropped bombs on us, but we knew what Commander Ga was talking about. Once we had to go north to get the biography of a guard at Prison 14-18. All day we rode north in the back of a crow, slush spraying up from the floorboards, our boots freezing solid, the whole time wondering if we were really going to interrogate a subject or if that was just what we'd been told to lure us to prison without a fuss. As the cold froze the turds inside our asses, we could only wonder if the Pubyok hadn't finally pulled the lever on us.

Commander Ga went on, "Because I was new, I was housed next to the infirmary, where people complained all night. One old man in there was a particular pain in the ass. He wasn't productive because his hands no longer worked. People might have covered for him, but he was hated—one of his eyes was cloudy, and he only knew how to accuse and demand. All night the guy would moan an endless series of questions. *Who are you?* he'd call to the night. *Why are you here? Why won't you answer?* Week after week, I'd wonder when the blood truck would finally come to shut him up. But then I started to think about his questions. Why was I there? What was my crime? Eventually, I began to answer him. *Why won't you confess?* he'd call out, and through my harmonica barracks, I'd shout, *I'm ready to confess, I'll tell everything.* These conversations made people nervous, and then one night, I got a visit from Mongnan. She was the oldest woman in the camp, and she'd long ago lost her hips and breasts to hunger. Her hair was cut like a man's, and she kept her palms wrapped with strips of cloth."

Commander Ga continued with his story of how he and Mongnan sneaked out of the barracks, past the mud room and water barrels, and if we perhaps didn't say it, we all must have been thinking that the name Mongnan meant "Magnolia," the grandest white flower of them all. That's what our subjects say they see when the autopilot takes them to the apex of pain—a wintry mountaintop, where from the frost a lone white blossom opens for them. No matter how their bodies contort, it is the stillness of this image they remember. It couldn't be so bad, could it? A single afternoon of pain . . . and then the past is behind you, every shortcoming and failure is gone, every last bitter mouthful of it.

"Outside, past my rising breath," Commander Ga continued, "I asked Mongnan where all the guards had gone. She pointed toward the bright lights of the administration buildings. *The Minister of Prison Mines must be coming tomorrow,* she said. *I've seen this before. They'll be up all night cooking the books.*

"*So?* I asked her.

"*The Minister is coming,* she said. *That's why they've worked us so hard, that's why all the weak have been thrown in the infirmary.* She pointed to the warden's complex, every light burning bright. *Look at all the electricity they're using,* she said. *Listen to that poor generator. The only way they can light this whole place is with the electric fence off.*

"*So what, escape?* I asked. *There's nowhere to run.*

"*Oh, we'll all die here,* she said. *Rest assured. But it won't be tonight.*

"And suddenly she was moving across the yard, stiff-spined but quick in the dark. I caught up with her at the fence, where we squatted. The fence was two fences, really, a parallel line of concrete posts strung with cables on brown ceramic insulators. Inside was a stretch of no-man's-land, teeming with wild ginger and radishes that nobody lived to steal.

"She moved to reach through the wires. *Wait,* I said. *Shouldn't we test it?* But Mongnan reached under the fence and pulled out two radishes, crisp and cold, which we ate on the spot. Then we began digging the wild ginger that grew there. All the old ladies in camp got placed on grave detail—they buried the bodies where they fell, just deep enough that the rain wouldn't seep them out. And you could always tell ginger plants whose tap root had penetrated a corpse: the blooms were large, iridescent yellow, and it was hard to jerk loose a plant whose roots had hooked a rib below.

"When our pockets could hold no more, we ate another radish and I could feel it cleaning my teeth. *Ah, the joys of a scarcity distribution,* Mongnan said and finished the radish—root, stem, and blossom. *This place is a lecture on supply and demand. Here is my blackboard,* she said, looking to the night sky. Then she put a hand on the electric fence. *And here is my final exam.*"

In the cafeteria, Q-Kee jumped up. "Wait," she said. "Is this Li Mongnan, the professor who was denounced, along with her students?"

Commander Ga stopped his story. "A professor?" he asked us. "What was her subject?"

It was a tremendous gaffe. The Pubyok just shook their heads. We had just given our subject more information than he'd given us. We dismissed both interns and asked Commander Ga to please continue.

"Were her students transported?" Ga asked. "Had Mongnan outlived them at Prison 33?"

"Please continue," we requested. "When you're done, we'll answer one question."

Commander Ga took a moment to digest this. Then he nodded and continued. "There was a pond in which the guards raised trout to feed to their families. The fish were counted every morning, and if one went missing, the whole camp would starve. I followed Mongnan to the low wall of the circular pool, where she crouched and reached over to snatch a fish from the black water. It took a couple tries, but she had a net rigged from a hoop of wire, and the fabric wrapped around Mongnan's hands gave her a good grip. She held a trout behind the pectoral fins—so healthy, so perfectly alive. *Pinch it here, just up from the tail,* she said. *Then massage it here, behind the belly. When you feel the egg pocket, squeeze.* Mongnan lifted the fish high and then milked an apricot-colored stream of eggs into her mouth. She tossed the fish back.

"Then it was my turn. Mongnan snatched another fish and showed me the slit that marked it as female. *Pinch hard,* she cautioned, *or you'll get fish shit.* I squeezed the fish, and a shot of eggs sprayed my face, surprisingly warm. Gelatinous, briny, unmistakably alive, I smelled it on my cheeks, then, wiping, licked my palms. With practice, I got the knack. We milked the eggs of a dozen fish, stars crossing the sky as we sat there, stunned.

"*Why are you helping me?* I asked her.

"*I am an old woman,* she said. *That's what old women do.*

"*Yes, but why me?*

"Mongnan rubbed her hands in the dirt, to get the smell off. *You need it,* she said. *The winter took ten kilos from you. You don't have that to give again.*

"*I'm asking, why do you care?*

"*Have you heard of Prison Number 9?*

"*I've heard of it.*

"*It's their most profitable prison mine—five guards run a prison of fifteen hundred. They just stand at the gate and never go inside. The whole prison is in the mine, there's no barracks, no kitchen, no infirmary—*

"*I said I've heard of it,* I told her. *Are you saying we should feel lucky we're in a nice prison?*

"Mongnan stood. *I heard there was a fire in Prison 9,* she said. *The guards wouldn't open the gates to let the prisoners out, so the smoke killed everyone inside.*

"I nodded at the gravity of her story, but said, *You're not answering my question.*

"*That minister is coming here tomorrow to inspect our mine. Think how his life is going right now. Think how much shit he's been eating.* She grabbed me by the shoulder. *You can't be talking to your hands and feet at self-criticism. You can't be throwing the guards stupid looks. You've got to stop debating the old man in the infirmary.*

"*Okay,* I said.

"*And the answer to your question is this: why I'm helping you is none of your business.*

"We made our way past the latrine benches and leaped the piers of the gravity sewer. There was a pallet where people who died in the night were stacked, but now it was empty. As we passed it, Mongnan said, *My tripod gets to sleep in tomorrow.* Still and clear, the night smelled of birch trees, which a detail of old men had been cutting into cane strips. Finally we came to the cistern and the ox that turned its great pump wheel. It had kneeled down on a bed of birch bark, very pungent. When the beast heard Mongnan's voice, it stood. She turned to me, whispering, *The fish eggs, that's once a year. I can show you where the tadpoles arrive in the streams, and when the trees by the west tower give their sap. There are other such tricks, but you can't count on them. There are only two constant sources of nourishment in the camp. One I'll show you later, when things get difficult, for it is quite distasteful. Here is the other.*

"She touched the beast on the nose, then patted the black plates between its horns. She fed him a piece of wild ginger—it breathed sharply through its nostrils, then chewed sideways. From deep in her pockets, Mongnan produced a medium-sized jar. *An old man showed me this,* she said. *The oldest man in the camp at the time. He must have been sixty, maybe more, but very fit. It was a cave-in that killed him, not hunger or weakness. He was strong when he went.*

"She ducked under the ox, already hanging long and red. With a tight grip, Mongnan began stroking him. The ox smelled my hands, looking for more ginger, and I looked into its wet, black eyes. *There was a man a few years back,* Mongnan said, from under the ox. *He had a little razor, and he would make cuts in the beast's hide, to drink the blood when it leaked. That was a different animal. The beast didn't complain, but the blood trickled out and froze, which the guards noticed, and that was the end of the little man. I photographed his body after the punishment. I went through all his clothes looking for that razor, but I never found it.*

"The ox snorted—its eyes were wide and uncertain, and it swung its head from side to side as if looking for something. Then it closed its eyes, and soon Mongnan emerged with a jar, nearly full and steaming. Mongnan drank half at one go and handed it to me. I tried to take a sip, but when a little rope of it went down my throat, the rest hung on, and it all swam down at once. The ox knelt again. *You'll be strong for three days,* she said.

"We looked at the lights glowing in the guard buildings. We looked toward China. *This regime will come to an end,* she said. *I have studied every angle, and it cannot last. One day all the guards will run away—they'll head that way, for the border. There will be disbelief, then confusion, then chaos, and finally a vacuum. You must have a plan ready. Act before the vacuum is filled.*

"We began to make our way back toward the barracks, our stomachs full, our pockets full. When we heard the dying man again, we shook our heads.

"*Why won't I tell them what they want to know?* the dying man moaned, his voice reverberating through the barracks. *What am I doing here? What is my crime?*

"*Allow me,* Mongnan said. She cupped her hands and moaned back, *Your crime is disturbing the peace.*

"Oblivious, the dying man moaned again. *Who am I?*

"Mongnan made her voice low and moaned, *You are Duc Dan, the camp's pain in the ass. Please die quietly. Die in silence, and I promise to take a flattering last photo of you.*"

In the cafeteria, one of the Pubyoks pounded the table. "Enough," he shouted. "Enough of this."

Commander Ga stopped his story.

The old interrogator knotted his hands. "Don't you know a lie when you hear one?" he asked us. "Can't you see the way this subject is playing you? He's talking about Kim Duc Dan, trying to make you think he's in prison. Interrogators don't go to prison, that's impossible."

Another old-timer stood. "Duc Dan's retired," he said. "You all went to his going-away party. He moved to the beach in Wonsan. He's not in jail, that's a lie that he's in jail. He's painting seashells right now. You all saw the brochure he had."

Commander Ga said, "I haven't gotten to the part about Commander Ga yet. Don't you want to hear the story of our first encounter?"

The first interrogator ignored him. "Interrogators don't go to prison," he said. "Hell, Duc Dan probably interrogated half the people in Prison 33, that's where this parasite got Duc Dan's name. Tell us where you heard this name. Tell us how you know about his milky eye. Confess to your lie. Why won't you tell us the truth?"

The Pubyok with the shoe stood. He had jagged scars in his neat gray hair. "Enough storytime," he said, and looked at our team with a disgust that left no doubt about his thoughts on our methods. Then he turned toward Ga. "Enough fairy tales," he said. "Tell us what you did with the actress's corpse, or by the blood of Inchon we'll make your fingernails tell us."

The look on Commander Ga's face made the old men grab him. They poured piping hot *pu-erh* in his facial wounds before dragging him off, leaving us to race to our office to begin filling out the forms that we hoped would get him back.

IT WAS MIDNIGHT before Division 42 approved our emergency memos. With our interrogation override authorization in hand, we went down into the torture wing, a place our team rarely went, to rescue Commander Ga. We had the interns check the hot boxes, even though the red lights were off. We checked the sense-dep cells and the time-out tanks, where subjects got some first aid and a chance to catch their breath. We lifted the floor hatch and descended down the ladders into the sump. There were many lost souls down there, all of them too far gone to be Ga, but still, we checked the names on their ankle bracelets and lifted their heads long enough to shine a light in their slow-to-dilate eyes. Finally, with trepidation, we checked a room the old-timers called the shop. It was dark when we swung open the door—there was only the occasional winking glint of a slowly turning power tool, suspended from the ceiling by its yellow pneumatic hose. When we threw the power switch, the air-recirc system started up and the banks of fluorescents flashed to life. The room—spotless, sterile—contained only chrome, marble, and the white clouds of our own breath.

Where we found Commander Ga was in his own room. While we were searching, he'd been replaced in his bed, head propped up on pillows. Someone had put him in his nightshirt. Here, he fixed the far wall with a quizzical stare. We took his vital signs and checked him for wounds, even though it was clear what had happened. On his forehead and scalp were pressure marks from the screws to the halo, a device that kept a subject from injuring his neck during the cranial administration of electricity.

We poured a paper cup of water and tried to give him a drink—it just dribbled out.

"Commander Ga," we said. "Are you okay?"

He looked up, as if he'd only now noticed us, even though we'd just taken his pulse, temp, and BP. "This is my bed?" he asked us. Then his eyes floated around the room, landing on his bedside table. "That is my peaches?"

"Did you tell them," we asked, "what happened to the actress?"

With a vague smile, he looked from each of us to the next, as if searching for the person who could translate the question into a language he understood.

We all shook our heads in disgust, then sat on the edges of Commander Ga's bed for a smoke, passing the ashtray above his outline in the sheets. The Pubyok had gotten what they needed to know out of him, and now there'd be no biography, no relationship, no victory for the thinking man. Our second in command was a man I thought of as Leonardo because he was baby-faced like the actor in *Titanic*. I'd seen Leonardo's real name in his file once, but I've never called him by either name. Leonardo set the ashtray on Commander Ga's stomach and said, "I bet they'll shoot him in front of the Grand People's Study House."

"No," I said. "That's too official. They'll probably shoot him in the market under Yanggakdo Bridge—that'll move the story by rumor."

Leonardo said, "If it turns out he did the unthinkable to her, then he'll just disappear. Nobody'll find so much as a little toe."

"If he'd been the real Commander Ga," Jujack said, "a famous person, a *yangban*, they'd fill the soccer stadium for it."

Commander Ga lay in the middle of us, sleepy as a rubella baby.

Q-Kee smoked like a singer, with the very tips of her fingers. Judging by the faraway look on her face, I figured she was warily pondering that unthinkable. Instead, she said, "I wonder what his question for us would have been?"

Jujack looked at Ga's tattoo, ghosting through his nightshirt. "He must have loved her," he said. "Nobody gets a tattoo like that unless it's love."

We weren't crime detectives or anything, but we'd been in the game long enough to know the kind of mayhem that came from the fount of love.

I said, "The rumors are that he stripped Sun Moon naked before he killed her. Is that love?"

When Leonardo cast his eyes down to our subject, you could see his long eyelashes. "I just wanted to find out his real name," he said.

I stubbed my cigarette out and rose. "I guess it's time to congratulate our betters and find out the resting place of our national actress."

The Pubyok lounge was two floors below us. When I knocked on the door, a rare silence followed. All those guys seemed to do was play table tennis, sing karaoke, and wing their throwing knives around. Finally, Sarge opened the door.

"It looks like you got your man," I told him. "The halo never lies."

Behind Sarge, a couple of Pubyok sat at a table, staring at their hands.

"Go ahead and gloat," I said. "I'm just curious about the guy's story. I just want to know his name."

"He didn't tell us," Sarge said.

Sarge didn't look so good. I understood he must have been under a lot of pressure with such a high-profile subject, and it was easy to forget that Sarge was in his seventies. But his color was off. It didn't look like he'd been sleeping. "No worries," I told him. "We'll piece all the details together from the crime scene. With the actress in hand, we'll know everything about this guy."

"He wouldn't talk," Sarge said. "He didn't give us anything."

I stared at Sarge in disbelief.

"We put the halo on him," Sarge said. "But he went to a place, some faraway place, we couldn't reach."

I nodded as it all sank in. Then I took a big breath.

"You understand that Ga's ours now," I told him. "You had your try."

"I don't think he's anybody's," Sarge said.

"That shit he said about Duc Dan," I said, "you know that's just a subject lying to survive. Duc Dan's building sandcastles in Wonsan right now."

"He wouldn't take it back," Sarge said. "No matter how much juice we put in that asshole's brain, he wouldn't take it back." Sarge looked up at me for the first time. "Why doesn't Duc Dan ever write? All these years, not one of them has ever dropped a line to their old Pubyok unit."

I lit a cigarette and handed it to Sarge. "Promise me that when you're on the beach, you won't ever think about this place again," I told him. "And don't ever let a subject get inside your head. You taught me that. Remember how green I was?"

Sarge half smiled. "Still are," he said.

I clapped him on the back and mimed a punch to the metal door-frame.

Sarge shook his head and laughed.

"We'll get this guy," I said, and walked away.

You can't believe how fast I can take a couple of staircases.

"Ga's still in play," I said when I burst through the door.

The team was only on its second cigarette. They all looked up.

"They didn't get anything," I told them. "He's ours now."

We looked at Commander Ga, mouth hanging open, as useful as a ly-chee nut.

Rations be damned, Leonardo lit a celebratory third cigarette. "We've got a few days till he gets his wits back," he said. "Assuming there aren't any memory-recovery issues. In the meantime, we should go out into the field, search the actress's house, see what we can dig up."

Q-Kee spoke up. "The subject responded to a mother figure in a captive environment. Is there any way we can get our hands on an older female interrogator, someone Mongnan's age, someone that might get through to him?"

"Mongnan," Ga echoed, staring straight ahead.

I shook my head no. There was no such animal.

It was true how much we were at a disadvantage for not having female interrogators. Vietnam was a pioneer in that department, and look at the great strides made by nations like Chechnya and Yemen. The Tamil Tigers in Sri Lanka used women exclusively for this purpose.

Jujack jumped in. "Why don't we bring Mongnan down here, put an extra bed in this room, and just record them for a week? I bet it would all come out."

Commander Ga seemed to notice us just then. "Mongnan's dead," he said.

"Nonsense," we told him. "No need to worry. She's probably just fine."

"No," he said. "I saw her name."

"Where?" we asked.

"On the master computer."

We were all seated around Commander Ga, like family. We weren't supposed to tell him, but we did. "There's no such thing as a master computer," we said. "It's a device, invented by us, to get people to reveal critical information. They're told that the computer has the location of everybody in Korea, North and South, and that as a reward for telling their stories, they get to enter a list of people they want to find. Do you understand us, Commander Ga? The computer has no addresses in it. It just saves the names that are typed in, so that we know everybody the subject cares about and then we can arrest them."

It kind of looked like some of that was sinking in, like Ga was coming around a little.

"My question," he said.

We did owe him the answer to a question.

At the Academy, they had an old adage about electricity therapy: "Voltage closes the attic but opens the cellar," meaning that it tends to disrupt a subject's working memory but leaves deep impressions intact and surprisingly easy to access. So maybe, if Ga was lucid enough, we had an opportunity. We'd take what we could get.

"Tell us your oldest memory," we said, "and then you get your question."

Ga began as the lobotomized begin, without calculation or consideration, speaking in a voice that was lifeless and rote:

"I was a boy," he said. "And I went for a long walk and got lost. My parents were dreamers and didn't notice I was gone. They came to look for me but it was too late—I had wandered too far. A cold wind rose and said, 'Come, little boy, sleep in my floating white sheets,' and I thought, *Now I will freeze to death.* I ran to escape the wind, and a mine shaft said, 'Come, shelter yourself in my depths,' and I thought, *Now I will fall down to death.* I ran into the fields where the filth is thrown and the sick are left. There, a ghost said, 'Let me inside, and I'll warm you from within,' and I thought, *Now I will die of fever.* Then a bear came and spoke to me, but I did not know his language. I ran into the woods and the bear followed me, and I thought, *Now I will be eaten to death.* The bear took me in his strong arm and held me close to his face. He used his great claws to comb my hair. He dipped his paw in honey and brought his claws to my lips. Then the bear said, 'You will learn to speak bear now, and you will become as the bear and you will be safe.'"

Everybody recognized the story, one that's taught to all the orphans, with the bear representing the eternal love of Kim Jong Il. So Commander Ga was an orphan. We shook our heads at the revelation. And it gave us chills the way he told the story, as if it actually was about him and not a character he had learned about, as if he personally had nearly died of cold, hunger, fever, and mine mishaps, as if he himself had licked honey from the Dear Leader's claws. But such is the universal power of storytelling.

"My question?" Ga asked.

"Of course," we told him. "Ask away."

Commander Ga pointed at the can of peaches on his bedside table. "Are those my peaches?" he asked. "Or your peaches or Comrade Buc's?"

Suddenly, we were quiet. We leaned in close.

"Who's Comrade Buc?" we asked.

"Comrade Buc," Ga said, looking into each of our faces, as if we were Comrade Buc. "Forgive me for what I did to you, I'm sorry about your scar."

Ga's eyes lost focus, then his head went back to the pillow. He felt cold, but when we checked his temperature again, it was normal—electricity can really throw off a body's thermal regulation. When we were sure it was just exhaustion, Jujack motioned us to the corner of the room, where he spoke in a hushed tone.

"I know that name, Comrade Buc," Jujack said. "I just saw it on an ankle bracelet, down in the sump."

That's when we lit a cigarette, placed it in Commander Ga's lips, and then began gearing up for another trip beneath the torture complex.

WHEN THE interrogators had left, Commander Ga lay in the dark, smoking. In pain school, they'd taught him to find his reserve, a private place he could go in unbearable moments. A pain reserve was like a real reserve—you put a fence around it, attended to its welfare, kept it pristine, and dealt with all trespassers. Nobody could ever know what your pain reserve was, even if you'd chosen the most obvious, rudimentary element of your life, because if you lost your pain reserve, you'd lost everything.

In prison, when rocks smashed his hands or a baton came down on the back of his neck, he'd attempt to transport himself to the deck of the *Junma* and its gentle rolling motion. When the cold made his fingers staticky with pain, he tried to get inside the opera diva's song, to enter her voice itself. He tried to veil himself in the yellow of the Second Mate's wife's dress or pull the cloak of an American quilt over his head, but none of them really worked. It was only when he'd seen Sun Moon's movie that he finally had a reserve—she saved him from everything. When his pickax struck frozen rock, in that spark, he felt her aliveness. When a wall of ore dust would sweep through a passage and double him over with cough, she gave him breath. When once he stepped in an electrified puddle, Sun Moon appeared and restarted his heart.

So it was that today, when the old Pubyok of Division 42 fitted him with the halo, he turned to her. Even before they'd fastened the thumbscrews to his scalp, he'd taken leave of them and was returning to the first day he'd physically stood in the presence of Sun Moon. He didn't believe that he might actually meet her until he'd made it out of the gates of Prison 33, until the Warden called for the guards to open the gate, and he stepped through its razor-wire threshold and then heard the gate slide shut behind him. He was wearing Commander Ga's uniform and was holding the box of photographs Mongnan had given him. In his pocket was the camera he'd watched over and a long-guarded DVD of *Casablanca*. Armed with these things, he walked through the mud to the car that would take him to her.

As he stepped into the Mercedes, the driver turned to him, shock and confusion on his face.

Commander Ga could see a thermos on the dashboard. A year without tea.

"I could use a cup of tea," he said.

The driver didn't move. "Who the hell are you?" he asked.

"Are you a homosexual?" was Commander Ga's answer.

The driver stared at him in disbelief, then shook his head.

"Are you sure? Have you been tested?"

"Yes," the driver said, confused. Then he said, "No."

"Get out," Commander Ga said. "I'm Commander Ga now. That other man is gone. If you think you belong with him, I can take you to him, what's left of him, down in the mine. Because you're either his driver or my driver. If you're my driver, you'll pour me a cup of tea, get me to a civilized place where I can bathe. Then you'll take me home."

"Home?"

"Home to my wife, the actress Sun Moon."

And then Ga was being driven to Sun Moon, the only person who could take away the pain he'd suffered in getting to her. A crow towed their Mercedes through the mountain roads, and in the backseat Ga looked through the box Mongnan had given him. It contained thousands of pictures. Mongnan had clipped together inmates' entrance and exit photos. Back to back, alive and dead, thousands of people. He flipped through the box so that all the exit images faced him—bodies crushed and torn and folded in unnatural angles. He recognized victims of cave-ins and beatings. In some pictures, he couldn't tell exactly what he was looking at. Mostly, the dead looked as if they'd gone to sleep, and children, because it was the cold that got them, were curled up in hard little discs, like lozenges. Mongnan was meticulous, and the catalog was complete. This box, he suddenly understood, was the closest thing his nation had to the phone book he'd seen in Texas.

He spun the box around, and now facing him were all the entrance photos, in which people were fearful and uncertain and hadn't quite let themselves imagine the nightmare they were in for, and these photos were even harder to look at. When at last he located his own entrance photo, he turned it slowly, seriously expecting to see himself dead. But it wasn't so. He took a moment to marvel at that. He studied the light in the trees as they flashed by. He watched the motion of the crow ahead, its tow chain tinkling with slackness before snapping taut. He remembered the egg-shells spinning whimsically in the crow that had brought him. In his photo, you couldn't see the dying people on cots around him. You couldn't see his hands dripping with bloody ice water. But the eyes—it's unmistakable how they are wide yet refusing to see what is before them. Such a boy he seems, as if he's still back in an orphanage, believing that all is well and that the fate which befalls all the orphan boys won't befall him. The chalk name on the slate he held seemed so foreign. Here was the only photo of that person, the person he used to be. He tore it slowly into strips before letting them flutter out the window.

The crow unhitched them in the outskirts of Pyongyang, and at the Koryo Hotel, the girls gave him Commander Ga's usual treatment—the deep soaking and cleansing he sought after every visit to a prison mine. His uniform was cleaned and pressed, and he was bathed in a grand tub, where the girls scrubbed the blood stains from his hands and tried to repair his nails, and they didn't care whose blood it was that tinted the soapy water, his or Commander Ga's or someone else's. In the warm, buoyant water he came to see that at some point in the last year, his mind and his flesh had separated, that his brain had sat high and frightened above the mule of his body, a beast of burden that hopefully would make it alone over the treacherous mountain pass of Prison 33. But now as a woman ran a warm washcloth along the arch of his foot, the sensation was allowed to rise up, up into his brain, and it was okay to perceive again, to recognize forgotten parts of his body as they hailed him. His lungs were more than air bellows. His heart, he believed now, could do more than move blood.

He tried to imagine the woman he was about to behold. He understood that the real Sun Moon couldn't be as beautiful as the one on the screen, the way her skin glowed, the radiance of her smile. And the particular way her desires took up residence about the eyes—it must be a product of projection, of some cinematic effect. He wanted to be intimate with her, to harbor no secrets, to have nothing between them. Seeing her projected on the wall of the infirmary, that's how it had felt, that there was no snow or cold between them, that she was right there with him, a woman who'd given everything, who'd abandoned her freedom and entered Prison 33 to save him. It had been a mistake to wait until the last moment to tell the Second Mate's wife about the replacement husbands that awaited her, Ga could see that now. So there was no way he was going to let a secret spoil things with Sun Moon. That was the great thing about their relationship: a new beginning, a chance to unburden all. What the Captain had said of getting his wife back would be true of him and Sun Moon as well: they'd be strangers for a while, there would be a period of discovery, but love, love would eventually return.

The women of the Koryo Hotel toweled him, dressed him. Finally, he took a number 7 haircut—the one they called Speed Battle, the Commander's signature style.

In the late afternoon, the Mercedes climbed the final, winding road that led to the peak of Mount Taesong. They passed the botanical gardens, the national seed bank, and the hothouses that contained the breeding stocks of kimilsungia and kimjongilia. They passed the Pyongyang Central Zoo, closed at this hour. On the seat beside him were some of Commander Ga's possessions. There was a bottle of cologne, and he quickly applied some. *This is the smell of me,* he thought. He picked up Commander Ga's pistol. *This is my pistol,* he thought. He pulled back the slide enough to see a bullet peek from the breech. *I am the kind of man who keeps one in the chamber.*

Finally, they passed a cemetery whose bronze-busted tombstones glowed orange in the light. This was the Revolutionary Martyrs' Cemetery, whose 114 occupants, all of whom had died before they could engender sons, gave names to every orphan in the nation. They reached the peak and here were three houses built for the ministers of Mass Mobilization, Prison Mines, and Procurement.

The driver came to a stop before the middle house, and Commander Ga walked through the gate himself, its low slats woven with cucumber vines and the blossoms of a magnificent melon. Nearing Sun Moon's door, he felt his chest tighten with pain, the pain of the Captain pressing him with inky needles, of the saltwater he splashed on the raw tattoo, of the Second Mate's wife weeping the infection out with a steaming towel. At the door, he took that breath, and knocked.

Almost immediately, Sun Moon answered. She wore a loose house robe, under which her breasts swung free. He'd seen such a house robe only once before, in Texas, hanging in the bath of his guest room. That robe was white and fluffy, while Sun Moon's was matted and stained with old sauces. She was without makeup, and her hair was down, falling across her shoulders. Her face was filled with excitement and possibility and, suddenly, he felt the terrible violence of this day leave him. Gone was the combat he'd faced at the hands of her husband. Gone was the look of doom on the Warden's face. Wiped away were the multitudes Mongnan had captured on film. This house was a good house, white paint, red trim. It was the opposite of the Canning Master's house—nothing bad had happened here, he could tell.

"I'm home," he said to her.

She looked past him, peering around the yard, the road.

"Do you have a package for me?" she asked. "Did the studio send you?"

But here she paused, taking in all the inconsistencies—the lean stranger in her husband's uniform, the man wearing his cologne and riding in his car.

"Who are you supposed to be?" she asked.

"I'm Commander Ga," he said. "And I'm finally home."

"You're telling me you've brought no script, nothing?" she asked. "You mean the studio dressed you up like this and sent you all the way up here, and you don't have a script for me? You tell Dak-Ho I said that's cold, even for him. He's crossed a line."

"I don't know who Dak-Ho is," he said and marveled at the evenness of her skin, at the way her dark eyes locked on him. "You're even more beautiful than I imagined."

She undid the belt of her house robe, then recinched it tighter.

Then she lifted her hands to the heavens. "Why do we live on this god-forsaken hill?" she asked the sky. "Why am I up here, when everything that matters is down there?" She pointed to Pyongyang far below, this time of day just a haze of buildings lining the silver Y of the Taedong River. She approached him and looked up into his eyes. "Why can't we live by Mansu Park? I could take an express bus to the studio from there. How can you pretend not to know who Dak-Ho is? Everybody knows him. Has he sent you here to mock me? Are they all down there laughing at me?"

"I can tell you've been hurting for a long time," he said. "But that's all over now. Your husband's home."

"You're the worst actor in the world," she said. "They're all down there at a casting party, aren't they? They're drunk and laughing and casting a new female lead, and they decided to send the worst actor in the world up the hill to mock me."

She fell down to the grass and placed the back of her hand against her forehead. "Go on, get out of here. You've had your fun. Go tell Dak-Ho how the old actress wept." She tried to wipe her eyes. Then, from her house robe, she produced a pack of cigarettes. She brazenly lit one—it made her look mannish and seductive. "Not a single script, an entire year without a script."

She needed him. It was completely clear how much she needed him.

She noticed that the front door was cracked and that her children were peeking out. She hooked loose a slipper and kicked it toward the door, which was quickly pulled shut.

"I don't know anything about the movie business," he said. "But I've brought you a movie, as a gift. It's *Casablanca,* and it's supposed to be the best."

She reached up and took the DVD case, dirty and battered, from his hands. She quickly glanced at it. "That one's black-and-white," she said, then threw it across the yard. "Plus I don't watch movies—they'd only corrupt the purity of my acting." On her back in the grass, she smoked contemplatively. "You really don't have anything to do with the studio?" she asked.

He shook his head no. She was so vulnerable before him, so pure—how did she stay so in this harsh world?

"So what are you, one of my husband's new flunkies? Sent to check on me while he goes on a secret mission? Oh, I know about his secret missions—he alone is brave enough to infiltrate a whorehouse in Minpo, only the great Commander Ga can survive a week in a Vladivostok card den."

He crouched beside her. "Oh, no. You judge him too harshly. He's changed. Sure, he's a man who's made some mistakes, he's sorry for those, but all that matters now is you. He adores you, I'm sure of it. He's completely devoted to you."

"Tell him I can't take much more of this. Please pass that along for me."

"I'm him now," he said. "So you can tell him yourself."

She took a deep breath and shook her head. "So you want to be Commander Ga, huh?" she asked. "Do you know what he'd do to you if he heard you assume his name? His taekwondo 'tests' are for real, you know. They've made an enemy of everyone in this town. That's why I can't get a role anymore. Just make up with the Dear Leader, won't you? Can't you just bow to him at the opera? Will you give my husband that request from me? That's all it would take, a single gesture, in front of everybody, and the Dear Leader would forgive all."

He reached to wipe her cheek, but she pulled away.

"These tears in my eyes," she said. "Do you see them? Can you tell my husband of these tears?" she asked. "Don't go on any more missions, please. Tell him not to send another flunky to babysit me."

"He already knows," he said. "And he's sorry. Will you do something for him, a favor? It would mean so much to him."

Lying on the grass, she turned to her side, her breasts lolling under the house robe, snot running freely from her nose. "Go away," she said.

"I'm afraid I can't do that," he said. "I told you it's been a long journey, and I've only just arrived. The favor is a small one, really, it's nothing to a great actress like yourself. You know that part from *A True Daughter of the Country*, where, to find your sister, you must cross the Inchon Strait, still aflame with the sinking battleship *Koryo*, and when you wade in, you're just a fishing-village girl from Cheju, but after swimming through the corpses of patriots in blood-red waters, you emerge a different person, now you are a woman soldier, a half-burned flag in your hands, and the line you say, you know it, will you say it to me now?"

She didn't say the words, but he thought he could see them pass through her eyes—*There is a greater love, one that from the lowest places calls us high.* Yes, they were there in her eyes, that's the sign of a true actress—being able to speak with just her expressions.

"Can you sense how right everything feels?" he asked her. "How everything's going to be different? When I was in prison—"

"Prison?" she asked. She sat up straight. "How exactly do you know my husband?"

"Your husband attacked me this morning," he said. "We were in a tunnel, in Prison 33, and I killed him."

She cocked her head. "What?"

"I mean, I believe I killed him. It was dark, so I can't be sure, but my hands, they know what to do."

"Is this one of my husband's tests?" she asked. "If so, it's his sickest one yet. Are you supposed to report back how I responded to that news, whether I danced for joy or hanged myself in grief? I can't believe he's stooped this low. He's a child, really, a scared little boy. Only someone like that would loyalty-test an old woman in the park. Only Commander Ga would give his own son a masculinity test. And by the way, his sidekicks eventually get tested, too, and when they fail, you don't see them anymore."

"Your husband won't be testing anyone ever again," he said. "You're all that matters in his life right now. Over time, you'll come to understand that."

"Stop it," she said. "This isn't funny anymore. It's time for you to leave."

He looked up to the doorway, and standing there silent were the children—a girl perhaps eleven, a boy a little younger. They held the collar of a dog with thick shoulders and a shiny coat. "Brando," Commander Ga called, and the dog broke free. The Catahoula bounded to him, tail wagging. It kept leaping high to lick his face, then flattening low to nip his heels.

"You got him," he said to her. "I can't believe you got him."

"Got him?" she asked. Her voice was suddenly serious. "How do you know its name?" she asked. "We've kept the dog a secret so he won't be taken by the authorities."

"How do I know his name? I named him," he said. "Right before I sent him to you last year. 'Brando' is the word that Texans use to say something is yours forever."

"Wait a minute," she said, and all the theatrics were gone. "Just who exactly are you?"

"I'm the good husband. I'm the one who's going to make everything up to you."

There was a look on her face that Ga recognized, and it was not a happy one. It expressed an understanding that everything would be different now, that the person you'd been and the life you'd been living were over. It was a tough knowledge to suddenly gain, but it got better with tomorrows. And it would be easier since she'd probably worn that look once before, when the Dear Leader gave her, as a prize, to the winner of the Golden Belt, the man who'd beat Kimura.

In his dark room in Division 42, the smoldering cigarette in Commander Ga's lips was nearly finished. It had been a long day, and the memory of Sun Moon had saved him yet again. But it was time to put her away in his mind—she'd always be there when he needed her. He smiled a last time at the thought of her, causing the cigarette to fall from his mouth into the well where his neck curved into collarbone. There it burned slowly against his skin, a tiny red glow in an otherwise black room.

Pain, what was pain?

CITIZENS, we bring good news! In your kitchens, in your offices, on your factory floors—wherever you hear this broadcast, turn up the volume! The first success we have to report is that our Grass into Meat Campaign is a complete triumph. Still, much more soil needs to be hauled to the rooftops, so all housing-block managers are instructed to schedule extra motivation meetings.

Also, this month's recipe contest is upon us, citizens. The winning recipe will be painted on the front wall of the central bus terminal for all to copy down. The winner will be the citizen who submits the best recipe for: Celery Root Noodles!

Now for world news. Naked aggression continues from America—currently, two nuclear attack groups are parked in the East Sea, while in the U.S. Mainland, homeless citizens lie urine-soaked in the streets. And in poor South Korea, our soiled little sister, there is more flooding and hunger. Don't worry, help is on the way—Dear Leader Kim Jong Il has ordered that sandbags and food shipments be sent south right away.

Finally, the first installment of this year's Best North Korean Story begins today. Close your eyes and picture for a moment our national actress Sun Moon. Banish from your minds the foolish stories and gossip that have lately swirled our city about her. Picture her the way she will live forever in our national consciousness. Remember her famous "With Fever" scene in *Woman of a Nation,* where, following her rape at the hands of the Japanese, the sweat ran from her brow to meet, with moonlight, the tears upon her cheek, only to tumble down to her patriotic breasts? How can one tear, tracing its brief journey, start as a drop of ruin, trail into a drip of resolution, and, finally, splash with national fervor? Certainly, citizens, fresh in your minds is the final image of *Motherless Fatherland,* in which Sun Moon, clad only in bloodied gauze, emerges from the battlefield having saved the national flag, while behind her, the American Army is in ruins, foundering and aflame.

Now imagine her house, perched on the scenic cliffs of Mount Taesong. From below rose the purifying scents of kimjongilia and kimilsungia being grown in the botanical garden's hothouses. And beyond that, the Central Zoo, the most profitable zoo in the world, with over four hundred animals available, live and preserved. Picture Sun Moon's children, their angelic natures filling the house with honorific *sanjo* music, courtesy of the boy's *taegum* and the girl's *gayageum*. Even our national actress must help the cause of the people, so she was canning kelp to prepare her family should another Arduous March occur. Kelp washes ashore in quantities to feed millions and, once dried, can also be used for bedding, insulation, masculine virility, and firing of local megawatt stations. See Sun Moon's glimmering *choson-ot* as she purged the jars, observe how the steam made glisteny the contours of her womanness!

There was a knock at the door. No one ever knocked at this door, so out of the way is their house. This is the safest nation in the world, where crime is unheard of, so she didn't fear for herself. Yet she hesitated. Her husband was the hero Commander Ga, often away on dangerous missions, as he was right now. What if something had befallen him, and here was a messenger of the state to deliver the bad news? She knew that he truly belonged to his nation, to his people, and that she shouldn't think of him as hers, and yet she did—such was her love. How could she help it?

When the door opened, there stood Commander Ga—his uniform was crisp and on his chest were pinned both the Ruby Star and the Eternal Flame of Juche. He stepped inside and at the sight of Sun Moon's great beauty, he brazenly undressed her with his eyes. Look at how he ogled her curves beneath her housecoat, how he studied the ways in which each small motion of her body heaved her chest. Look at how this coward treated the great Korean modesty of Sun Moon like rubbish!

The good citizen is thinking, How can you call the hero Commander Ga a coward? Did Commander Ga not famously complete six assassination missions via the tunnels under the DMZ? Does he not hold the Golden Belt in taekwondo, the most deadly martial art in the world? Did Ga not win for his bride the cinema actress Sun Moon, star of the movies *Immortally Devoted* and *Oppressors Tumble*?

The answer, citizens, is that this was not the genuine Commander Ga! Look at the photo of the real Commander Ga on the wall behind this imposter. The man in the picture had broad shoulders, a crenellated brow, and teeth worn down from aggressive grinding. Now look at the spindly man wearing the Commander's uniform—sunken chest, girl's ears, barely the notion of a noodle in his trousers. Certainly it is an insult to do this imposter the honor of being called Commander Ga, but for the beginning of this story, it will suffice.

He commanded, "I am Commander Ga, and you will treat me as such."

Even though all her instincts told her this was not true, she was wise to set aside her own feelings and trust the guidance of a government official, for he bore the rank of minister. When in doubt, always look to your leaders for proper behavior.

For two full weeks, though, she was wary of him. He had to sleep in the tunnel with the dog, and he was only allowed out to taste of the broth that she prepared once daily for him. His body was lean, but he did not complain of the thin soup. Every day, she drew a hot bath for him, and he was allowed to enter the house from the tunnel to cleanse his body. Then, like a dutiful wife, Sun Moon bathed in his leftover wash water. Finally, it was back to the tunnel with the canine, an animal not meant to be domesticated. For an entire year, this beast had chewed the furniture and urinated at will. No amount of beatings from Sun Moon's husband could get the dog to obey. Now, Commander Ga spent his time in the tunnel training the animal to "sit" and "lie down" as well as other indolent phrases from capitalism. Worst of the commands was "hunt," which encouraged the beast to poach game from the public lands of the people.

For two weeks, this is the routine they kept, as if by maintaining it, the real husband would simply enter one day and all would be as if he never disappeared. As if the current man in her house were nothing but a smoker's intermission in one of her epic film performances. Certainly this was difficult for the actress—look at her posture, observe how she stood flat-footed, arms crossed. But did she think the pain in her movies was pretend, did she think the portrayal of national suffering was fiction? Did she think she could be the face of a Korea that has been dealt a thousand years of blows without losing a husband or two?

For Commander Ga, or whoever he really was, he thought he'd finished with a life of tunnels. This tunnel was a small one—large enough to stand inside, sure, but barely fifteen meters in length, just enough to travel under the front yard and perhaps under the road. Inside were barrels of supplies for the next Arduous March. There was a single lightbulb and a single chair. There was a large collection of DVDs, though no sign of a screen on which to view them. Yet he was happy listening to the boy above blow the wobbly notes of his *taegum*. It was bliss to hear the pluckings of a mother teaching her daughter the melancholy way of the *gayageum*—he could picture their *choson-ots* spread wide across the floor as they leaned into the sorrowful notes. Late at night, the actress paced behind the closed doors of the bedroom, and in his tunnel, Commander Ga could almost watch her feet fall, so closely did he follow her movements. In his mind, he mapped the bedroom based on how many steps she took between the window and the door, and by the way she moved around certain objects, he was sure of the location of her bed and wardrobe and vanity. It was almost as if he were in the chamber with her.

On the morning of the fourteenth day, he had accepted that this was how his life might continue for a long time, and he was at peace with that, but little did he know a dove was headed his way with a most glorious message in its beak. Loosed from the capital, the dove's wings fluttered above the Taedong River, turning in its bends sweet and green, while along the banks patriots and virgins strolled hand in hand. The dove swooped through girls from a Juche Youth Troop, skipping along in their darling uniforms, axes over their shoulders, heading to chop wood in Mansu Park. With delight, the white bird barrel-rolled through the May Day Stadium, largest in the world, then clapped its wings in pride over the great red flame of the Tower of Juche! Then up, up Mount Taesong, bending a wing in greeting toward the flamingos and peacocks in the Central Zoo, before veering wide from the electric fences surrounding the botanical gardens, ready to repel the next American sneak attack. A single, patriotic tear was shed above the Revolutionary Martyrs' Cemetery, and then the dove was on Sun Moon's windowsill, dropping the note in her hand.

Commander Ga looked up when the trapdoor to the tunnel was opened and Sun Moon leaned down, her robe opening slightly, the glory of a whole nation seemingly enbosomed in her generous womanliness. She read the note: "It is time, Commander Ga, to return to work."

The driver was waiting to take Commander Ga into the most beautiful city in the world—observe its wide streets and tall buildings, try to find a single item of trash or stray mark of graffiti! Graffiti, citizens, is the name for the way capitalists deface their public buildings. Here are no annoying advertisements, cellular phones, or planes in the sky. And try to take your eyes off our traffic girls!

Soon Commander Ga was on the third floor of Building 13, the most modern office complex in the world. *Whoosh, whoosh* went the vacuum tubes all around him. Flicker, flicker went the green computer screens. He found his desk on the third floor, then turned his nameplate inward, as if to remind himself that he was Commander Ga and his job was Minister of Prison Mines, that it was he who was in charge of the finest prison system in the world. Ah, there is no prison like a North Korean prison—so productive, so conducive to personal reflection. Prisons in the South are filled with jukeboxes and lipstick, places where men sniff glue and ripen each other's fruit!

A whoosh dropped a vacuum tube into the hopper on Commander Ga's desk. He opened the tube and removed a note, scribbled on the back of a requisition form. It read, "Prepare for the Dear Leader." He looked around the room for the author of the note, but all the phone sweepers were hard at work typing what they heard over their blue headsets, and the procurement teams had their heads buried under the black cloth of their computer hoods.

Out the window, light rain had begun to fall, and Commander Ga could make out an old woman in a shift, now nearly see-through, making her way through the upper branches of an oak tree, hunting down acorns, which all citizens know is forbidden until acorn-harvesting season is officially declared. Perhaps years of prison inspection had given the Commander a soft spot for our older citizens.

It was then that the entire vacuum system came to a halt, and in the eerie silence that followed, everyone looked up to the maze of clear tubes overhead, knowing what was to follow: the system was being prepared for a personal delivery from the Dear Leader himself. Suddenly, the sucking whistle began again, and all eyes watched as a golden tube snaked its way through the system to land in the hopper at the edge of Commander Ga's desk.

Commander Ga removed the golden tube. The note inside read only, "Would you do us the courtesy of your presence?"

The tension in the room was palpable. Was it possible that Commander Ga was not leaping high to run to the aid of his glorious leader? No, instead, he fumbled with the items on his desk, choosing to inspect more closely a device called a Geiger counter, made to detect the presence of nuclear materials, for our country is rich in deeply buried nuclear materials. Did he make a plan to put this valuable piece of equipment to work? Did he assign it a guardian for safekeeping? No, citizens, Commander Ga took this detector and climbed out the window, where he stepped onto a wet oak bough. Climbing high, he handed it to the old woman, saying, "Sell this at the night market. Then buy yourself a proper meal."

Of course, citizens, he lied: there's no such thing as a night market!

What's important is that no one looked up when Ga returned through the window. All kept working as he brushed wet leaves from his uniform. In the South, workers would be tittyweeping that someone had broken the "rules" by giving away government property. But here, discipline reigns, and people know that nothing happens without a purpose, that no task goes unnoticed, that if a man gives an old woman in an oak tree a nuclear detector, he does so because the Dear Leader wishes him to. That if there are two Commander Gas or one or none, it is as the Dear Leader desires.

Walking toward his destiny, Commander Ga caught the eye of Comrade Buc, who threw him the thumbs-up sign. Some people may find Comrade Buc humorous or even jaunty. Sure, he has an adorable scar splitting his brow that, owing to his wife's inability to sew, no longer connected. But remember that the thumbs-up was the signal the Yanks gave before dropping their payloads upon the innocents of North Korea. Just watch the movies, and you'll see the smiles, the thumbs-up, and then the bombs falling on Mother Korea. Watch *Sneak Attack,* starring Ga's own lovely wife. Watch *The Last Day of March,* which dramatizes the day in 1951 in which the Americans dropped a hundred and twenty thousand tons of napalm, leaving only three buildings standing in Pyongyang. So give Buc a thumbs-down and pay no more attention to him! His name, regrettably, will be heard from time to time, but he is no longer a character in this story and you are to henceforth ignore him.

And of Commander Ga? However lacking, however feeble you have judged his character, know that this is a story of growth and redemption, one in which enlightenment is gained by the lowliest of figures. Let this story be an inspiration when dealing with the weak-minded who share your communal housing blocks and the selfish who use all the soap in your group bathing wells. Know that change is achievable and that happy endings do come, for this story promises to have the happiest ending you will ever hear.

An elevator was waiting for Commander Ga. Inside was a beautiful woman in a white-and-navy uniform with blue-tinted sunglasses. She did not speak. The elevator had no controls, and she made no movement. How it descended, and whether she operated it, Ga couldn't tell, but soon they were dropping deep under Pyongyang. When the doors opened, he found himself in a glorious room, where gifts from other world leaders adorned the walls. There were rhino-horn bookends from Robert Mugabe, Supreme President of Zimbabwe; a black-lacquered longevity mask from Guy de Greves, Foreign Minister of Haiti; and a silver "Happy Birthday" platter signed to the Dear Leader by every member of Myanmar's Central Junta.

Suddenly, there was a bright light. Emerging from this was the Dear Leader, so confident, so tall, striding toward Commander Ga, and Commander Ga felt all his earthly worries fall away as a sense of well-being overtook him. It was as if his very being were cupped within the Dear Leader's own protective hands, and he felt only an urge to serve the glorious nation that had spawned such confidence in him.

Commander Ga bowed deeply and with total supplication.

The Dear Leader clasped him firmly and spoke, "Please, enough bowing, my good citizen. It has been too long, Ga, too long. Your nation needs you now. I have a delicious bit of mischief planned for our American friends. Are you willing to help?"

Why, citizens, did the Dear Leader show no distress at the appearance of this imposter? What is the Dear Leader's plan? Will the extended sadness of the actress Sun Moon be lifted? Find out tomorrow, citizens, when we deliver the next installment of this year's Best North Korean Story!

THE ELEVATOR plummeted deep into Bunker 13, where Commander Ga would meet the Dear Leader. Ga felt a sharp pain in his eardrums and his body felt limp, as if he were free-falling back into a prison mine. Seeing Comrade Buc—his smile, his thumbs-up—had opened a void in Commander Ga between the person he used to be and the person he'd become. Comrade Buc was the only person who existed on both sides of Commander Ga's void, who knew both the young hero who'd gone to Texas and the new husband of Sun Moon, the most dangerous man in Pyongyang. Now Ga felt rattled. He felt newly aware that he wasn't invincible, that it wasn't destiny in control of him but danger.

When the elevator doors opened, deep in Bunker 13, a team of elite bodyguards gave Commander Ga an eleven-point body search, though it was nothing worse than what he'd experienced each time he'd returned from Japan. The room was white and cold. They took a cup of urine from him and a clipping of hair. He barely got his clothes back on before he heard the clacking of heels growing louder in the hall outside as guards saluted the approach of the Dear Leader. Then the door simply opened, and in stepped Kim Jong Il. He wore a gray jumpsuit and designer glasses that amplified the playfulness in his eyes.

"There you are, Ga," he said. "We missed you."

Commander Ga gave a long, deep bow, fulfilling his first promise to Sun Moon.

The Dear Leader smiled. "That wasn't so hard," he said. "That didn't cost you anything, did it?" He placed a hand on Ga's shoulder and looked up into his eyes. "But the bow must come in public. Isn't that what I told you?"

Commander Ga said, "Can't a man practice?"

"There's the Ga I love," the Dear Leader said. On the table was a mounted Siberian fox posed mid-pounce above a white vole, a gift of

Constantine Dorosov, mayor of Vladivostok. The Dear Leader looked as though he might admire the fur of the fox, but instead he stroked the vole, its teeth bared against the threat above. "I should still be cross with you, Ga," he said. "I can't even count your wrongdoings. You let our most productive prison burn, along with fifteen hundred of our best inmates. I'm still trying to explain to the Chinese Premier your episode at that bathhouse in Shenyang. My driver of twenty years, he's still in a coma. The new one drives fine, but I miss the old one—his loyalty had been tested many times." Here, the Dear Leader returned to him. With a hand on the shoulder, the Dear Leader pressed Ga to his knees, so the Dear Leader now towered above. "And what you said to me at the opera, that cannot be unsaid. Your head would be the only way to restore the injury. And what leader wouldn't wish you gone, to disappear forever for all the trouble you cause? Do you forget that I gave you Sun Moon? Still, I have a soft spot for your antics. Yes, I will give you one more chance. Do you accept a new mission from me?"

Commander Ga looked down and nodded.

"Up, then," the Dear Leader said. "Dust yourself off, grab hold of your dignity again." He indicated a platter from the table. "Dried tiger meat?" he asked. "Do eat, and pocket some for that son of yours—that boy could use some tiger. When you eat of the tiger, you become like the tiger. That's what they say."

Commander Ga took a piece—it was hard and tasted sweet.

"I can't eat the stuff," the Dear Leader said. "It's the teriyaki flavor, I think. The Burmese have sent this as a gift. You know my collected works are being published in Rangoon? You must write your works, Commander. There will be volumes on taekwondo, I hope." He clapped Commander Ga on the back. "We sure have missed your taekwondo."

The Dear Leader led Commander Ga out of the room and down a long white hallway that slowly serpentined back and forth—should the Yanks attack, they'd get no line of fire longer than twenty meters. The tunnels under the DMZ slowly curved the same way—otherwise a single South Korean private, shooting through a mile of darkness, could counter an entire invasion.

They passed many doors, and rather than offices or residences, they seemed to house the Dear Leader's many ongoing projects. "I have a good feeling about this mission," the Dear Leader said. "When was the last time we embarked on one together?"

"It has been too long to remember," Commander Ga said.

"Eat, eat," the Dear Leader said as they strolled. "It's true what they say—your prison work has taken a toll on you. We must get your strength back. But you still have the Ga good looks, yes? And that beautiful wife, I'm sure you're glad to have her back. Such a fine actress—I'll have to compose a new movie role for her."

From the flat ping of his footsteps echoing back, Ga knew hundreds of meters of rock were above him. You could learn to perceive such depth. In the prison mines, you could feel the ghostly vibration of ore carts moving through other tunnels. You couldn't exactly hear the roto-hammers biting in the other shafts, but you could feel them in your teeth. And when there was a blast, you could tell its location in the mountain by the way dust was slapped off the walls.

"I have called you here," the Dear Leader said as they walked, "because the Americans will be visiting soon, and they must be dealt a blow, the kind that hits under the ribs and takes the breath away but leaves no visible mark. Are you up for this task?"

"Does the ox not yearn for the yoke when the people are hungry?"

The Dear Leader laughed. "This prison work has done wonders for your sense of humor," he said. "So tense you used to be, so serious. All those spontaneous taekwondo lessons you delivered!"

"I'm a new man," Ga said.

"Ha," the Dear Leader said. "If only more people visited the prisons."

The Dear Leader stopped before a door, considered it, then moved on to the next. Here he knocked, and with the buzz of an electric bolt, the door opened. The room was small and white. Only boxes were stacked inside.

"I know you keep close tabs on the prisons, Ga," the Dear Leader said, ushering him in. "And here is our problem. In Prison 33, there was a certain inmate, a soldier from an orphan unit. Legally, he was a hero. He has gone missing, and we need his expertise. Perhaps you met him and perhaps he shared some of his thoughts with you."

"Gone missing?"

"Yes, I know—it's embarrassing, no? The Warden has already paid for this. In the future, this won't be a problem, as we have a new machine that can find anyone, anywhere. It's a master computer, if you will. Remind me to show it to you."

"So, who is this soldier?"

The Dear Leader started to sort through boxes, opening some, tossing others aside, looking for something. One box was filled with barbecue tools, Ga observed. Another was filled with South Korean Bibles. "The orphan soldier? An average citizen, I suppose," the Dear Leader said. "A nobody from Chongjin. Ever visit that place?"

"Never had that pleasure, Dear Leader."

"Me, either. Anyway, this soldier, he went on a trip to Texas—had some security skills, language talents, and so on. The mission was to retrieve something the Americans took from me. The Americans, it seems, had no intention of returning this item. Instead, they subjected my diplomatic team to a thousand humiliations, and when the Americans visit us, I will subject them to a thousand in return. To do this right, I must know exact details of this visit to Texas. The orphan soldier, he is the only one who knows these."

"Certainly there were other diplomats on the visit. Why not ask them?"

"Sadly, they are no longer reachable," the Dear Leader said. "The man I speak of, he is currently the only one in our nation who's been to America."

Then the Dear Leader found what he was looking for—a large revolver. He hefted it around in the direction of Commander Ga.

"Ah, I suddenly remember," Ga said, looking at the pistol. "The orphan soldier. A lean, good-looking man, very smart and humorous. Yes, he was certainly in Prison 33."

"So you know him?"

"Yes, we often spoke late into the night. We were like brothers, he told me everything."

The Dear Leader handed Ga the revolver. "Do you recognize this?"

"It looks just like the revolver the orphan soldier described, the one they used in Texas to shoot cans off the fence. A forty-five-caliber Smith & Wesson, I believe."

"You do know him—now we are getting somewhere. But look closer, this revolver is North Korean. It was constructed by our own engineers and is actually a forty-six-caliber, a little bigger, a little more powerful than the American model—do you think it will embarrass them?"

Inspecting it, Commander Ga could see that the parts had been hand-milled on a lathe—on the barrel and cylinder were notches the smith had used to align the action. "It most certainly will, Dear Leader. I would only add that the American revolver, as my good friend the orphan soldier described it, had little grooves on the hammer, and the grips were not pearl, but carved antler of deer."

"Ah," the Dear Leader said. "This is exactly the kind of thing we're looking for, exactly." Then, from another box, he produced an Old West–style gun belt, hand-tooled and low-slung, and this he placed himself around Commander Ga's waist. "There are no bullets yet," the Dear Leader said. "These the engineers are at pains to produce, one shell at a time. For now, wear the gun, get the feel. Yes, the Americans are going to see that we can make their guns, only bigger and more powerful. We are going to serve them American biscuits, but they will discover that Korean corn is more hearty, that honey from Korean bees is more sweet. Yes, they will trim my lawn and they will ingest whatever foul cocktail I concoct, and you, Commander Ga, you will help us construct an entire Potemkin Texas, right here in Pyongyang."

"But Dear Lea—"

"The Americans," he said with a flash of anger, "will sleep with the dogs from the Central Zoo!"

Commander Ga waited a moment. When he was sure the Dear Leader felt he had been heard and understood, he said, "Yes, Dear Leader. Just tell me when the Americans visit."

"Whenever we want," the Dear Leader said. "We haven't actually contacted them yet."

"My good friend the orphan soldier, once when I visited his prison, he told me that the Americans were very reluctant to make contact with us."

"Oh, the Americans are coming," the Dear Leader said. "They're going to deliver what they took from me. They're going to get humiliated. And they're going home with nothing."

"How?" Ga asked. "How will you bring them here?"

Now the Dear Leader smiled. "That's the best part," he said.

He led Ga to the end of the curving hall, where there was a staircase.

They took metal stairs down several floors, with the Dear Leader trying to hide a limp. Soon, seeps of water ran down the walls, and the metal rail became rusted and loose. When Commander Ga leaned over the rail to see how far down the steps went, there was nothing but darkness and echoes. The Dear Leader at last stopped on a landing and opened a door to a new hall, this one much different. Here, each door they passed had a small, reinforced window and a swing-arm lock. Commander Ga knew a prison when he saw one.

"Seems pretty lonely down here," he said.

"Don't feel that way," the Dear Leader said without looking back. "You've got me."

"What about you?" Ga asked. "You come down here alone?"

The Dear Leader stopped before a door and pulled out a solitary key. He looked at Commander Ga and smiled. "I'm never alone," he said, and opened the door.

Inside the room was a tall, skinny woman, her face hidden by shaggy dark hair. Before her were spread many books, and she was writing by the light of a lamp whose cord disappeared into a hole in the cement ceiling. Silent, she gazed up at them.

"Who is she?" Commander Ga asked.

"Ask her yourself. She speaks English," the Dear Leader said, then turned to the woman. "*You bad girl*," he told her. He had a grand smile on his face. "*Bad, bad, bad girl*."

Ga approached and crouched down, so they were at eye level. "*Who are you?*" he asked in English.

She eyed the gun on his hip and shook her head, as if revealing anything might bring harm upon her.

Here, Ga saw that the books before the woman were English versions of the eleven-volume *Selected Works of Kim Jong Il*, which she was transcribing into notebooks, stacks of them, word for word. He cocked his head and saw she was transcribing a tenet from volume five, called *On the Art of the Cinema*.

"'*The Actress cannot play a role*,'" Ga read. "'*She must, in an act of martyrdom, sacrifice herself to become the character*.'"

The Dear Leader smiled in approval at the sound of his own words. "She's quite the pupil," he said.

The Dear Leader motioned for her to take a break. She set her pencil down and began rubbing her hands. This caught Commander Ga's attention. He leaned in close.

"*Will you show me your hands?*" he asked.

He extended his own hands, palms up, to demonstrate.

Slowly, she revealed them. Her hands were thick with gray, pitted calluses, rows of them, right to the pads of her fingertips. Commander Ga closed his eyes and nodded in recognition at the thousands of hours at the oars that had made her hands this way.

He turned to the Dear Leader. "How?" he asked. "Where did you find her?"

"A fishing boat picked her up," the Dear Leader said. "It was just her alone in her rowboat, no friend in sight. She'd done a bad thing to her friend, a very bad thing. The captain rescued her and set the boat ablaze." With some delight, the Dear Leader pointed a finger of naughtiness at the girl. "*Bad girl, bad,*" he said. "But we forgive her. Yes, what's past is past. Such things happen, it can't be helped. Do you think the Americans will visit now? Do you think the Senator will soon regret making my ambassadors eat without cutlery, outside, among dogs?"

"We'll have to get many specific items," Commander Ga said. "If our American welcome party is to succeed, I'll need the help of Comrade Buc."

The Dear Leader nodded.

Commander Ga returned to the woman. "*I hear you've talked to whale sharks,*" he said to her. "*And navigated by the glow of jellyfish.*"

"*It didn't happen the way they say it did,*" she said. "*She was like my sister, and now I'm alone, it's just me.*"

"What's she saying?" the Dear Leader asked.

"She says she's alone."

"Nonsense," the Dear Leader said. "I'm down here all the time. I offer her comfort."

"*They tried to board our boat,*" she said. "*Linda, my friend, she fired flares at them; it's all we had to defend ourselves with. But they kept coming, they shot her right there, right in front of me. Tell me, how long have I been down here?*"

Commander Ga removed the camera from his pocket. "May I?" he asked the Dear Leader.

"Oh, Commander Ga," the Dear Leader said, shaking his head. "You and your cameras. At least this time it's a female you're taking a picture of."

"Would you like to meet a senator?" Ga asked her.

Guardedly, she nodded.

"You keep your eyes open in this place," he said. *"No more rowing with your eyes closed. Do that and I'll bring you a senator."*

The girl flinched as Commander Ga reached to pull the hair from her face, and she was wild-eyed with fear as the camera's tiny motor whirred her into focus. And then came the flash.

WHEN OUR interns first arrived at Division 42, they were issued the standard items—field smocks, which buttoned in the front, interrogation smocks, which buttoned in the back, clipboards, and, finally, mandatory eyeglasses, which lend us an air of authority, thus further intellectually intimidating our subjects into compliance. All the members of the Pubyok team had been issued gear bags that contained items designed to brutalize and punish—abrasion gloves, rubber mallets, stomach tubes, and so on—and it's true that our interns looked disappointed when we broke the news that our team had no need for such things. But tonight, we handed Jujack a pair of bolt cutters, and you could see his face light with a sense of mission. He hefted the cutters before his eyes to find their balance point. And Q-Kee took possession of a cattle prod by rapid-firing the trigger so fast that our room strobed blue. I didn't exactly travel in elite *yangban* circles, so I had no way of knowing who this Comrade Buc fellow would turn out to be, but I was sure he'd be an important chapter in our biography of Commander Ga.

Then we all donned headlamps and surgical masks and took turns buttoning up the backs of each other's smocks before descending the ladders that led into the heart of the torture wing. As we were unscrewing the hatch that led down into the sump, Jujack asked us, "Is it true that old interrogators get sent to prison?"

Our hands stopped turning. "The Pubyok are right about one thing," we told him. "Don't ever let a subject get inside your head."

Once we were through the hatch, we sealed it behind us. Then we descended many metal rungs, protruding from the cement wall. Down here were four great pumps that pulled water from bunkers even deeper below. They activated a couple of times an hour, running for only a few minutes, but the heat and noise they generated was tremendous. This is where the Pubyok stored recalcitrant subjects, ones that were being softened by time and a humidity that steamed our lenses. A bar that ran the length of the room was bolted to the floor, and to this thirty-odd subjects were chained. The floor was sloped, for drainage, so that the poor fools on the lower side of the room slept in a skein of standing water.

Few people roused as we crossed the room through a light drizzle of warm water that dripped from a concrete ceiling that was slick with green. We held our masks tight. Last year diphtheria stole into the sump, taking all subjects and pocketing a few interrogators as well.

Q-Kee placed the prongs of the cattle prod against the iron bar and crackled off some juice—that got everyone's attention. Most of the subjects covered their faces on instinct or rolled into a baby position. A man at the end of the bar, down in the water, sat up and barked in pain. He wore a torn, soaked dress shirt, underwear, and sock suspenders around his calves. This was Comrade Buc.

We approached him and saw the vertical scar above his left eye. The wound had split the eyebrow in two, and it had healed so badly the halves of the brow missed each other. Who marries a woman that can't sew?

"Are you Comrade Buc?" we asked him.

Buc looked up, blinded by the headlamps. "What are you, the night shift?" he asked, and laughed a feeble, unconvincing laugh. He put his hands up in mock defense. "I confess, I confess," he said, but the laugh broke into a long cough—a sure sign of cracked ribs.

Q-Kee put the end of the prod in the water and pulled the trigger.

Comrade Buc was seized, while the naked man next to him rolled to one side and defecated into the black water.

"Look, we don't like this," we told Buc. "When we're in charge, we're going to close this place down."

"Oh, that's rich." Comrade Buc laughed. "You're not even in charge."

"How'd you get that scar?" we asked.

"What, this?" he asked, pointing to the wrong eyebrow.

Q-Kee lowered the prod again, but we caught her hand. She was new, she was a woman, and we understood the pressure to prove oneself, but this was not our way.

We clarified: "How'd you get that scar from Commander Ga?" we asked, and signaled Jujack to cut the chain. "Answer that question for us and we'll answer any question you like."

"A yes-or-no question," Q-Kee added.

"Yes or no?" Comrade Buc asked in confirmation.

It was a bold move from Q-Kee, ill-advised, but we had to present a unified front, so we all nodded, and with a grunt from Jujack, the good comrade's chains fell.

Comrade Buc's hands went straight to his face, to massage his eyes. We poured clean water on a handkerchief and handed it to him.

"I worked in the same building with Commander Ga," Buc said. "I did procurement, so I had my head under a black hood all day, ordering supplies on the computer. China mostly, Vietnam. Ga, he had his nice desk and a window, and he didn't do any work. This was before he began his feud with the Dear Leader, before Prison 9 burned. Back then, he didn't know anything about prisons or mines. The post was just a reward for winning the Golden Belt and for going to Japan to fight Kimura. That was a big deal after Ryoktosan went to Japan to fight Sakuraba and defected. Ga would bring me lists of things he needed, stuff like DVDs and rare bottles of rice wine."

"Did he ever ask you to order fruit?"

"Fruit?"

"Peaches, perhaps? Did he want canned peaches?"

Buc studied us. "No, why?"

"Nothing, continue."

"One day, I had worked late, it was just me and Commander Ga on the third floor. He often wore a white fighting *dobok* with a black belt, like he was in the gym, ready to spar. This night, he was leafing through magazines about taekwondo from South Korea. He liked to read illegal magazines right in front of us, saying he was studying the enemy. Just knowing about such a magazine could get you sent to Prison 15, the prison for families, the one they call Yodok. I often did the procurement for that prison. Anyway, these magazines have fold-out posters of fighters from Seoul. Ga was holding one up, appraising the fighter, when he caught me looking at him. I'd been warned about him, so I was nervous."

Q-Kee interrupted. "Was it a man who warned you or a woman?"

"Men," Comrade Buc said. "Commander Ga then stood. He had the poster in his hand. He grabbed something out of his desk and started walking toward me, and I thought, okay, I have been beaten up before, I can do this. I'd heard that once he beat you up, he never bothered you again. He began walking toward me. He was famous for his composure—

when he fought, he never showed emotion. The only time he smiled was when he executed the *dwi chagi,* where he turned his back to the opponent, inviting his offense.

"*Comrade,* Ga said to me in a very mocking tone. Then he stands there, appraising me. People think I am a sycophant to go by 'Comrade,' but I am a twin, and as is custom, we both have the same name. Our mother called us Comrade Buc and Citizen Buc to identify us. People thought it was cute—to this day, my brother is Citizen Buc."

Ah, we should have seen this information in his file. Missing it was a mistake on our part. Most people hate twins because of the procreation bonuses their families receive from the government. This explains much of Buc's exterior, and constitutes an advantage we should have exploited.

"Commander Ga," Buc continued, "held the poster out for me to view. It was just a young black belt with a dragon tattooed on his chest. *Do you like this?* Commander Ga asked. *Does it interest you?* He asked these questions in a way that implied a wrong answer, but I didn't know what that might be. *Taekwondo is an ancient and noble sport,* I told him. *And I must get home to my family.*

"*All the lessons you need to learn in life,* he said, *will be taught to you by your enemy.* Then, for the first time, I noticed that what he'd brought with him was a *dobok.* This he tossed to me. It was damp and smelled of groin. I'd heard that if you didn't fight him, he beat you up. But if you did fight back, he might do something much worse to you, something unthinkable.

"Very crisply, I said, *I do not wish to wear a dobok.*

"*Of course,* he said. *It is optional.*

"I just looked at him, trying to see in his eyes what would happen next.

"*We are vulnerable,* he told me. *We must always be ready. First let's check your core strength.* He unbuttoned my shirt and then pulled it open. He put his ear to my chest and thumped me on the sides and back. He repeated this with my stomach. He would thump me hard and say something like *Lungs clear, kidneys strong, avoid the alcohol.* Then he had to check my symmetry, he said. He had a little camera, very small, and he photographed my symmetry."

We asked Buc, "Did Commander Ga wind the film or was there a sound of a camera motor winding the film?"

"No," he said.

"No whir or anything?"

"It beeped," Buc said. "Then Commander Ga said, *The foreigner's first impulse is toward aggression.* He told me I needed to learn how to fight off this force. *Repelling foreign impulses from without is how you prepare yourself to repel them from within,* he said. The Commander then presented several scenarios like, *what would I do if the Americans landed on the roof and rappelled down the air shafts?* And *what would I do if confronted with a Japanese man attack?*

"*A man attack?* I asked him.

"He put his hand on my shoulder, pulled my arm straight, and got ahold of my hip. *A homosexual attack,* Ga said, as if I was stupid. *The Japanese are famous for this. In Manchuria, the Japanese raped everything, men, women, the pandas in the zoo.* He tripped me, and I went down, cutting my eye on the corner of a desk. That's the story, that's how I got this scar. And now the answer to my question."

Here Comrade Buc stopped, as if he knew it drove us crazy not to get an ending. "Please do continue," we suggested.

"I must have my answer first," he said. "The other interrogators, the old ones, they are always lying to me. They say, *Tell us your means of secret communication. Your children would like to see you, they're right upstairs. Talk and you may visit with your wife. She is waiting for you. Tell us your role in the plot and you can go home with your family.*"

"Our team does not use deception," we told him. "We'll answer your question, and if you like, you can verify it for yourself." We'd brought Comrade Buc's file. Jujack held it up, and Buc recognized the folder's official blue sleeve and red tab.

Comrade Buc stared at us a moment, then said, "When I fell, it was face first, and Commander Ga landed on my back. He just sat there, lecturing me. Blood filled my eye. Using his leverage, Commander Ga wrestled my right hand out, then twisted it back."

Q-Kee, wide-eyed with the story, said, "That move's called a reverse Kimura."

"You can't believe how it hurt—my shoulder, it was never the same. *Please,* I called out. *I was just working late, please, Commander Ga, let me go.* He released the hold, but continued to sit on my back. *How can you not fight off a man attack?* he asked. *For the love of everything, there's nothing worse, there's nothing more base that can happen to a man—in fact, he's not even a man after it. How could you not die trying to stop it, no matter what . . . unless you wanted it, unless you secretly wanted a man attack and that's why you failed to repel it. Well, you're lucky it was only me and not some Japanese. You're lucky I was strong enough to protect you, you should be thanking your stars I was here to stop it."*

"And that's it?" we asked. "That's where it stopped?"

Comrade Buc nodded.

"Did Commander Ga show any remorse?"

"The last thing I remember was the flash of that camera again. I was facedown, there was blood everywhere." For a moment Comrade Buc was silent—the whole room was quiet, nothing but the sound of urine trickling downhill. Then Buc asked, "Is my family alive?"

This is where the Pubyok are better at handling some things.

"I have prepared myself," Comrade Buc said.

"The answer is no," we said. We moved Buc out of the water and re-chained him uphill. Then we began gathering our gear and heading for the ladders. His eyes were looking inward, a look we're trained to recognize as a signifier of sincerity, since it's nearly impossible to fake. True self-searching cannot be imitated.

Then Buc looked up. "I will look at the file," he said.

We held it out to him. "Be careful," we warned. "There is a photo."

He paused, at the cusp of taking the folder.

We said, "The investigator said it was probably carbon monoxide poisoning. They were found in the dining room, near the heater, where they were all overtaken, before succumbing together."

"My daughters," Comrade Buc said. "Were they wearing white dresses?"

"One question," we said. "That was the deal. Unless you want to help us understand why Commander Ga pulled this stunt with the actress?"

Comrade Buc said, "Commander Ga didn't have anything to do with the missing actress—he went into Prison 33 and didn't come out. He died down there in the mine." Buc then cocked his head at us. "Wait, which Commander Ga are you talking about? There are two of them, you know. The Commander Ga who gave me the scar is dead."

"You were talking about the real Commander Ga?" we asked. "Why would the false Commander Ga apologize for what the real Commander Ga did to you?"

"He apologized?"

"The imposter told us he was sorry for your scar, for what he did to you."

"That's ridiculous," Buc said. "Commander Ga has nothing to be sorry for. He gave me the thing I wanted most, the one thing I couldn't procure for myself."

"And what was that?" we asked.

"Why, he killed the real Commander Ga, of course."

We all exchanged a glance. "So in addition to killing the actress and her children, you're saying he killed a DPRK commander as well?"

"He didn't kill Sun Moon and her children. Ga turned them into little birds and taught them a sad song. Then they flew away toward sunset, to a place where you'll never find them."

We suddenly wondered if it wasn't true, if the actress and her children weren't in hiding someplace. Ga was alive, wasn't he? But who had her, where was she being held? It was easy to make somebody disappear in North Korea. But making them reappear—who has that kind of magic?

"If you helped us, we would find a way to help you," we told Buc.

"Help you? My family is gone, my friends are gone, I'm gone. I won't ever help you."

"Okay," we said and began gathering our gear. It was late and we were wiped.

I'd noticed that Comrade Buc was wearing a wedding ring, one made of gold. I told Jujack to take it.

Jujack looked back with trepidation, then took Buc's hand and tried to shimmy it off.

"It's too tight," Jujack said.

"Hey," Comrade Buc said. "Hey, that's all I have left of them, of my wife and daughters."

"Come on," I told Jujack. "The subject doesn't need it anymore."

Q-Kee hefted the bolt cutters. "I'll get that ring off," she said.

"I hate you," Comrade Buc said. He twisted hard, cutting skin, and then the ring was in my pocket. We turned to go.

"I won't ever tell you anything," Comrade Buc yelled at us. "You have no power over me now, nothing. Do you hear me? I'm free now. You have no power over me. Are you listening to me?"

One by one, we began climbing the rungs that led out of the sump. They were slippery and required caution.

"Eleven years," Comrade Buc called out, his voice echoing off the wet cement. "Eleven years I procured for those prisons. The uniforms come in children's sizes, you know. I've ordered thousands of them. They even make a half-sized pickax. Do you have children? For eleven years, the prison doctors order no bandages and the cooks ask for no ingredients. We ship them only millet and salt, tons and tons of millet and salt. No prison has ever requested a pair of shoes or even a single bar of soap. But they must have transfusion bags right away. They must have bullets and barbed wire tomorrow! I prepared my family. They knew what to do. Are you prepared? Do you know what you would do?"

Climbing hand over hand up the galvanized steps, those of us with children tried to keep focus, but the interns, always the interns think they are invincible, right? Q-Kee led the way with her headlamp. When she stopped and looked down at the rest of us, we all stopped, too. We looked up at her, a halo of light above us.

She asked, "Ryoktosan defected?"

We were all silent. In the quiet, you could hear Buc preaching about children being stoned and hanged, going on and on.

Q-Kee let out a groan of pain and disappointment. "Ryoktosan, too," she said, shaking her head. "Is there anyone left who's not a coward?"

Then the pumps kicked in, and thankfully, we couldn't hear anything.

WHEN Commander Ga returned to Sun Moon's house, he was wearing the Western pistol on his hip. Before he could knock on the door, Brando alerted the house to his presence. Sun Moon answered in a simple *choson-ot*—its *jeogori* was white and the *chima* was patterned with pale blossoms. It was the peasant-girl dress she'd worn in the movie *A True Daughter of the Country*.

Today, she did not banish him to the tunnel. He'd been to work and now he was home, and he was greeted as a normal husband returning from the office. The son and daughter were standing at attention in their school uniforms, though they hadn't been going to school. She hadn't let them out of her sight since he'd arrived. He called the girl *girl* and the boy *boy* because Sun Moon refused to tell him their names.

The daughter held a wooden tray. On it was a steaming towel, which he used to wipe the dust from his face and neck, the backs of his hands. Upon the boy's tray were various medals and pins placed there by his father. Commander Ga emptied his pockets onto the tray—some military won, subway tickets, his Ministry ID card—and in the commingling of these everyday objects, the two Commander Gas were one. But when a coin fell to the floor, the boy flinched in fear. If the ghost of Commander Ga was anywhere, it was here, in the worried posture of the children, in the punishment they seemed convinced was continually at hand.

Next his wife held open a *dobok* like a drape, so that he could disrobe before them in privacy. When the *dobok* was cinched, Sun Moon turned to the children.

"Go," she told them. "Go practice your music."

When they were gone, she waited for the sounds of their warm-up scales before speaking, and then, when their notes seemed too soft, she made for the kitchen, where the loudspeaker was playing, and she was sure not to be overheard. He followed her, watched her cringe when she recognized that over the loudspeaker the new opera diva was singing *Sea of Blood.*

Sun Moon relieved him of his weapon. She opened the cylinder and assured herself the chambers were empty. Then she gestured at Ga with the butt of the gun. "I must know how you came by this pistol," she said.

"It's custom made," he said. "One of a kind."

"Oh, I recognize the gun," she said. "Tell me who gave it to you."

She pulled a chair to the counter and climbed atop it. She reached high to place the gun in the top cupboard.

He watched her body elongating, taking a different shape under her *choson-ot.* Its hem lifted to show her ankles, and there she was, the whole weight of her balanced upon poised toes. He regarded that cabinet, wondering what else it might contain. Commander Ga's pistol was in the backseat of the Mercedes, yet he asked, "Did your husband carry a gun?"

"Does," she said.

"Does your husband carry a gun?"

"You're not answering my question," she said. "I know the gun you brought home, we've used it in a half-dozen movies. It's the pearl-handled pistol that the cold-blooded, cowboyish American officer always uses to shoot civilians."

She stepped off the chair, and dragged it back to the table. There were marks on the floor showing this had happened many times before.

"Dak-Ho gave this to you from the prop warehouse," she said. "Either he's trying to send me some kind of message, or I don't know what's going on."

"The Dear Leader gave it to me," he said.

A pain crossed Sun Moon's face. "I can't stand that voice," she said. The new diva had made it to the aria celebrating the martyred sniper teams of Myohyang. "I have to get out of here," she said and stepped outside onto the deck.

He joined her in the warm afternoon sunlight, the view from the top of Mount Taesong encompassing all of Pyongyang. Below them swallows turned in the air above the botanical gardens. In the cemetery, old people prepared for their deaths by opening lantern-paper parasols and visiting the graves of others.

She smoked a cigarette as her eyes got wet, her makeup soon running. He stood next to her at the rail. He didn't know if you could tell whether an actress was really crying. He only knew, real or fake, the tears were not for her husband. Perhaps she wept because she was thirty-seven now or because friends no longer visited, or for the way her children in their play theater punished the puppets for talking back.

"The Dear Leader told me he was writing a new movie role for you."

Sun Moon turned her head to exhale smoke. "The Dear Leader only has room in his heart for opera now," she said, and offered him the last draw of her cigarette.

Ga took it and inhaled.

"I knew you were from the country," she said. "Look at how you hold that cigarette. What do you know of the Dear Leader or whether a new movie will happen or not?"

Ga reached for her cigarettes and lit a new one, for himself.

"I used to smoke," he said. "But in prison, I lost the habit."

"Is that supposed to mean something to me, prison?"

"They showed us a movie in there. It was *A True Daughter of the Country*."

She planted her elbows against the balcony rail and leaned back. It lifted her shoulders high, made visible the blades of her pelvis through the white of her *choson-ot*. She said, "I was just a kid when I made that movie, I didn't know anything about acting."

She gave him a look, as if to ask, how was the movie received?

"I used to live by the sea," he said. "For a short time, I almost had a wife. I mean, maybe. It could have been. She was the wife of a shipmate, quite beautiful."

"But if she was a wife, she was already married," Sun Moon said and looked at him, confused. "Why are you telling me this?"

"Oh, but her husband disappeared," Commander Ga said. "Her husband just went off into the light. In prison, when things were not so good, I tried to think of her, my almost wife, my maybe wife, to keep me strong." An image of the Captain came to him, of the Captain's wife tattooed on the Captain's ancient chest—how the once-black ink had turned blue and hazy as it migrated under the old man's skin, a watercolor where indelibility had been, leaving only the stain of the woman he loved. That's what had happened to the Second Mate's wife in prison—she'd gone out of focus, she'd seeped from his memory. "Then I saw you on the movie screen, and I realized how plain she had been. She could sing, she had ambitions, but you showed me that she was only an almost beauty, a maybe beauty. The truth was that when I thought of the missing woman in my life, it was your face that I saw."

"This almost-maybe wife," she said. "What happened to her?"

He shrugged.

"Nothing?" she asked. "You never saw her again?"

"Where would I see her?" he asked.

Though he hadn't noticed, Sun Moon perceived her children had stopped playing their instruments. She went to the door and shouted until they resumed.

She turned to him. "You should probably tell me why you were in prison."

"I went to America, where my mind was soiled by capitalist ways."

"California?"

"Texas," he said. "Where I got the dog."

She crossed her arms. "I don't like any of this," she said. "You must be part of my husband's plan, he must have sent you as some kind of stand-in—otherwise, his friends would have killed you. I don't know why you're here, saying these things to me, and no one has killed you."

She gazed toward Pyongyang, as if the answer were there. He watched emotions cross her face like weather—uncertainty, like clouds blotting the sun, gave way to a wince of regret, eyes twitching, as with the first drops of rain. She was a great beauty, it was certainly true, but he saw now that what made him fall in love with her in prison was this, the way what was felt in her heart came instantly to her face. That was the source of her great acting, this thing that couldn't be faked. You'd have to have twenty tattoos, he realized, to capture her moods. Dr. Song had made it to Texas, where he'd eaten barbecue. Gil had gotten to sip scotch and make a Japanese bartender laugh. And here he was, on Commander Ga's balcony with Sun Moon, tear streaks on her face, backdropped by Pyongyang. It didn't matter what happened to him now.

He leaned toward her. That would make the moment perfect, to touch her. Everything would be worth it if he could wipe a tear from her cheek.

She eyed him warily. "You said the husband of your almost wife. You said he disappeared, that he went off into the light. Did you kill him?"

"No," he told her. "That man defected. He escaped on a life raft. When we went to look for him, the morning sun off the ocean was so bright, it was like the light had swallowed him. He had the image of his wife tattooed on his chest, so he would always have her, even if she didn't have him. But don't worry, I won't let you become a hazy memory."

She didn't like the answer or the way he told it, he could tell. But his story was part of her story now. It couldn't be helped. He reached to touch her cheek.

"Stay away from me," she said.

"Your own husband, if you want to know, it was the darkness for him," he said. "Your husband went off into the dark."

From somewhere below came the sound of a truck engine. Vehicles rarely came up the mountain, so Ga peered down into the woods, hoping to catch sight of it through a break in the trees.

"You don't have to worry," Ga said to her. "The truth is that the Dear Leader has an assignment for me, and when that's over, I expect you won't see me again."

He looked at her, to see if she'd registered what he'd said.

"I've worked with the Dear Leader for many years," she told him. "Twelve motion pictures. I wouldn't be so sure about what he does or doesn't have in mind."

The sound grew until the engine was unmistakable, a heavy diesel with a low grind in the gearing. From the house next door, Comrade Buc stepped out onto his balcony and stared down into the woods, but he didn't need to spot the truck for a grim look to cross his face. He and Ga caught each other's eyes in a long, wary glance.

Comrade Buc called to them, "Come join us, there's little time."

Then he went inside.

"What is it?" Sun Moon asked.

Ga said, "It's a crow."

"What's a crow?"

At the railing, they waited for the truck to pass into a visible stretch of road. "There," he said when the black canvas of its canopy flashed through the trees. "That's a crow." For a moment the two of them watched the truck slowly climb the switchbacks toward their house.

"I don't get it," she said.

"There's nothing to get," he said. "That's the truck that takes you away."

In 33, he'd often fantasized about what he'd have grabbed from the aircraft hangar if he'd had even a minute's notice that he was headed for a prison mine. A needle, a nail, a razor, what he wouldn't have given for those things in prison. A simple piece of wire, and he'd have had a bird snare. A rubber band could have triggered a rat trap. How many times he longed for a spoon to eat with. But now he had other concerns.

"You take the kids into the tunnel," Ga said. "I'll go and meet the truck."

Sun Moon turned to Ga with a look of horror on her face.

"What's happening?" she asked. "Where does that truck take you?"

"Where do you think it takes you?" he asked. "There's no time. Just take the kids down. It's me they're after."

"I'm not going down there alone," she said. "I've never even been down there. You can't abandon us in some hole."

Comrade Buc came onto his balcony again. He was buttoning his collar. "Come over," he said and threw a black tie around his neck. "We are ready over here. Time is short, and you must join us."

Instead, Ga went to the kitchen and stood before the washtub on the floor. The washtub was fixed to a trapdoor that lifted to reveal the ladder down to the tunnel. Ga took a deep breath and descended. He tried not to think of the minehead of Prison 33, of entering the mine in darkness every morning and emerging from the mine in darkness each night.

Sun Moon brought the boy and the girl. Ga helped them down and pulled a string that turned on the lightbulb. When it was Sun Moon's turn at the ladder, he told her, "Get the guns."

"No," she said. "No guns."

Ga helped her down, and then closed the trapdoor. Her husband had rigged a wire that pulled the pump handle, and in this way, Ga was able to fill the tub with a few liters of water to disguise the entrance.

The four of them stood by the ladder a moment, their eyes unable to adjust as the bulb swung from its wire. Then Sun Moon said, "Come, children," and took their hands. They began walking into the darkness, only to realize that, after just fifteen meters, barely enough to get beyond the house and the road out front, the tunnel came to an end.

"Where's the rest of it?" Sun Moon asked. "Where's the way out?"

He walked a little into the darkness toward her, but stopped.

"There's no escape route?" she asked. "There's no exit?" She came to him, her eyes wheeling in disbelief. "What have you been doing down here all these years?"

Ga didn't know what to say.

"Years," she said. "I thought there was a whole bunker down here. I thought there was a system. But this is just a hole. What have you been spending your time on?" Lining the tunnel were some bags of rice and a couple of barrels of grain, their U.N. seals still unbroken. "There's not even a shovel down here," she said. Midway into the tunnel was the sole furnishing, a padded chair and a bookcase filled with rice wine and DVDs. She grabbed one and turned to him. "Movies?" she asked. Ga could tell she would scream next.

But then they all looked up—there was a vibration, the muted sound of a motor, and suddenly dirt loosened from the roof of the tunnel and fell into their faces. A sort of terror came over the children as they coughed and clutched their dirt-filled eyes. Ga walked them back toward the ladder and the light. He wiped their faces with the sleeve of his *dobok*. In the house above, they heard a door open, followed by footsteps crossing the wood floors, and suddenly the trapdoor was lifting. Sun Moon's eyes went wide with shock, and she took hold of him. When Ga looked up, there was a bright square of light. In it appeared the face of Comrade Buc.

"Please, neighbors," Comrade Buc said. "This is the first place they'll look."

He lowered a hand to Ga.

"Don't worry," Comrade Buc said. "We'll take you with us."

Commander Ga took the hand. "Let's go," he said to Sun Moon, and when she didn't move, he yelled, "Now." The little family snapped to and scrambled out of the tunnel. Together, they cut through the side yard and into Buc's kitchen.

Inside, Buc's daughters sat around a table covered in white embroidery. Buc's wife was pulling a white dress over the last daughter's head while Comrade Buc brought extra chairs for the guests. Ga could tell that Sun Moon was at the edge of unraveling, but the calmness of Buc's family wouldn't allow her to do so.

Ga and Sun Moon sat across from the Buc family, with the boy and the girl between them, the four of them dusted with dirt. In the center of the table was a can of peaches and the key to open it. They all ignored the crow idling out front. Comrade Buc passed a stack of glass dessert bowls around, and then he passed the spoons. Very carefully, he opened the peaches, so quietly you could hear the key punch and cut, punch and cut, the tin complaining as the key went around the rim in its jagged circle.

Very carefully, Buc peeled back the tin lid with a spoon, so as not to come in contact with the syrup. The nine of them sat in silence looking at the peaches. Then a soldier entered the house. Under the table, the boy took Ga's hand, and Ga gave the small hand a reassuring squeeze. When the soldier came to the table, no one moved. He had no chrome Kalashnikov, no weapon at all that Ga could tell.

Comrade Buc pretended not to see him. "All that matters is that we are together," he said, then spooned a single slice of peach into a glass bowl. This he passed, and soon a circle of glass bowls, a single peach slice in each, was rounding the table.

The soldier stood there a moment, watching.

"I'm looking for Commander Ga," he said. He seemed unwilling to believe that either of these men could be the famous Commander Ga.

"I'm Commander Ga."

Outside, they could hear a winch operating.

"This is for you," the soldier said, and handed Ga an envelope. Inside was a car key and an invitation to a state dinner that evening upon which someone had handwritten, *Would you do us the pleasure of your company?*

Outside, a classic Mustang, baby blue, was being lowered from the back of the crow. With a winch, the car crawled backward down two metal ramps. The Mustang was just like the classic cars he'd seen in Texas. He approached the car, ran a hand down its fender—though you couldn't quite see it, there were dimples and troughs attesting to how the body had been fashioned from raw metal. The bumper wasn't chrome, but plated in sterling silver, and the taillights were made from blown red glass. Ga stuck his head underneath the body—it was a web of improvised struts and welded mounts connecting a handmade body to a Mercedes engine and a Soviet Lada frame.

Comrade Buc joined him by the car. He was clearly in a great mood, relieved, exuberant. "That went great in there," he said. "I knew we wouldn't need those peaches, I just had a feeling. It's good for the kids though, dry runs like that. Practice is the key."

"What did we just practice?" Ga asked him.

Buc just smiled with amazement and handed Ga an unopened can of peaches.

"For your own rainy day," Buc said. "I helped close down Fruit Factory

49 before they burned it. I got the last case on the canning line." Buc was so impressed he shook his head. "It's like no harm can come to you, my friend," he said. "You've managed something I've never seen before, and I knew we'd be okay. I knew it."

Ga's eyes were red, his hair dusted with dirt.

"What have I managed?" he asked.

Comrade Buc gestured at the car, the house. "This," he said. "What you're doing."

"What am I doing?"

"There's no name for it," Buc said. "There's no name because no one's ever done it before."

*

The rest of the day, Sun Moon locked herself in the bedroom with the children, and there was the silence that comes only from sleep. Even the afternoon news on the loudspeaker did not wake them. Down in the tunnel, it was just Commander Ga and his dog, whose breath was foul from eating a raw onion, executing trick after trick.

Finally, when the lowering sun was rust-colored and waxen, amber-bright off the river, they emerged. Sun Moon wore a formal *choson-ot* the color of platinum, so exquisite the silk shone like crushed diamonds in one flash, then dark as lamp smudge the next. Seed pearls trimmed the *goreum*. While she prepared the tea, the children positioned themselves on elevated pallets to play their instruments. The girl began with her *gaya-geum*, obviously an antique from the days of court. Wrists erect, she plucked in the old *sanjo* way. The boy tried his best to accompany on the *taegum*. His lungs were not quite strong enough to play the demanding flute, and because his hands were too small to finger the high notes, he sang them instead.

Sun Moon kneeled before Commander Ga and began the Japanese tea ritual. She spoke as she removed the tea from an alderwood box and infused it in a bronze bowl. "These items," she said, indicating the tray, the cups, the whisk, the ladle. "Do not be fooled by them. They are not real. They are only props from my last movie, *Comfort Woman*. Sadly, it never premiered." She steeped the tea, making sure it turned clockwise in a bamboo cup. "In the movie, I must serve afternoon tea to the Japanese officers who will afterward make me their business for the rest of the evening."

He asked, "Am I the occupying force in this story?"

She turned his cup slowly in her hands, awaiting the proper infusion. Before handing it to him, she cast her breath once upon the tea, rippling the surface. The cape of her *choson-ot* spread in a shimmer around her. She passed him his tea and then bowed, down to the wooden floor, the full form of her body displaying itself.

Her cheek against the wood, she said, "It was only a movie."

While Sun Moon retrieved his finest uniform, Ga drank and listened. In the sideways light, the windows to the west gave the illusion that he could see all the way to Nampo and the Bay of Korea. The song was elegant and clean, and even the children's off notes made the music pleasingly spontaneous. Sun Moon dressed him, and then standing, pinned the appropriate medals to his chest. "This one," she said, "came from the Dear Leader himself."

"What was it for?"

She shrugged.

"Pin it at the top," he said.

She raised her eyebrows at his wisdom and complied. "And this one was presented by General Guk for unspecified acts of bravery."

Her attention and beauty had distracted him. He forgot who he was and his situation. "Do you think," he asked, "that I am brave and unspecified?"

She buttoned the breast pocket of his uniform and gave a final pull on his tie.

"I do not know," she said, "if you are a friend of my husband or an enemy. But you are a man, and you must promise to protect my children. What almost happened today, it can't happen again."

He pointed at a large medal she had not pinned on him. It was a ruby star with the golden flame of Juche behind it. "What's that one?" he asked.

"Please," she said. "Just promise me."

He nodded, and he did not leave her eyes.

"That medal was for defeating Kimura in Japan," she said. "Though really it was for not defecting afterward. The medal was just part of a package."

"A package of what?"

"This house," she said. "Your position, other things."

"Defect? Who would leave you?"

"That is a good question," she said. "But at the time, my hand was not yet Commander Ga's."

"So I beat Kimura, huh? Go ahead and pin it on me."

"No," she said.

Ga nodded, trusting her judgment.

"Should I wear the pistol?" he asked.

She shook her head.

Before leaving, they stopped to regard, behind a casing of glass and illuminated by a spotlight, the Golden Belt. The display was positioned to be the first thing a visitor noticed when entering the house. "My husband," Sun Moon said . . . but did not finish the thought.

*

Her mood lightened in the car. The sun was going down but the sky was still pale blue. Ga had driven only trucks in the military, but he got the hang of it, despite how the Mercedes engine jammed the little Lada gearbox. The interior, though, was beautiful—mahogany dash, mother-of-pearl gauges. At first, Sun Moon had wished to sit in the backseat by herself, but he talked her into the front, saying that in America the ladies drive with their men. "Do you like this car, the Mustang?" he asked her. "The Americans make the best cars. This one is quite revered there."

"I know this car," she said. "I have been in it before."

"I doubt that," Ga said. They were winding down the mountain, driving just fast enough to elude the dust cloud behind them. "This is surely the only Mustang in Pyongyang. The Dear Leader had it custom built to embarrass the Americans, to show them we could make their own car, only better, more powerful."

Sun Moon ran her hands across the upholstery. She flipped down the passenger visor, looked at herself in the mirror. "No," she said. "This is the car I was in. It was a prop in one of my movies, the one where the Americans are repelled and MacArthur is caught fleeing. This was the car the coward tried to escape in. I had a scene right here, in this seat. I had to kiss a traitor to get information. That was years ago, that movie."

Talk of movies had fouled her mood, he could tell.

They drove alongside the Revolutionary Martyrs' Cemetery. The Son-gun guard with their golden rifles had gone home for the day and in the long shadows cast by the bronze headstones moved occasional men and women. In the growing dark, these ghostly figures, keeping low and moving quickly, were gathering all the flowers from the graves.

"Always they are stealing flowers," Sun Moon remarked as they passed by. "It sickens me. My great-uncle is in there, you know. Do you know what that says to our ancestors, how it must insult them?"

Ga asked her, "Why do you think they steal the flowers?"

"Yes, that's the question, isn't it? Who would do that? What's happening to our country?"

He stole a brief glance, to confirm her disbelief. Had she never been hungry enough to eat a flower? Did she not know that you could eat daisies, daylilies, pansies, and marigolds? That hungry enough, a person could consume the bright faces of violas, even the stems of dandelions and the bitter hips of roses?

They crossed the Chongnyu Bridge, drove through the south of the city, and crossed again on the Yanggakdo. It was dinnertime, and there was wood smoke in the air. In the twilight, the Taedong River reminded him of mineshaft water, ore-dark and cold. She instructed him to take Sosong Street toward the Putong, but amid the thick apartment buildings that lined Chollima, something slammed onto the hood of their car. A gun had gone off, that's what he thought at first, or some kind of collision. Commander Ga stopped in the road, and he and Sun Moon got out, leaving their doors open.

The road was wide and unlit, there were no other cars. It was the time of evening when blues and grays grew together. People had been grilling turnips at the curb—a band of bitter smoke stood in the air, waist high. They congregated around the car to see what had happened. There on the hood was a baby goat, its horns just stubs and its eyes loose and wet. Some people looked up to the rooftops where other animals continued to graze as the first stars appeared above. There was no gore, but you could see the goat's little eyes go milky and fill with blood. Sun Moon covered her face, and Ga put his hand on her shoulder.

Suddenly, a young woman broke from the crowd. She snatched the baby goat and bolted down the street. They watched her run, the goat's bouncing head, its blood-spittle streaking down her back. The crowd, he realized, was now staring at him. He was a *yangban* in their eyes, with his fancy uniform and beautiful wife.

*

They arrived late to the Grand People's Opera House, empty save for a few dozen couples in small groups, their conversations reduced to murmurs by the huge ceilings and cascades of black silk curtains and mulberry-colored carpets. In one of the upper balconies stood a tenor. With his hands clasped, he sang "Arirang" while below, despite the drinks and delicacies, the guests attempted to find some pleasure in the hollow time before they were rewarded with the Dear Leader's spirited company.

"*Arirang, Arirang,*" the tenor sang, "*ah-rah-ree-yoh.*"

"That," Sun Moon said, "is Dak-Ho. He runs the Central Cinema Studio. But his voice, no other man's is his match."

Commander Ga and Sun Moon moved watchfully toward the couples. How beautiful she was crossing the room, taking quick, small steps, her shape so perfectly implied in the drape of Korean silk.

The men were the first to acknowledge her. In their dress uniforms and Assembly suits, they showed their gold smiles as if Sun Moon hadn't been absent from the *yangban* set for so long. They seemed indifferent to the cancellation of her movie premiere or to her arrival with a strange man in her husband's uniform, as if all these weren't signs they'd lost one of their own. The women, however, broadcast open scorn—perhaps they believed if they closed ranks against her, Sun Moon might not transmit to them the malady they feared most.

Sun Moon stopped suddenly and turned to Ga, as if overcome by an impulse to kiss him. Showing her back to those women, she looked into Ga's eyes as if looking for her own reflection. "I am a talented actress and you are my husband," she said. "I am a talented actress and you are my husband."

Ga looked into her uncertain, unseeing eyes.

"You are a talented actress," he said. "And I am your husband."

Then she turned, smiled, and they strode forward.

One man broke from the group to intercept them.

At his approach, Sun Moon stiffened. "Commander Park," she said. "How have you been?"

"Fine, thank you," he said to Sun Moon, and with a jackknife bow, he kissed her hand. Rising, he said, "And Commander Ga, how long has it been?"

Park's face was marked from a naval firefight with an ROK patrol boat.

"Too long, Commander Park, much too long."

"True," Park said. "But tell me, have you noticed something different about me?"

Ga looked at Park's uniform, at his fat rings and tie, but really he couldn't help being drawn to the striated scars on one side of his face.

"Certainly," Ga said. "The change is for the better."

"Really," Commander Park said. "I thought you would be angry—you are the most competitive person."

Ga glanced over at Sun Moon.

He thought she might be relishing this moment, but her face was fixed, wary.

Commander Park fingered a medal on his chest. "You will win your own Songun Cross one day," he said. "True, it's only given once a year, but don't let that deter you."

Ga said, "Perhaps I will be the first to win two in a row, then."

Commander Park laughed. "That's a good one, Ga. That is so like you." He placed a hand on Ga's shoulder, as if to whisper something humorous in his ear. Instead, he grabbed Ga's collar, pulling him down to deliver a vicious uppercut to Ga's midsection, a liver punch that knuckled under the ribs. Then Park strode away.

Sun Moon took hold of Ga and tried to usher him to a seat, but no, he wished to stand.

"Always men must come to that," she said.

Between shallow breaths, Commander Ga asked, "Who was that?"

Sun Moon said, "That was your best friend."

People returned to their conversations, standing in clusters near the food.

Ga held his side, then nodded. "I think I will sit," he said, and they took chairs at an empty table. Sun Moon observed every move the party-goers made, attempting, it seemed, to read their conversations by gestures only.

A woman came their way alone. She wore a cautious look on her face, but she brought Ga a glass of water. She wasn't much older than Sun Moon, yet she had tremors, so the water kept coming over the rim. In her other hand was a cocktail plate stacked with shrimp.

Ga took the glass and drank, though it hurt when the water went down.

The woman pulled from her pocket a piece of waxed paper and began placing the shrimp in it. "My husband," she said. "He is my age. He has such a good heart, that man. By heart I mean he would have intervened in that spectacle we just witnessed. No, he couldn't stand to see someone get hurt without getting involved."

Ga watched her place the shrimp one at a time on the paper. He stared at their opaque white shells and black bead eyes—these were the blind, deep-water shrimp they'd risked their lives for aboard the *Junma*.

"I can't say my husband has any distinguishing features," she continued. "Like a scar or a birthmark. He is a normal man, about forty-five, with hair going white."

Ga held his side in pain. Sun Moon, impatient, said, "Please leave us."

"Yes, yes," the woman said. She looked at Ga. "Do you think you ever saw him, in that place where you were?"

Ga set the glass down. "In the place where I was?" he asked.

"There are rumors," the woman said. "People know where you came from."

"You confuse me with someone else," he told her. "I'm not a prisoner. I'm Commander Ga. I'm the Minister of Prison Mines."

"Please," the woman said. "I must have my husband back, I can't . . . there's no point without him. His name was—"

"Don't," Sun Moon said. "Don't tell us his name."

She looked from Sun Moon to Ga. "Is it true, I mean, have you heard there's a lobotomy prison?" she asked. She held a shrimp in her shaking hand, and it wriggled mindlessly.

"What?" Ga asked.

"No," said Sun Moon. "Stop."

"You've got to help me find him. I've heard all the men are given lobotomies when they enter—they work like zombies forever."

"No surgery is needed to make a man work like that," he told her.

Sun Moon stood. She took Ga by the arm and led him away.

They blended into the crowds, mingling near the food. Then the lighting dimmed and the band began to tune its instruments. "What's happening?" he asked her.

She pointed to a yellow curtain that hung across a second-floor balcony.

"The Dear Leader will emerge there," she said and took a step away. "I must go talk to people about my movie. I must learn what happened to *Comfort Woman*."

A spotlight hit the yellow curtain, and instead of "We Shall Follow You Forever," the band began a rousing version of "The Ballad of Ryoktosan." The tenor began singing of Ryoktosan, the baby-faced giant from South Hamgyong! The farmer's boy who became the fighting king of Japan! The baby-faced giant who bested Sakuraba! Belt on his waist, all he longed for was home. His only desire a hero's return to his sweet place of birth, Korea! But our champion was stolen and murdered, stabbed by the shamefaced Japanese. A Japanese knife, dripping with urine, brought the great Ryoktosan to his knees.

Soon, the crowd joined in. They knew when to stomp their feet and double clap. A throng of cheers rose when people heard the rolling, blast-proof doors open behind the curtain. And when the yellow parted, there stood a figure, short of stature, round-bellied, wearing a white *dobok* and a mask fashioned to resemble the big baby face of Ryoktosan. The crowd went wild. Here the tiny taekwondo fighter made his way down the steps on nimble feet to run a victory lap through the crowd. He grabbed someone's cognac and swilled it through the hole in his mask. Then he made his way to Commander Ga, bowing with the utmost formality before assuming a taekwondo stance.

Commander Ga didn't know what to do. The guests began forming a large, loose circle around himself and this short man with his fists high. A spotlight was suddenly on them. The little man bobbed up and down, then approached Ga quickly, within striking distance, before backing away. Ga looked around for Sun Moon, but all he could see were the bright lights. The tiny fighter danced up to Ga and performed a series of air strikes and shadow kicks. Then, out of nowhere, the imp punched him—a quick, snapping shot to the throat.

A cheer went up, people began singing along with the ballad.

Ga grabbed his windpipe and bent over. "Please, sir," he said, but the little man had moved to the edge of the circle, where he leaned against someone's wife to catch his breath and have another drink.

Suddenly the little man backcircled in for another shot—should Ga block the punch, try to reason with the man, run?—but it was too late. Ga felt knuckles rake his eye and then his mouth was stinging and fat and then his nose went electric. He felt the hot flush, inside his head, and then the blood poured out his nose and back into his throat. Then little Ryok-tosan did a dance for everyone's pleasure, such as the Russian sailors do when on night leave from their submarines.

Ga's eyes had watered, and he couldn't see well. Yet again the small man came close—he connected with a left hook to Ga's body. Ga's pain responded on its own, sending a fist into the man's nose.

You could hear the plastic mask crumple. He took a few stagger-steps backward as blood trickled from the nostril holes and a collective gasp went up from the assembled guests. They placed him in a chair, fetched a glass of water, and then lifted his mask to reveal not the Dear Leader but a small man, weak-featured, disoriented.

The spotlight lifted to the balcony. There, clapping, was the true Dear Leader.

"Did you think it was me?" he called. "Did you think that was me?"

The Dear Leader Kim Jong Il came down the stairs, laughing, shaking people's hands, and accepting congratulations for a prank well done. He stopped to check on the little man in the *dobok*, leaning in close to inspect his wounds. "He is my driver," the Dear Leader said and shook his head at the man's nose. But a pat on the back was in order, and the Dear Leader's personal physician was summoned.

People grew quiet as the Dear Leader approached Commander Ga.

Ga saw Sun Moon turn sideways to make her way closer, so she could hear.

"No, no," the Dear Leader said. "You must stand up straight to stop the blood," and despite the pain in his midsection, Ga straightened. Then the Dear Leader took hold of Ga's nose, pinched the nostrils shut above the bridge, and drew his fingers down to squeeze out all the blood and snot.

"Did you think it was me?" he asked Ga.

Ga nodded. "I thought it was you."

The Dear Leader laughed and slung the mess off his hands. "Do not worry," he said. "The nose is not broken."

A handkerchief was handed to the Dear Leader. He wiped his hands as he addressed his guests—"He thought it was me," he announced to the delight of the room. "But I am the real Kim Jong Il, I am the real me." He pointed at his driver, whose eyes went suddenly wide. "He is the imposter, he is the one who pretends. I am the real Kim Jong Il."

The Dear Leader folded the cloth and gave it to Ga for his nose. Then he lifted Ga's arm. "And here is the real Commander Ga. He has beaten Kimura, and now he will defeat the Americans."

The Dear Leader's voice rose, as if he were speaking to all of Pyong-yang, all of North Korea. "In need of a real hero, I give you Commander Ga," he said. "In need of a national defender, I give you Commander Ga. Let's hear it for the holder of the Golden Belt!"

The applause was grand and sustained. Within it, the Dear Leader spoke to him in a low voice. "Take a bow, Commander," he said.

Hands at his sides, he bent at the waist, holding it a moment, observing drops of blood as they fell from his nose to the opera house carpet. When he rose, as if on cue a small fleet of beautiful servants emerged with trays of champagne. Above, Dak-Ho began singing "Unsung Heroes," the theme song from Sun Moon's first starring role.

Commander Ga looked to Sun Moon, and her face confirmed that she now understood that it didn't matter if her husband was alive or dead—he had been replaced and she would never see him again.

She turned, and he followed.

He caught her at an empty table, where she took a seat amid other people's coats and bags. "What about your movie?" he asked. "What did you find out?"

Her hands were shaking in front of her. "There will be no movie," she said. The sadness was pure on her face, it was the opposite of acting.

She was going to cry. He tried to comfort her, but she wouldn't have it.

"Nothing like this has ever happened to me," Sun Moon said. "And now everything has gone wrong."

"Not everything," he said.

"Yes, everything," she said. "You just don't know the feeling. You don't know what it's like to lose a movie you worked on for a year. You've never lost all your friends or had your husband taken from you."

"Don't speak this way," he told her. "There's no need to talk like this."

"This is what hunger must feel like," she said, "this hollowness inside. This is what people must feel in Africa, where they have nothing to eat."

He was suddenly repulsed by her.

"You want to know the flavor of hunger?" he demanded.

From the table's floral centerpiece, he plucked a petal from a rose. He tore off its white base, then placed the petal to her lips. "Open," he said, and when she didn't, he was rough with the word. "Open," he demanded. She parted her lips and allowed the flower in. She looked up at him with welling eyes. And here the tears spilled as slowly, slowly, she began to chew.

CITIZENS, come, gather 'round the loudspeakers in your kitchens and offices for the next installment of this year's Best North Korean Story. Have you missed an episode? They are available for playback in the languages lab of the Grand People's Study House. When last we saw the coward Commander Ga, he had been treated to his own taekwondo demonstration by the Dear Leader! Don't be fooled by the Commander's dashing uniform and cleanly parted hair—he is a tragic figure, who has far, far to fall before talk of redemption can begin.

For now, our dazzling couple was crossing Pyongyang late after an opulent party as, neighborhood by neighborhood, substation power switches were being thrown to cast our sweet city into slumber. Commander Ga drove, while Sun Moon leaned with the turns.

"I'm sorry about your movie," he said.

She didn't respond. Her head was turned toward the darkening buildings.

He said, "You can make another."

She dug through her purse, and then in frustration closed it.

"My husband never let me run out of cigarettes, not once," she said. "He had some special hiding place for the cartons, and every morning, there was a fresh pack under my pillow."

The Pyongchon eating district extinguished as they drove through it, and then one, two, three, the housing blocks along Haebangsan Street went black. Nighty-night, Pyongyang. You earned it. No nation sleeps as North Korea sleeps. After lights-out, there is a collective exhale as heads hit pillows across a million households. When the tireless generators wind down for the night and their red-hot turbines begin to cool, no lights glare on alone, no refrigerator buzzes dully through the dark. There's just eye-closing satisfaction and then deep, powerful dreams of work quotas fulfilled and the embrace of reunification. The American citizen, however, is wide awake.

You should see a satellite photo of that confused nation at night—it's one grand swath of light, glaring with the sum of their idle, indolent evenings. Lazy and unmotivated, Americans stay up late, engaging in television, homosexuality, and even religion, anything to fill their selfish appetites.

The city was in full darkness as they drove by the Hyoksin line's Rakwan station. Their headlights momentarily illuminated an eagle owl atop the subway's vent shaft, its beak at work on a fresh lamb. It would be easy, dear citizens, to feel for the poor lamb, plucked so young from life. Or the mama sheep, all her love and labor for nothing. Or even the eagle owl, whose duty it is to live by devouring others. Yet this is a happy story, citizen: by the loss of the inattentive and disobedient lamb, the ones on other rooftops are made stronger.

They began making their way up the hill, passing the Central Zoo, where the Dear Leader's own Siberian tigers were on display next to the pen that housed the zoo's six dogs, all gifts from the former king of Swaziland. The dogs were kept on a strict diet of soft tomatoes and kimchi to lessen that animal's inherent danger, though they will become meat-eaters again when it comes time for the Americans to visit!

In the headlights they saw a man running from the zoo with an ostrich egg in his hands. Chasing him up the hill with flashlights were two watchmen.

"Do you feel for the man hungry enough to steal?" Commander Ga asked as they drove by. "Or for the men who must hunt him down?"

"Isn't it the bird who suffers?" Sun Moon asked.

They passed the cemetery, which was dark, as was the Fun Fair, its gondola chairs hanging pure black against a blue-black sky. Only the botanical gardens were lighted. Here, even at night, work on the hybrid crop program continued, the precious seed vault protected from an American invasion by a grand electric fence. Ga glanced at a cone of moths, high in protein, circling in a security light, and he became melancholy as he drove slowly up this last stretch of dirt road.

"This is a fine automobile," he said. "I will miss it."

By this, the Commander meant that, though our nation produces the finest vehicles in the world, life is transient and subject to hardships, which is the entire reason the Dear Leader has given us Juche philosophy.

"I'll pass your sentiments along," Sun Moon said, "to the next man who finds himself driving it."

Here, the good actress is agreeing that the car is not theirs, but rather is the property of the citizens of the Democratic People's Republic of Korea and the Dearest General who leads us. She is wrong, however, to suggest that she does not belong to her husband, for a wife has certain obligations, and to these she is bound.

Commander Ga pulled up before the house. The dust cloud that had been trailing them now caught up, ghostly in the headlights and the front door they illuminated. Sun Moon stared at this door with uncertainty, trepidation.

"Is this a dream?" Sun Moon asked. "Tell me it's only a movie I'm in."

But enough of your moods, the two of you! It's time for sleep. Off to bed, now . . .

Oh, Sun Moon, our heart never stops going out to you!

Let us all repeat together: We miss you, Sun Moon!

Finally, citizens, a warning that tomorrow's installment contains an adult situation, so protect the ears of our littlest citizens as the actress Sun Moon decides whether she will open herself fully to her new husband Commander Ga, as is required by law of a wife, or whether she will make a misguided declaration of chastity.

Remember, female citizens, however admirable it may be to remain chaste to a missing husband, such a sense of duty is misplaced. Whenever a loved one disappears, there is bound to be a lingering hurt. The Americans have the saying "Time heals all wounds." But this is not true. Experiments have shown that healing is hastened only by self-criticism sessions, the inspirational tracts of Kim Jong Il, and replacement persons. So when the Dear Leader gives you a new husband, give yourself to him. Still: We love you, Sun Moon!

Again: We love you, Sun Moon!

Show your vigor, citizens.

Repeat: We admire you, Sun Moon!

Yes, citizens, that's better.

Louder: We emulate your sacrifice, Sun Moon!

Let the Great Leader Kim Il Sung himself hear you in heaven!

All together: We will bathe in the blood of the Americans who came to our great nation to hurt you!

But we get ahead of ourselves. That is for a future episode.

HOME FROM the Dear Leader's party, Commander Ga studied Sun Moon's evening routine. First, she lit an oil lantern, the kind they place on the beaches of Cheju so night fishermen can navigate their skiffs. She let the dog inside, then checked the bedroom to see that the children were asleep. When she did, she left the doors open for the first time. Inside, by the glow of her lamp, he saw a low mattress and rolled ox-hair mats.

In the dark kitchen, he pulled a bottle of Ryoksong from the cool place under the sink. The beer was good, and the bottle soothed his stiffening hand. He didn't want to see what his face looked like. She inspected his knuckles, a little fan of yellow beginning to show.

"I have nursed many broken hands," she said. "This is only a sprain."

"You think that driver was okay? It looked like I broke his nose."

She shrugged. "You have chosen to impersonate a man dedicated to violence," she said. "These things happen."

"You've got it backward," he answered. "Your husband chose me."

"Does it matter? You're him now, aren't you? Commander Ga Chol Chun—is that what I should call you?"

"Look at how your children hide their eyes, how they're afraid to move. I don't want to be the man who taught them that."

"Tell me, then. What should I call you?"

He shook his head.

Her face agreed it was a difficult problem.

The lamp's light cast shadows that gave form to her body. She leaned against the counter and stared at the cabinets as if she were seeing the contents inside. But really she was looking the other way, into herself.

"I know what you're thinking," he said.

"That woman," she said. "I haven't been able to get her out of my head."

He'd thought, by the look on her face, that she was somehow blaming herself for things, which was something the Captain said his wife always did. But the moment she mentioned that woman, he knew exactly what Sun Moon was talking about.

"That was foolish, that talk about lobotomies," he said. "There is no such prison. People start rumors like that out of fear, out of not knowing."

He took a drink of beer. He opened and closed his jaw, moved it side to side to assess the damage to his face. Of course there was a zombie prison—he knew it must be true the second he'd heard it. He wished he could ask Mongnan about it—she'd know, she'd tell him all about the lobotomy factory, and she'd tell it in a way that made you certain you were the luckiest person in the world, that your lot in life was pure gold compared to others'.

"If you're worried about your husband, about what happened to him, I'll tell you the story."

"I don't want to talk about him," she said. She bit one of her fingernails. "You mustn't let me run out of cigarettes again, you must promise." She retrieved a glass from the cupboard and set it on the counter. "This is the time of evening when you pour me some rice wine," she told him. "That is one of your duties."

With the lamp, he went down into the tunnel to retrieve a bottle of rice wine, but he found himself looking at the DVDs instead. He ran his fingers along the movies, looking for one of hers, but there were no Korean films, and soon titles like *Rambo, Moonstruck,* and *Raiders of the Lost Ark* flipped the switch in his brain to read English and he couldn't stop skimming the rows. Suddenly, Sun Moon was by his side.

"You left me in the dark," she said. "You have a lot to learn about how to treat me."

"I was looking for one of your movies."

"Yes?"

"But there aren't any."

"Not one?" She studied the rows of titles. "All these movies he had and not one by his own wife?" she asked, confused. She pulled one off the shelf. "What movie is this?"

Ga looked at the cover. "It's called *Schindler's List.*" "Schindler" was a difficult word to say.

She opened the case and looked at the DVD, how its surface shined against the light.

"These are stupid," she said. "Movies are the property of the people, not for a single person to hoard. If you'd like to see one of my films go to the Moranbong Theater, they never stop playing there. You can see a Sun Moon film with peasant and politburo alike."

"Have you seen any of these?"

"I told you," she said. "I'm a pure actress. These things would only corrupt me. I'm perhaps the only pure actress in the world." She grabbed another movie and waved it at him. "How can people be artists when they act for money? Like the baboons in the zoo who dance at their tethers for heads of cabbage. I act for a nation, for an entire people." She looked suddenly crestfallen. "The Dear Leader said I was going to act for the world. You know he gave me this name. In English, Sun means *hae* and Moon means *dal,* so I'd be night and day, light and dark, celestial body and its eternal satellite. The Dear Leader said that would make me mysterious to American audiences, that the intense symbolism would speak to them."

She stared at him.

"But they don't watch my movies in America, do they?"

He shook his head. "No," he said. "I don't believe they do."

She returned *Schindler's List* to the shelf. "Get rid of these," she said, "I don't want to see them again."

"How did he watch them, your husband?" he asked. "You don't have a player."

She shrugged.

"Did he have a laptop?"

"A what?"

"A computer that folds up."

"Yes," she said, "but I haven't seen it in a while."

"Wherever the laptop is hiding," he told her, "I bet your cigarettes are there, too."

"It's too late for wine," she said. "Come, I will turn down the sheets."

*

The bed faced a large window that displayed the darkness of Pyongyang. She left the lamp burning on a side table. The children slept on a pallet at the foot, the dog between them. On the mantel above, out of the children's reach, was the can of peaches Comrade Buc had given them. In the low light, they undressed, stripping to their undergarments. When they were under the sheets, Sun Moon spoke.

"Here are the rules," she said. "The first is that you will begin work on the tunnel, and you will not stop until there is a way out. I'm not getting trapped again."

He closed his eyes and listened to her demand. There was something pure and beautiful about it. If only more people in life said, *This is what I must have.*

She eyed him, to make sure he was listening. "Next, the children will reveal their names to you only when they decide."

"Agreed," he said.

Far below, dogs began baying in the Central Zoo. Brando whimpered in his sleep.

"And you cannot ever use taekwondo on them," she said. "You will never make them prove their loyalty, you will never test them in any way." She trained her eyes on him. "Tonight you discovered that my husband's friends are happy to hurt you in public. It is still within my power to have one person crippled in this world."

From the botanical gardens down the hill came an intense blue flash that filled the room. There's no arc quite like a human meeting an electric fence. Sometimes birds set off the fence in Prison 33. But a person—a deep-humming blue snap—that was a light that came through your eyelids and a buzz that entered your bones. In his barracks, that light, that sound, woke him up every time, though Mongnan said after a while you stop noticing.

"Are there other rules?" he asked.

"Only one," she said. "You will never touch me."

In the dark, there was a long silence.

He took a deep breath.

"One morning, they lined up all the miners," he said. "There were about six hundred of us. The Warden approached. He had a black eye, a fresh one. There was a military officer with him—tall-brimmed hat, lots of medals. This was your husband. He told the Warden to have us all re-move our shirts."

He paused, waiting to see if Sun Moon would encourage the story or not.

When she didn't speak, he went on. "Your husband had an electronic device. He went down the rows of men, pointing it at their chests. When held up to most men, the box was silent. But for some, it made a staticky sound. This was what happened to me, when he aimed the device at my lungs, it crackled. He asked me, *What part of the mine do you work in?* I told him the new tier, down in the subfloor. He asked me, *Is it hot down there, or cold?* I told him *Hot.*

"Ga turned to the Warden. *That's enough proof, yes? From now on, all work will focus on that part of the mine. No more digging for nickel and tin.*

"*Yes, Minister Ga,* the Warden said.

"It was only then that Commander Ga seemed to notice the tattoo on my chest. A disbelieving smile crossed his face. *Where did you get that?* he asked me.

"*At sea,* I said.

"He reached out and held my shoulder so that he could get a good look at the tattoo over my heart. I hadn't bathed in almost a year, and I'll never forget the look of his white, buffed fingernails against my skin. *Do you know who I am?* he asked. I nodded. *Do you want to explain that tattoo to me?*

"All the choices that came to me seemed like bad ones. *It's pure patriotism,* I finally said, *toward our nation's greatest treasure.*

"Ga took some pleasure in that answer. *If you only knew,* he told me. Then he turned to the Warden. *Did you hear that?* Ga asked him. *I think I have discovered the only damn heterosexual in this whole prison.*

"Ga took a closer look at me. He lifted my arm and noticed the burn marks from my pain training. *Yes,* he said in recognition. Then he took hold of my other arm. He turned it so he could study the circle of scars. Intrigued, he said, *Something happened here.*

"Then Commander Ga took a step back, and I could see his rear foot go light. I lifted my arm just in time to block a lightning-fast head kick. *That's what I was looking for,* he said.

"By resetting his teeth, Commander Ga made a piercing whistle, and we could see that on the other side of the prison gate, Ga's driver opened the trunk to his Mercedes. The driver pulled something out of the trunk, and the guards opened the gate for him. He came our way, and whatever he had, it was extremely burdensome.

"*What's your name?* Ga asked me. *Wait, I don't need it. I'll know you by this.* He touched my chest with a lone finger. He said to me, *Have you ever seen the Warden set foot in the mine?*

"I looked at the Warden, who glared at me. *No,* I told Commander Ga.

"The driver came to us, carrying a large white stone. It must have weighed twenty-five kilos. *Take it,* Commander Ga told the Warden. *Lift it up, so everyone can see it,* and with much difficulty, the Warden worked the stone up to his shoulder, where it perched, bigger than his head. Commander Ga then pointed the detector at the stone, and we all heard the machine go wild, ticking with energy.

"Commander Ga said to me, *Look how it's white and chalky. This rock is all we care about now. Have you seen some rock like it in the mine?* I nodded. That made him smile. *The scientists said this was the right kind of mountain, that this stuff should be down there. Now I know it is.*

"*What is it?* I asked him.

"*It's the future of North Korea,* he said. *It's our fist down the Yankees' throat.*

"Ga turned to the Warden. *This inmate is now my eyes and ears around this place,* he said. *I'll be back in a month, and nothing will happen to him in the meantime. You're to treat him how you'd treat me. Do you hear? Do you know what happened to the last warden of this prison? Do you know what I had done to him?* The Warden said nothing.

"Commander Ga handed me the electronic machine. *I want to see a white mountain of this when I return,* he said. *And if the Warden sets this rock down before I get back, you're to tell me. For nothing is he to let go of that rock, you hear? At dinner, that rock sits on his lap. When he sleeps, it rises and falls on his chest. When he takes a shit, the rock shits, too.* Ga pushed the Warden, who stumbled to keep his balance under the load. Then Commander Ga made a fist—"

"Stop," Sun Moon said. "That's him. I recognize my husband."

She was quiet a moment, as if digesting something. Then she turned to him in the bed, bridging the space between them. She lifted the sleeve of his nightshirt, fingered the ridges of the scars on his biceps. She put her hand flat on his chest, spreading her fingers across the cotton.

"It's here?" she asked. "Is this the tattoo?"

"I'm not sure you want to see it."

"Why?"

"I'm afraid it will frighten you."

"It's okay," she said. "You can show me."

He pulled off his shirt, and she leaned close to observe in the low light this portrait of herself, forever fixed in ink, a woman whose eyes still burned with self-sacrifice and national fervor. She studied the image as it rose and fell on his chest.

"My husband. A month later he came back to the prison, yes?"

"He did."

"And he tried to do something to you, something bad, didn't he?"

He nodded.

She said, "But you were stronger."

He swallowed.

"But I was stronger."

She reached to him, her palm coming lightly to rest on his tattoo. Was it this image of the woman she once was that made her fingers tremble? Or did she feel for this man in her bed who'd quietly started weeping for reasons she didn't understand?

I ARRIVED home from Division 42 tonight to discover that my parents' vision had become so bad that I had to inform them night had fallen. I helped them to their cots, placed side by side near the stove, and, once settled, they stared at the ceiling with their blank eyes. My father's eyes have gone white, but my mother's are clear and expressive, and I sometimes suspect that maybe her vision isn't as ruined as his. I lit a bedtime cigarette for my father. He smokes Konsols—that's the kind of man he is.

"Mother, Father," I said. "I have to go out for a while."

My father said, "May the everlasting wisdom of Kim Jong Il guide you."

"Obey the curfew," my mother said.

I had Comrade Buc's wedding ring in my pocket.

"Mother," I said. "Can I ask you a question?"

"Yes, son."

"How come you never found a bride for me?"

"Our first duty is to country," she said. "Then to leaders, then to—"

"I know, I know," I said. "Then to Party, then to the Charter of the Workers' Assembly, and so on. But I was in the Youth Brigade, I studied Juche Idea at Kim Il Sung University. I did my duty. It's just that I have no wife."

"You sound troubled," my father said. "Have you spoken to our housing block's Songun advisor?" I saw the fingers twitch on his right hand. When I was a boy, one of his gestures was to reach out with that hand to ruffle my hair. That's how he would reassure me when neighbors went away or we witnessed MPSS men pulling citizens off the subway. So I knew he was still in there, that despite the distemper of his patriotism, my father was still my father, even if he felt the need to hide his true self from everyone, even me. I blew out the candle.

When I left, though, when I stepped out into the hall and closed the door and turned the lock, I didn't walk away. Quietly, I placed my ear to the door and listened. I wanted to know if they could be themselves, if they could let down their guard when they were finally alone in a dark and silent room and could speak as husband and wife. I stood like that a long time, but heard nothing.

Outside on Sinuiju Street, even in the dark, I could see that troops of Juche girls had chalked the sidewalks and walls with revolutionary slogans. I heard a rumor that one night an entire troop fell into an unmarked construction pit on Tongol Road, but who knows if that's true. I headed for the Ragwon-dong district, where long ago the Japanese built slums to house the most defiant Koreans. That's where there's an illegal night market at the base of the abandoned Ryugyong Hotel. Even in the darkness, the outline of the hotel's rocket-shaped tower stands black against the stars. As I crossed the Palgol Bridge, pipes were dumping sewage from the backs of pastel housing blocks. Like gray lily pads, shit-streaked pages of the *Rodong Sinmun* newspaper slowly spread across the water.

The deals take place around the rusted elevator shafts. Guys on the ground floor arrange terms and then yell up the shaft to cohorts who deliver the goods—medicines, ration books, electronics, travel passes—with buckets on ropes. A few guys didn't like the looks of me, but one was willing to talk. He was young, and his ear had been notched by MPSS agents who'd picked him up for pirating before. I handed him Commander Ga's phone.

Real quick, he opened the back, pulled the battery, licked its contacts, then checked the number on the internal card. "This is good," he said. "What do you want for it?"

"We're not selling it. We need a charger for it."

"We?"

"Me," I said. I showed him Comrade Buc's ring.

He laughed at the ring. "Unless you're selling the phone, get out of here."

Several years ago, after an April Fifteenth ceremony, the whole Pubyok team got drunk, and I took the opportunity to lift one of their badges. It came in handy every now and then. I pulled it out now and let it gleam in the dark. "We need a phone charger," I said. "You want your other ear notched?"

"Little young to be a Pubyok, aren't you?"

The kid was half my age.

With my authority voice, I said, "Times change."

"If you were Pubyok," he said, "my arm would already be broke."

"Pick the arm, and I'll oblige," I said, but even I didn't believe me.

"Let me see this," he said and took the badge. He studied its image of a floating wall, felt the weight of the silver, ran his thumb against the leather backing. "Okay, Pubyok," he said. "I'll get your phone charger, but keep the ring." He flashed the badge at me. "I trade for this."

∗

The next morning, a pair of dump trucks pulled up and offloaded mounds of dirt on the sidewalks outside the Glory of Mount Paektu Housing Block, 29 Sinuiju Street. My work at Division 42 usually got me out of tasks like this, but not this time, the housing committee manager told me. Grass into Meat was a citywide campaign, it was out of his hands. The manager was generally leery of me because I'd had a few of the tenants sent away, and he thought I lived on the top floor out of paranoia, rather than to protect my parents from some of the building's bad influences.

I found myself in a two-day human chain that moved buckets and jerry cans and shopping bags filled with earth up the stairwell to the roof. Sometimes there was a voice in my head that narrated events as they unfolded, as if it were writing my biography as I was living it, as if the audience for such a life's story was only me. But I rarely got the chance to put this voice to paper—by the end of the second day, when I got down to the first floor and found myself last in line to bathe in what was now cold, gray water, the voice had vanished.

For my parents, I cooked spicy turnips with some mushrooms that an old widow on the second floor grew in kimchi jars. The power was spotty, so it seemed as though the amber light on the phone charger would never switch to green. My mother informed me that on the golf course, with the Foreign Minister of Burundi, Kim Jong Il had shot eleven holes in one. News of all the poverty in South Korea had my father depressed. The loudspeaker had broadcast a big story about starvation down there. *The Dear Leader is sending them aid,* he told me. *I hope they can hang on until reunification.* The mushrooms made my urine rusty pink.

Now that the roof was covered with twenty centimeters of soil, all I could think about was getting back to Division 42 to see if Commander Ga was on the road to recovery.

"Not so fast," my housing-block manager told me the next morning. He pointed off the edge of the roof to a truck full of goats below. Because my parents were infirm, I'd have to do their share. Certainly a rope and pulley would have worked best. But not everybody around here went to Kim Il Sung University. Instead, we carried them over our shoulders, holding their legs out in front like handles. They'd fight like mad for about ten floors, but then succumb to the darkness of the cement stairwell and finally lower their heads in closed-eyed resignation. Even though the goats appeared to be in a state of total submission, I could tell they were alert and alive because of what you couldn't see, what you could only feel against the back of your neck: their fast little hearts, fluttering like mad.

It would take weeks for the grass to grow, so a team was formed to make daily missions to Mansu Park to gather foliage for the goats to eat. The manager knew not to push his luck with me. We watched the goats warily circle the roof. One of the little ones got boxed against the ledge and was squeezed off. It was vocal all the way down, but the rest of the goats acted as if it never happened.

I skipped my bath so I could race to the Yanggakdo market. It was shameful how little I got for Comrade Buc's ring. It seemed that everyone had a wedding ring for sale. Reeking of goat, I rode the subway home with a summer squash, some dried squid, a paper bag filled with Chinese peanuts, and a five-kilo sack of rice. You can't help but notice how people on the metro have a way of giving you the stink-eye without even glancing your way.

I made a feast for my parents, and we were all in high spirits. I lit a second candle for the occasion. In the middle of dinner, the amber light on the charger turned green. I guess I'd imagined standing on the roof under the stars when I placed my first call with Commander Ga's phone, like I'd behold the whole universe as I first employed a device that could reach any person on earth. Instead, I toyed with it while we ate, scrolling through the menus. The phone used the Roman alphabet, but I was only looking for numbers, and there was no record of calls coming in or going out.

My father heard the tones that the buttons made. "Have you got something there?" he asked.

"No," I told him.

For a moment, it felt as though my mother glanced at the phone, but when I looked, she was staring straight ahead savoring the fluffy white rice—ration cards for rice had stopped months ago, and we'd been living a long time on millet. They used to ask where I got the money for black-market food, but they don't anymore. I leaned toward my mother. I held the phone up and slowly passed it back and forth before her eyes. If she perceived the phone, she showed no sign.

I returned to the keypad. It wasn't that I didn't know anyone's phone number—I didn't—it was that only at this moment did I realize I had no one to call. There wasn't a woman, a colleague, or even a relative that I had to contact. Didn't I have a single friend?

"Father," I said. He was eating the salty peanuts toasted with chilies that he loved. "Father, if you were to contact someone, anyone, who would it be?"

"Why would I contact anyone?" he asked. "I have no need."

"It's not need," I said. "It's want, like you'd want to call a friend or a relative."

"Our Party comrades fulfill all our needs," my mother said.

"What about your aunt?" I asked my father. "Don't you have an aunt in the South?"

My father's face was blank, expressionless. "We have no ties to that corrupt and capitalist nation," he said.

"We denounce her," my mother said.

"Hey, I'm not asking as a state interrogator," I told them. "I'm your son. This is just family talk."

They ate in silence. I returned to the phone, moving through its functions, all of which seemed disabled. I dialed a couple of random numbers, but the phone wouldn't connect to the network, even though I could see the cellular tower from our window. I turned the volume up and down, but the ringer wouldn't sound. I tried to employ the little camera feature, but it refused to snap a photo. It looked like I would be selling the thing after all. Still, it irked me that I couldn't think of one person to call. I went through a mental list of all my professors, but my two favorites got sent to labor camps—it really hurt to add my signature to their writ of sedition, but I had a duty, I was already an intern at Division 42 by then.

"Hey, wait, I remember," I said. "When I was a boy, there was a couple. They'd come over and the four of you would play cards late into the night. Aren't you curious what happened to them? Wouldn't you contact them if you could?"

"I don't believe I've heard of these people," my father said.

"I'm sure of it," I told him. "I remember them clearly."

"No," he said. "You must be mistaken."

"Father, it's me. There's no one else in the room. No one is listening."

"Stop this dangerous talk," my mother said. "We met with no one."

"I'm not saying you met with anyone. The four of you would play cards after the factory closed. You would laugh and drink *shoju*." I reached to take my father's hand, but the touch surprised him, and he recoiled. "Father, it's me, your son. Take my hand."

"Do not question our loyalties," my father said. "Is this a test?" he asked me. He looked white-eyed around the room. "Are we being tested?" he asked the air.

There is a talk that every father has with his son in which he brings the child to understand that there are ways we must act, things we must say, but inside, we are still us, we are family. I was eight when my father had this talk with me. We were under a tree on Moranbong Hill. He told me that there was a path set out for us. On it we had to do everything the signs commanded and heed all the announcements along the way. Even if we walked this path side by side, he said, we must act alone on the outside, while on the inside, we would be holding hands. On Sundays the factories were closed so the air was clear, and I could imagine this path ahead stretching across the Taedong Valley, a path lined with willows and vaulted by singular white clouds moving as a group. We ate berry-flavored ices and listened to the sounds of old men at their *chang-gi* boards and slapping cards in a spirited game of go-stop. Soon my thoughts were of toy sailboats, like the ones the *yangban* kids were playing with at the pond. But my father was still walking me down that path.

My father said to me, "I denounce this boy for having a blue tongue."

We laughed.

I pointed at my father. "This citizen eats mustard."

I had recently tried mustard root for the first time, and the look on my face made my parents laugh. Everything mustard was now funny to me.

My father addressed an invisible authority in the air. "This boy has counterrevolutionary thoughts about mustard. He should be sent to a mustard-seed farm to correct his mustardy thinking."

"This dad eats pickle ice with mustard poop," I said.

"That was a good one. Now take my hand," he told me. I put my small hand in his, and then his mouth became sharp with hate. He shouted, "I denounce this citizen as an imperialist puppet who should be remanded to stand trial for crimes against the state." His face was red, venomous. "I have witnessed him spew capitalist diatribes in an effort to poison our minds with his traitorous filth."

The old men turned from their game to observe us.

I was terrified, on the verge of crying. My father said, "See, my mouth said that, but my hand, my hand was holding yours. If your mother ever must say something like that to me, in order to protect the two of you, know that inside, she and I are holding hands. And if someday you must say something like that to me, I will know it's not really you. That's inside. Inside is where the son and the father will always be holding hands."

He reached out and ruffled my hair.

*

It was the middle of the night. I couldn't sleep. I'd try to sleep, but I'd just lie on my cot puzzling over how Commander Ga had managed to change his life and become someone else. With no record of who he'd been. How do you escape your Party Aptitude Test score or elude twelve years of your teachers' Rightness of Thinking evaluations? I could sense that Ga's hidden history was chaptered with friends and adventures, and I was jealous of that. It didn't matter to me that he had probably killed the woman he loved. How had he found love itself? How had he pulled that off? And had love made him become someone else, or, as I suspected, had love suddenly appeared once he took on a new identity? I suspected that Ga was the same person on the inside but had a whole new exterior. I could respect that. But wouldn't the real change be, if a person was to go all the way, to get a new inner life?

There wasn't even a file for this Commander Ga character—I only had Comrade Buc's. I'd toss and turn for a while, wondering how Ga was so at peace, and then I'd relight my candle and pore over Buc's file. I could tell my parents were awake, lying perfectly still, breathing evenly, listening to me as I rifled Comrade Buc's file for any insight into Ga's identity. I was jealous for the first time of the Pubyok, of their ability to get answers.

And then there came a single clear sound from the phone. *Bing,* it rang.

I heard the creak of canvas as my parents stiffened in their cots.

The phone on the table began to blink with a bright green light.

I took the phone in my hands and opened it. On its little screen was an image, a photo of a sidewalk, and set in the pavement was a star and in the star were two words in English, "Ingrid" and "Bergman." It was daylight where this photo was taken.

I turned again to Comrade Buc's file, looking for any images that might contain such a star. There were all the standard photos—his Party commission, receiving his Kim Il Sung pin at sixteen, his oath of eternal affiliation. I flipped to the photo of his dead family, heads thrown back, contorted on the floor. And yet so pure. The girls in their white dresses. The mother draping an arm over the older girls while holding the hand of the youngest. I felt a pang at the sight of her wedding ring. It must have been a hard time for them, their father newly arrested, and here at some formal family moment without him, they succumbed to "possibly carbon monoxide." It's hard to imagine losing a family, to have someone you love just disappear like that. I understood better now why Buc had warned us in the sump to be ready, to have a plan in place. I listened to the silence of my parents in that dark room, and I wondered if I shouldn't have a plan in place for when I lost one of them, if that's what Buc meant.

Because Comrade Buc's family was clustered on the floor, the eye was naturally drawn there. For the first time I noticed that sitting on the table above them was a can of peaches, a small detail in relation to the entire photo. The can's jagged lid was bent back, and I understood then that the method Commander Ga would use to excuse himself from the rest of his biography, whenever he felt like it, was sitting on his bedside table.

*

At Division 42, a strip of light was shining underneath the door to the Pubyok lounge. I slipped quietly past—with those guys, you never knew if they were staying late or arriving early.

I found Commander Ga sleeping peacefully, but his can of peaches was gone.

I shook him awake. "Where are the peaches?" I asked him.

He rubbed his face, ran a hand through his hair. "Is it day or night?" he asked.

"Night."

He nodded. "Feels like night."

"Peaches," I said. "Is that what you fed to the actress and her kids? Is that how you killed them?"

Ga turned to his table. It was empty. "Where are my peaches?" he asked me. "Those are special peaches. You've got to get them back before something terrible happens."

Just then, I saw Q-Kee walk past in the hall. It was three thirty in the morning! The shock-work whistles wouldn't blow for another two hours. I called to her, but she kept going.

I turned to Ga. "You want to tell me what a Bergman is?"

"A Bergman?" he asked. "I don't know what you're—"

"How about an Ingrid?"

"There's no such word," he said.

I stared at him a moment. "Did you love her?"

"I still love her."

"But how?" I asked him. "How did you get her to love you back?"

"Intimacy."

"*Intimacy*? What is that?"

"It's when two people share everything, when there are no secrets between them."

I had to laugh. "No secrets?" I asked him. "It's not possible. We spend weeks extracting entire biographies from subjects, and always when we hook them up to the autopilot, they blurt out some crucial detail we'd missed. So getting every secret out of someone, sorry, it's just not possible."

"No," Ga said. "She gives you her secrets. And you give her yours."

I saw Q-Kee walk past again, this time she was wearing a headlamp. I left Ga to catch up with her—she had a hallway-length lead on me. "What are you doing here in the middle of the night?" I called to her.

Echoing through the halls, I heard her answer, "I'm dedicated."

I caught up with her in the stairwell, but she wasn't slowing. In her hands, she had a device from the shop, a hand pump connected to a section of rubber tubing. It's used to irrigate and drain a subject's stomach—organ swelling from force-induced fluids being the third most painful of all coercion tactics.

"Where are you going with that?" I asked.

Flight after flight, we spiraled deeper into the building.

"I don't have time," she said.

I grabbed her hard by the elbow and spun her. She didn't look used to that treatment.

"I made a mistake," she said. "But really, we have to hurry."

Down two more flights, we came to the sump and the hatch was open.

"No," I said. "Don't tell me."

She disappeared down the ladder, and when I followed, I could see Comrade Buc writhing on the floor, a spilled can of peaches beside him. Q-Kee was fighting his convulsions to get the tube down his throat. Black saliva streamed from his mouth, his eyes were drooping, sure signs of botulism poisoning.

"Forget it," I said. "The toxin's already in his nervous system."

She grunted in frustration. "I know, I screwed up," she said.

"Go on."

"I shouldn't have, I know," she said. "It's just that, he knows everything."

"Knew."

"Yes, knew." She looked like she wanted to kick Buc's shuddering body. "I thought if I could take a crack at him, then we'd figure this whole thing out. I came down here and asked him what he wanted, and he told me peaches. He said it was the last thing he wanted on earth." Then she did kick him, but it seemed to bring no satisfaction. "He said if I brought him the peaches last night, he'd tell me everything in the morning."

"How did he know night from day?"

She shook her head. "Another screwup. I told him."

"It's okay," I told her. "Every intern makes that mistake."

"But in the middle of the night," she said, "I got this gut feeling something was wrong, so I came down to find him like this."

"We don't work on gut feelings," I said. "Pubyok do."

"Well, what did we get out of Buc? Basically nothing. What have we got from Commander Ga? A fucking fairy tale and how to jerk off an ox."

"Q-Kee," I said. I put my hands on my hips and took a deep breath.

"Don't be mad at me," she said. "You're the one who asked Comrade

Buc about canned peaches. You're the one who told him Commander Ga was in the building. Buc just put two and two together."

She looked ready to storm off. "There's one more thing," she said. "Remember how Commander Ga asked whether those peaches were his or Comrade Buc's? When I handed Comrade Buc the can of peaches, he asked me the same question."

"What did you tell him?"

"What did *I* tell *him*? Nothing," she said. "I'm the interrogator, remember?"

"Wrong," I told her. "You're the intern."

"That's right," she said. "Interrogators are people who get results."

*

Behind the cells where new subjects are first processed is the central property locker. It's on the main floor, and before leaving I went there to snoop around. Anything of real value was looted by the MPSS agents long before bringing the subjects in. Up and down the rows I studied the meager possessions that people were carrying before their final visit here. Lots of sandals. Enemies of the state tended to wear a size seven, was my initial observation. Here were the acorns from people's pockets, the twigs they used to clean their teeth, rucksacks filled with rags and eating utensils. And next to a piece of tape bearing Comrade Buc's name, I found a can of peaches with a red-and-green label, grown in Manpo, canned in Fruit Factory 49.

I took the can of peaches and headed home.

The subway had started running, and jammed in one of the cars, I looked no different than the legions of gray-clad factory workers as we involuntarily leaned against one another in the turns. I kept seeing Buc's family, beautiful in their white dresses. I kept hoping my mother, cooking breakfast blind, didn't burn the apartment down. Somehow she always managed not to. And even one hundred meters underground we all heard the shock-work whistle's five morning blasts.

COMMANDER GA'S eyes opened to see the boy and the girl at the foot of the bed, staring at him. They were really just the shine of first light in their hair, a thin blue across cheekbones. He blinked, and though it seemed like a second, he must have slept because when he opened his eyes again, the boy and the girl were gone.

In the kitchen he found the chair balanced against the counter, and here they were, up high, staring into the open door of the top cabinet.

He lit the burner under a carbon steel skillet, then quartered an onion and spooned in some oil.

"How many guns are in there?" he asked them.

The boy and the girl shared a look. The girl held up three fingers.

"Has anyone shown you how to handle a pistol?"

They shook their heads no.

"Then you know not to touch them, right?"

They nodded.

The smell of cooking brought barking from the dog on the balcony.

"Come, you two," he said. "We need to find where your father keeps your mother's cigarettes before she wakes mad as a dog in the zoo."

With Brando, Commander Ga scoured the house, toe-tapping the baseboards and inspecting the undersides of furniture. Brando sniffed and barked at everything he touched, while the children hung back, wary but curious. Ga didn't know what he was looking for. He moved slowly from room to room, noticing a patched-over flue hole where an old heating stove had been. He observed a patch of swollen plaster, perhaps from a roof leak. Near the front door, he saw marks in the hardwood floor. He ran his toes over the scratches, then looked up.

He fetched a chair, stood upon it, discovered a section of molding that was loose. He reached behind it, into the wall, and removed a carton of cigarettes.

"Oh," the boy said. "I understand now. You were looking for hiding places."

It was the first time the child had spoken to him.

"That's right," he told the boy.

"There's another one," the boy said. He pointed toward the portrait of Kim Jong Il.

"I'm sending you on a secret mission," Ga told them and handed over a pack of cigarettes. "You must get these cigarettes under your mother's pillow, and she must not wake."

The girl's expressions, in contrast to her mother's, were subtle and easily missed. With a quick lip flare, she suggested this was much beneath her spying abilities, but still she accepted the mission.

When the oversized portrait of the Dear Leader was removed, Commander Ga found an old shelf recessed in the wall. A laptop computer occupied most of it, but on the top shelves, he found a brick of American hundred-dollar bills, vitamin supplements, protein powder, and a vial of testosterone with two syringes.

The onions had sweetened and clarified, turning black at the edges. He added an egg, a pinch of white pepper, celery leaves, and yesterday's rice. The girl set out the plates and chili paste. The boy served. The mother emerged, half asleep, a lit cigarette in her lips. She came to the table, where the children suppressed knowing smiles.

She took a drag and exhaled. "What?" she asked.

Over breakfast, the girl asked, "Is it true that you went to America?"

Ga nodded. They ate from Chinese plates with silver chopsticks.

The boy said, "I heard you must pay for your food there."

"That's true," Ga said.

"What about an apartment?" the girl asked. "Does that cost money?"

"Or the bus," the boy asked. "Or the zoo—does it cost to see the zoo?"

Ga stopped them. "Nothing is free there."

"Not even the movies?" Sun Moon asked, a little offended.

"Did you go to Disneyland?" the girl asked. "I heard that's the best thing in America."

The boy said, "I heard American food tastes horrible."

Ga had three bites left, but he stopped, saving them for the dog.

"The food's good," he answered. "But the Americans ruin everything with cheese. They make it out of animal milk. Americans put it on everything—on their eggs at breakfast, on their noodles, they melt it on ground meat. They say Americans smell like butter, but no, it is cheese. With heat, it becomes an orange liquid. For my work with the Dear Leader, I must help Korean chefs re-create cheese. All week, our team has been forced to handle it."

Sun Moon still had a little food left on her plate, but with the talk of the Dear Leader, she extinguished her cigarette in the rice.

This was a signal that breakfast was over, but still the boy had one last question to ask. "Do dogs really have their own food in America, a kind that comes in cans?"

The idea was shocking to Ga, a cannery dedicated to dogs. "Not that I saw," he said.

*

Over the next week, Commander Ga oversaw a team of chefs constructing the menu for the American delegation. Dak-Ho was enlisted to use props from the Central Movie Lot to construct a Texas-style ranch, based on Ga's drawings of the lodgepole corral, mesquite fences, branding hearth, and barn. A site was chosen east of Pyongyang, where there was more open space and fewer citizens. Comrade Buc acquired everything from patterns for guayabera shirts to cobbler molds for cowboy boots. Procuring a chuck wagon proved Buc's greatest challenge, but one was located at a Japanese theme park, and a team was sent to get it.

It was determined that a North Korean Weedwacker would not be engineered since tests showed that a communist scythe, with a 1.5-meter razor-sharp blade, was the more effective tool at clearing brush. A fishing pond was constructed and filled with eels from the Taedong River, a most voracious and worthy opponent for the sport of fishing. Teams of volunteer citizens were sent into the Sobaek Mountains to capture a score of rock mamushi, the nation's most poisonous snake, for target practice.

A group of stage mothers from the Children's Palace Theater was enlisted to make the gift baskets. While calfskin could not be found for the making of gloves, the most supple replacement—puppy—was chosen. In place of bourbon, a potent snake whiskey from the hills of Hamhung was selected. The Junta in Burma donated five kilos of tiger jerky. Much debate was given to the topic of which cigarettes best bespoke the identity of the North Korean people. In the end, the brand was Prolot.

But it wasn't all work. Each day, Commander Ga took a long lunch at the Moranbong Theater, where, alone, he watched a different Sun Moon movie. He beheld her fierce resilience in *Oppressors Tumble,* felt her limitless capacity to suffer in *Motherless Fatherland,* understood her seductive guile from *Glory of Glories,* and went home whistling patriotic tunes after *Hold the Banner High!*

Each morning before work, when the trees were alive with finches and wrens, Commander Ga taught the children the art of fashioning bird snares from delicate loops of thread. With a deadfall stone and a trigger twig, they each set a snare on the balcony rail and baited it with celery seeds.

After he arrived home in the afternoons, Commander Ga taught the children work. Because they'd never tried work before, the boy and the girl found it new and interesting, though Ga had to show them everything, like how to use your foot to drive a shovel into dirt or how you must go to your knees to swing a pick in a tunnel. Still, the girl liked to be out of her school uniform and she wasn't afraid of tunnel dust. The boy relished hauling buckets of dirt up the ladder and muscling them out back to the balcony, where he slowly poured them down the mountainside.

While Sun Moon sang the children nightly to sleep, he explored the laptop, which mostly consisted of maps he didn't understand. There was a file of photographs, though, hundreds of them, which were hard to look at. The pictures were not so different than Mongnan's: images of men regarding the camera with a mixture of trepidation and denial toward what was about to happen to them. And then there were the "after" pictures, in which men—bloodied, crumpled, half-naked—clung to the ground. The images of Comrade Buc were especially hard.

Each night, she slept on her side of the bed, and he slept on his.

Time to get some shut-eye, he'd say to her, and she'd say, *Sweet dreams.*

Toward the end of the week, a script arrived from the Dear Leader. It was called *Ultimate Sacrifices.* Sun Moon left it on the table where the messenger had placed it, and all day she approached it and retreated, circling with a fingernail fixed in the space between her teeth.

Finally, she sought the comfort of her house robe and took the script into the bedroom, where with the aid of two packs of cigarettes she read it over and over for an entire day.

In bed that night, he said, *Time to get some shut-eye.* She said nothing.

Side by side, they stared at the ceiling.

"Does the script trouble you?" he asked. "What is the character the Dear Leader wishes you to play?"

Sun Moon pondered this awhile. "She is a simple woman," Sun Moon said. "In a simpler time. Her husband has gone off to fight the imperialists in the war. He had been a nice man, well liked, but as manager of the farm collective he was lenient and productivity suffered. During the war, the peasants almost starved. Four years pass, they assume he is dead. It is then that he returns. The husband barely recognizes his wife, while his own appearance is completely different—he has been burned in battle. War has hardened him and he is a cold taskmaster. But the crop yields increase and the harvest is bountiful. The peasants fill with hope."

"Let me guess," Commander Ga said. "It is then that the wife begins to suspect this is not her real husband, and when she has her proof, she must decide whether to sacrifice her personal happiness for the good of the people."

"Is the script that obvious?" she asked. "So obvious that a man who has seen but one movie can guess its content?"

"I only speculated on the ending. Perhaps there is some twist by which the farm collective meets its quota and the woman can be fulfilled."

She exhaled. "There is no twist. The plot is the same as all the others. I endure and endure and the movie ends."

Sun Moon's voice in the dark was freighted with sorrow, like the final voice-over of *Motherless Fatherland* during which the Japanese tighten the chains to prevent the character from hurting herself during all the future escapes she would attempt.

"People find your movies inspiring," he said.

"Do they?"

"I find them inspiring. And your acting shows people that good can come from suffering, that it can be noble. That's better than the truth."

"Which is?"

"That there's no point to it. It's just a thing that sometimes has to be done and even if thirty thousand suffer with you, you suffer alone."

She said nothing. He tried again.

"You should be flattered," he told her. "With all that demands the Dear Leader's attention, he has spent the week composing a new movie for you."

"Have you forgotten that this man's prank got you beaten in front of all the *yangbans* of Pyongyang? Oh, it will give him no end of delight to watch me act my heart out in another movie that he will never release. It will be of endless amusement to him to see how I play a woman who must submit to a new husband."

"He's not trying to humiliate you. The Americans are coming in two weeks. He's focused on humiliating the greatest nation on earth. He replaced your husband in public. He took *Comfort Woman* from you. He's made his point. At this stage, if he really wanted to hurt you, he'd really hurt you."

"Let me tell you about the Dear Leader," she said. "When he wants you to lose more, he gives you more to lose."

"His grudge was with me, not you. What reason could he have to—"

"There," she said. "There is the proof that you don't understand any of this. The answer is that the Dear Leader doesn't need reasons."

He rolled to his side, so he faced her eye to eye.

"Let's rewrite the script," he said.

She was silent a moment.

"We'll use your husband's laptop, and we'll give the new version a plot twist. Let's have the peasants meet their quotas and the wife find her happiness. Perhaps we'll have that first husband make a surprise return in the third act."

"Do you know what you're talking about?" she asked. "This is the Dear Leader's script."

"What I know about the Dear Leader is this: satisfaction matters to him. And he admires crafty solutions."

"What's it matter to you?" she asked. "You said after the Americans came, he was going to get rid of you."

He rolled to his back. "Yeah," he said. "There's that."

Now he was quiet.

"I don't think I'd have the first husband return from the war," she said. "Then there would be a showdown, and that would appeal to the viewer's sense of honor, rather than duty. Let's say that the manager of another farm collective is jealous of the burned man's success. This other manager is corrupt and he gets a corrupt Party official to sign a warrant for the woman's husband to be sent to a reeducation camp as punishment for his previous low quotas."

"I see," Commander Ga said. "Instead of the woman being trapped, now it is the burned man who has a choice. If he admits he is an imposter, he may leave freely with his shame. But if he insists he is her husband, with honor he goes to the camp."

Sun Moon said, "The wife's almost positive that beneath the burns this husband is not hers. But what if she's wrong, what if he's just been hardened by the savagery of war, what if she lets the father of her children be sent away?"

"Now there is a story of duty," he said. "But what happens to the woman? In either outcome, she is alone."

"What happens to the woman?" Sun Moon asked the room.

Brando stood. The dog stared into the dark house.

Commander Ga and Sun Moon looked at one another.

When the dog started growling, the boy and the girl woke. Sun Moon pulled on her robe while Commander Ga cupped a candle and followed the dog to the door of the balcony. Outside, the bird snare had tripped, and in the loop a small wren thrashed wildly, flashes of brown and gray feathers, streaks of pale yellow. He handed the candle to the boy, whose eyes were wide with amazement. Ga took the bird in his hands and removed the slipknot from its leg. He spread its wings between his fingers and showed them to the children.

"It worked," the girl said. "It really worked."

In Prison 33, it was dangerous to get caught with a bird, so you learned to dress one in seconds. "Okay, watch close," Ga told the children. "Pinch the back of the neck, then pull up and turn." The bird's head snapped off, and he tossed it over the rail. "Then the legs come off with a twist, as do the wings at the first joint. Then put your thumbs on the breast and slide them away from one another." The friction tore the skin and exposed the breast. "This meat is the prize, but if you have time, save the rest. You can boil the bones, and the broth will keep you healthy. For that, just send your finger into the abdomen, and by rotating the bird, all the insides come out at once." Ga slung his finger clean, and by turning the skin inside out, it stripped all at once.

"There," he said. Ga held the bird out for them again. It was beautiful, the meat pearlescent and pink, fanned over the finest white bones, the tiny tips of which leaked red.

With a thumbnail he scraped along the sternum and removed a perfect almond of translucent breast meat. This he placed in his mouth and savored, remembering.

He offered the other breast, but the children, stunned, shook their heads. This, too, Ga ate, then tossed the carcass to the dog, who crunched it right down.

CONGRATULATE one another, citizens, for high praises are in order on the occasion of the publication of the Dear Leader's latest artistic treatise, *On the Art of Opera*. This is a sequel to Kim Jong Il's earlier book *On the Art of the Cinema*, which is required reading for serious actors worldwide. To mark the occasion, the Minister of Collective Child Rearing announced the composition of two new children's songs—"Hide Deeply" and "Duck the Rope." All week, expired ration cards may be used to gain admittance to matinee opera performances!

Now, an important word from our Minister of Defense: Certainly the loudspeaker in each and every apartment in North Korea provides news, announcements, and cultural programming, but it must be reminded that it was by Great Leader Kim Il Sung's decree in 1973 that an air-raid warning system be installed across this nation, and a properly functioning early-warning network is of supreme importance. The Inuit people are a tribe of isolated savages that live near the North Pole. Their boots are called mukluk. Ask your neighbor later today, what is a mukluk? If he does not know, perhaps there is a malfunction with his loudspeaker, or perhaps it has for some reason become accidentally disconnected. By reporting this, you could be saving his life the next time the Americans sneak-attack our great nation.

Citizens, when last we saw the beauty Sun Moon, she had closed herself off. Our poor actress was handling her loss badly. Why won't she turn to the inspirational tracts of the Dear Leader? Kim Jong Il is someone who understands what you're going through. Losing his brother when he was seven, his mother after that, and then a baby sister a year later, not to mention a couple of stepmothers—yes, the Dear Leader is someone who speaks the language of loss.

Still, Sun Moon did understand the role of reverence in a good citizen's life, so she packed a picnic lunch to take to the Revolutionary Martyrs'

Cemetery, just a short walk from her house on Mount Taesong. Once there, her family spread a cloth on the ground, where they could relax at their meal, knowing Taepodong-II missiles stood at the ready, while high above, North Korea's BrightStar satellite defended them from space.

The meal, of course, was *bulgogi*, and Sun Moon had prepared all manner of *banchan* to accompany the feast, including some *gui, jjim, jeon,* and *namul*. They thanked the Dear Leader for their bounty and dug in!

As he ate, Commander Ga asked about her parents. "Do they live here in the capital?"

"It's just my mother," Sun Moon said. "She retired to Wonsan, but I never hear from her."

Commander Ga nodded. "Yes," he said, "Wonsan."

He stared off into the cemetery, no doubt thinking of all the golf and karaoke to be found in that glorious retirement community.

"You've been there?" she asked.

"No, but I've seen it from the sea."

"Is it beautiful, Wonsan?"

The children were fast at their chopsticks. Birds eyed them from the trees.

"Well," he said, "I can say the sand is especially white. And the waves are quite blue."

She nodded. "I'm sure," she said. "But why, why doesn't she write?"

"Have you written her?"

"She never sent me her address."

Commander Ga certainly knew that Sun Moon's mother was having too much fun to write. No other nation on earth has an entire city, right on the beach, dedicated to the comfort of its retired persons. Here, there is surf casting, watercolor, handicrafts, and a Juche book club. Too many activities to name! And Ga also knew that if more citizens volunteered at the Central Postal Bureau in their evenings and weekends, less mail would be lost in transit across our glorious nation.

"Stop worrying about your mother," he told her. "It's the young ones you should focus on."

After lunch, they spilled the leftover food into the grass for the cute little birds to eat. Then Ga decided the children needed some education. He took them to the top of the hill, and while Sun Moon looked on with pride, the good Commander indicated the most important martyr in the cemetery, Kim Jong Suk, wife of Kim Il Sung and mother of Kim Jong Il. The busts of all the martyrs were larger-than-life bronzes whose burnished hues seemed to bring their subjects to life. Ga explained at length Kim Jong Suk's anti-Japanese heroics and how she was kindly known for carrying the heavy packs of older revolutionary guerrillas. The children wept that she died so young.

Then they walked a few meters to the next martyrs, Kim Chaek, An Kil, Kang Kon, Ryu Kyong Su, Jo Jong Chol, and Choe Chun Guk, all patriots of the highest order who fought at the Great Leader's side. Then Commander Ga pointed out the tomb of the hot-blooded O Jung Hup, commander of the famed Seventh Regiment. Next was the eternal sentinel Cha Kwang Su, who froze to death during a night watch at Lake Chon. The children rejoiced in their new understandings. And here was Pak Jun Do, who took his own life in a test of loyalty to our leaders. Don't forget Back Hak Lim, who earned his nickname Eagle Owl one imperialist at a time. Who hadn't heard of Un Bo Song, who'd packed his ears with earth before charging a Japanese gun emplacement? *More*, the children called, *more!* Thus they walked the rows, taking note of Kong Young, Kim Chul Joo, Choe Kwang, and O Paek Ryong, all too heroic for medals. Ahead was Choe Tong O, father of South Korean commander Choe Tok Sin, who defected to North Korea in order to pay his respects here. And here is Choe Tong O's brother by marriage Ryu Tong Yol! Next was the bust of tunnel master Ryang Se Bong and the assassination trio of Jong Jun Thaek, Kang Yong Chang, and "the Sportsman" Pak Yong Sun. Many Japanese orphans still feel the burn of Kim Jong Thae's long patriotic shadow.

Such education was the kind that brought milk to women's breasts!

Sun Moon's skin was flush, so nakedly had Commander Ga aroused her patriotism.

"Children," she called. "Go play in the woods."

Then she took the arm of Commander Ga and led him downhill to the botanical gardens. They passed the experimental farm, with its tall corn and bursting soybeans, the guards with their chrome Kalashnikovs ever at the ready to defend the national seed bank against imperial aggression.

She paused before what is perhaps our greatest national treasure, the twin greenhouses that exclusively cultivate kimjongilia and kimilsungia.

"Pick your hothouse," she told him.

The buildings were translucent white. One glowed with the full fuchsia of kimjongilia. The breeding house of kimilsungia radiated an operatic overload of lavender orchid.

It was clear she couldn't wait. "I choose Kim Il Sung," Sun Moon said. "For he is the progenitor of our entire nation."

Inside, the air was warm, humid. A mist hung. As this husband and wife strolled the rows arm in arm, the plants seemed to take notice—their swiveling blossoms followed in our lovers' wake, as if to drink in the full flavor of Sun Moon's honor and modesty. The couple stopped, deep in the hothouse, to recumbently enjoy the splendor of North Korea's leadership. An army of hummingbirds hovered above them, expert pollinators of the state, the buzzing thrum of their wing beats penetrating the souls of our lovers, all the while dazzling them with the iridescent flash of their throats and the way their long flower-kissing tongues flicked in delight. Around Sun Moon, blossoms opened, the petals spreading wide to reveal hidden pollen pots. Commander Ga dripped with sweat, and in his honor, grop-ing stamens emanated their scent in clouds of sweet spoor that coated our lovers' bodies with the sticky seed of socialism. Sun Moon offered her Juche to him, and he gave her all he had of Songun policy. At length, in depth, their spirited exchange culminated in a mutual exclaim of Party understanding. Suddenly, all the plants in the hothouse shuddered and dropped their blossoms, leaving a blanket upon which Sun Moon could recline as a field of butterflies ticklishly alighted upon her innocent skin.

Finally, citizens, Sun Moon has shared her convictions with her hus-band!

Savor the glow, citizens, for in the next installment, we take a closer look at this "Commander Ga." Though he is remarkable at satisfying the political needs of a woman, we will look closely at the ways in which he has defiled all seven tenets of North Korean Good Citizenship.

SUN MOON announced that the day to honor her great-uncle was upon them. Even though it was Saturday, a workday, they'd make the walk to the Revolutionary Martyrs' Cemetery to lay a wreath. "We'll make it a picnic," Commander Ga told her. "And I'll cook my favorite meal."

Ga had refused to let any of them eat breakfast. "An empty stomach," he told them, "is my secret ingredient." For the picnic, Ga brought only a pot, some salt, and Brando on a lead.

Sun Moon shook her head at the sight of the dog. "He's not legal," she said.

"I'm Commander Ga," he told her. "If I want to walk a dog, I walk a dog. Besides, my days are numbered, right?"

"What's that mean?" the boy asked. "His days are numbered."

"Nothing," Sun Moon said.

They walked downhill under the Fun Fair's idle gondola. With the children of Pyongyang hard at work, the lift chairs creaked in place above them. The zoo, however, was crowded with peasants bused in for their once-a-year trip to the capital. The four of them cut through the woods, dense this time of year, and left Brando tied to a tree so as not to offend any of the veterans paying their respects.

This was the first time he'd entered the cemetery. Sun Moon ignored all the other markers and led them right to the bust of her great-uncle. The bust depicted a man whose face looked Southern in its angles and abruptness of brow. His eyes were almost closed in an expression of certainty and calm.

"Ah," Ga said. "It's Kang Kung Li. He charged across a mountain bridge under enemy fire. He took the door off Kim Il Sung's car and carried it as a shield."

"You've heard of him?" she asked.

"Of course," Ga said. "He saved many lives. People who break the rules in order to do good are sometimes named after him."

"Don't be so sure," Sun Moon said. "I fear the only people named after him these days are a few measly orphans."

Commander Ga wandered the rows in stunned recognition. Here were the names of all the boys he'd known, and looking at their busts, it seemed as though they'd made it to adulthood—here they had mustaches and strong jaws and broad shoulders. He touched their faces and ran his fingers in the hangul characters of their names carved in the marble pedestals. It was as if, instead of starving at nine or falling to factory accidents at eleven, they'd all lived into their twenties and thirties like normal men. At the tomb of Un Bo Song, Commander Ga traced the features of the bronze bust with his hand. The metal was cold. Here Bo Song was smiling and bespectacled, and Ga touched the martyr's cheek, saying, "Bo Song."

There was one more bust he needed to see, and Sun Moon and the children trailed him through the tombs until he came to it. The bust and the man faced one another but bore no resemblance. He hadn't known what he'd feel when he finally faced this martyr, but Ga's only thought was, *I'm not you. I'm my own man.*

Sun Moon approached him. "Is this martyr special to you?" she asked.

"I used to know someone with his name," he told her.

"Do you know this one's story?"

"Yeah," he said. "It's a pretty simple tale. Though descended from impure bloodlines, he joined the guerrillas to fight the Japanese. His comrades doubted his loyalties. To prove they could trust him with their lives, he took his own."

"That story speaks to you?"

"This guy I used to know," he said. "It spoke to him."

"Let's get out of here," Sun Moon said. "Once a year is all I can take of this place."

*

The boy and the girl each held a hand on Brando's lead as he pulled them deep into the woods. Commander Ga started a fire and showed the children how to notch a tripod to hold a pot over the flames. The pot they filled with water from a stream, and when they found a little pool, they narrowed the water's exit with rocks, and Ga held his shirt at the pinch point like a sieve while the children walked the pool, trying to scare any fish downstream. They caught a ten-centimeter fingerling in the shirt. Or perhaps it was an adult and the fish here were stunted. He scaled the fish with the back of a spoon, gutted it, and fixed it on a stick for Sun Moon to grill. Once charred, it would go into the stock with the salt.

There were many flowers growing wild, probably owing to the proximity of the cemetery's bouquets. He showed the children how to identify and pick *ssukgat*; together they softened the stalks between two stones. Behind a boulder was an ostrich fern, its succulent buds begging to be stripped from their fanlike leaves. As luck would have it, growing at the bottom of the boulder was stone-ear *seogi*—sharp with the brine of seaweed. They scraped these lichen free with a sharp stick. He showed the boy and the girl how to spot yarrow, and searching together, they managed to find one wild ginger, small and pungent. As a final touch, they picked *shiso* leaves, a plant left behind by the Japanese.

Soon the pot was steaming, three dots of fish oil turning on the surface as Ga stirred the wild herbs. "This," Ga said, "is my favorite meal in the world. In prison, they kept us right at the edge of starvation. You could still do work, but you couldn't think. Your mind would try to retrieve a word or thought, but it wouldn't be there. There's no sense of time when you're hungry. You just labor and then it's dark, no memory. But on logging details, we could make this. By building a fishfall at night, you could gather minnows all day while you worked. Herbs were everywhere up in the hills, and every bowl of this added a week to your life."

He tasted the broth, bitter still. "More time," he said. His wet shirt hung in a tree.

"What about your parents?" Sun Moon asked. "I thought when people were sent to the labor camps, their parents went with them."

"It's true," he told her. "But that wasn't a concern for me."

"Sorry to hear that," she said.

"I guess you could say my folks lucked out," he said. "What of your parents? Do they live here in the capital?"

Sun Moon's voice went grave. "I only have my mother left," she said. "She's in the east. She retired to Wonsan."

"Oh, yes," he said. "Wonsan."

She was quiet. He stirred the soup, the herbs rising now.

"How long ago was this?" he asked.

"A few years," she said.

"And she's busy," he said. "Probably too busy to write."

It was hard to read her face. She looked at him expectantly, as if hoping that he would offer reassuring news. But deeper in her eyes, he could see a darker knowing.

"I wouldn't worry about her," he said. "I'm sure she's fine."

Sun Moon didn't look comforted.

The children took turns tasting the soup and making faces.

He tried again. "Wonsan has plenty to keep a person busy," he added. "I've seen it with my own eyes. The sand is especially white. And the waves are quite blue."

Sun Moon gazed absently into the pot.

"So don't believe the rumors, okay?" he told her.

"What are the rumors?" she asked.

"That's the spirit," he said.

In Prison 33, all of a person's self-deceit was slowly broken down, until even the fundamental lies that formed your identity faltered and fell. For Commander Ga, this happened at a stoning. These took place near the river, where there were banks of round, water-polished rocks. When a person was caught trying to escape, he was buried to his waist at the water's edge and at dawn, a slow, almost endless procession of inmates filed by. There were no exceptions—everyone had to throw. If your toss was lackluster, the guards would shout for vigor, but you didn't have to throw again. He'd been through it three times, but deep in the line, so that what he stoned was not a person but a mass, bent unnaturally to the ground, no longer even steaming.

But one morning, by chance, he was near the front of the line. Traversing the round stones was dangerous for Mongnan. She needed an arm to steady her, and she had him up early, near the front of the line, none of which he minded until he came to understand that the man they were to stone would be awake and have an opinion. The rock was cold in his hand. He could hear the rocks ahead of them finding their homes. He steadied Mongnan as they neared the half-buried man, whose arms were up in a mime of self-defense. He was trying to speak, but something other than words was coming out, and the blood that ran from his wounds was still hot.

Nearing, he saw the bleeding man's tattoos, and it took him a moment to realize they were in Cyrillic, and then he saw the face of the woman inked on his chest.

"Captain," he called, dropping his rock, "Captain, it's me."

The Captain's eyes rolled in recognition, but he could not make words. His hands still moved, as if he was trying to clear imaginary cobwebs. His fingernails had somehow torn during his escape attempt.

"Don't," Mongnan said as he let go her arm and crouched by the Captain, taking the sailor's hand. "It's me, Captain, from the *Junma*," he said.

There were only two guards, young men with hard-set faces and ancient rifles. They began shouting, their words coming in sharp claps, but he wouldn't let go of the old man's hand.

"The Third Mate," the Captain said. "My boy, I told you I'd protect all of you. I saved my crew again."

It was unnerving how the Captain looked toward him, yet his eyes didn't quite find him.

"You must get out, son," the Captain said. "Whatever you do, get out."

A warning shot was fired, and Mongnan scrambled to him, pleading with him to return to the line. "Don't let your friend see you get shot," she told him. "Don't let that be the last thing he sees."

With these words, she pulled him back in line. The guards were quite agitated, barking orders, and Mongnan was almost yelling above them. "Throw your stone," she commanded. "You must throw it," and as if offering her own incentive, she dealt the Captain a hard, glancing shot to the head. It loosed a tuft of hair into the wind. "Now!" she commanded, and he hefted his rock and dealt his blow hard to the Captain's temple, and that was the last thing the Captain saw.

Later, behind the rain barrels, he broke down.

Mongnan brought him to the ground, held him.

"Why wasn't it Gil?" he asked her. He was weeping uncontrollably. "The Second Mate I could understand. Even Officer So. Not the Captain. He followed every rule, why him? Why not me? I have nothing, nothing at all. Why should he go to prison twice?"

Mongnan pulled him to her. "Your Captain fought back," she told him. "He resisted, he wouldn't let them take his identity. He died free."

He couldn't get hold of his breathing, and she pulled him close, like a child. "There," she said, rocking him. "There's my little orphan, my poor little orphan."

Meekly, through tears, he said, "I'm not an orphan."

"Of course you are," she said. "I'm Mongnan, I know an orphan, of course you are. Just let go, let it all out."

"My mother was a singer," he told her. "She was very beautiful."

"What was the name of your orphanage?"

"Long Tomorrows."

"Long Tomorrows," she said. "Was the Captain a father to you? He was a father, wasn't he?"

He just wept.

"My poor little orphan," she said. "An orphan's father is twice as important. Orphans are the only ones who get to choose their fathers, and they love them twice as much."

He put his hand over his chest, remembering how the Captain had worked the image of Sun Moon into his skin.

"I could have given him his wife back," he told her, weeping.

"But he wasn't your father," she said. She took his chin and tried to lift his head so she could get through to him, but he pulled his head back to her breast. "He wasn't your father," she said, stroking his hair. "What's important now is that you let go of all your illusions. It's time to see the truth of things. Like the fact that he was right, that you have to get out of here."

In the pot, little flakes of fish were floating off the spine, and Sun Moon, lost in thought, slowly stirred. Ga thought of how difficult it was to come to see the lies you told yourself, the ones that allowed you to function and move forward. To really do it, you needed someone's help. Ga leaned over to smell the broth—it cleared his mind, this perfect meal. Eating such a meal at sunset, after a day of logging the ravines above 33, it was the definition of being alive. He removed Wanda's camera and took a photo of the boy and the girl and the dog and Sun Moon, all of them casting their eyes the way people do into a fire.

"My stomach's growling," the boy said.

"Perfect timing," Commander Ga answered. "The soup's ready."

"But we don't have bowls," the girl said.

"We don't need them," he told her.

"What about Brando?" the boy asked.

"He'll have to find his own lunch," Ga said and removed the loop of rope from the dog's neck. But the dog didn't move—he sat there, staring at the pot.

They began passing a single spoon around, and the taste of the charred fish was magnificent with the yarrow and hint of *shiso.*

"Prison food's not so bad," the girl said.

"You two must be wondering about your father," Commander Ga said.

The boy and the girl didn't look up; instead, they kept the spoon in motion.

Sun Moon threw him a harsh look, warning him that he was in dangerous territory.

"The wound of not knowing," Ga said to her. "That's the one that never heals."

The girl cast him a thin, measured glance.

"I promise to tell you about your father," Ga went on. "After you've had more time to adjust."

"To adjust to what?" the boy asked.

"To *him,*" the girl told her brother.

"Children," Sun Moon said, "I told you, your father's just on a long mission."

"That's not true," Commander Ga said. "But I'll tell you the whole story soon."

Quietly, through her teeth, Sun Moon said, "Don't you take their innocence."

From the woods came a rustle. Brando stood at attention, his hair bristling.

The boy got a smile on his face. He had seen all of the dog's tricks and here was a chance to try one out. "Hunt," the boy said.

"No," Ga called, but it was too late—the dog was already sprinting into the trees, his bark describing a hectic path through the brush. He barked on and on. And then they heard the shriek of a woman. Ga grabbed the rope lead and began running. The boy and the girl were right behind him. Ga followed the small stream for a while, and he could see that the water was muddy from the dog. Soon, he came upon a family, backed against a boulder by Brando's barking. The family was eerily like theirs—a man and woman, a boy and girl, an older aunt. The dog was very agitated, snapping its teeth in mock charges, shifting its attention from one ankle to another, as if it would take all their legs in turn. Slowly Ga approached, slipped the loop around the dog's neck.

Ga backed the dog up and took a look at the family. Their fingernails were white with malnutrition, and even the girl's teeth had gone gray. The boy's shirt hung empty on him as from a wire hanger. Both women had lost much hair, and the father was nothing but cords under taut skin. Ga suddenly realized the father had something behind his back. Ga rattled the rope around the dog's neck to get it lunging.

"What are you hiding?" Ga shouted. "Show it. Show it before I let the dog loose."

Sun Moon came up breathing heavily as the man produced a dead squirrel, its tail snapped away.

Ga couldn't tell if they'd stolen it from the dog or if the dog was trying to steal it from them.

Sun Moon took a hard look at them. "My word," she said. "They're starving. There's nothing to them."

The girl turned to her father. "We're not starving, are we, Papa?"

"Of course not," the father said.

"Right before our eyes," Sun Moon said. "Starving to death!"

Sun Moon flashed them the back of her hand and pointed at a ring. "Diamond," she said, and after wresting it off, she placed it in the hands of the frightened mother before her.

Ga advanced and took back the ring. "Don't be a fool," he told Sun Moon. "This ring was a gift from the Dear Leader. Do you know what would happen if they got caught with a ring like this?" In his pocket, Ga had some military won, not much else. He took his boots off. "If you want to help them," Ga told Sun Moon, "they need simple things they can barter at the market."

The boy and the girl removed their shoes, and Ga also offered his belt. Sun Moon contributed earrings. "There's a pot of soup," Sun Moon said. "It's good. Just follow the stream. Keep the pot."

"That dog," the father said. "I thought it was escaped from the zoo."

"No," Ga told him. "He's ours."

"You don't have an extra one, do you?" the father asked.

*

That night, Commander Ga hummed along as Sun Moon sang the children to sleep. "*The cat's in the cradle*," she sang, "*the baby's in the tree.*" Later, when they'd climbed into bed, Sun Moon said to him, "Do you think the Dear Leader's line should be read 'Love knows *no* replacement,' as if it's unthinkable to search for a substitute for love, or 'Love *knows* no replacement,' suggesting that love is sentient and is itself at a loss to comprehend its absence?"

"I have to tell you the truth," he said to her.

"I'm an actress," she said. "The truth is all that matters to me."

He didn't hear her roll to her side, so he knew they both stared into the same darkness above. He was suddenly scared. His hands gripped the sheets.

"I've never been to Wonsan," he said. "But I've sailed past it many times. There are no umbrellas in the sand. There are no lounge chairs or fishing poles. There are no old people. Wherever the grandparents of North Korea go, it's not Wonsan."

He tried to listen for her breathing, but couldn't even hear that.

At last, she spoke to him.

"You're a thief," she said. "You are a thief who came into my life and stole everything that mattered to me."

*

The next day, she was silent. For breakfast, she murdered an onion and served it raw. The children were deft at quietly migrating to whatever room she wasn't in. Once, she ran out of the house screaming, only to lie weeping in her garden. She came back in to argue with the loudspeaker. Then she threw them out of the house so she could bathe, and standing in the grass together, Commander Ga and the children and the dog stared at the front door, behind which they could hear her furiously scrubbing every inch of her skin. The children soon wandered down the hill, practicing "hunt" and "fetch" with Brando by tossing melon rinds into the trees.

Commander Ga stood to the side of the house, where Comrade Buc found him. Buc kept his Ryoksong beer in a shady patch of tall, cool grass. He offered Ga one. Together they drank and stared up at Sun Moon's balcony. She was up there in her house robe, smoking and running lines from *Ultimate Sacrifices*, but every word she read with anger.

"What happened?" Buc asked him.

"I told her the truth about something," Ga answered.

"You've got to stop doing that," Buc said. "It's bad for people's health."

Sun Moon held the script with one hand and raised the other high. Cigarette in her mouth, she tried to find her motivation in a line:

"The *true* first husband of all women is the Great Leader Kim Il Sung!

"The true *first* husband of all women is the Great Leader Kim Il Sung!

"The true first husband of *all* women is the Great Leader Kim Il Sung!"

"Did you hear what the Dear Leader wants to do now?" Buc asked him. "He wants to give the Americans a branding demonstration."

"Ha," Commander Ga said. "I'm sure the cattle are lining up to volunteer."

At the sound of his laugh, Sun Moon stopped reading and turned. Seeing him standing there, she threw the script off the balcony and went inside.

Ga and Buc watched the cloud of paper flutter through the trees.

Comrade Buc shook his head in disbelief. "You really upset her," he said. "You know how long she's been waiting for this movie?"

"She'll be rid of me soon enough, and her life will return to normal," Ga said, and despite himself, there was a sadness to his voice.

"Are you joking?" Buc asked. "The Dear Leader has declared you the real Commander Ga. There's no way he can get rid of you now. And why would he want to? His nemesis is gone."

Ga drank from his beer.

"I found his computer," he said.

"Are you serious?" Buc asked.

"Yeah. It was hidden behind a painting of Kim Il Sung."

"Is there anything on there you can use?"

"It's mostly loaded with maps," Ga said. "There's a lot of technical data, flowcharts, blueprints, things I can't make sense of."

"Those maps are the uranium mines," Buc said. "Your predecessor was in charge of every excavation site. Plus, he oversaw the entire processing network—ore to refinement. I procured everything for him. You ever try to buy aluminum centrifuge tubes over the internet?"

"I thought being the Minister of Prison Mines was supposed to be a symbolic post, nothing more than signing the paperwork to keep the convict labor coming."

"That was before the uranium was discovered," Buc said. "You think the Dear Leader would hand Ga the keys to the nuclear program? If you want, I'll explain it all. We can go through the laptop together."

"You don't want to see it," Ga said. "There are also pictures."

"Of me?"

Ga nodded. "And a thousand other men."

"He didn't do to me what those photos make it look like."

"You don't have to talk about it."

"No, this is something you should hear," Buc said. "He was going to man-attack me, he said. But once he beat me down, once he had me where he could do anything he wanted, he lost interest. All he wanted then was an image to remember me by. I can't imagine how good it must have felt, to take the life from that man. He tried to do it to you, right?"

Ga didn't say anything.

Buc said, "You can tell me, can't you? How you finished him off? Seeing as you're in the mood to tell the truth."

"It's not a big story," Ga said. "I was in the bottom level of the mine. The ceilings were low, and there was only one droplight in each chamber. Water rained through cracks in the ceiling, and it was hot, everything was steam. There were several men down there, and we were looking at a vein of white rock. That was the goal, getting the white rock out. Then Commander Ga appeared in the room. Suddenly he was there, dripping with sweat.

"*You've got to know the men under you,* Ga said to me. *You've got to know their hearts. Victory from without comes from victory within.*

"I pretended I didn't hear him.

"*Grab a man,* Commander Ga told me. *That one there, let's know the heart of that one.*

"I beckoned one of the men over.

"*Grab him!* Commander Ga shouted. *Grab him so he believes it. Take him so there's no doubt in his mind.*

"I approached the man. He saw the look on my face, and I saw the look on his. He turned from me and I took his back, wrapping him with my arms. When I looked back to see if this was sufficient for the Commander, I saw that he was now naked, his uniform a pile on the ground.

"Commander Ga spoke as if nothing was different. *You've got to do it like you mean it, he's got to believe there's no escape. That's the only way you'll know if he likes the idea.* Commander Ga put his arms around the midsection of another inmate. *You've got to get ahold of him. He's got to know you're stronger, that there's no way out. Maybe it's only when you grab him by the backside that he gives in to what he really wants and then his arousal betrays him.*

"Commander Ga grabbed the man in a way that made him wince in fear.

"*Stop*, I told him.

"Commander Ga turned to me, amazement on his face. *That's right. That's what you say to him. Stop. I knew you were the only real man here.*

"Commander Ga took a step toward me, and I took a step back.

"*Don't do this*, I said.

"*That's right, that's exactly what you say.* Commander Ga had a strange light in his eyes. *But he doesn't listen, that's the point. He's stronger than you are, and he keeps coming.*

"*Who keeps coming?*

"*Who?* Ga asked, then gave a smile. *Him.*

"I began moving backward. *Please*, I said. *Please, there's no need for this.*

"*Yes*, Commander Ga said. *Yes, you're resisting, you're doing everything to keep it from happening, it's clear you don't want it, that's why I like you, that's why I'm teaching you the test. But what if it's going to happen anyway? What if your words mean nothing to him? What if when you fight him, he fights harder?*

"Commander Ga closed on me, and I took a swing. It was a weak punch. I was scared to really hit him. Ga batted my fist to the side, then nailed me with a crisp jab. *What if you fight all the way*, he asked, *but it's just going to happen? What does that make you?*

"I landed a swift leg kick that made Commander Ga lose his footing, and excitement crossed his face. Ga flashed a high kick that came so fast it swiveled my head—I'd never seen a kick so fast.

"*This isn't going to happen*, I said. *I'm not going to let it happen.*

"*That's why I chose you.* Ga doled a searing left kick to my midsection, and I could feel my liver bruise over. *Of course you're going to give it your all, of course you're going to struggle with all your might. You don't know how I respect you. You're the only one, in all this time, that's really fought back, you're the only one who knows me, who really understands me.* I glanced down and saw that the Commander was aroused, his prick fiercely curving. Still, there was a sweet, childlike smile on his face. *I'm about to show my soul, the big scar on my soul*, Ga said, advancing upon me, his hips charging for a kick. *It will hurt—I won't lie to you, it's never going to stop hurting, really. But think of it—soon we'll both have the same scar. Soon, we'll be like brothers that way.*

"I backed away to his right, until I was under the droplight that illuminated the chamber. With a jumpkick, my foot swept through the bulb, and in the flash, a mist of glass hung frozen in the air. Then it was dark. I could hear Commander Ga shuffling. That's how people move when they're not used to the dark."

"And then what happened?" Buc asked.

"Then I went to work," Ga answered.

*

Sun Moon spent that evening in the bedroom. Commander Ga made the children cold noodles for dinner, which the boy and the girl kept dangling above Brando's nose so they could witness the dog's powerful teeth snapping them down. Only when the dishes were cleared did Sun Moon emerge in her bathrobe, puffy-faced, smoking. She told the children it was time to sleep, then spoke to Ga.

"I must see this American movie," she said. "The one that's supposed to be the best."

That night, the children slept with the dog on a pallet at the foot of the bed, and when Pyongyang went black, they lay side by side on the bed and inserted *Casablanca* into the laptop. The battery indicator said they had ninety minutes, so there would be no stopping.

Right away, she shook her head at the primitive nature of black-and-white photography.

He translated on the fly for her, converting the English to Korean as fast as he could, and when the words wouldn't come, he simply had to move his fingers, and they transcribed the lines.

For a while, her face was sour. She criticized the movie for moving too quickly. She labeled everyone in it an elite, drinking all day in fancy clothes. "Where are the common people?" she asked. "With real problems?" She laughed at the premise of a "letter of transit" that allowed anyone who possessed it to escape. "There is no magic letter that gets you out."

She told him to stop the movie. He wouldn't. *But it was giving her a headache.*

"I cannot tell what this movie glorifies," she said. "And when will the hero make his appearance? If no one breaks into song soon, I am going to bed."

"Shh," he said to her.

It was hurting her to watch, he could tell. Every image was a challenge to her life. The complicated looks and shifting desires of the characters were breaking her down, yet she had no power to stop it. As the beautiful actress Ingrid Bergman spent more time on screen, Sun Moon began questioning her, coaching her. "Why doesn't she settle down with the nice husband?"

"The war is coming," Ga told her.

"Why does she gaze at the immoral Rick that way?" she asked, even as she gazed at him, too. Soon, she stopped seeing the ways he profiteered off others and filled his safe with currency and spread bribes and lies. She only saw how he reached for a cigarette when Ilsa entered the room, how he drank when she left it. The ways in which no one seemed happy spoke to Sun Moon. She nodded at how all the characters' problems originated in the dark capital of Berlin. When the movie went back in time to Paris, where the characters smiled and wanted only bread and wine and each other, Sun Moon was smiling through her tears, and Commander Ga stopped translating for whole passages when all that was needed were the emotions crossing the faces of this man Rick and the woman Ilsa who loved him.

At the end of the movie, she was inconsolable.

He placed a hand on her shoulder, but she did not respond.

"My whole life is a lie," she said through tears. "Every last gesture. To think I acted in color, every garish detail captured in color." She rolled to him, so she was looking up into his eyes. She grabbed his shirt, wrenching the fabric in both hands. "I must make it to the place where this movie was made," she said. "I have to get out of this land and make it to a place where real acting exists. I need a letter of transit and you must help me. Not because you killed my husband or because we will pay the price when the Dear Leader casts you aside, but because you are like Rick. You are an honorable man like Rick in the movie."

"But that was just a movie."

"No it wasn't," she said, defiance in her eyes.

"But how would I get you out?"

"You are a special man," she said. "You can get us out. I'm telling you you must."

"But Rick made his own decision, that was his to make."

"That's right, I have told you what I need of you, and you have a decision to make."

"But what about us?" he asked.

She looked at him as if now she understood how it would work. That she now knew her fellow actor's motivation, and the plot would follow from that.

"What do you mean?" she asked.

"When you say, get us out, do you mean *us*, does that include me?"

She pulled him closer. "You are my husband," she said. "And I am your wife. That means us."

He stared into her eyes, hearing the words he hadn't known he'd been waiting his whole life to hear.

"My husband used to say that one day it would all end," she said. "I'm not waiting for that day."

Ga placed his hand on her. "Did he have a plan?"

"Yes," she said. "I discovered his plan—passport, cash, travel passes. The plan included only him. Not even his children."

"Don't worry," he said. "My plan won't be like that."

I WAS AWAKE in the middle of the night. I could feel that my parents were, too. For a while, I heard the boots of a Juche Youth Troop heading toward one of those dark, all-night shock rallies in Kumsusan Square. Heading to work in the morning, I knew I'd pass those girls on the way home, faces blacked by fire smoke, slogans painted down their thin arms. Most of all, those wild eyes. I stared at the ceiling, imagining the nervous hooves of baby goats above, always taking shuffle steps since it was too dark for them to see the edge of the roof.

I kept thinking how much Commander Ga's biography was like my own. Both our names were essentially unknown—there was nothing by which friends and family could call us, there was no word to which our deepest selves could respond. And then there was the way I was coming to believe that he didn't know the fates of the actress and her children. True, he seemed to move forward under the belief that all was well with them, but I don't think he had any idea. Much like myself—I created biographies of my subjects, which basically documented their lives up to the point they met me. Yet I had to admit, I'd never followed up on a single person who left Division 42. Not one biography had an epilogue. Our most important connection was how, to be given a new life, Ga had to take one away. I proved that theorem every day. After years of failure, I now understood that by writing Commander Ga's biography, maybe I was also writing my own.

I stood at the window. By the merest of starlight, I urinated into a wide-mouthed jar. A sound rose from the street below. And then something happened to let me know, despite the darkness, despite the kilometers between me and the nearest farm, that the nation's rice stalks were golden-tipped and it was harvest season again: two dump trucks pulled up across Sinuiju Street, and with bullhorns, the Minister of Mass Mobilization's men rousted all the occupants of the Worker's Paradise Housing

Block. Below, my neighbors in their bedclothes were slowly packed into trucks. By dawn they would be bent over, ankle deep in paddy water, receiving a daylong remedial lesson on the word "toil," which is the source of all food.

"Father," I spoke into the dark room. "Father, is it just about survival? Is that all there is?" I could feel the jar warm in my hand as I carefully screwed the lid back on. When the trucks pulled away, the only sound left was the slight whistle of my father breathing through his nose, a sure sign he was awake.

*

In the morning, another member of my team was missing. I can't say his name, but he was the one with the thin mustache and the lisp. He'd been out a week, and I had to assume it was more than being pressed into a harvest detail. It was likely I wouldn't see him again. He was the third this month, the sixth this year. What happened to them, where did they go? How were we going to replace the Pubyok when they retired if we were only a couple of men and a pair of interns?

Nonetheless, we took the gondola to the top of Mount Taesong. While Jujack and Leonardo searched Comrade Buc's house, Q-Kee and I swept Commander Ga's residence, though it was hard to focus. Every time you looked up, there through the grand windows was the skyline of Pyongyang below. You had to gasp at the sight of it. The whole house had a dreamlike quality to it—Q-Kee just shook her head at the way these people had their own bedroom and kitchen. They shared a commode with no one. Dog hair was everywhere, and it was clear they kept such an animal simply for personal amusement. The Golden Belt, in its glowing case, was something we were frightened to inspect. Even the Pubyok hadn't touched it on their initial sweep.

Their garden had been picked clean—there wasn't so much as a pea to take home to my parents. Had Commander Ga and Sun Moon taken fresh food with them, expecting a journey, perhaps? Or did Ga intend the food for his getaway? In their scrap heap was the rind of a whole melon and the fine bones of songbirds. Had they been more deprived than their fancy *yangban* house suggested?

Under the house, we found a thirty-meter tunnel stocked with rice sacks and American movies. The escape hatch was across the road, behind some bushes. Inside the house, we discovered some standard hiding compartments in the wall, but they were mostly empty. In one, we found a stack of South Korean martial-arts magazines, very illegal. The magazines were well worn and depicted fighters whose bodies rippled with combat. With the magazines was a lone handkerchief. This I lifted, looking for a monogram. I turned to Q-Kee. "I wonder what this handkerchief is doing—"

"Drop it," Q-Kee told me.

Right away, I let go, and the handkerchief fell to the floor. "What?" I asked.

"Don't you know what Ga must have used that for?" she asked me. She looked at me like I was one of the blind new puppies in the Central Zoo. "Didn't you have brothers?"

In the bathroom, Q-Kee indicated how Sun Moon's comb and Commander Ga's razor shared the edge of the sink. She'd come to work sporting a black eye, and I'd pretended not to notice, but in front of a mirror, there was no way to avoid it.

"Did someone try to hurt you?" I asked her.

"What makes you think it wasn't love?"

I laughed. "That would be a new way to show affection."

Q-Kee cocked her head and regarded me in the mirror.

She lifted a single glass from the sink ledge and held it to the light.

"They shared a rinse cup," she said. "That's love. There are many proofs."

"Is it proof?" I asked her. I shared a rinse cup with my parents.

In the bedroom, Q-Kee surveyed things. "Sun Moon would sleep on this side of the bed," she said. "It is closer to the toilet." Then Q-Kee went to the little table on that side of the bed. She opened and closed its drawer, knocked on the wood. "A smart woman," Q-Kee said, "would keep her condoms taped to the underside of this table. They wouldn't be visible to her husband, but when she needed one, all she had to do was reach."

"Condoms," I repeated. All forms of birth control were strictly illegal.

"You can get them at any night market," she said. "The Chinese make them in every color."

She turned over Sun Moon's bedside table, but there was nothing underneath.

I turned over Commander Ga's bedside table as well—nothing.

"Trust me," Q-Kee said. "The Commander had no need for birth control."

Together, we pulled the sheets from the bed and got down on our knees to identify hairs on the pillows. "They both slept here," I declared, and then we ran our fingertips across each centimeter of the mattress, sniffing and eyeballing everything for even the smallest sign of spoor. It was about halfway down the mattress that I came across a scent the likes of which I'd never encountered. I felt something primal in my nostrils, and then a bright light flashed in my mind. The scent was so sudden, so foreign, that I couldn't find the words, I couldn't have alerted Q-Kee even if I'd wanted to.

At the foot of the bed, we both stood.

Q-Kee crossed her arms in disbelief. "They slept together, but no *fucky-fucky*."

"No what?"

"It's English for 'sex,'" she said. "Don't you watch movies?"

"Not those kinds of movies," I said, but the truth was I hadn't seen any.

Opening the wardrobe, Q-Kee ran a finger across Sun Moon's *choson-ots* until it came to rest at an empty dowel. "This is the one she took," Q-Kee said. "It must have been spectacular, if these are the ones she left behind. So Sun Moon wasn't planning on being gone long, yet she wanted to look her best." She gazed at the lustrous fabrics before her. "I know every dress she wore in every movie," she said. "If I stood here long enough, I'd figure out the missing dress."

"But harvesting the garden," I said. "That suggests they *were* planning on being gone a long time."

"Or maybe it was a last meal, in her best dress."

I said, "But that only makes sense if—"

"—if Sun Moon knew what was going to happen to her," Q-Kee added.

"But if Sun Moon knew Ga meant to kill her, why dress up, why go along?"

Q-Kee considered the question as her touch lingered on all those beautiful dresses.

"Perhaps we should impound them as evidence," I told her, "so that you could more closely inspect them at your leisure."

"They are beautiful," she said. "Like my mother's dresses. But I clothe myself. Plus, dressing like a tour guide at the International Friendship Museum, that isn't my style."

Leonardo and Jujack returned from Comrade Buc's.

"Nothing much to report," Leonardo said.

"We found a hidden compartment in the kitchen wall," Jujack added. "But inside were only these."

He held up five miniature Bibles.

The light changed as the sun flashed off the steel of the distant May Day Stadium, and for a moment, we were newly stunned to be in such a residence, one without common walls or shared faucets, without cots that folded up and rolled into the corner, without a twenty-story trot down to a communal washtub.

Behind the security of Pubyok crime-scene tape, we began divvying up all of Commander Ga's rice and movies. *Titanic*, our interns agreed, was the best movie ever made. I told Jujack to throw the Bibles off the balcony. You could maybe explain a satchel full of DVDs to an MPSS officer, but not those things.

*

At Division 42, I went through my daily session with Commander Ga, and except for what happened to the actress and her children, he was all too happy to give the whats and whys and wheres and whens of everything. Once again, he went over how Mongnan had implored him to put on the dead Commander's uniform, and he reviewed the conversation with the Warden, sagging under the weight of a great rock, that allowed him to walk out of a prison camp. It's true that when I first imagined Ga's biography, it was the big moments that loomed large in the chapters, such as an underground showdown with the holder of the Golden Belt. But now it was a much more subtle book I was constructing, and only the hows mattered to me.

"I understand that you talked your way out of prison," I said to Commander Ga. "But how did you summon the nerve to go to Sun Moon's house? What did you say to her on the heels of killing her husband?"

Commander Ga had forsaken the bed by now. We leaned against opposite walls of the small room, smoking.

"Where else could I go?" he asked me. "What could I say but the truth?"

"And how did she respond?"

"She fell down and wept."

"Of course she did. How did you get from there to sharing a cup?"

"Sharing a cup?"

"You know what I'm saying," I told him. "How do you get a woman to love you, even though she knows you hurt people?"

"Is there someone you love?" Commander Ga asked me.

"I ask the questions around here," I said, but I couldn't let him think I had no one. I gave him a slight nod, one that suggested, *Are we not both men?*

"Then she loves you despite what you do?"

"What I do?" I asked him. "I help people. I save people from the treatment they'd get from those Pubyok animals. I've turned questioning into a science. You have your teeth, don't you? Has anyone wrapped wire around your knuckles until your fingertips swelled purple and went dead? I'm asking how she loved you. You were a replacement husband. Nobody truly loves a replacement husband. It's only their first family they care about."

Commander Ga began speaking on the topic of love, but suddenly his voice became static in my ears. I couldn't hear anything, for a notion had risen in my mind, the thought that maybe my parents had had a first family, that there were children before me that they lost and that I was a late, hollow replacement. That would account for their advanced ages and for the way that, when they looked at me, they seemed to see something that was lacking. And the fear in their eyes—might it not be the unbearable fear of losing me, too, a fear of the knowledge that they couldn't handle going through such loss again?

I took the underground trolley to Central Records and pulled my parents' files. All afternoon I read through them, and here I saw another reason that citizen biographies were needed: the files were filled with dates and stamps and grainy images and informant quotes and reports from housing blocks, factory committees, district panels, volunteer details, and Party boards. Yet there was no real information in them, no sense of who these two old people were, what brought them from Manpo to be line workers for life at the Testament to the Greatness of Machines Factory. In the end, though, the file's only stamp from the Pyongyang Maternity Hospital was mine.

Back in Division 42, I headed to the Pubyok lounge, where I moved my placard "Interrogator Number 6" from "On Duty" to "Off." Q-Kee and Sarge were laughing together, but when I entered, they went silent. So much for sexism. Q-Kee wasn't wearing her smock, and there was no missing her figure as she leaned back in one of the Pubyok recliners.

Sarge held up a hand freshly wrapped with tape. Even with a head of silver hair, even in the year of his retirement, he'd broken his hand anew. He made a voice, like his hand was talking. "Did the doorjamb hurt me?" his hand asked. "Or did the doorjamb love me?"

Q-Kee could barely suppress her laughter.

Instead of interrogation manuals, the Pubyok bookcases were filled with bottles of Ryoksong, and I could guess how their night would go: faces would start to glow red, a few patriotic songs would get belted from the karaoke machine, and soon Q-Kee would be playing drunken table tennis with the Pubyok, all gathered 'round to watch her breasts as she leaned over, prowling her end of the table, swatting that red-hot paddle of hers.

"You about to clear a name from the board?" Q-Kee asked me.

Now it was Sarge who had his laugh.

At this point, I'd missed preparing my parents' dinner, and since the trains had stopped, I'd have to cross the whole city in darkness in order to help them make their bedtime trip to the bathroom. But then I had a look at the big board, my first moment in weeks to really take a look at my workload. I had eleven active cases. All of the Pubyok together had one—some guy they were softening up till morning in the sump. The Pubyok close cases in forty-five minutes just by dragging people into the shop and helping them hold the confession pen in the moments before they expire. But here, looking at all those names, I understood how far my obsession with Ga had gone. My longest open case was my military nurse from Panmunjom, accused of flirting with an ROK officer across the DMZ. It was said she gave him pinkie waves and even blew kisses hard enough to float over the minefields. It was the easiest case on the board, really, which is why I kept putting it off. Her location on the board was marked as the "Down Cell," and I realized I'd left her there for five days. I slid my placard back to "On Duty" and got out of there before the sniggering could set in.

The nurse didn't smell so good when I pulled her out. The light was devastating to her.

"I'm so glad to see you," she said, wincing. "I'm really ready to talk. I've been doing a lot of thinking, and I have some things to say."

I took her to an interrogation bay and warmed up the autopilot. The whole thing was a shame, really. I had her biography half written—I'd probably wasted three afternoons on that. And her confession would practically write itself, but it wasn't her fault—she'd just fallen through the cracks.

I reclined her on one of our baby-blue chairs.

"I'm ready to denounce," she said. "There were many bad citizens who attempted to corrupt me, and I have a list, I'm ready to name them all."

I could only think of what would happen if I didn't get my father to a bathroom in the next hour. The nurse was wearing a medical gown, and I ran my hands along her torso to ensure that she was harboring no objects or jewelry that would interfere with the autopilot.

"Is that what you want?" she asked.

"What?"

"I'm ready to mend my relationship with my country," she said. "I'm prepared to do whatever it takes to show my good citizenship."

She lifted her gown so that it rose above her hips and the dark frost of her pubic hair was unmistakable. I was aware of how a woman's body was constructed and of its major functions. And yet I didn't feel in control again until the nurse was in her restraints, and I could hear the thrum of the autopilot's initial probings. There is always that initial involuntary gasp, that full-body tense when the autopilot administers its first licks. The nurse's eyes focused far away, and I ran my hand along her arm and across her collarbones. I could feel the charge moving through her. It entered me, made the hairs stand on the back of my hand.

Q-Kee was right to tease me; I'd let things slide, and here was our nurse, paying the price. At least we had the autopilot. When I first arrived at Division 42, the preferred method of reforming corrupted citizens was the lobotomy. As interns, Leonardo and I performed many. The Pubyok would grab whatever subjects were handy and in the name of training, we'd do a half-dozen in a row. All you needed was a twenty-centimeter nail. You'd lay the subject out on a table and sit on his chest. Leonardo, standing, would steady the subject's head, and with his thumbs, hold both eyelids open. Careful not to puncture anything, you'd run the nail in along the top of the eyeball, maneuvering it until you felt the bone at the back of the socket. Then with your palm, you gave the head of the nail a good thump. After punching through the orbital, the nail moved freely through the brain. Then it was simple: insert fully, shimmy to the left, shimmy to the right, repeat with other eye. I wasn't a doctor or anything, but I tried to make my actions smooth and accurate, not gruff like the Pubyok, whose broken hands made any delicate work apelike. I found a strong light proved most humane as the subjects were blinded to what was happening.

We were told there were whole lobotomy collectives where former subversives now knew nothing but good-natured labor for the benefit of all. But the truth proved far different. I went with Sarge once, when I was but a month in the smock, to interrogate a guard at one of these collectives, and we discovered no model labor farm. The actions of all were blunted and stammering. The laborers would rake the same patch of ground countless times and witlessly fill in holes they'd just dug. They cared not whether they were clothed or naked and relieved themselves at will. Sarge wouldn't stop commenting on what he thought was the indolence of the lobotomized, their group sloth. Shock-work whistles meant nothing to them, he said, and it seemed impossible to engender any notion of Juche spirit. He said, "Even children know how to step to the wheel!"

But it was the slack faces of the braincut you never forget—the babies in the jars on display in the Glories of Science Museum have more life. That trip proved to me that the system was broken, and I knew one day I'd play a role in fixing it. Then along came the autopilot, developed by a deep-bunker think tank, and I jumped at the chance to field-test it.

The autopilot is a hands-free piece of electronic wizardry. It's not some brutal application of electricity like one of the Pubyok's car batteries. The autopilot works in concert with the mind, measuring brain output, responding to alpha waves. Every consciousness has an electrical signature, and the autopilot's algorithm learns to read that script. Think of its probing as a conversation with the mind, imagine it in a dance with identity. Yes, picture a pencil and an eraser engaged in a beautiful dance across the page. The pencil's tip bursts with expression—squiggles, figures, words— filling the page, as the eraser measures, takes note, follows in the pencil's footsteps, leaving only blankness in its wake. The pencil's next seizure of scribbles is perhaps more intense and desperate, but shorter lived, and the eraser follows again. They continue in lockstep this way, the self and the state, coming closer to one another until finally the pencil and the eraser are almost one, moving in sympathy, the line disappearing even as it's laid down, the words unwritten before the letters are formed, and finally there is only white. The electricity often gives male subjects tremendous erections, so I'm not convinced the experience is all bad. I looked at the empty blue chair next to the nurse—to catch up, I'd probably have to start doing two at a time.

But back to my nurse. She was in a deep cycle now. The convulsions had hiked her gown again, and I hesitated before pulling it back down. Before me was her secret nest. I leaned over and inhaled deeply, breathing in—crackling bright—the ozone scent that rose from her. Then I loosened her restraints and turned out the light.

WHEN Commander Ga arrived at the site of the artificial Texas, a morning mist hung in the air. The landscape was rolling and tree-covered, so the area's watchtowers and surface-to-air-missile ramps couldn't be seen. They were downstream from Pyongyang, and though you could not see the Taedong River, you could smell it in every breath, swollen and green. It had been raining recently, an early monsoon off the Yellow Sea, and with the mud and dripping willow trees, it seemed a far cry from the desert of Texas.

He parked the Mustang and stepped out. There was no sign of the Dear Leader's entourage. Only Comrade Buc was here, sitting alone at a picnic table with a cardboard box. Buc beckoned him over, where Ga could see that the table's slats had been carved with initials in English. "Every last detail," he said to Buc.

Buc nodded at the box. "I've got a surprise for you," he said.

When Commander Ga looked at the box, he had a sudden feeling that inside was an object that had once belonged to the real Commander Ga. He didn't have a sense of whether it was a jacket or a hat or why Buc would be in possession of such a thing, he only felt that what was inside had belonged to his predecessor and that when he opened the box and came in contact with the thing, when he touched it and accepted it, the real Commander Ga would hold a power over him.

"You open it," he said to Buc.

Comrade Buc reached into the box and removed a pair of black cowboy boots.

Ga took them, turned them in his hands—they were the same pair he'd held in Texas.

"How'd you find these?" he asked.

Buc didn't answer, but gave a grin of pride that he could find any item on earth, anywhere, and fetch it to Pyongyang.

Ga removed his dress shoes, which, he now realized, actually had belonged to his predecessor. They'd been at least a size too large. When he sank his feet into the cowboy boots, they fit perfectly. Buc took one of Commander Ga's dress shoes and studied it.

"He was always such an ass about his shoes," Buc said. "He made me procure them for him in Japan. *They had to be from Japan.*"

"What should we do with them?"

"They're fine shoes," Buc said. "They'd be worth a small fortune at a night market."

But then Buc tossed them into the mud.

Together, the two men began walking the site, making sure everything was in order for the Dear Leader's inspection. The Japanese chuck wagon looked convincing enough, and there was no end of fishing poles and scythes. Near the shooting stand was a bamboo cage that contained the dark motion of poisonous snakes.

"Does it feel like Texas to you?" Comrade Buc asked.

Commander Ga shrugged. "The Dear Leader's never been to Texas," he said. "He'll think it looks like Texas, that's all that matters."

"That's not what I asked," Buc said.

Ga looked up to see if it would rain. This morning the rainfall had been heavy, obscuring everything out the windows, so the light was faint when Sun Moon shifted to his side of the bed. "I have to know if he's really gone," she said. "So many times my husband disappeared, only to reappear days or weeks later, in ways that would surprise you, test you. If he came back now, if he saw what we were planning . . . you don't even know." Here she paused. "When he really hurts people," she added, "he doesn't take snapshots."

Her hand was on his chest. He reached for her shoulder, the skin warm from the covers. "Trust me," he told her. "You'll never see him again." He ran his hand down her side, feeling the soft skin travel under his fingers.

"No," she said and pulled back. "Just tell me he's dead. Ever since we decided on our plan, now that we're risking everything, I can't shake this feeling that he's coming back."

"He's dead, I promise," he told her. But it wasn't so simple. It wasn't so simple because it had been dark and chaotic in the mine. He'd sunk a rear scissors choke on Commander Ga and held it for the full count and then some. When Mongnan came and found him, she told him to put on Ga's uniform. He got dressed and listened when she told him what to say to the Warden. But when she told him to crush the naked man's skull with a rock he shook his head no. Instead, he rolled the body into a shaft. It turned out to be a shallow one. They heard the body tumble briefly before sliding to a rest, and with the seed of doubt Sun Moon had placed in his chest, he, too, now had the feeling that he'd only *almost* killed the real Commander Ga, that the man was out there somewhere, recovering, regaining his strength, that when he was himself again, he'd be coming.

Ga walked to the corral. "This is the only Texas we've got," he said to Buc, then climbed the poles to sit on the top rung. A lone water ox was penned inside. A few fat, widely spaced raindrops fell, but they weren't followed by others.

Comrade Buc was busy lighting a fire in the pit, but mostly he was making smoke. From where he sat atop the corral, Ga could see eels gulping air along the surface of the fishing pond and hear the flap of a Texas state flag, hand-painted on Korean silk. The ranch looked enough like Texas to make him think of Dr. Song. But when he thought of what had happened to Dr. Song, the place suddenly looked nothing like America. It was hard to believe the old man was gone. Ga still saw him sitting there in the dark moonlight of a Texas night, holding his hat against the wind. He could still hear Dr. Song's voice in the aircraft hangar, *A most fascinating journey, never to be repeated.*

Comrade Buc splashed more fuel oil on the fire, raising a dark column.

"Wait till the Dear Leader brings the Americans out here," Buc said. "When the Dear Leader's happy, everyone's happy."

"About that," Ga said. "Don't you think your work's about done here?"

"What?" Buc asked. "What do you mean?"

"Looks like you got your hands on all the stuff you had to get. Shouldn't you move on to the next project and forget about all of this?"

"You upset about something?" Comrade Buc asked him.

"What if it turns out the Dear Leader isn't happy? What if something goes wrong and he ends up very unhappy? Have you thought of that?"

"That's what we're here for," Buc said. "To not let that happen."

"And then there's Dr. Song, who did everything right, and look what they did to him."

Buc turned away, and Ga could tell that the man did not want to talk about his old friend.

Ga said, "You've got a family, Buc. You should get some distance from this."

"But you still need me," Buc said. "I still need you." Buc walked to the fire pit and retrieved the Dear Leader's branding iron, which had just begun to heat. Buc used both arms to heft the thing—he held it up for Ga's inspection. In English, the letters running backward, the brand read: "PROPERTY OF THE DEMOCRATIC PEOPLES REPUBLIC OF KOREA."

The letters were big, making the brand almost a meter long. Red hot, it would sear an animal's entire side.

"It took the guys at the foundry a week to make this," Buc said.

"So?"

Buc looked impatient. "*So?* I don't speak English. I need you to tell me if we spelled it right."

Commander Ga carefully read the letters in reverse. "It's right," he said. Then he slipped through the corral rungs and went to the ox, tethered by a ring in its nose. He fed the beast watercress from a bin, then rubbed the black plate between its horns.

Comrade Buc neared, and by the way he warily eyed the large animal, it was pretty clear he'd never been commandeered to help with the harvest.

"You know how I told you about defeating Commander Ga in a prison mine?"

Buc nodded.

"He was lying there naked, and he looked pretty dead. A friend told me to drop a large rock on his skull."

"Wise friend," Buc said.

"But I couldn't do it. Now, I keep thinking, you know—"

"—that Commander Ga is still alive? Impossible. If he were alive, we'd know it, he'd be on top of us right now."

"I know he's dead. The only point is this," Ga said. "I keep having this feeling that something bad is ahead. You've got a family. You should think about them."

"There's something you're not telling me, isn't there?" Buc asked.

"I'm just trying to help you," Ga told him.

"You're planning something, I can tell," Buc said. "What are you up to?"

"I'm not," Ga said. "Let's just forget I said anything."

Buc stopped him. "You've got to tell me," he said. "Look, when the crow came, I opened my house, we extended our exit plan to you. I've said nothing to anyone about your real identity. I gave you my peaches. If something's up, you have to tell me."

Ga didn't say anything.

"Like you said, I have a family. What about them?" Buc asked. "How am I supposed to protect them if you leave me in the dark?"

Commander Ga looked around the ranch, at the pistols, the pitchers for lemonade, the gift baskets on the picnic tables. "When the American plane leaves, we'll be on it, Sun Moon, the kids, me."

Comrade Buc cringed. "No, no, no," he said. "You don't tell anyone, ever. Don't you know that? You never tell. Not your friends, not your family, especially not me. You could get everyone killed. If they interrogate me, they'll know I knew. And that's assuming you make it. Do you know the cushy promotion I'd get for turning you in?" Buc threw his hands up. "You don't ever tell. Nobody tells. Never."

Commander Ga stroked the ox's black neck, then patted it twice, dust rising from its greasy coat. "That branding iron will probably kill it, you know. That wouldn't impress the Americans."

Comrade Buc began lining fishing poles up against a tree. His hands were shaky. When he had them all set, a line snagged, and the poles fell over again. He looked at Ga, as if it were his fault. "But you," he said. "You're the one who tells." He shook his head. "That's why you're different. Somehow the rules are different for you, and that's why you maybe have a shot at making it."

"You believe that?"

"Is the plan simple?"

"I think so."

"Don't tell me anything more. I don't want to know." There was thunder, and Buc looked up, gauging whether rain was imminent. "Just answer this—are you in love with her?"

"Love," that was a very big word.

"If something happened to her," Buc asked, "would you want to go on without her?"

Such a simple question—how had he not asked himself this? He felt her steady hand on his tattoo from the other night, the way she let him quietly weep in bed beside her. She didn't even turn down the lantern so she wouldn't have to look upon his vulnerability. She'd just watched him, concern in her eyes, until sleep drew near.

Ga shook his head no.

Headlights appeared in the distance. Buc and Ga turned to see a black car navigating the muddy ruts on the road. It wasn't the Dear Leader's caravan. As it neared, they could see its wipers were still on, so it had come from the direction of the storm.

Buc turned to him, so they were close. He spoke with urgency. "I'll tell you what I know about how this world works. If you and Sun Moon go together with the kids, *maybe* there's a chance you'll make it, *maybe*." The first drops of rain fell. The ox lowered its head. "But if Sun Moon and the kids somehow get on that plane, yet you're by the Dear Leader's side, directing his focus, making excuses, diverting his attention, they'll *probably* make it." And here Comrade Buc let go of his permanent grin and laughing squint. When his face went slack, it was clear its natural state was seriousness. "It also means," he said, "that you'll *absolutely* be around to pay the price for this, rather than dutiful citizens like myself and my children."

A lone figure was walking toward them. He was military, they could tell. As the rain thickened, he made no effort to shield himself, and they watched his uniform darken as he neared. Ga opened his spectacles and peered through them. For some reason, he could make out nothing of the man's face, but the uniform was unmistakable: he was a commander.

Comrade Buc regarded the figure nearing them. "Fuck me," he said, and turned to Ga. "You know what Dr. Song said about you? He said you had a gift, that you could say a lie while speaking the truth."

"Why'd you tell me that?"

"Because Dr. Song never got the chance to tell you," Buc said. "And here's something I have to say to you. There's probably no way you could pull this off without me. But if you stick around after this happens, if you stay and bear the burden, I'll help you."

"Why?"

"Because Commander Ga did the worst thing that's ever been done to me. Then he went right on living next door. And I had to go on working on the same floor with him. I had to bend over and check his shoe size before I ordered his slippers from Japan. Every time I closed my eyes, I saw him coming at me. When I lay with my wife, I felt Ga's weight atop me. But you, you came along and fixed him for me. When you arrived, he vanished."

Comrade Buc stopped and turned. Ga turned, too.

Then from the rain appeared the scarred face of Commander Park.

"Forget about me?" Park asked.

"Not at all," Ga said. He watched beads of rain trace the wounds in Park's face and wondered if this wasn't the inspiration for the disfigured man in the Dear Leader's script.

"There's been a turn of events," Commander Park said. "Comrade Buc and I are going to take inventory of the situation here." He fixed his eyes on Ga. "And you, the Dear Leader will brief you himself. And after this is all said and done, perhaps you and I will have a chance to rekindle our friendship."

*

"Ah, you've just come from Texas," the Dear Leader said when he saw Commander Ga's muddy boots. "What do you think? Is the ranch convincing?"

The Dear Leader was in a white hallway, deep underground, deciding which of two identical doors he should open. When the Dear Leader reached for one, the knob buzzed, and Ga could hear an electric lock unbolt.

"It was uncanny," Ga said. "Like stepping into the Old West."

Ga's ears were still pulsing from the elevator's plunge. His uniform was wet, and the underground cold penetrated him. How far below Pyongyang he was, he had no way of knowing. The bright fluorescent lights looked familiar, as did the white cement walls, but he could only wonder if they were on the same level as last time.

"Sadly," the Dear Leader said, "I might not get a chance to behold it."

Inside, the room was filled with gifts, awards, platters, and plaques, all with blank areas where inscriptions and occasions were to be engraved across the silver or bronze. The Dear Leader placed his hand on a rhinoceros horn, one in a set of bookends. "Mugabe keeps giving us these," he said. "The Americans would piss Prozac if we surprised them with a pair of these. But that raises the question: what gift do you give a guest who travels a great distance to visit but won't accept your hospitality?"

"I'm afraid I don't follow," Ga said.

The Dear Leader felt the tip of the rhino's horn. "The Americans have informed us that this will not be a diplomatic mission after all. *It is an exchange,* they now say, which will take place at the airport. They ask that we bring our pretty rower there, and it will be on the runway, provided we supply a forklift, that they return what they stole from me."

Ga was suddenly offended. "They won't taste our corn biscuits or fire our pistols?"

The Dear Leader's laugh lines went slack, and he regarded Ga with eyes so serious that a stranger would take them for sad. "In doing this, they steal from me something much larger."

"What about the Texas ranch?" he asked the Dear Leader. "We've built it complete."

"Dismantle it, move it to the airport," he said. "Put it in a hangar where we can access it if we decide we can still use some of it."

"Everything? The snakes, the river eels?"

"You have eels? Now I'm really sorry I missed it."

Ga tried to visualize taking a hearth apart or a branding pit. That monstrous branding iron now seemed like a labor of love, and he couldn't imagine it packed away in the cinema house's property lot, as likely to see the light of day again as a hand-painted, silken flag of Texas.

"Do the Americans offer a reason?"

The Dear Leader's eyes panned the room, trying, Ga could tell, to find a gift that might match his humiliation. "The Americans say there is a window two days from now in which no Japanese spy satellites will be flying over. The Americans fear the Japanese would be furious to learn that— Oh, fuck them!" the Dear Leader said. "Do they not know that on my soil they play by my rules! Do they not know that when their wheels touch the ground they are beholden to me, to my tremendous sense of duty!"

"I know the gift," Commander Ga said.

The Dear Leader eyed him with suspicion.

"When our delegation left Texas, there were a couple of surprises at the airport."

The Dear Leader said nothing.

"There were two pallets, the kind a forklift would use. The first was loaded with food."

"A pallet of food? This was not in the report I read. No one confessed to that."

"The food was not from the Senator, but from his church. There were barrels of flour and hundred-kilo sacks of rice, burlap bags of beans, all stacked up in a cube and wrapped tight with plastic."

"Food?" the Dear Leader asked.

Ga nodded.

"Go on," the Dear Leader said.

"And on another skid were little Bibles, thousands of them, shrink-wrapped in plastic."

"Bibles," the Dear Leader said.

"Very small ones, with green vinyl covers."

"How have I not heard any of this?"

"Of course we didn't accept it, we left it on the runway."

"*On the runway,*" the Dear Leader said.

"There was one other thing," Commander Ga said. "A dog, a baby one. It was given to us by the Senator's wife herself, bred from her own stock."

"Food aid," the Dear Leader said, his eyes darting about, thinking. "Bibles and a dog."

"The food is already prepared," Ga said.

"And of the Bibles?"

Ga smiled. "I know an author whose thoughts on opera should be required reading in all civilized nations. A thousand copies could easily be obtained."

The Dear Leader nodded. "About the dog, what Korean pet would be the equivalent? A tiger, perhaps? A tremendous snake?"

"Why not give them a dog back—we'll say it's the Senator's dog, and say we're returning it because it's selfish, lazy, and materialistic."

"This dog," the Dear Leader said, "must be the most vicious, snarling cur in all the land. It must have tasted the blood of baboons in the Central Zoo and chewed on the bones of half-starved prisoners in Camp 22." The Dear Leader looked off, as if he wasn't at the bottom of a bunker, but on a plane, watching the Senator being ravaged by a rabid canine for the sixteen hours it took to return to Texas.

"I know just the dog," Commander Ga said.

"You know," the Dear Leader said, "you broke my driver's nose."

Ga said, "The nose will heal back stronger."

"Spoken like a true North Korean," the Dear Leader said. "Come, Commander, there's something I've been meaning to show you."

*

They moved to another floor, to another room that looked just like the last one. Ga understood that sameness was meant to confuse an invading force, but wasn't the effect worse on those who must daily endure it? In the halls, he could feel the presence of security teams, always just out of sight, making the Dear Leader seem eternally alone.

In the room was a school desk with a lone computer monitor, its green cursor blinking. "Here's the machine I promised to show you," the Dear Leader said. "Were you secretly mad at me for making you wait?"

"Is this the master computer?" Ga asked.

"It is," the Dear Leader answered. "We used to have a dummy version, but that was only for interrogations. This one contains the vital information for every single citizen—it tells you date of birth or date of death, current location, family members, and so on. When you type in a citizen's name, all this information is sent to a special agency that dispatches a crow right away."

The Dear Leader ushered Commander Ga into the chair. Before him was only the black of the screen, that green flash. "Everyone's in here?" Ga asked.

"Every man, woman, and child," the Dear Leader said. "When a name is typed on this screen, it is sent to our finest team. They act with great dispatch. The person in question will be found and transported right away. There is no evading its reach."

The Dear Leader pushed a button, and on the screen appeared a number: 22,604,301.

He pressed the button again, and the number changed: 22,604,302.

"Witness the miracle of life," the Dear Leader said. "Do you know we are fifty-four-percent female? We didn't discover that until this machine. They say that famine favors the girls. In the South, it's the opposite. They have a machine that can tell if a baby will be a boy or a girl, and the girls they dispose of. Can you imagine that, killing a girl baby, still in the mother?"

Ga said nothing—all babies in Prison 33 were killed. Every couple of months, there was a termination day in which rows of pregnant inmates had their bellies injected with saline. The guards had a wooden box on casters that they pushed around with their feet. Into this went, one by one, purple and dogpaddling, the partly developed babies as they came.

"But we will have the last word," the Dear Leader said. "A version is being created with every South Korean's name inside, so that there will be no one beyond our reach. That's real reunification, don't you think, being able to place a guiding hand on the shoulder of every Korean, North or South? With good infiltration teams, it will be like the DMZ doesn't exist. In the spirit of One Korea, I offer you a gift. Type in the name of a person you'd like found, for whom resolution is lacking, and they will be dealt with. Go ahead, any name. Perhaps someone who wronged you during the Arduous March or a rival from the orphanage."

The parade of people came to Ga, all those whose absences hung like empty dry docks in his memory. Throughout his life, he'd felt the presence of people he'd lost, eternally just out of reach. And here he was, seated before the collected fates of everyone. Yet he did not know his parents' names, and the only information an orphan's name gives is that he's an orphan. Since Sun Moon had come into his life, he'd stopped wondering what had happened to Officer So and the Second Mate and his wife. The Captain's name is the one he would have typed, but there was no need for that now. And Mongnan and Dr. Song, those were the last names he'd enter, as he wanted them to live forever in his memory. In the end, there was only one person who was haunting him, whose fate and location he had to know about. Commander Ga put his fingers to the keys and typed "Commander Ga Chol Chun."

When the Dear Leader saw this, he was beside himself. "Oh, that's rich," he said. "Oh, that's a new one. You know what this machine does, right, you know what kind of team waits for these names? It's good, too good, but I can't let you do it." The Dear Leader hit the Delete button and shook his head. "He typed his own name. Wait till I tell everyone at dinner tonight. Wait till they hear the story of how the Commander entered his own name into the master computer."

The green blinked at Ga like a faraway pulse in the dark.

The Dear Leader clapped him on the shoulder. "Come," he said. "One last thing. I need you to translate something for me."

*

When they reached the Girl Rower's cell, the Dear Leader paused outside. He leaned against the wall, tapping the key against the cement. "I don't want to let her go," he said.

Of course a deal had been struck, the Americans would be here in a few days and breaking a deal like this would never be forgiven. But Ga didn't mention any of that. He said, "I understand exactly how you feel."

"She has no idea what I'm talking about when I speak to her," the Dear Leader said. "But that's okay. She has a curious mind, I can tell. I've been visiting her for a year. I've always needed someone like that, someone I can say things to. I like to think she enjoys my visits. Over time I think I have grown on her. How she makes you work for a smile, but when she gives you one, it's real, you know it."

The Dear Leader's eyes were small and searching, as if he was trying not to see the fact that he would have to give her up. It was the way your eyes could scan the sloshing water in the bottom of a skiff because to look anywhere else—at the beach or the duct tape in your hands or Officer So's stony face—was to acknowledge you were trapped, that very soon you'd be forced to do the thing you abhorred the most.

"I have read that there is a syndrome," the Dear Leader said. "In this syndrome, a female captive begins to sympathize with her captor. Often it leads to love. Have you heard of this?"

The idea seemed impossible, preposterous, to him. What person could shift allegiance toward their oppressor? Who could possibly sympathize with the villain who stole your life?

Ga shook his head.

"The syndrome is real, I assure you. The only problem is they say it sometimes takes years to work, which it seems we don't have." He looked at the wall. "When you said you understood how I felt, did you mean that?"

"I did," he said. "I do."

The Dear Leader studied closely the ridges of the key in his hand. "I suppose you do," he said. "You have Sun Moon. I used to confide in her. Yes, I used to tell her everything. That was years ago. Before you came and took her." He looked at Ga now, shaking his head. "I can't believe you're still alive. I can't believe I didn't throw you to the Pubyok. Tell me, where am I going to find another girl rower? One who's tall and beautiful and who listens, a girl whose heart is true and yet she still knows how to take the blood out of her friend with her bare hands?" He stuck the key in the lock. "So she doesn't understand the words I say to her—she gets the meaning, I'm sure of it. And she doesn't need words—everything she feels crosses her face. Sun Moon was that way. Sun Moon was exactly like that," he said, and turned the key in the lock.

*

Inside, the Girl Rower was at her studies. Her notebooks were stacked high, and she was silently transcribing an English version of *The Vigorous Zeal of the Revolutionary Spirit* by Kim Jong Il.

The Dear Leader stood leaning against the open doorframe, admiring her at a distance.

"She's read every word I've written," he said. "That's the truest way to know the heart of another. Can you imagine it, Ga, if that syndrome is real, an American in love with me? Wouldn't that be the ultimate victory? A brawny, beautiful American girl. Wouldn't that be the last word?"

Ga knelt next to her and slid the lamp across the table so he could get a better look. Her skin was so pale it seemed translucent. There was a rattle when she breathed from the damp air.

The Dear Leader said, "Ask her if she knows what a *choson-ot* is. I honestly doubt it. She hasn't seen another woman in a year. I bet the last woman she saw was being killed by her own hands."

Ga got her to lock eyes with him. *"Do you want to go home?"* he asked her.

She nodded.

"Excellent," the Dear Leader said. "So she does know what a *choson-ot* is. Tell her I'll have someone come fit her for one."

"This is very important," Ga said to her. *"The Americans are going to try to come get you. Right now, in your notebook, I need you to write what I say: Wanda, accept—"*

"Tell her she will get her first bath, too," the Dear Leader interrupted. "And assure her it will be a woman that helps her."

Ga went on. *"Write exactly what I say: Wanda, accept food aid, dog, and books."*

While she wrote, he looked back at the Dear Leader, backlit by the corridor lights.

The Dear Leader said to him, "Maybe I should let her out, take her to that spa treatment at the Koryo Hotel. She might start to look forward to things like that."

"Excellent idea," Ga told him, then turned to the girl. Quietly, clearly, he said, "*Add: Hidden guests bring a valuable laptop.*"

"Maybe I should spoil her a little," the Dear Leader mused, looking at the ceiling. "Ask her if there's anything she wants, anything."

"*When we leave, destroy that paper,*" Ga told her. "*Trust me, I'm going to get you home. In the meantime, is there anything you need?*"

"*Soap,*" she said.

"Soap," he told the Dear Leader.

"Soap?" the Dear Leader asked. "Didn't you just tell her that she was getting a bath?"

"*Not soap,*" Ga told her.

"*Not soap?*" she asked. "*Toothpaste, then. And a brush.*"

"She meant the kind of soap you clean your teeth with," Ga told him. "You know, toothpaste and a brush."

The Dear Leader stared first at her, then at him. He pointed the cell key at Ga.

"She grows on a person, doesn't she?" the Dear Leader asked. "How can I give her up? Tell me, what do you think the Americans would do if they came here, returned my property, got humiliated, and left with nothing but bags of rice and a mean dog?"

"I thought that was the plan."

"Yes, that was the plan. But all my advisors, they're like mice in a munitions factory. They tell me not to anger the Americans, that I can only push them so far, that now that the Americans know the Girl Rower's alive, they'll never relent."

"The girl is yours," Ga said. "That is the only fact. People must understand that whether she stays or goes or becomes a cinder in Division 42, it is as you wish it. If the Americans receive a tutorial in this fact, it doesn't matter what happens to her."

"True, true," the Dear Leader said. "Except I don't want to let her go. Is there a way, you think?"

"If the girl met with the Senator and told him herself that she wished to stay, then maybe there would be no incident."

The Dear Leader shook his head at that distasteful suggestion. "If only I had another girl rower," he said. "If only our little killer here hadn't done away with her friend, then I could have sent home the one I liked the least." Here he laughed. "That's all I need, right? *Two* bad girls on my hands." He wagged his finger at her. *"Bad girl, bad girl,"* he said, laughing. *"Very bad girl."*

Commander Ga produced his camera. "If she's going to get cleaned up and fitted for a *choson-ot,*" he said, "I'll need to get a 'before' photo." He neared her and squatted low to snap the picture. "And maybe an action shot," he announced, "of how our guest has documented the amassed knowledge of our glorious leader Kim Jong Il."

He nodded to her. *"Now hold up the book."*

Commander Ga was squinting to make sure everything fit perfectly, the woman and her book, the note to Wanda—everything had to be in focus—when he saw through the viewfinder that the Dear Leader was crouching down and squeezing into the frame, his hand pulling her close by her shoulder. Ga stared at the strange and dangerous image before him and decided it was right that cameras were illegal.

"Tell her to smile," the Dear Leader said.

"Can you smile?" he asked.

She smiled.

"The truth is," Ga said, his finger on the button, "that eventually everyone goes away."

That these words should come from the lips of Commander Ga made the Dear Leader grin. "Isn't that the truth of it," he responded.

In English, Ga said, *"Say 'Cheese.'"*

And then the Dear Leader and his dear rower were blinking together from the flash.

"I want copies of those," the Dear Leader said, straining to get back to his feet.

I'D STAYED LATE at Division 42; my body felt weak. It was like there was some nourishment I was missing, like my body was hungering for some kind of food I'd simply never run across. I thought of the dogs in the Central Zoo that lived only on cabbage and old tomatoes. Had they forgotten the taste of meat? I felt like there was something, some sustenance that I'd simply never known. I breathed deeply, but the air smelled no different—grilled onion stalks, boiling peanuts, millet in the pan, dinner in Pyongyang. There was nothing to do but go home.

Much of the city's electricity was being diverted to run industrial rice dryers south of town, so the subway was shut down. And the line for the Kwangbok express bus was three blocks long. I started walking. I didn't make it two blocks before I heard the bullhorns and knew I was in trouble. The Minister of Mass Mobilization and his cadres were moving through the district, sweeping up any citizen unlucky enough to be out on the street. Just the sight of their yellow insignia sickened me. You couldn't run—if they even thought you were trying to avoid "volunteering" for harvest duty, it was off to a Redeemability Farm for a month of labor and group criticism. It was, however, the kind of thing a Pubyok badge could get you out of. Without it, I found myself in the back of a dump truck headed to the countryside to harvest rice for sixteen hours.

We drove northeast by moonlight, toward the silhouetted Myohyang Range, a dump truck filled with city folks in professional attire, the driver flashing on his headlamps when he thought he saw something in the road, but there was nothing in the road, no people, no cars, nothing but empty highways lined with tank traps and large Chinese excavators—their orange arms frozen in extension—abandoned by the canals for want of parts.

In the dark, we found a peasant village somewhere along the Chongchon River. We city folk, about a hundred of us, climbed down to sleep on the open ground. I had a smock to keep me warm and my briefcase for a pillow. The stars above seemed placed for my pleasure, and it was a welcome change from sleeping under dirt and goats. For five years, I'd used a badge to escape harvest details, so I'd forgotten the sounds of crickets and frogs in the summer, the pungent mist that rises off the rice water. I heard children somewhere playing a game in the dark, and I heard the sounds of a man and a woman engaged in what must have been intercourse. What followed was my best night of sleep in years.

There was no breakfast, and my hands blistered before the sun was fully up. For hours I did nothing but dig open irrigation dams and backfill running canals. Why we drained one field and flooded another, I had no idea, but light dawned hard on the peasants of Chagang Province. They all wore cheap, ill-fitting vinalon clothes, they had nothing but black sandals, and their bodies were rail thin with cracked, dark skin and teeth translucent to their black cores. Every woman with a hint of beauty had been siphoned to the capital. It turned out I showed too little promise as a rice harvester and was instead sent to empty latrine pots, raking the contents in between layers of rice hull. Then I dug ruts through the village that I was told would be of use when the rains came. An old woman, too old to work, watched me dig. She smoked her own kind of cigarette, rolled in corn husks, and told me many stories, but because she lacked teeth, I could not understand them.

In the afternoon, a city woman was struck by a grand snake, long as a man. They gave her wound a poultice. I tried to quiet her screams by stroking her hair, but that snakebite must have done something to her—she started hitting me and pushing me away. The peasants by then had caught the twisting snake, black as the befecaled water that had concealed it. Some wanted to take its gall bladder, others wished to milk its venom for liquor. They appealed to the old woman, who motioned for them to free it. I watched the snake swim away through a paddy field cleared of rice. The shallow water was both dark and flashing with sunset. The snake took its own course, away from all of us, and I had a feeling there was another black snake out across the water, waiting for this broad swimmer to make its way home to her.

*

It was midnight when I made it home. Though the key turned in the lock, the door wouldn't open. It was somehow barricaded from within. I pounded on the door. "Mother," I called. "Father, it's me, your son. There's something wrong with the door. You must open it for me." I pleaded for a while, then put my shoulder to the wood, leaning into it some, but not too hard. Breaking down a door would cause much discussion in the building. Finally, I buttoned my smock and lay down in the hall. I tried to think of the sounds of the crickets and the children running in the dark, but when I closed my eyes I could imagine only cold cement. I thought of the peasants with their ropy bodies and harsh manner of speaking, of how, except for starvation, they didn't have a care in the world.

In the dark, I heard a sound—*bing!* It was the red cell phone.

I found the phone, its green light flashing. On the tiny screen was a new picture: a Korean boy and a Korean girl stood half-stunned, half-smiling against a sunny blue sky. They wore black caps with ears that made them look like mice.

Come morning, the door was standing open. Inside, my mother was cooking porridge while my father sat at the table. "Who's there?" my father asked. "Is someone there?"

I could see that one of the chairs had a shiny spot on its back where the doorknob had rubbed.

"It's me, Father, your son."

"Thank goodness you're back," my father said. "We were worried about you."

My mother said nothing.

On the table were the files I'd pulled on my parents. I'd been studying them all week. They looked like they'd been rifled.

"I tried to get in last night but the door was blocked," I said. "Didn't you hear me?"

"I didn't hear anything," Father said. He spoke to the air. "My wife, did you hear anything?"

"No," she said from the stove. "I heard nothing, nothing at all."

I straightened the files. "I suppose you two have gone deaf, now, as well."

My mother shuffled to the table with two bowls of porridge, her feet sliding in baby steps lest she stumble in her darkness.

I asked, "But why was the door blocked? You aren't afraid of me, are you?"

"Afraid of you?" my mother asked.

"Why would we be afraid of you?" asked my father.

My mother said, "The loudspeaker said the American Navy was conducting aggressive military exercises off the coast."

"You can't take any chances," my father said. "With the Americans, you must take measures."

They blew on their food and took quiet spoonfuls.

"How is it," I asked my mother, "that you cook so well without your sight?"

"I can feel the heat that comes off the pan," she said. "And as the food cooks, the smell changes."

"What about the knife?"

"Using the knife is easy," she said. "I guide it with my knuckles. Stirring food in the pan is the hardest. I always spill."

In my mother's file was a photo of her when she was young. She was a beauty, perhaps the reason she was brought to the capital from the countryside, but what got her sentenced to a factory, rather than assigned as a singer or a hostess, was not in her record. I ruffled the folders, so they could be heard.

"There were some papers on the table," my father said, his voice nervous.

"They fell to the floor," my mother said. "But we picked them up."

"It was an accident," my father added.

"Accidents happen," I told them.

"Those papers," my mother said. "Were they work related?"

"Yes," Father said. "Were they part of a case you're working on?"

"Just research," I said.

"They must be important files if you brought them home," my father said. "Is anyone in trouble? Perhaps someone we know?"

"What's going on here?" I asked. "Is it about Mrs. Kwok? Are you still mad at me for that? I didn't want to turn her in. She was the one stealing coal from the furnace. In winter, we were all colder because of her selfishness."

"Don't get mad," my mother said. "We were just showing concern for the unlucky souls in your files."

"Unlucky?" I asked. "What makes you call them unlucky?"

They both went silent. I turned toward the kitchen and looked at the can of peaches perched above the top cabinet. I had a feeling the can had been moved a little, inspected perhaps by this blind duo, but I couldn't be sure of the direction I'd left the can facing.

Slowly, I waved my mother's file once before her eyes, yet she made no track of it. Then I fanned her with the file, so the breeze moved across her face, surprising her.

My mother recoiled, inhaling with fright.

"What is it?" my father asked her. "What happened?"

She said nothing.

"Can you see me, Mother?" I asked. "It's important that I know if you can see me."

She faced my direction, though her eyes were focusless. "Can I see you?" she asked me. "I see you as I first saw you, in glimpses, through darkness."

"Spare me the riddles," I warned her. "I have to know."

"You were born at night," she said. "I labored all day, and when darkness fell, we had no candles. You came by feel into your father's hands."

My father lifted his hands, scarred by mechanical looms. "These hands," he said.

"Such was the year Juche 62," my mother said. "Such was life in a factory dormitory. Your father lit match after match."

"One after another, until they were gone," my father said.

"I touched every part of your body, at first to see if you were whole and then to know you. So new you were, so innocent—you could have become anyone. It took a while, until first light, that we got a look at what we had created."

"Were there other children?" I asked. "Was there another family?"

My mother ignored this. "Our eyes do not work. That is the answer to your question. But then as now, we do not need sight to see what you have become."

ON SUNDAY, Commander Ga strolled with Sun Moon along the Chosun Relaxation Footpath, which followed the river to the Central Bus Terminal. In this public place, they thought they might not be overheard. Old people filled the benches, and because a new book had been published that month, young people lay in the grass reading copies of the novel *All for Her Country.* Commander Ga could smell the hot ink from the presses of the *Rodong Sinmun,* which, rumor had it, printed on Sunday afternoons all the newspaper editions for the week to come. Whenever Ga spotted a hungry-eyed urchin crouched in the bushes, he'd toss him a couple of coins. Sun Moon's children seemed oblivious to these orphans hiding in their midst. The boy and the girl ate flavored ice and wandered through willows whose late-summer arms hung low enough to sweep the gravel path.

Commander Ga and Sun Moon had been speaking in abstractions and half notions, dancing around the facts of the very real thing they had set in motion. He wanted to put a name to what they were doing, to call it escape, defection. He wanted to outline the steps, to memorize them and practice out loud how they would go. Like a script, he said. He asked her to say she understood that the worst could happen. She would speak of none of this. Instead, she remarked on the crunch of the gravel under her feet, of the groan of the river dredges as they bent their rusty booms below the surface. She stopped to smell an azalea as if it were the last azalea, and as she walked, she wove fine purple bracelets from wisteria. She wore a white cotton *choson-ot* that outlined her body with shifts in the breeze.

"I want to tell the children before we leave," he said.

This, perhaps because it seemed so preposterous to her, moved her to speak.

"Tell them what?" she asked. "That you killed their father? No, they're going to grow up in America believing that their dad was a great hero whose remains rest in a faraway land."

"But they have to know," he said, then was silent a moment as a brigade of soldiers' mothers passed by, shaking their red cans to intimidate Songun donations from people. "Those kids have to hear it from me," he went on. "The truth, an explanation—these are the most important things for them to hear. This is all I have to give them."

"But there will be time," she said. "This decision can be made later, when we're safe in America."

"No," he told her. "It must be now."

Commander Ga looked back at the boy and the girl. They were watching this conversation, even though they were too far away to make out the words.

"Is something wrong?" Sun Moon asked. "Does the Dear Leader suspect something?"

He shook his head. "I don't think so," he said, though the question conjured the Girl Who Rowed in the Dark and the notion that the Dear Leader might not relinquish her.

Sun Moon stopped by a cement water barrel and lifted its wooden cover. She drew a ladle and drank, her hands cupping the silver dipper. Commander Ga watched a trickle of water darken the front of her *choson-ot*. He tried to imagine her with another man. If the Dear Leader didn't let go of his Girl Rower, then the plan was off, the Americans would leave in outrage, and something bad would soon happen to Commander Ga. As for Sun Moon, she would become a prize once more, to whatever replacement husband was found. And what if the Dear Leader was right, what if over the years she came to love this new husband, real love, not the promise of love or the potential for love—could Commander Ga leave this world knowing her heart was destined for another?

Sun Moon plunged the ladle deep into the barrel to get the cool water at the bottom before holding the dipper for Ga to drink. The water tasted mineral and fresh.

He wiped his mouth. "Tell me," he said to her. "Do you think it's possible for a woman to fall in love with her captor?"

She observed him a moment. He could tell she was looking for signs as to how to answer.

He said, "It's impossible, right? The idea is completely insane, don't you think?" He saw in his mind a parade of all the people he'd captured, their wide eyes and abraded faces, the white of their lips when the duct tape was torn off. He saw those red toenails rearing to strike. "I mean, all they can have is contempt for you, for taking everything from them. Tell the truth, say there can be no such syndrome."

"Syndrome?" she asked.

He looked over at the children, frozen in mid-stride. They often played a game to see which one could be the most statue-like.

"The Dear Leader has read of a syndrome, and he believes that if he keeps a certain woman imprisoned long enough, she will come to love him."

"A certain woman?" Sun Moon asked.

"It's not important who she is," he said. "All that matters is that she's American. A delegation is coming for her, and if the Dear Leader doesn't hand her over, our plan is ruined."

"You said she was a captive. What—is she in a cage or a prison? How long has this been going on?"

"She's in his private bunker. She was going around the world but had a problem on her boat. They plucked her out of the sea, and now the Dear Leader's infatuated with her. He goes down there at night and plays her operas composed in his honor. He wants to keep her down deep until she develops feelings for him. Have you ever heard of anything like this? Tell me there's no such thing."

Sun Moon was quiet a moment. Then she said, "What if a woman had to sleep in the same bed as her captor?"

Ga eyed her to see what she was getting at.

Sun Moon said, "What if she depended on her captor for every necessity—food, cigarettes, clothes—and he could indulge or deprive her at his whim?"

She looked at him as though she truly wanted an answer, but he could only wonder if she was speaking of himself or his predecessor.

"What if a woman had children with her captor?"

Ga took the ladle from her hands and drew water for the boy and the girl, but they were now assuming the poses of the hammer and sickle bearers on the frieze of the Party Foundation Monument, and even the heat of the day could not make them break from their personas.

"That man is gone," he said. "I'm here now. I'm not your captor. I'm liberating you. It's easy to talk about prisoners, but I'm the one trying to get you to say the word 'escape.' That's what the Dear Leader's captive wants. She might be locked in a cell, but her heart is restless. She will leap at the chance to get out, trust me."

"You sound like you know her," Sun Moon said.

"There was a time," he told her. "It seems like another life. I had a job transcribing radio transmissions on the sea. I listened from sunset to sunrise, and in the darkest hour, I'd hear her, the Girl Rower. She and her friend were rowing around the world, but this one, she was the one that rowed all night, without the horizon to steer toward or the sun to mark her progress. She was forever bound to the other rower, yet completely alone. She labored forward solely on duty, her body bowing to the oars, but her mind, the broadcasts she made, never had a woman sounded so free."

Sun Moon cocked her head and tried on those words. "Forever bound to another," she whispered. "Yet totally alone," she added in self-reflection.

"Is that how you want to live?" he asked.

She shook her head.

"Are you ready to talk about the plan?"

She nodded.

"Okay," he said. "Just remember, forever bound yet alone—that could be a good thing. If for some reason we ended up separated, if somehow we didn't get out together, we could be bound, even if we weren't together."

"What are you talking about?" she asked. "There will be no alone. That's not how it's going to go."

"What if something goes wrong, what if in getting the three of you out, I am left behind?"

"Oh no," she said. "There is going to be none of that. I need you. I don't speak English, I don't know where to go, I don't know which Americans are informants and which are not. We're not going around the world with just the clothes on our backs."

"Believe me—if something went wrong, I'd eventually join you. Somehow I'd make it. And you wouldn't be alone. The Senator's wife would help you until I made my way to you."

"I don't need someone's wife," she told him. "I need you. It's you I must have. You don't understand what my life has been like, how I've been baited and tricked before."

"You must believe me that I'll follow," Ga said. "After you get safely out, I'll be right behind you. I've been to South Korea twelve times in my life, Japan nine times, Russia twice, and I have seen the sun rise and set on Texas soil. I will join you."

"No, no, no," she said. "You never do that to me, you never disappear on me. We all go together. Your job is to make that happen. Is it the *Casablanca* movie that's got you confused?" Her voice was rising now. "You don't stay behind like a martyr, like Rick. Rick failed at his job, his job was to . . ." She stopped herself before she became too upset. Instead, she gave him that voluptuous actress smile of hers. "You can't leave me. I'm your captive," she said. "What good's a captive without her captor? Won't we need a lot of time together if we're to prove once and for all if the Dear Leader's syndrome is true?"

He could hear the lie in her voice. Her acting, he could recognize it now. But he saw the desperation and vulnerability underneath, and he loved her all the more for it.

"Of course I am going with you," Ga told her. "I'll always be with you."

And then came the kiss. It started with the tilt of her head, her eyes flashing to his mouth, a hand slowly reaching to his collarbone, where it rested, and then she leaned in, the slowest lean in the world. He recognized the kiss. It was from *Hold the Banner High!*, the one she planted on the weak-minded South Korean border guard, distracting him while her band of freedom fighters cut the power to the sentry tower and began the liberation of South Korea from the hands of its capitalist oppressors. He'd dreamed of that kiss and now it was his.

Into his ear, she whispered, "Let's escape."

CITIZENS! Open your windows and cast your eyes upward, for a crow flies above Pyongyang, its raked beak twitching at every possible threat to the patriotic populace below. Hear the black wings beat, flinch at its sharp call. Observe this master of the air swooping into the schoolyards to sniff all the children for traces of cowardice, then dive, claws extended, to gauge the loyalty of the doves that adorn the statue of Kim Il Sung. Being the only animal with eyes sharp enough to spot virginity, witness our crow circle a Juche Youth Troop, and nod in approval as this illustrious avian performs an aerial inspection of their reproductive purity.

But America's what's really on this crow's mind. It's not hunting chestnut thieves or peering in housing-block windows for the telltale paw-prints of illegal dog farming. No, citizens, the Americans have accepted the Dear Leader's invitation to visit Pyongyang, the most glorious capital in the world. So the dark wings that protectively cast their shadow upon the fields of Arirang are hunting for any hint of capitalist sympathizers. One traitor is all it would take to disillusion a land so pure it knows nothing of materialist greed or war-crime sneak attacks. Luckily, citizens, no animal keeps its benevolent eye on the Korean people like the crow. It won't let ours become a nation where people give names to canines, oppress others because of the color of their skin, and eat pharmaceutically sweetened pills to abort their babies.

But why, you ask, does this crow circle the Chosun Relaxation Footpath? Isn't this where our finest citizens come to stroll, where young people gather to wash the feet of the old and where on a hot day wet nurses volunteer their paps to refresh Pyongyang's finest *yangban* babies? The keen-eyed crow is here, citizens, because it spotted a man tossing a shiny object into the bushes, where some scrambling orphans fought to obtain it. Not only does the giving of coins to orphans rob them of their self-respect and Juche Spirit, it violates a central rule of good citizenship: Practice Self-Sufficiency.

Looking more closely, the crow noted that as this man spoke to a woman, he made certain gestures that were clear indicators of the discussion of a plan. Tomorrow is a concern of the state, citizens. Tomorrow is the business of your leaders, and you must leave what's to come in their hands. So another rule of good citizenship had been violated: Refrain from the Future. It was then that this crow recognized the violator as Commander Ga, a man who had recently been observed disregarding all the rules of good citizenship: Devote Yourself Eternally to Our Glorious Leaders, Treasure Criticism, Obey Songun Policies, Pledge Yourself to Collective Child Rearing, and Conduct Regular Martyrdom Drills.

It was here, spellbound by beauty, that the crow almost fell from the sky when it realized that the woman speaking to this loathsome citizen was none other than Sun Moon. Wings arresting a free fall, the bird dropped between our mismatched couple. There was a message in the crow's beak, and when Commander Ga bent to retrieve it, the bird leaped high—*Caw!*—and lashed its wings at Ga's face. The bird then turned to face Sun Moon. The note, she saw, was intended for her. When she unfolded the strip of paper, it bore only the name of our Dear Leader Kim Jong Il.

A black Mercedes suddenly appeared, and a man with a splint on his nose hurried to open the door for Sun Moon. She was on her way to visit the Great General who had discovered her, who had written all her movies, who had spent many a long night counseling her on the proper ways of depicting our nation's triumphs over adversity. Great leader, diplomat, strategist, tactician, athlete, filmmaker, author, and poet—all this, and yes, Kim Jong Il was a friend, too.

Passing through the streets of Pyongyang, Sun Moon leaned her head against the car window and regarded as if with sadness the rays of sunlight glowing golden in the millet-dusted air of the Central Ration Depot. It looked as though she might weep passing the Children's Theater, where as a girl she had learned the accordion, the art of puppetry, and mass gymnastics. *Whatever became of my old teachers?* her eyes seemed to ask, and it was not without tears that she beheld the fanciful spires of the ice rink, one of the rare places her mother, ever mindful of American sneak attacks, would dare to venture. No one upon the ice in those days could do anything but cheer for young Sun Moon, her girl limbs flaring through the leaps, the joy on her face dazzling through a spray of her blades' ice crystals. Poor Sun Moon! It was almost as if she knew she would never see these sights again, as if she had some kind of premonition of what the savage, remorseless Americans had in store for her. What woman wouldn't weep all along Reunification Boulevard to think she'd never again see a street so clean, a ration line so perfectly straight, or hear again the crimson banners fluttering a thousand strong in a chain of red flags that extolled every word of Kim Il Sung's great speech of October 18, Juche 63!

Sun Moon was brought before the Dear Leader in a room that had been designed to put the visiting Americans at ease. Its muted lamps, dark mirrors, and wooden tables were reminiscent of an American "speakeasy," which is a type of establishment that Americans frequent in order to evade the eyes of their repressive government. Behind the heavy doors of a speakeasy, Americans are free to abuse alcohol, fornicate, and violence each other.

Over his smart jumpsuit, the Dear Leader wore an apron. On his forehead, he sported a green visor, while a rag was draped over his shoulder. He came from behind the bar with his arms extended. "Sun Moon," he called. "What can I serve you?"

Their embrace was filled with the zest of socialist comradeship.

"I don't know," she said.

He told her, "You're supposed to say, 'The usual.'"

"The usual," she said.

Here he poured for them modest snifters of North Korean cognac, which is known for its medicinal properties.

Looking more closely, the Dear Leader saw that there was sadness in her eyes.

"What's got you down?" he asked her. "Tell me the story—I'll give it a happy ending."

"It's nothing," she said. "I'm just practicing for my new movie role."

"But this movie is a happy one," he reminded her. "Your character's undisciplined husband is replaced with a highly efficient one—soon all the farmers have increased their yields. Something else must be bothering you. Is it a matter of the heart?"

"I only have room in my heart for the Democratic People's Republic of Korea," she said.

The Dear Leader smiled. "That's my Sun Moon," he said. "That's the girl I miss. Come, look, I have a present for you."

From behind the bar, the Dear Leader produced an American musical instrument.

"What is it?" she asked.

"It's called a *gui-tar*. It's used to perform American rural music. It's said to be especially popular in Texas," he told her. "It's also the instrument of choice for playing 'the blues,' which is a form of American music that chronicles the pain caused by poor decision making."

Sun Moon ran her delicate fingers across the strings of the *guitar*. It produced a muted groan, as if a vibrant *gayageum* had been wrapped in a blanket and doused with a bucket of water. "The Americans have much to be sad about," she said, plucking another string. "But listen to it. I can make no song with this."

"But you must, you must," said the Dear Leader. "Please make it perform for me."

She strummed. "I regret that my heart ..." she sang, "... is not as big as my love ..."

"That's it," he said.

She strummed. "For the most democratic nation ..." she went on, "... the Democratic People's Republic of Korea."

"That's good," he said. "Now less birdlike. Sing with the heat of your blood."

On the bar, she placed the *guitar* flat on its back, the way a proper stringed instrument is played. She tried to finger the strings so that different notes might sound.

"The Yankees are happy," she sang and strummed hard. "The Yankees are sad."

The Dear Leader beat the rhythm on the bar top with his fist.

"Our nation doesn't see the difference," she belted. "Satisfaction's all we've ever had."

Together, they laughed. "I miss all this," he said. "Remember how we used to speak of movie scripts late into the night? How we professed our love of country and embraced reunification?"

"Yes," she said. "But all that changed."

"Did it? I used to wonder if," the Dear Leader said, "if something happened to your husband on one of his many dangerous missions, if we'd become friends again. Of course your husband is alive and well and your marriage is better than ever, I'm sure. But if something had happened to your husband, if he'd been lost on one of his many heroic missions for our nation, would I have been right to think that we would become close again, that we would again stay up into the night sharing notions of Juche and Songun scholarship?"

She pulled her hand from the *guitar*. "Is something going to happen to my husband? Is that what you're trying to tell me? Is there a dangerous mission you must send him on?"

"No, no, banish the thought," said the Dear Leader. "Nothing could be further from the truth. Of course I could never say for sure. It must be stated that the world is a dangerous place, and the future is known only to high-ranking officials."

Sun Moon said, "Your fatherly wisdom always did have the power to soothe my female fears."

"It is one of my gifts," replied the Beneficent Leader Kim Jong Il in all his Glory. "I must make note," he continued, "that you do call him *husband*."

"I don't know what else to call him."

The Dear Leader nodded. "But you do not answer my question."

Sun Moon crossed her arms and turned from the bar. She took two steps, then turned back. "I, too, yearn for our late-night conversations," she said. "But those days are past, now."

"But why?" the Dear Leader asked. "Why must they be past?"

"Because I hear you have a new confidante now, a new young pupil."

"I see someone has been speaking to you, sharing certain things."

"When a citizen is given a replacement husband, it is her duty to share certain things with him."

"Have you?" the Dear Leader asked. "Have you been *sharing* with him?"

"Only high-ranking officials know the future," she said, and smiled.

The Dear Leader nodded in appreciation. "See, that's what I've missed. That right there."

Sun Moon took a first sip of her drink.

"So who is this new pupil?" she asked. "Does she appreciate your subtleties, your humor?"

The Dear Leader leaned forward some, happy to have her engage him again. "She is no you, I can tell you that. She has none of your beauty, your charm, your way with words."

Sun Moon feigned being startled. "She has no way with words?"

"You tease me now," he said. "You know she speaks only English. She is no Sun Moon, I grant you that, but don't underestimate her, this American girl. Don't think my Rower Girl doesn't have her own special qualities, her own dark energy."

Now Sun Moon leaned forward, so that over the bar, the two were close.

"Answer me this, my Dearest Leader," she said. "And please, speak from the heart. Can a spoiled American girl handle the grand notions that emanate from a mind as great as yours? Can this girl from a land of corruption and greed comprehend the purity of your wisdom? Is she worthy of you, or should she be sent home so that a real woman can take her place?"

The Dear Leader reached behind the bar. He produced for Sun Moon a bar of soap, a comb, and a *choson-ot* that seemed cut from pure gold.

"That's what you're going to tell me," he said.

*

Citizens, observe the hospitality our Dear Leader shows for all peoples of the world, even a subject of the despotic United States. Does the Dear Leader not dispatch our nation's best woman to give solace and support to this wayward American? And does Sun Moon not find the Girl Rower housed in a beautiful room, fresh and white and brightly lit, with a pretty little window affording a view of a lovely North Korean meadow and the dappled horses that frolic there? This is not dingy China or soiled little South Korea, so do not picture some sort of a prison cell with lamp-blacked walls and rust-colored puddles on the floor. Instead, notice the large white tub fitted with golden lion's feet and filled with the steaming restorative water of the Taedong.

Sun Moon approached her. Though the Rower was young, her skin had been marred by the sun and the sea. Still, her spirit seemed strong—perhaps her year as a guest of our great nation had given her life focus and conviction. Undoubtedly, it had provided this American the only chastity she'd ever known. Sun Moon helped her disrobe, holding the Rower's garments as she removed them. The girl's shoulders were broad and strong cords were visible in her neck. There was a small, circular scar on the Rower's upper arm. When Sun Moon touched this, words came from the Rower that Sun Moon couldn't understand. And yet a look crossed the Girl Rower's face that reassured Sun Moon that the mark was a sign of something good, if such a wound was possible.

In the water, the American reclined, and Sun Moon sat at the head of the tub, wetting the Rower's dark, straight hair one ladle at a time. The last inch of her hair was distressed and needed to come off, but Sun Moon had no scissors. Instead, Sun Moon massaged the soap into her scalp, raising a lather. "So you're the woman of endurance, of aloneness, the survivor," Sun Moon said as she rinsed and soaped and rinsed again. "The girl that has captured the attention of all the males. You are a female who struggles, yes, a student of solitude? You must think we know nothing of adversity in our happy little nation of plenty. Perhaps you think I am a doll on a shelf in a hall of *yangbans*. That my life will be a diet of shrimp and peaches until I retire to the beaches of Wonsan."

Sun Moon moved to the foot of the tub, where she began washing the Rower's long toes and ungainly feet. "My grandmother was a great beauty," Sun Moon said. "During the occupation, she was singled out to become the comfort woman for Emperor Taisho, the decadent predecessor to Hirohito. The dictator was short and sickly, with thick glasses. She was kept in a fortress by the sea, which the emperor visited at the end of each week. He would ravage her at the bay window, where with binoculars, he could also keep track of his fleet. Such was his need to control her that the evil little man insisted that she act happy."

Sun Moon soaped the Rower's taut ankles and withered calves.

"When my grandmother attempted to leap from the window, the Emperor tried to cheer her up with a paddle boat shaped like a swan. Then he bought her a mechanical horse that circled a pole on a metal track. When she tried to throw herself on the ocean's jagged reef, a shark rose. *Endure,* the shark said. *I must dive each day to the bottom of the sea for my dinner—surely you can find a way to survive.* When she placed her neck in the gears of the mechanical horse, a finch landed and implored her to keep living. *I must fly around the world to find my little seeds—certainly you can last another day.* In her room, as she waited for the arrival of the Emperor, she stared at the wall. Gazing at the mortar binding the wall's stones, she thought, I can hold fast a little longer. The Dear Leader turned her story into a screenplay for me, so I know what my grandmother felt. I have tasted her words and stood waiting by her side for the Japanese dictator's inevitable arrival."

Sun Moon motioned for the Rower to stand, and she washed the girl's entire body, like a giant child, skin glistening above the gray-skeined water in which she stood. "And the choices my own mother had to make are things about which I can't even speak. If I am alone in this world, stripped of my siblings, it is because of the decisions she had to make."

There were freckles along the Girl Rower's arms and down her back. Sun Moon had never seen freckles before. Even just a month before, she would have viewed them as flaws marring otherwise even skin. But now the freckles suggested there were other kinds of beauty in the world than simply striving to be made from Pyongyang porcelain. "Perhaps adversity has skipped my generation," Sun Moon told her. "Maybe it's true that I don't know real suffering, that I haven't stuck my head in mechanical gears or rowed around the world in the dark. Maybe I am untouched by loneliness and sorrow."

They were silent as Sun Moon helped the Rower step from the tub, and they didn't speak as she toweled the American's body. The *choson-ot,* utterly golden, was exquisite. Sun Moon pinched the fabric here and there until the dress fell perfectly. Finally, Sun Moon began weaving the Rower's hair into a single braid. "I do know that my turn at suffering will come," she said. "Everyone's does. Mine might be just around the corner. I wonder of what you must daily endure in America, having no government to protect you, no one to tell you what to do. Is it true you're given no ration card, that you must find food for yourself? Is it true that you labor for no higher purpose than paper money? What is California, this place you come from? I have never seen a picture. What plays over the American loudspeakers, when is your curfew, what is taught at your child-rearing collectives? Where does a woman go with her children on Sunday afternoons, and if a woman loses her husband, how does she know the government will assign her a good replacement? With whom would she curry favor to ensure her children got the best Youth Troop leader?"

Here, Sun Moon realized she had gripped the Girl Rower's wrists, and her questions had become demands, leveled into the Rower's wide eyes. "How does a society without a fatherly leader work?" Sun Moon implored. "How can a citizen know what is best without a benevolent hand to shepherd her? Isn't that endurance, learning how to navigate such a realm alone—isn't that survival?"

The Girl Rower took her hands back and gestured toward some unknown distance. Sun Moon had a feeling this woman was asking about the end of the story, of what became of the Emperor's comfort woman, his private *kisaeng*. "She waited until she was older, my grandmother," Sun Moon said. "She waited until she was back in her village and all her children had been grown and married away, and that's when she unsheathed her long-hidden knife and took her honor back."

Whatever was going through the Girl Rower's mind, the strength of Sun Moon's words moved her to act. The Rower, too, began speaking with some force, trying to get Sun Moon to understand something vital. The American went to a small table with a lamp and many notebooks. She brought to Sun Moon one of the inspirational works of Kim Jong Il in a clear attempt to help guide Sun Moon to the only wisdom that had a chance of alleviating the actress's woes. The Rower shook the book and then began speaking fast, a rapid gibberish that was impossible for Sun Moon to make out.

Citizens—what was this poor American Rower saying? We didn't need a translator to understand she was despondent at the prospect of leaving North Korea, which had become a second home to her. No one needed an English dictionary to feel her anguish at the idea of being torn from a paradise where food and shelter and medical care were free. Citizens—feel her sadness at having to return to a land where doctors chase pregnant women with ultrasounds. Sense her outrage at being sent back to a crime-laden land of materialism and exclusion, where huge populations languish in jail, sprawl urine-soaked in the streets, or babble incoherently about God on the sweatpants-polished pews of megachurches. Think of the guilt she must feel after learning how the Americans, her own people, devastated this great nation during the imperialists' sneak-attack war. But despair no more, Rower Girl, even this small taste of North Korean compassion and generosity might see you through the dark days of your return to Uncle Sam's savagery.

I WAS tired when I arrived at Division 42. I hadn't slept well the night before. My dreams were filled with dark snakes whose hissing sounded like the peasants I'd heard doing intercourse. But why snakes? Why would snakes haunt me so, with their accusing eyes and folded fangs? None of the subjects I put in the autopilot ever visited me in my sleep. In the dream, I had Commander Ga's cell phone, and on it kept flashing pictures of a smiling wife and happy children. Only it was *my* wife and *my* children, the family I've always felt I should have had—all I had to do was discover their location and make my way through the snakes to them.

But what did the dream mean? That's what I couldn't fathom. If only a book could be written to help the average citizen penetrate and understand a dream's mysteries. Officially, the government took no position on what occurred while its citizens were asleep, but isn't something of the dreamer to be found in his dream? And what of the extended open-eyed dream I afforded our subjects when I hooked them up to the autopilot? I've sat for hours watching our subjects in this state—the oceany eye sweep, the babyish talk, the groping, the way they were always reaching for something seen with a faraway focus. And then there are the orgasms, which the doctors insist are actually seizures. Either way, something profound takes place inside these people. In the end, all they can remember is the icy mountain peak and the white flower to be found there. Is a destination worth reaching if you can't recall the journey? I'd say so. Is a new life worth living if you can't recollect the old one? All the better.

At work, I discovered a couple of guys from Propaganda sniffing around our library, looking for a good story, one they could use to inspire the people, they said.

I wasn't about to let them near our biographies again.

"We don't have any good stories," I told them.

Man, they were slick, with their gold-rimmed teeth and Chinese cologne.

"Any story would do," one said. "Good or bad, it doesn't matter."

"Yeah," his sidekick added. "We'll add the inspiration later."

Last year they swiped the biography of a lady missionary who'd snuck
in from the South with a satchel full of Bibles. We were told to find out
who she'd given Bibles to and if more like her walked amongst us. She was
the one person the Pubyok couldn't crack, except for Commander Ga, I
suppose. Even when I hooked her up to the autopilot, she had the strang-
est smile on her face. She had a thick set of spectacles that magnified her
eyes as they pleasantly roamed the room. Even when the autopilot was in
its peak cycle, she hummed a Jesus song and beheld the last room she'd
ever see as if it were filled with goodness, as if in the eyes of Jesus all places
were created equal and with her own eyes she saw that this was so and
thought it good.

When the Propaganda boys got done with her story, though, she was a
monstrous capitalist spy bent on kidnapping loyal children of the Party to
work as slaves in a Bible factory in Seoul. My parents were addicted to the
story. Every night I had to listen to their summary of the loudspeaker's
latest installment.

"Go write your own tales of North Korean triumph," I told the boys
from Propaganda.

"But we require real stories," one told me.

"Don't forget," the other added. "These stories are not yours—they're
the property of the people."

"How'd you like me to take your biographies?" I asked them, and they
didn't miss the implied threat.

They said, "We'll be back."

I stuck my head in the Pubyok lounge, which was empty. The place was
littered with empty bottles, which meant they'd pulled an all-nighter. On
the floor was a pile of long black hair. I knelt down and lifted a lock, silken
in the light. Oh, Q-Kee, I thought. Inhaling slowly and deeply, I smelled
her essence. Looking up to the big board, I saw that the Pubyok had cleared
my cases, every one of them except for Commander Ga. All those people.
All their stories, lost.

That's when I noticed Q-Kee in the doorway, watching me. Her head was indeed buzzed, and she wore a Pubyok-brown shirt, military pants, and Commander Ga's black boots.

I dropped the swirl of hair, and rose from my knees.

"Q-Kee," I said. "Good to see you."

She said nothing.

"I see a lot has changed since I was conscripted to help with the harvest."

"I'm sure it was voluntary," she said.

"Of course it was." Pointing at the pile of hair, I added, "I was just using my investigative skills."

"To determine what?"

There was an awkward silence.

"It looks like you've got the Commander's boots there," I said. "They should fetch a good barter at the night market."

"Actually, they fit me pretty well," she said. "I think I'll keep them."

I nodded, admired her boots a moment. Then I caught her eye.

"Are you still my intern?" I asked. "You didn't switch sides, did you?"

She reached out to me. There was a folded slip of paper in her fingers.

"I'm handing you this, aren't I?" she said.

I opened the paper. It was some kind of hand-drawn map. There were sketches of a corral, a fire pit, fishing poles, and guns. Some of the words were in English, but I could make out the word "Texas."

Q-Kee said, "I found this inside Ga's right boot."

"What do you think it is?" I asked her.

"It might be the place where we find our actress." Q-Kee turned to go, but then she looked back. "You know, I've seen all her movies. The Pubyok, they don't seem to care about really finding her. And they couldn't get Ga, or whoever he is, to talk. But you'll get results, right? You'll find Sun Moon. She needs a proper burial. Results, that's the side I'm on."

*

I studied the map a long time. I had it spread across the Pubyok Ping-Pong table and was contemplating every word and line, when Sarge came in. He was soaking wet.

"Been doing some waterboarding?" I asked him.

"Actually, it's raining," he said. "A big storm's coming in from the Yellow Sea."

Sarge rubbed his palms together. Though he smiled, I could tell his hands were hurting.

I pointed at the big board. "I see there was a mass confession while I was out."

Sarge shrugged. "We got a whole team of Pubyok with time on their hands. And here you were with ten open cases, just you and two interns. We were only showing some solidarity."

"Solidarity?" I asked. "What happened to Leonardo?"

"Who?"

"My team leader, the baby-faced one. He left work one night and never came back. Like the rest of the guys who used to be on my team."

"You're asking me to solve one of life's mysteries," he said. "Who's to say what becomes of people? Why does rain fall down and not up? Why was the snake created cowardly while the dog was born vicious?"

I couldn't tell if he was mocking me or not. Sarge wasn't exactly a philosopher. And since Leonardo's disappearance, Sarge had acted strangely civil toward me.

I returned to the crudely penciled sketch of the Texas village.

He stood there, massaging his hands.

"My joints," he said. "They're murder when it rains."

I ignored him.

Sarge looked over my shoulder. "What do you have there, some kind of map?"

"Some kind."

He looked closer. "Oh, yeah," he said. "The old military base west of town."

"What makes you say that?"

He pointed. "There's the road to Nampo, and look, here's the fork in the Taedong." He turned to me. "This have to do with Commander Ga?"

Finally, the kind of lead we'd been looking for, the chance to crack this case wide open. I folded the map. "I've got work to do," I said.

Sarge stopped me from leaving. "You know," he said, "you don't have to write an entire book about every citizen that comes through the door."

But I did have to. Was anyone else going to tell a citizen's story, was there going to be any other proof that someone ever existed? If I took the time to learn everything about them, if I made a record, then I was okay with the kinds of things that happened to them afterward. The autopilot, the prison mines, the soccer stadium at dawn. If I wasn't a biographer, then who was I, what did I really do for a living?

"Am I getting through to you?" Sarge asked. "Nobody even reads those books. They gather dust in a dark room. So quit killing yourself. Try it our way for once. Knock out a few quick confessions, and then come have a beer with the guys. We'll let you load the karaoke machine."

"What about Commander Ga?" I asked.

"What about him?"

"His biography is the most important one."

Sarge stared at me with cosmic frustration.

"First of all," he said, "that's not Commander Ga. Did you forget that? Second, he wouldn't talk. He's had pain training—the halo didn't even touch him. Most important, there is no mystery to solve."

"Of course there is," I said. "Who is he? What happened to the actress? Where's her body, her kids?"

"You think the guys at the top," Sarge said, pointing down to the bunker below, "you think they don't know the real story? They know where the Americans were hosted—they were *there*. You think the Dear Leader doesn't know what happened? I bet Sun Moon was probably standing to his right, while Commander Ga was to his left."

Then what was our purpose, I wondered. *What was it we were interrogating, and why?*

"If they have all the answers," I said, "what are they waiting for? How long can the people wonder why our national actress has gone missing? And what about our national hero, the holder of the Golden Belt? How long can the Dear Leader not acknowledge they've mysteriously vanished?"

"Don't you think the Dear Leader has his reasons?" Sarge asked me. "And just so you know: you don't get to tell people's stories, the state does. If a citizen does something worthy of a story, good or bad, then it's up to the Dear Leader's people. They're the only ones who get to tell a story."

"I don't tell people's stories. My job is to listen and write down what I hear. And if you're talking about the boys from Propaganda, everything they say is a lie."

Sarge stared at me in wonderment, as if only now did he realize the size of the gulf between us. "Your job . . ." he started to say. Then he started to say something else. He kept shaking his hands, trying to expel the pain. Finally, he turned to leave, pausing only a moment in the doorway.

"I did my training at that base," he said. "You don't want to be anywhere near Nampo during a storm."

When he was gone, I called the Central Motor Pool and told them we'd need a vehicle to take us toward Nampo. Then I gathered Q-Kee and Jujack. "Round up some rain slickers and shovels," I told them. "We're going to fetch an actress."

*

It turned out the only vehicle that could get us down the road to Nampo in the rain was an old Soviet Tsir. When it pulled up, the driver was none too happy, since someone had stolen his windshield wipers. Jujack shook his head at the sight and backed away.

"No way," he said. "My father told me never to get in a crow."

Q-Kee had a shovel in her hand. "Shut up and get in the truck," she told him.

Soon, the three of us were headed west, into the storm. The dark canopy was made of oiled canvas, which kept the rain out, though sprays of muddy water rose through the slats in the bed. The bench seats we sat on had been carved with people's names. It was probably the work of folks being transported to faraway prison mines like 22 or 14-18, voyages that would give a person lots of time to think. Such was the human urge to be remembered.

Q-Kee ran her fingers over the carvings, tracing one name in particular.

"I knew a Yong Yap-Nam," she said. "He was in my Evils of Capitalism class."

"It's probably a different Yong Yap-Nam," I reassured her.

She shrugged. "If a citizen goes bad, he goes bad. What else should he expect?"

Jujack wouldn't look at any of the names. "Why don't we wait till after the storm?" he kept saying. "What's the point of going out there now? We probably won't find anything. There's probably nothing to find."

The wind started to rattle the black canopy, its metal ribs groaning. A cascade of water poured from the road, sluicing over the sewage ditches.

Q-Kee leaned her head on her shovel handle, staring out the back of the truck at the two channels our tires cut through the water.

Q-Kee asked me, "You don't think Sun Moon could have gone bad, do you?"

I shook my head. "No way."

"I want to find Sun Moon as much as anybody," she said. "But then she'll be dead. It's like, until our shovels unearth her, she still seems alive."

It's true that when I'd been imagining finding Sun Moon, I'd been picturing the radiant woman on all the movie posters. It was only now that I visualized my shovel raising up pieces of decomposed children, of the shovel's blade sinking into the abdomen of a corpse.

"When I was a girl, my father took me to see *Glory of Glories*. I'd been acting out a lot, and my father wanted me to see what happened to women who challenged authority."

Jujack said, "That the movie where Sun Moon gets her head cut off?"

"It's about more than that," Q-Kee said.

"Good special effects, though," Jujack added. "The way Sun Moon's head rolls away and everywhere the blood spills, the flowers of martyrdom spring from the ground and blossom. That had me, man, I was there."

Of course everyone knew the movie. Sun Moon plays a poor girl who confronts the Japanese officer who controls her farming village. The peasants must relinquish their harvest to the Japanese, but some rice goes missing and the officer decrees that all will starve until the culprit is caught. Sun Moon stands up to the officer and tells him it is his own corrupt soldiers who have stolen the rice. For this affront, the officer has her beheaded in the town square.

"Never mind what the movie was really about, or what my father thought it was about," Q-Kee said. "All around Sun Moon were powerful men, yet she was without fear. I registered that. I saw the strength with which she accepted her fate. I saw how she changed the terms of men into her own. That I am here right now, in Division 42, I owe to her."

"Oh, when she kneels down to take the sword," Jujack said, as if he could see the moment before him. "Her back arches, her heavy chest swings forward. Then her perfect lips part and her eyelids slowly, slowly close."

The movie is filled with famous scenes, as when the old women in the village stay up all night sewing the beautiful *choson-ot* that Sun Moon will wear to her death. Or how, before dawn, when Sun Moon is gripped by fear and falters in her resolve, a sparrow flies to her—the bird holds kim-ilsungia blossoms in its beak to remind her that she does not sacrifice alone. The moment I remember, the point of the story at which no citizen could hold back tears, is when, in the morning, her parents bid her a final farewell. They say to her what has always gone unspoken, how she is the thing that gives meaning to their lives, that without her they will be lessened, that their love is of no use if not for her.

I looked to Q-Kee, deep in contemplation, and I wished for a moment that we weren't about to discover the decomposed remains of her hero.

The crow left the road and drove into a basin, a field of shallow water as far as one could see. When I questioned the driver, he pointed to the map I'd given him. "This is it," he said.

We looked out the back of the crow. The sky flashed white.

Jujack said, "We'll get diphtheria in all this runoff. Look, I bet there's nothing out there, this is a probably a wild goose chase."

"We won't know until the shovel hits the mud," I told him.

"But we're probably just wasting our time," Jujack said. "I mean, what if they moved it at the last minute?"

"What are you talking about, moved it?" Q-Kee asked him. "Do you know something you're not telling us?"

Jujack looked warily at the darkening sky.

Q-Kee pressed him. "You do know something, don't you?"

"Enough," I told them. "We only have a couple of hours of light."

Then the three of us jumped from the crow into ankle-deep water that was sheened with oil and sewage foam. Everywhere around us was muddy water, as far as you could see. The map, long since soaked, pointed us toward a stand of trees. Using our shovels as probes, we made our way. Passing between us were the humps of river eels wrestling through the shallow water. The beasts were like biceps with teeth, some two meters long.

The trees, it turned out, were filled with snakes. Their heads hung down to watch us splash from tree trunk to tree trunk. It was straight out of my awful dreams, as though the snakes from my sleep were visiting me here. Or did it work the other way—would these snakes visit me again tonight? How I hoped not. Endure what one must during the day. But please, can I not have some peace when darkness falls?

"Those are rock mamushi," Q-Kee said.

"Can't be," Jujack said. "Those only live in the mountains."

Q-Kee turned to him. "I know my deadly snakes," she said.

When distant lightning flashed, you could see them all, silhouetted in the branches, hissing, poised to drop on unsuspecting citizens as they went about their civic duties.

"A snake is a fucking snake," I said. "Just don't provoke them."

We looked around, but there was no sign of a fire pit or a corral. There was no chuck wagon, no guns or fishing poles, no stack of scythes.

"We're in the wrong place," Jujack said. "We should get out of here before we get electrocuted."

"No," Q-Kee said. "We dig."

"Where?" Jujack asked.

"Everywhere," Q-Kee said.

Jujack stomped the blade of his shovel into the mud. With great effort, he pulled a single scoop of mud, sucking from a hole that filled with water. When he turned the shovel upside-down, the mud stuck.

Rain battered my face. I kept spinning the map, trying to see if I'd made a mistake. This should've been the place—the trees, the river, the road. What we needed was one of the dogs from the Central Zoo. It's said their savage instincts can detect bones, even ones long under the earth.

"This is impossible," Jujack said. "It's all just water. Where's the crime scene? Where's any scene?"

"That might work to our advantage," I told them. "If a body were in the mud, the water might help float it free. All we need to do is go around loosening the soil."

So we went our ways, individually probing the mud for any sign of an actress below.

I started turning shovels of mud, one after the other. Each time I did I could visualize success, each time I felt discovery was at hand and I'd be able to leverage the actress to get Commander Ga's story, and then his biography would be mine, with Ga's real name in gold on the spine, and then Sarge's office would become mine. As the rain fell and fell, I kept coming up with pithy lines I'd say as Sarge placed his meager possessions in an old food-aid box and removed them from my new office.

Finally, I felt, here was an event in my life worthy of inclusion in my own biography.

The crow's drivers watched us from behind their windshield. It grew dark enough to see the red glow of their cigarettes. As my arms weakened, I switched from my right hand to my left. Every bone I struck turned out to be a tree root. If only a piece of silk would float up, or a shoe, perhaps. The eels kept striking at things in the muddy water, and thinking they were onto something, I began digging wherever they slashed their teeth and battled over unseen prey. Every clump of mud brought my spirits lower, and soon the day seemed less like the life I wanted and more like the one I had—slogging, for nothing, the failures mounting. It was like my whole university experience—when I first arrived, I wondered which of these thousands of women was for me, yet one by one, over time, I realized the answer was none. No, today certainly wasn't a chapter to include in my biography.

In the dark, the only thing I could hear was Q-Kee grunting each time she brought her weight to bear on the shovel. Finally I shouted into the darkness, "Let's pack it in."

When Q-Kee and I made it back to the crow, we discovered Jujack already inside.

We were soaked and shivering, our hands blistered from working wet handles, the soles of our feet sore from spading the heads of shovels a thousand times into the mud.

Q-Kee stared at Jujack the entire drive back to Division 42.

"You knew she wasn't there, didn't you?" Q-Kee kept saying to him. "You knew something, and you didn't tell us."

*

Right away, when we'd descended the stairs to Division 42, Q-Kee marched up to Sarge.

"Jujack's holding out on us," she said. "He knows something about this Commander Ga case he's not telling us."

A grave look crossed Sarge's face. He studied Q-Kee. Then he studied Jujack.

"That's a big accusation," Sarge said to her. "You have any proof?"

Q-Kee pointed to her heart. "I can feel it," she said.

Sarge considered this, then nodded. "Okay," he said. "Let's get the truth out of him."

A couple of Pubyok moved to grab Jujack.

"Whoa," I said, stepping in. "Let's slow down. A 'feeling' isn't proof."

I put my hand on Jujack's shoulder. "Tell the truth, son," I said. "Just say what you know, and I'll stand by you."

Jujack looked at our feet. "I don't know anything, I swear."

We all turned to Q-Kee. "Don't take my word for it," she said. "Look in his eyes. It's right there for everyone to see."

Sarge bent and looked in the boy's eyes. For the longest time, Sarge just stared. Then he nodded and said, "Take him away."

A couple of the Pubyok put their hands on Jujack. A look of terror filled his eyes.

"Wait," I told them, but there was no stopping the floating wall. Soon Jujack was kicking as they dragged him toward the shop.

Jujack screamed, "I'm the son of a minister."

"Save it for your biography," Sarge called after him, laughing.

I said, "There's got to be some kind of mistake."

Sarge seemed not to hear me. "Fucking disloyalty," he said, shaking his head. Then he turned to Q-Kee. "Good work," he said to her. "Get your smock on. You'll be the one to get the truth out of him."

*

Jujack was concealing something, and the only other person who knew what that might be was Commander Ga. I raced to the tank where we were holding him. Inside, Ga was shirtless, staring at his chest's reflection in the stainless-steel wall.

Without looking at me, Ga said, "You know, I should have had them ink her image in reverse."

"There's an emergency," I said. "It's my intern, Jujack. He's in trouble."

"But I didn't know then," Ga said. "I didn't know my destiny." He turned to me, indicating his tattoo. "You see her as she is. I'm forced to see her backward. I should have had them ink her image in reverse. But back then, I thought it was for others to see. When really, the whole time, she was for me."

"I need some information," I told him. "It's really important."

"Why are you so intent on writing my biography?" Commander Ga asked me. "The only people in the world who'd want to read it are gone now."

"I just need to know one thing. It's life and death," I said. "We went to the military base, on the road to Nampo, but there was no corral or fire pit or ox. I know you made a village there, to make the Americans feel at home. But the actress wasn't there. Nothing was."

"I told you, you'll never find her."

"But where was the picnic table, the chuck wagon?"

"We moved those."

"Where?"

"I can't tell you."

"Why, why not?"

"Because this mystery is the only reminder to the Dear Leader that what happened to him is real, that something happened that was out of his control."

"What happened to him?"

"That would be a good question to ask him."

"But this isn't about the Dear Leader, it's about a kid who made a mistake."

"It's also the only thing keeping me alive."

I appealed to his reason. "You're not going to live through any of this," I said.

He nodded in acknowledgment. "None of us will," he said. "Do you have a plan? Have you taken steps? You still have time, you can choose your terms."

"In whatever time you have left," I said, "you can save this kid, you can atone for whatever heinous thing you did to the actress." I pulled his phone from my pocket. "The pictures that arrive on this phone," I asked him. "Are they meant for you?"

"What pictures?"

I turned on the phone, let him see the blue glow of its charged battery.

"I must have that," he told me.

"Then help me," I said.

I held the phone in front of his face, showing him the image of the star on the sidewalk.

He took the phone from my hand. "The Americans refused the Dear Leader's hospitality," he said. "They wouldn't leave their plane, so we moved the Texas village to the airport."

"Thank you," I said, and just as I turned, the door flew open.

It was Q-Kee on the threshold, the rest of the Pubyok behind her.

There was gore on her smock. "They moved to the airport," she declared. "That's where the actress disappeared."

"Makes sense he'd know what was going on at the airport," one of the Pubyok said. "His dad is the Minister of Transportation."

"What about Jujack?" I demanded. "Where is he, what's happened to him?"

Q-Kee didn't answer. She looked to Sarge, who nodded his approval.

Steeling her eyes, Q-Kee turned to face the Pubyok assembled in the doorway. She assumed a taekwondo stance. The men backed up, gave her a moment to compose herself. Then, together, they said *Junbi. Hana, dul, set,* they counted, and when they shouted *Sijak!* Q-Kee's hand struck the stainless-steel door.

There was a long, shuddering inhale, and then she drew several sharp breaths.

Slowly, she pulled her broken hand to her chest and sheltered it there.

Always the first break is a chopping strike to the outside of the palm. There will be plenty of time to break the knuckles, a couple at a time, later.

Calmly, carefully, Sarge took her arm and extended it, placing her broken hand in his. With great care, he gripped her wrist with one hand then pinched her last two fingers with the other. "You're one of us now," he said. "You're an intern no more. You no longer have use for a name," he added as he pulled hard on her fingers, snapping the cracked bones straight for a proper heal.

Sarge nodded his head my way, as a sign of respect. "I was against having a woman in the Division," he told me. "But you were right—she's the future."

IT WAS afternoon, the sun bright and heatless through the windows. Commander Ga sat between the boy and the girl, the three of them watching Sun Moon restlessly wander the house, her hands lifting certain objects that she seemed to consider anew. The dog followed her, sniffing at everything she touched—a hand mirror, a parasol, the kettle in the kitchen. It was the day before the Americans were to arrive, the day before the escape, though the children didn't know that.

"What's wrong with her?" the boy asked. "What's she looking for?"

"She acts like this before she starts a new movie," the girl said. "Is there a new movie?"

"Something like that," Ga told them.

Sun Moon came to him. In her hands was a hand-painted *chang-gi* board. The look on her face said, *How can I abandon this?* He'd told her that they could take nothing with them, that any keepsake might signal their plan.

"My father," she said. "It's all I have of him."

He shook his head. How could he explain to her that it was better this way, that yes, an object could hold a person, that you could talk to a photograph, that you could kiss a ring, that by breathing into a harmonica, you can give voice to someone far away. But photographs can be lost. In your sleep, a ring can be slipped from your finger by the thief in your barracks. Ga had seen an old man lose the will to live—you could see it go out of him—when a prison guard made him hand over a locket. No, you had to keep the people you loved safer than that. They had to become as fixed to you as a tattoo, which no one could take away.

"Nothing but the clothes on my back?" she asked him.

Then a look of dawning crossed her face. She turned and moved quickly to her wardrobe. Here, she stared into the row of *choson-ots,* each folded over its own dowel. The setting sun was tinted and rich through the bedroom. In this golden, yolk-colored light, the dresses glowed with life.

"How will I choose?" she asked him. She ran her fingers over them. "I wore this one in *Motherless Fatherland*," she said. "But I played a politician's wife. I can't leave here as that. I can't be her forever." Sun Moon studied a simple *choson-ot* whose *jeogori* was white and *chima* was patterned with pale blossoms. "And here's *A True Daughter of the Country*. I can't arrive in America dressed as a peasant girl." She leafed through all the dresses—*Oppressors Tumble, Tyrants Asunder, Hold the Banner High!*

"All of your dresses have come from your movies?"

She nodded. "Technically, they're the property of Wardrobe. But when I act in them, they become a part of me."

"You have none of your own?" he asked.

"I don't need my own," she said. "I've got these."

"What about the dresses you wore before you were in the movies?"

She stared at him a moment.

"Oh, I cannot decide," she said and closed her eyes. "I'll leave it for later."

"No," he told her. "This one."

She removed the silver *choson-ot* he'd selected, held it to her figure.

"*Glory of Glories*," she said. "You wish me to be the opera singer?"

"It is a story of love," he told her.

"And tragedy."

"And tragedy," he acknowledged. "Wouldn't the Dear Leader love to see you dressed as an opera star? Wouldn't that be a nod to his other passion?"

Sun Moon wrinkled her nose at this idea. "He got me an opera singer to help me prepare for that role, but she was impossible."

"What happened to her?"

Sun Moon shrugged. "She vanished."

"Vanished where?"

"She went where people go, I guess. One day she just wasn't there."

He touched the fabric. "Then this is the dress to wear."

*

They spent the remaining light harvesting the garden, preparing a feast to eat raw. The flowers they turned to tea, and the cucumbers they sliced and let brine in vinegar and sugar water with shredded red cabbage. The girl's prize melon they broke open on a rock, so that the meat inside tore along the seed lines. Sun Moon lit a candle, and at the table, they started their final dinner with beans, which they shelled and rolled in coarse salt. Then the boy had a treat—four songbirds he'd snared and dressed and cured in the sun with red pepper seeds.

The boy started to tell a story he'd heard over the loudspeaker about a laborer who thought he'd found a precious gem. Instead of sharing the discovery with the leader of his detachment, the laborer swallowed the gem in the hopes of keeping it for himself.

"Everyone's heard that story," his sister said. "It turned out to be a piece of glass."

"Please," Sun Moon said. "Let's have a happy story."

The girl said, "What about the one where the dove flew into the path of an imperialist bullet and saved the life of a—"

Sun Moon raised a hand to stop her.

It seemed the only stories the children knew of had come from the loudspeaker. When Commander Ga was young, sometimes all the orphans had to fill themselves with at the dinner table were stories. In an offhanded way, Commander Ga said, "I'd tell the story about the little dog from Pyongyang who went into space, but I'm sure you've heard that one."

With uncertainty on her face, the girl looked from her brother to her mother. Then she shrugged. "Yeah, sure," she said. "Who hasn't heard that one?"

The boy also feigned knowledge of the story. "Yeah, that's an old one," he added.

"Let me see if I remember how it goes," Commander Ga said. "The best scientists got together and built a gigantic rocket. On its fuselage, they painted the blue star and red circle of the Democratic People's Republic of Korea. Then they filled it full of volatile fuel and rolled it out to the launch pad. The rocket was designed to go up. If it worked, they would try to make the next rocket capable of coming back down. Even though the scientist that piloted it would be declared a martyr, no one was brave enough to climb inside."

Ga stopped his story there. He sipped his tea, and looked at the children, who could not tell what this story was designed to glorify.

Hesitantly, the girl said, "That's when they decided to send the dog."

Ga smiled. "That's right," he said. "I knew you'd know the story. Now where was it they found the dog again?"

Once more, there was silence. "At the zoo," the boy finally said.

"Of course," Ga said. "How could I forget? And what did that dog look like?"

"He was gray," the girl said.

"And brown," the boy said.

"With white paws," the girl said. "He had a long, slim tail. They chose him because he was skinny and could fit in the rocket."

"Old tomatoes," the boy said. "That's all the mean zookeeper fed him."

Sun Moon smiled to see her children engage in the tale. "At night, the dog would consider the moon," was her contribution.

"The moon was his only friend," the girl said.

"The dog would call and call," the boy added, "but he never heard back."

"Yes, it is an old story, but a good one," Commander Ga said, smiling. "Now, the dog agreed to ride the rocket into space—"

"—to be closer to his friend the moon," the girl said.

"Yes, to be closer to his friend the moon," Ga said. "But did they tell the dog he would never be coming back?"

A look of betrayal crossed the boy's face. "They didn't tell him anything," he said.

Ga nodded at the wrongness of this injustice. "The scientists, as I recall, allowed the dog to bring one thing with him."

"It was a stick," the boy said.

"No," the girl said. "It was his bowl."

And suddenly the two of them were racing to discover the item the dog chose to take into space, but Ga nodded in approval at all their proposals.

"The dog brought along a squirrel," the boy said. "So he wouldn't get lonely."

"He chose to bring a garden," the girl countered. "So he wouldn't be hungry."

On and on they went—a ball, a rope, a parachute, a flute he could play with his paws.

Ga halted them with a hand, letting a silence fall over the table. "Secretly," he whispered, "the dog brought along all those things, the weight of which changed the course of the rocket when it launched, sending it on a new trajectory . . ."

Ga gestured up in the air, and the children looked above them, as if the answer would materialize on the ceiling.

". . . to the moon," the girl said.

Ga and Sun Moon now listened as the children spun the rest of the story for themselves, how on the moon, the dog discovered another dog, the one who howled at the earth every night, how there was a boy on the moon, and a girl, and how the dogs and the children began building their own rocket, and Ga watched how the candlelight played on their faces, how Sun Moon's eyes lowered with delight, how the children relished their mother's attention, and how they kept trying to outdo one another for it, and how, as a family, they turned that melon to rind, saving the seeds in a small wooden bowl, smiling together as the sweet pink juice ran down their fingers and wrists.

The boy and the girl implored their mother to create a ballad for the dog who went to the moon, and since Sun Moon wouldn't play her *gaya-geum* in house clothes, she soon emerged in a *choson-ot* whose *chima* was cut from plum-colored satin. On the wooden floor, she placed the crown of the instrument on a pillow while its base rested sidesaddle on her folded legs. She bowed to the children, and they lowered their heads to her.

At first she plucked its strings high, creating notes that were fast and bright. She strummed the sounds of the rocket blast, her voice laced with humor and rhyme. As the dog left gravity for space, her playing became ethereal, the strings reverberating, as if sounding together in a void. Candlelight was alive in the fall of Sun Moon's hair, and when she pursed her lips to play more difficult chords, Ga felt it in his chest, in the out-chambers of his heart.

He was stricken anew by her, overcome with the knowledge that in the morning he would have to relinquish her. In Prison 33, little by little, you relinquished everything, starting with your tomorrows and all that might be. Next went your past, and suddenly it was inconceivable that your head had ever touched a pillow, that you'd once used a spoon or a toilet, that your mouth had once known flavors and your eyes had beheld colors beyond gray and brown and the shade of black that blood took on. Before you relinquished yourself—Ga had felt it starting, like the numb of cold limbs—you let go of all the others, each person you'd once known. They became ideas and then notions and then impressions, and then they were as ghostly as projections against a prison infirmary. Sun Moon appeared to him now like this, not as a woman, vital and beautiful, making an instrument speak her sorrow, but as the flicker of someone once known, a photo of a person long gone.

The story of the dog became more lonesome now and melancholy. He tried to control his breathing. There was nothing beyond the light of the candle, he told himself. The glow included the boy, the girl, this woman, and himself. Beyond that, there was no Mount Taesong, no Pyongyang, no Dear Leader. He tried to diffuse the pain in his chest across his body, the way his pain mentor Kimsan had once taught him, to feel the flame not on the part but the entire, to visualize the flow of his blood spreading, diluting the hurt in his heart across the whole of him.

And then he closed his eyes and imagined Sun Moon, the one that was always within him—she was a calm presence, open-armed, ready to save him at all times. She wasn't leaving him, she wasn't going anywhere. And here the sharp pain in his chest subsided, and Commander Ga understood that the Sun Moon inside him was the pain reserve that would allow him to survive the loss of the Sun Moon before him. He began to enjoy the song again, even as it grew increasingly sad. The sweet glow of the puppy's moon had given way to an unfamiliar rocket on an uncertain course. What had started as the children's song had become her song, and when the chords became disconnected, the notes wayward and alone, he understood that it was his. Finally, she stopped playing and leaned slowly forward until her forehead came to rest against the fine wood of an instrument she would never play again.

"Come, children," Ga said. "It's time for bed."

He ushered them to the bedroom and closed the door.

Then he tended to Sun Moon, helping her to the balcony for some fresh air.

The lights of the city below were glowing beyond their usual hour.

She leaned against the rail, turning her back to him. It was quiet, and they could hear the children through the wall as they made rocket noises and gave the dog its launch instructions.

"You okay?" he asked her.

"I just need a cigarette, that's all," she said.

"Because you don't have to go through with it, you can back out and nobody will ever know."

"Just light it for me," she said.

He cupped his hand and lit the cigarette, inhaling.

"You're having second thoughts," he said. "That's natural. Soldiers have them before every mission. Your husband probably had them all the time."

She glanced at him. "My husband never had a second thought about anything."

When he extended the cigarette to her, she looked at the way he held it in his fingers and turned again to face the city lights. "You smoke like a *yangban* now," she said. "I like the way you used to smoke, when you were still a boy from nowhere."

He reached to her, pulling her hair aside so he could see her face.

"I'll always be a boy from nowhere," he told her.

She shook her hair back in place, then reached for her cigarette, the V of her fingers indicating where it should be placed.

He took her by the arm, turned her to him.

"You can't touch me," she said. "You know the rules."

She tried to pull loose, but he didn't let her.

"Rules?" he asked. "Come tomorrow, we'll have broken every rule there is."

"Well, tomorrow's not here yet."

"It's on its way," he told her. "Sixteen hours, that's how long the flight is from Texas. Tomorrow's in the air right now, circling the world to us."

She took the cigarette. "I know what you're after," she said. "I know what you want with your talk of *tomorrow*. But there'll be plenty of time, a forever's worth. Don't lose focus on what we have to do. So much has to go right before that plane takes off with us."

He held his grip on her arm. "What if something goes wrong? Have you thought of that? What if today is all there is?"

"Today, tomorrow," she said. "A day is nothing. A day is just a match you strike after the ten thousand matches before it have gone out."

He let go of her, and she turned to the rail, smoking now. Neighborhood by neighborhood, the lights of Pyongyang extinguished themselves. As the landscape blacked out, it became easier to see the headlights of a vehicle that was climbing the switchbacks of the mountain toward them.

"You want me?" she eventually said. "You don't even know me."

He lit his own cigarette. The lights of the May Day Stadium had stayed on, along with the Central Cinema Studio north of town, on the road to the airport. Other than that, the world had gone dark.

"Your hand reaches for mine when you sleep," he said. "I know that."

Sun Moon's cigarette burned red as she inhaled.

"I know that you sleep curled up tight," he added, "that whether you're a *yangban* or not, you didn't grow up with a bed. You probably slept as a child on a small cot, and though you've never spoken of siblings, you probably reached out to touch the brother or sister asleep in the next one."

Sun Moon stared ahead, as if she hadn't heard him. In the silence, he could just make out the sound of the car below, but couldn't guess at what kind. He checked to see if Comrade Buc had heard the car and was on his balcony, but the house next door was dark.

Commander Ga went on, "I know you pretended to be asleep one morning to give me more time to study you, to allow me to see the knot in your collarbone where someone had hurt you. You let me see the scars on your knees, scars that tell me you once knew real work. You wanted me to know the real you."

"I got those from dancing," she said.

"I've seen all your movies," he said.

"I'm not my movies," she snapped at him.

"I've seen all your movies," he went on, "and in all of them, you hair is the same—straight, covering your ears. And yet by pretending to be asleep . . ." Here he reached into her hair again, fingers finding her earlobe. ". . . you let me see where your ear had been notched. Did an MPSS agent catch you stealing from a market stall, or were you picked up for begging?"

"Enough," she said.

"You'd tasted a flower before, hadn't you?"

"I said stop it."

He reached to the small of her back, pulling her till their bodies touched. He threw her cigarette over the balcony, then he held his to her lips so she would understand that they would now share and that each inhale would come from him.

Their faces were close. She looked up, into his eyes. "You don't know the first thing about me," she said. "Now that my mother, now that she's gone, only one person knows who I really am. And it's not you."

"I'm sorry about your husband. What happened to him, what I did— I had no choice. You know that."

"Please," she said. "I'm not talking about him. He didn't know himself, let alone me."

He placed a hand on her cheek and stared into her eyes. "Who, then?"

A black Mercedes pulled up, parking to the side of the house. Sun Moon glanced over at the driver, who stepped out to hold the door open for her. The driver no longer wore a bandage, but the bend in his nose would be there forever.

"Our real problem has arrived," she said. "The man who knows me, he wants me back."

She went into the house and retrieved the *chang-gi* board.

"Don't tell the children anything," she said, and then Ga watched her climb into the car, her face impassive, as if such a car had come for her many times before. Slowly the car backed out, and as its tires shifted from grass to gravel, he heard the grab of the road and knew that the ultimate had been taken from him.

The Orphan Master had bent his fingers back and removed food from his very hand. And the other boys at Long Tomorrows, as they died in turn, stole from him the notion that your shoulder should be turned against death, that death shouldn't be treated as just another latrine mate, or the annoying figure in the bunk above who whistled in his sleep. At first, the tunnels had given him nothing but terror, but after a while, they began to take it away until suddenly gone was his fear, and with it inclinations toward self-preservation. Kidnapping had reduced everything to either death or life. And the mines of Prison 33 had drained, like so many bags of blood, his ability to tell the difference. Perhaps only his mother had taken something grander by depositing him at Long Tomorrows, but this was only speculation, because he'd never found the mark it had left . . . unless the mark was all of him.

And yet, what had prepared him for this, for the Dear Leader tugging at the string that would finally unravel him? When the Dear Leader wanted you to lose more, he gave you more to lose. Sun Moon had told him that. And here it was. To what bunker would she be taken? With what lighthearted stories would she be regaled? What elixir would they sip while the Dear Leader readied himself for more serious amusement?

Beside him, Ga suddenly noticed, were the children, barefoot on the wet grass. The dog was between them, a cape around its neck.

"Where did she go?" the boy asked him.

Ga turned to the two of them.

"Has a car ever come for your mother at night?" he asked.

The girl stared straight ahead at the dark road.

He crouched down, so he was at their level.

"The time has come to tell you a serious story," he told them.

He turned them back toward the light of their home.

"You two climb into bed. I'll be there in a few minutes."

Then he turned to face Comrade Buc's house. He had to find a few answers first.

*

Commander Ga entered through the side door. In Buc's kitchen, he struck a match. The chopping table was clean, the washing tub empty and up-turned for the night. He could still smell fermented beans. He moved to the dining room, which felt heavy and dark. With his thumbnail, he sparked another match and here loomed old furniture, portraits on the wall, military regalia, and the family celadon, all things he hadn't noticed when they'd sat around the table and passed bowls of peaches. Sun Moon's home contained none of these things. On Buc's wall hung a rack of long, thin smoking pipes that formed a history of the family's male ancestry. Ga had always thought it was random, who lived and died, who was rich or poor, but it was clear these people's lineage went back to the Joseon Court, that they were descended from ambassadors and scholars and people who'd fought the guerrilla war alongside Kim Il Sung. It wasn't luck that nobodies lived in army barracks while somebodies lived in homes on the tops of mountains.

He heard a mechanical sound in the next room, and here he found Comrade Buc's wife pumping the foot pedal of a sewing machine as she stitched a white dress by candlelight.

"Yoon has outgrown her dress," she said, then inspected the seam she'd just sewn by passing the candle down its length. "I suppose you're looking for my husband."

He noted her calm, the kind that came from befriending the unknown.

"Is he here?"

"The Americans are coming tomorrow," she said. "All week he has been working late, preparing the final details of your plan to welcome them."

"It's the Dear Leader's plan," he said. "Did you hear a car arrive? It took Sun Moon away."

Comrade Buc's wife turned the dress inside-out to inspect it again. "Yoon's dress will now go to Jia," she said. "Jia's dress will soon fit Hye-Kyo and Hye-Kyo's will wait for Su-Kee, who barely seems to grow." She started working the pedal again. "Soon, I'll be able to fold up another one of Su-Kee's dresses and put it away. That's how I mark our life. When I'm old, it's what I hope to leave behind—a chain of unworn white dresses."

"Is Comrade Buc with the Dear Leader? Do you know where they might be? I have a car, if I knew where she was I could—"

"We don't tell each other anything," she said. "That's how we keep the family safe. That's how we protect one another." She snipped a thread, then turned the dress under the needle. "My husband says I shouldn't worry, that you made a promise to him, that because of your word, none of us is in danger. Is this true, did you give him your promise?"

"I did."

She looked at him, nodded. "Still, it's hard to know what the future holds. This machine was a bridal gift. I didn't imagine making this kind of garment back when I took my vows."

"When it's time, when that comes," he said, "does it matter what you're wearing?"

"I used to have my sewing machine in the window," she said, "so I could look out upon the river. When I was a girl, we used to catch turtles in the Taedong and release them with political slogans painted on their backs. We used to net fish and deliver them each evening to the war veterans. All the trees they now chop down? We planted them. We believed we were the luckiest people in the luckiest nation. Now all the turtles have been eaten and in place of fish there are only river eels. It has become an animal world. My girls will not go as animals."

Ga wanted to tell her that in Chongjin, there was no such thing as the good old days. Instead, he said, "In America, the women have a kind of sewing in which a story is told. Different kinds of fabric are sewn together to say something about a person's life."

Comrade Buc's wife took her foot off the pedal.

"And what story would that be?" she asked him. "The one about a man who comes to town to destroy everything you have? Where would I find the fabric to tell of how he kills your neighbor, takes his place, and gets your husband caught up in a game that will cost you everything?"

"It's late," Commander Ga told her. "I apologize for bothering you."

He turned to go, but at the door, she stopped him.

"Did Sun Moon take anything with her?" she asked.

"A *chang-gi* board."

Comrade Buc's wife nodded. "At night," she said, "that's when the Dear Leader seeks inspiration."

Ga took a last look at the white fabric and thought of the girl who would wear it.

"What do you tell them?" he asked. "When you pull the dresses over their heads? Do they know the truth, that you're practicing for the end?"

She left her eyes on him a moment. "I would never steal the future from them," she said. "That's the last thing I want. When I was Yoon's age, ice cream used to be free in Mansu Park on Sundays. I would go there with my parents. Now the ice-cream van snatches children and sends them to 9-27 camps. Kids shouldn't have to contemplate that. To keep my girls away from the van, I boast that peaches are the best dessert, that we have the last canned peaches in Pyongyang and that someday, when the Buc family is at its absolute happiest, we'll have a feast of peaches that will taste better than all the ice cream in Korea."

*

Brando raised his head when Ga entered the bedroom. The dog no longer wore a cape. The boy and the girl were at the foot of the bed, worry on their faces. Ga sat on the floor beside them.

Above, on the mantel, was the can of peaches he would take with him tomorrow. How in the world to tell them what he had to tell them? He decided to just take a breath and begin.

"Sometimes people hurt other people," he said. "It's an unfortunate fact."

The children stared at him.

"Some people hurt others for a living. No one takes pleasure from it. Well, most don't. The story I have to tell is about what happens when two of these people, these men who hurt others, meet."

"Are you talking about taekwondo?" the boy asked.

Ga had to find a way to explain to them how it was he'd killed their father, ugly as that would be. If they left for America believing the lie that their father was still alive, that he loomed as large as the propaganda about him, then, in the children's memory, that's who he would become. He'd turn to bronze and bear little resemblance to the real man. Without the truth, he'd be just another famous name, so much chiseling at the base of a statue. Here was the one chance to know who their father really was, a chance Ga never got himself. It was the same with their home—without learning of the hidden DVDs, the contents of the laptop, the meaning of the blue flashes at night, their house on Mount Taesong would turn to watercolor in their memories, becoming as staged as a picture postcard. And if they didn't know his true role in their lives, he himself would become in their recollections nothing more than a guest who came to stay for some foggy reason, for some vague length of time.

Yet he didn't want to hurt them. And he didn't want to go against Sun Moon's wishes. Most of all, he didn't want to put them in danger by changing how they might behave tomorrow. If only he could reveal the truth to them in the future, to somehow have a conversation with their older selves. What he needed was a bottle with a message inside that they'd only be able to decipher years from now.

The girl spoke. "Did you find out about our mother?" she asked.

"Your mother is with the Dear Leader," he told them. "I'm sure she's safe and will be home soon."

"Maybe they're meeting about a movie," the girl said.

"Maybe," Ga said.

"I hope not," the boy said. "If she makes a new movie, we'll have to go back to school."

"I want to go back to school," the girl said. "I had perfect marks in Social Theory. Do you want to hear Kim Jong Il's speech from April Fifteenth, Juche 86?"

"If your mother goes on location," Ga asked, "who will watch you?"

"One of our father's flunkies," the girl said. "No offense."

"Your father," Ga said. "That's the first I've heard you speak of him."

"He's on a mission," the girl said.

"Those are secret," the boy added. "He goes on lots."

After a silence, the girl spoke up. "You said you'd tell us a story."

Commander Ga took a breath. "To understand the story I'm about to tell you, you need to know a few things. Have you heard of an incursion tunnel?"

"An incursion tunnel?" the girl asked, a look of distaste on her face.

Ga said, "What about uranium ore?"

"Tell us another dog story," the boy said.

"Yeah," said the girl. "This time make him go to America, where he eats food out of a can."

"And bring back those scientists," the boy added.

Commander Ga thought about it a moment. He wondered if he couldn't tell a story that seemed natural enough to them now, but upon later consideration might contain the kind of message he was looking for.

"A team of scientists was ordered to find two dogs," he began. "One must be the smartest dog in North Korea, the other the bravest. These two dogs would be sent on a top-secret mission together. The scientists went to all the dog farms in the land, and then they inspected canine warrens in all the prisons and military bases. First the dogs were asked to work an abacus with their paws. Then they had to fight a bear. When all the dogs had failed the tests, the scientists sat on the curb, heads in their hands, afraid to tell the ministers."

"But they hadn't checked Brando," the boy said.

At the mention of his name, Brando twitched in his sleep but did not wake.

"That's right," Commander Ga said. "Just then, Brando happened to be walking down the street with a chamber pot stuck on his head."

Peals of laughter came from the boy, and even the girl showed a smile. Suddenly, Ga saw a better use for the story, one that would help them now, rather than later. If in the story he could get the dog to America by stowing itself in a barrel being loaded onto an American plane, he could implant in the children basic instructions for the escape tomorrow—how to enter the barrels, how to be quiet, what kind of movement to expect, and how long they should wait before calling to be let out.

"A chamber pot," the boy said. "How did that happen?"

"How do you think?" Ga answered.

"Yech," the boy said.

"Poor Brando didn't know who had turned out the lights," Ga said. "Everything echoed inside the pot. He wandered down the road, bumping into things, but the scientists thought he had come to take the tests. How brave of a dog to voluntarily face a bear, the scientists thought. And how smart to put on armor!"

Both the boy and the girl laughed large, natural laughs. Gone was the worry on their faces, and Ga decided that perhaps it was better for the story to have no purpose, that it be nothing other than the thing it was, spontaneous and original as it wandered toward its own conclusion.

"The scientists hugged each other in celebration," Ga continued. "Then they radioed Pyongyang, reporting that they'd found the most extraordinary dog in the world. When the American spy satellites intercepted this message, they—"

The boy was tugging Ga's sleeve. The boy was still laughing, there was a smile on his face, but he had turned serious somehow.

"I want to tell you something," the boy said.

"I'm listening," Ga said.

But then the boy went silent and looked down.

"Go on," the girl said to her brother. When he wouldn't answer, she said to Ga, "He wants to tell you his name. Our mother said it was okay, if that's what we wanted to do."

Ga looked at the boy. "Is that it, is that what you want to tell me?"

The boy nodded.

"What about you?" Ga asked the girl.

She, too, glanced down. "I think so," she said.

"There's no need," Ga said. "Names come and go. Names change. I don't even have one."

"Is that true?" the girl asked.

"I suppose I have a real one," Ga said. "But I don't know what it is. If my mother wrote it on me before she dropped me off at the orphanage, it faded away."

"Orphanage?" the girl asked.

"A name isn't a person," Ga said. "Don't ever remember someone by their name. To keep someone alive, you put them inside you, you put their face on your heart. Then, no matter where you are, they're always with you because they're a part of you." He put his hands on their shoulders. "It's you that matter, not your names. It's the two of you I'll never forget."

"You talk like you're going somewhere," the girl said.

"No," Ga said. "I'm staying right here."

The boy finally lifted his eyes. He smiled.

Ga asked, "Now, where were we?"

"The American spies," the boy said.

SAD NEWS, citizens, for our nation's oldest comrade has died at the age of one hundred and thirty-five. Have a safe journey to the afterlife, old friend, and remember fondly your days in the most contented, most long-lived nation on earth! Consider taking a moment today, citizens, to offer a respectful gesture for an older person in your housing block. Carry their ice blocks up the stairs or surprise them with a bowl of chive-blossom soup. Remember: not too spicy!

And a warning, citizens, against touching any balloons that float across the DMZ. The Minister of Public Safety has determined that the gas which floats these balloons and the propaganda messages they carry is actually a deadly nerve agent meant to slay innocent civilians who encounter them.

But there is good news, citizens! The city's notorious windshield-wiper thief has been apprehended. The presence of all citizens is requested tomorrow morning in the soccer stadium. And more good news—shipments of sorghum have begun arriving from the countryside. See your ration stations for ample portions of this delicious starch. Not only does sorghum fortify the bowel, it also assists with male virility. Distillation of sorghum into *goryangju* liquor is not allowed this year. Be prepared for random crockery inspections.

Perhaps the best news of all, citizens: the next installment of this year's Best North Korean Story is here. As we near our tale's conclusion, already there are cries from the populace for more! But there will be no sequel, citizens. The conclusion of this story is one of eternal finality.

Forget for a moment, citizens, that you're fabricating vinalon clothing or running an industrial lathe. Picture instead this scene—it is late, the moon's a sliver above, while beneath it Pyongyang slumbers. One car threads its beams through the city's towering structures, heading north, on the road to the airport. Looming ahead is the Central Cinema Studio, the largest film-production facility on earth. Here, hectares of Quonset huts link in a chain of unparalleled cinematic capacity. And it is here that the vehicle halted. From it emerged none other than Sun Moon, the woman for whom this facility exists.

The corrugated bay doors parted for her, and a great light emanated from inside. Bathed in this warm glow, waiting to greet her, was none other than the most charismatic figure in all the world, the Reverend General Kim Jong Il. He threw his arms wide to her, and together they exchanged gestures of socialist support.

Strong was the smell of Texan cooking—great slabs of pork torso and the noodle called the *mac-a-roni*. When the Dear Leader led her inside, Sun Moon discovered music, gymnastics, and synchronized forklifts!

"I thought the extravaganza to welcome the Americans would take place at the airport," she said.

"It will," the Dear Leader told her. "But our preparations must occur indoors." He pointed to the sky. "To safeguard against spying eyes."

The Dear Leader took her arms and squeezed them through the satin. "You are healthy, yes? You are doing well?"

"I want of nothing, Dear Leader," she said.

"Splendid," he responded. "Now tell me of the American. How many bars of soap did it take to clean our dirty, dirty girl?"

Sun Moon started to speak.

"No, don't tell me, not yet," the Dear Leader interrupted. "Save your opinions of her for later. First I have something to show you, a little treat, if you will."

The two began crossing the studio. Near the blast-proof film vaults, the Pochonbo Electronic Ensemble had set up and were playing their latest hit, "Reunification Rainbow." To this music, a forklift ballet performed with pallets of food aid for America, their loads hoisted high as they circled, spun, and reversed in gay synchronicity with the lively tune. Most impressive, however, was an army of child gymnasts in colorful uniforms. Each limber tot held as his dance partner a hundred-liter barrel. The children had these white plastic barrels spinning like tops, rotating as if on their own and—*surprise!*—the children were atop them, logrolling them in unison toward the forklifts where they were to be stacked and loaded onto the American cargo plane. Tell us, citizens—have the hungry ever been fed with such precision and joy?

When they neared three *choson-ots* displayed on seamstress's dummies, Sun Moon caught her breath at the sight of their stunning beauty. She stopped before them.

"The gift is too much," she said, admiring the trio of satin dresses, each flashing almost metallic—one white, one blue, one red.

"Oh, these," the Dear Leader said. "These are not the treat. These you'll wear tomorrow as you dress in the colors of the DPRK flag. The white one when we greet the Americans, the blue one while you perform your blues composition in honor of the Girl Rower's departure. And red as you escort the Girl Rower to her American fate. That is what will happen, right? Is that what you've chosen?"

"I'm not to wear a dress of my own?" she asked. "I've already picked which one."

"I'm afraid it's been decided," he told her. "So please, no sad faces."

From his pocket, he withdrew an envelope and handed it to her.

Inside, she discovered two tickets. "What's this?" she asked.

"It's part of the treat," he said. "A sample of what's ahead for you."

Examining them, she saw they were official tickets to the premiere of *Comfort Woman.*

"These are for next Saturday," she said.

"An opera had to be canceled," he said. "But we must have priorities, yes?"

"My movie," she said. In disbelief, she asked, "My movie will finally be screened?"

"All of Pyongyang will be in attendance," the Dear Leader assured her. "If for some reason duty calls your husband on a mission, would you do me the honor, would you join me in my box?"

Sun Moon gazed into the Dear Leader's eyes. She was almost without comprehension that someone so powerful and generous would assist a citizen as humble as herself. But with the Dear Leader, citizens, remember, everything is possible. Remember that his only desire is to protectively clasp each and every one of you in his everlasting embrace.

"Come," the Dear Leader said. "There's more."

Sun Moon could see that across the studio, a small orchestra was assembled. The two of them walked in that direction, passing through fields of props, all of which were familiar to her—a row of American jeeps and racks of GI uniforms, pulled from dead imperialists during the war. And here was a scale model of Mount Paektu, birthplace of the glorious leader

Kim Jong Il, born so close to the sun! Paektusan, may your magisterial peaks ever extend to the heavens!

As they strolled further, the Dear Leader said, "Now it's time to speak of your next film."

"I have been practicing my lines," she told him.

"For *Ultimate Sacrifices*?" he asked. "Throw that script away. I have changed my mind—a story of replacement husbands isn't for you. Come, come see your new projects."

They came to three easels surrounded by musicians in tuxedos. And here in his tuxedo stood Dak-Ho, the state movie producer. Because of his resonant tenor's voice, he'd performed the voice-overs on all her movies. Dak-Ho removed the linen from the first easel, and here was the lobby card for Sun Moon's next movie. It depicted a ravishing Sun Moon, barely contained in her uniform, wrapped in the embrace of a naval officer, the two of them shrouded by a halo of torpedoes. But surprise, citizens, the officer she embraces wears a South Korean uniform!

"*The Demon Fleet*," Dak-Ho announced, his voice robust and deep.

The orchestra began playing a theme for the movie-to-be that was tense and brooding.

"In a world of danger and intrigue," Dak-Ho continued, "one woman will discover that a pure heart is the only weapon that can repel the imperialist menace. The sole survivor of an illegal South Korean assault on her submarine, Sun Moon is 'rescued' by her sneak-attacker's gunship. As a captive of the dashing ROK captain, she is pressed to reveal the defenses of the DPRK fleet. Slowly, however, she begins showing her handsome captor how he is actually the imprisoned one—jailed by the manipulations of the American regime. In the stunning climax, he turns his guns toward the real enemy."

The Dear Leader smiled broadly. "The submarine we'll use for the opening scenes is already moored in the Taedong," he said. "And as we speak, there's an entire naval detachment in the disputed waters searching for the appropriate ROK gunship to capture."

The Dear Leader snapped his fingers, and the sheet came off the second lobby card.

Soaring violins began a refrain that was strong and inspiring.

"*The Floating Wall*," Dak-Ho began, but the Dear Leader cut him off.

"This is a bio-pic about the first female Pubyok," the Dear Leader said, pointing at the beautiful, determined woman on the movie poster. He indicated the way her badge shone brightly and her eyes were fixed on a better horizon. "In this role, you will get results—cracking cases and proving that a woman can be as strong as any man."

The Dear Leader turned to her for a reaction.

Sun Moon pointed to the poster. "But her hair," she said. "It's so short."

"Did I mention it's a true story?" he asked. "A woman really was hired at Division 42 not long ago."

Sun Moon shook her head. "I cannot act with hair of this length," she said.

"The character is Pubyok," the Dear Leader said. "So it must be short. You've never been one to shy from authenticity, you practically live your roles." He reached and touched her hair. "It's beautiful, but sacrifices must be made."

The last movie poster remained veiled as Sun Moon's face saddened. Despite her best efforts, she began to weep. Arms crossed, she started walking away.

Look, citizens, at how delicate are her sensibilities. The attentive citizen can see that no one else is pure enough to play these roles, that if anyone thieved Sun Moon from us, they would be stealing these powerful characters as well. Why, the movies themselves would be swiped from posterity. Kidnapped would be the very future of our nation's cinema, which belongs not only to our patriotic citizens, but to the entire world!

The Dear Leader neared her. "Please say that these are tears of joy."

Weeping, Sun Moon nodded.

"What is it?" he asked. "Come, you can tell me."

"I weep only that my mother won't be able to make the premiere of *Comfort Woman*," she said. "Since retiring to Wonsan, she never writes, not once. I was just imagining her at the reception for *Comfort Woman*, seeing her own mother's story large across the screen."

"Don't worry, I'll solve this. Your mother probably lacks only for typing paper, or perhaps the stamp deliveries to the east coast have been delayed. I'll make a call tonight. Trust me, I can make anything happen. You'll have typed letters from your mother by sunset tomorrow."

"Is it true?" she asked. "Can you really do anything?"

With his thumbs, the Dear Leader wiped away her tears. "It's hard to believe how far you've come," he said. "Sometimes I forget that. Do you remember when I first laid eyes on you?" He shook his head at the memory of some long-ago moment. "You weren't even named Sun Moon then." He reached into her hair and touched her ear. "Remember that you have no secrets from me. That's what I'm here for, I'm the one you reveal yourself to. Just tell me what it is you need."

"Please," she said. "Give me the joy of seeing my mother at the premiere."

Citizens, citizens. Ours is a culture that respects the elderly, that grants them their need of rest and solitude in the final years. After a life of labor, haven't they earned some remote quietude? Can't the greatest nation on earth spare a little silence for the aged? Certainly, we all wish our parents were spry forever, that they'd never leave our side. But Sun Moon, listen to the people cluck their tongues at you. See how selfish it is to burden your mother with an arduous journey, one on which she might perish, simply to satisfy your own personal pleasures? But we throw up our hands. Who can deny Sun Moon? Ever the exception, so pure of emotion is she.

"She'll be sitting in the front row," the Dear Leader told her. "I guarantee."

Citizens, if the Dear Leader says it, that settles it. Nothing could prevent Sun Moon's mother from attending that movie premiere now. Only an utterly unforeseeable occurrence—a train mishap, possibly, or regional flooding—could stand in the way of this joyous reunion. Nothing short of a diphtheria quarantine or a military sneak attack could keep Sun Moon's dreams from coming true!

In a gesture of socialist support, the Dear Leader placed his hand upon her.

"Haven't I followed all the rules?" he asked.

She was silent.

"I have to have you back," he said to her. "We must return to our arrangement."

"It was an agreement," she said.

"So it was, and haven't I lived up to my side, haven't I followed your rules?" he asked. "That I never force you to do anything, isn't that rule number one? Answer me, have I ever gone against your will? Can you name one thing I've made you do?"

She shook her head.

"That's right," he told her, his voice rising. "That's why you must choose to come back, you must choose right now. The time has come." His voice had turned sharp, such was his paternal concern for her. He gave himself a moment of pause and soon his charming smile returned. "Yes, yes, you'll have a new set of rules, I'm sure. They'll be whoppers, impossibly complicated rules—already I can imagine the joy on your face when you spell them out to me, but I agree to them right now, I accept all your new rules in advance." He held his arms wide with possibility. "Just come back. It will be like old times. We'll play Iron Chef with the kitchen staff, and you'll help me open my fan mail. We'll ride my train to no place in particular and spend all night in the karaoke car. Inventing new kinds of sushi rolls, don't you miss that? Remember playing *chang-gi* by the lake? We could have a tournament, this weekend, while your children zoom past on my Jet Skis. Did you bring it?"

"It's in the car," she said.

The Dear Leader smiled.

"Where were we in our series?" he asked. "I can't remember our tally."

"When we left off, I think I was down a few games."

"You weren't letting me win, were you?" he asked.

"Assure yourself, I show no mercy," she said.

"That's my Sun Moon."

He wiped the residue of her tears.

"Compose a song of departure for our Night Rower. Please sing her away from us. Wear that red *choson-ot* for me, won't you? Tell me you'll wear it. Just try on, try it on and tomorrow we'll send that American girl back to whatever forsaken place it was that bred her."

Sun Moon cast her eyes downward. Slowly, she nodded.

The Dear Leader, too, slowly nodded. "Yes," he said softly.

Then he lifted a finger, and who should briskly arrive astride a forklift but Comrade Buc, sweat dripping from his brow. Do not gaze upon him, citizens! Avert your eyes from the puppetry of his traitorous smile.

"To guard the modesty of Sun Moon," the Dear Leader said, "she'll need some type of changing station at the airport."

Comrade Buc took a deep breath. "Nothing but the finest," he said.

The Dear Leader took her by the arm and turned her toward the lights and music.

"Come," he said. "I have a last movie to show you. The American visit has got me thinking about cowboys and frontier justice. So I have composed a Western. You'll play the long-suffering wife of a Texas cattle driver who's being exploited by capitalist landowners. When a corrupt sheriff accuses the cattle driver of rustling—"

She stopped him.

"Promise me nothing bad will happen to him," Sun Moon said.

"Who? The cattle driver?"

"No, my husband. Or whoever he is," she said. "He has a good heart."

"In this world," the Dear Leader told her, "no one can make such a promise."

COMMANDER GA smoked on the balcony, eyes narrowed to the dark road below, searching for any sign of the car that might return Sun Moon to him. He heard the faraway bark of a dog in the zoo, and he recalled a dog on a beach long ago, standing sentinel at the waves for someone who would never return. There were people who came into your life and cost you everything. Comrade Buc's wife was right about that. It had felt pretty shitty being one of those people. He had been the person who took. He'd been the one who was taken. And he'd been the one left behind. Next he would find out what it was like to be all three at once.

He extinguished his cigarette. There were stray celery seeds on the rail from the boy's bird snare. Ga rolled them under his finger as he gazed upon a city whose surface was black, but below was a labyrinth of brightly lit bunkers, one of which, he was certain, held Sun Moon. Who had thought up this place? Who had concocted its existence? How ugly and laughable was the idea of a quilt to Comrade Buc's wife. Where was the pattern, with what fabric, would someone sew the story of life in this place? If he had learned anything about the real Commander Ga by living in his clothes and sleeping in his bed, it was the fact that this place had made him. In North Korea, you weren't born, you were made, and the man that had done the making, he was working late tonight. The stray seeds on the balcony rail led the way to a mound of seeds. Ever so slowly, Ga extended his hand to them. Where was it, he wondered, that Comrade Buc's wife got her calm in the face of it all? How was it she knew what had to be done? Suddenly, a twig twitched, a stone fell, a thread tightened, and then a little noose cinched itself around Ga's finger.

He searched the house, looking for information—for what purpose, of what kind, he didn't know. He went through Commander Ga's rice-wine collection, laying hands on each bottle. He stood on a chair, and with the use of a candle, studied a variety of pistols, haphazard in the upper cabinet. In the tunnel, he ran his eyes across all the DVDs, looking for one that might address his situation, but it didn't seem Americans made such movies. He studied the pictures on their covers and read their descriptions, but where was the film that had no beginning, an unrelenting middle, and ended over and over? Reading English made his eyes hurt and then it started him thinking in English, which forced him to think of tomorrow, and, for the first time in a long time, he was filled with great fear. There would be English in his head until he heard the voice of Sun Moon.

When at last her car arrived, he was lying flat in the bed, letting the breathing of the children—unconscious, elemental—soothe him. He listened to her enter in the dark and in the kitchen ladle herself a glass of water. When she opened the door to the bedroom, he felt for the box of matches and drew one.

"Don't," she said.

He feared that she had somehow been damaged or marked, that she was trying to hide something that had been inflicted upon her.

"Are you all right?"

"I'm fine," she said.

He listened to her change into her bedclothes. Despite the darkness, he could visualize her, the way she removed garments and draped them across a chair back, how she balanced herself, hand against the wall, to step into the shift she would wear to sleep. He could sense her in the dark, touching the children's faces, making sure they were safe and dreaming deep.

When she was under the covers, he lit the candle, and there she was, illuminated in golden light.

"Where did he take you?" he asked. "What did he do to you?"

He studied her face, looking for a sign of what she might have gone through.

"He didn't hurt me," she said. "He simply gave me a glimpse of the future."

Ga saw the three *choson-ots* hanging red, white, and blue against the wall.

"Is that part of it?" he asked.

"Those are the costumes I'm to wear tomorrow. Won't I look like one of those patriotic tour guides in the War Museum?"

"You're not to wear your own dress, the silver one?"

She shook her head.

"So you'll leave here looking like the showgirl he wants you to be," he said. "I know that's not how you wanted to go, but the important thing is that you get out. You're not having second thoughts, are you? You're still going, right?"

"We're still going, right?" she said. Then something caught her eye. She looked up to the empty mantel. "Where are the peaches?"

He paused. "I threw the can off the balcony," he told her. "We won't need them anymore."

She stared at him.

"What if someone finds them and eats them?" she asked.

"I cut open the lid first," he said, "so they'd all spill out."

Sun Moon cocked her head. "Are you lying to me?"

"Of course not."

"Can I still trust you?"

"I threw them away because we're not taking that path," he said. "We're choosing a different one, one that leads to a life like the one in the American movie."

She rolled to her back and stared at the ceiling.

"What about you?" he asked. "Why won't you tell me what he did to you?"

She pulled the sheet higher and kept ahold of the fabric.

"Did he put his hands on you?"

"There are things that happen in this world," she said. "And what is there to say about them?"

Ga waited for her to elaborate, but she didn't.

After a while, she exhaled.

"The time has come for me to be intimate with you," she said. "There are many things that the Dear Leader knows about me. When we're safe on a plane, I'll tell you my story, if that's what you want. Tonight I'm going to tell you the things he doesn't know."

She craned her neck toward the candle and blew it out.

"The Dear Leader doesn't have a clue about how my husband and Commander Park plotted against him. The Dear Leader doesn't know that I hate his constant karaoke, that I've never sung a song for pleasure in my life. He has no idea that his wife used to send me notes—she put his seal on them to get me to open them, but I never did. He could never know how I turn my hearing off when he starts to confide his vile secrets to me. I would never tell him how much I hated you for making me eat a flower, how I loathed you for forcing me to break my vow never to eat as a starving person again."

Ga wanted to light the candle, to see if she was angry or afraid. "If I'd known—"

"Don't interrupt me," she told him. "I won't be able to say these things if you stop me. He doesn't know my mother's prized possession was a steel zither. It had seventeen strings, and you could see yourself in the black lacquer of its finish. The night before my younger sister died, my father filled the room with the steam of boiling herbs, while my mother flooded us with *sanjo* music, fierce through the darkness, sweat coming off her, the metal strings flashing. It was a sound meant to challenge the light that come morning would take her little girl. The Dear Leader doesn't know that I reach for my sister at night. Not finding her, every time, wakes me. I would never tell him how that music is still stuck in my head.

"The Dear Leader knows my basic story, the facts of it. He knows my grandmother was taken to Japan to serve as a comfort woman. But he could never understand what she went through, why she came home having learned only songs of despair. Because she couldn't speak of those years, it was important that her daughters know these songs. And she had to convey them without the lyrics—after the war, just knowing Japanese could get you killed. She taught the musical notes, though, and how to transfer to the notes the feeling of the missing words. That's what Japan had taught her to do—to make the pluck of a string contain a missing thing, to store in a struck chord what had been swallowed by war. The Dear Leader doesn't understand that the skill he prizes me for is this.

"He doesn't know that when he first heard me singing, it was to my mother, locked in another train car, a song to keep her from despairing. There were hundreds of us on a relocation train to a redeemability camp, all with freshly bleeding ears. This was after my older sister was siphoned to Pyongyang for her beauty. This was after we'd agreed as a family that my father would try to smuggle out my little sister. This was after the attempt failed, after we'd lost her, after my father had been labeled a defector and we'd become the family of a defector, my mother and I. It was a long journey, the train moving so slowly that crows landed on the roof of the boxcar, where they paced back and forth between the vent holes to stare down at us like we were crickets they couldn't quite get. My mother was in another boxcar. Talking wasn't allowed, but singing was. I would sing 'Arirang' to let her know I was okay. She would return the song to say she was still with me.

"Our train pulled onto a side track to let another pass. It turned out to be the Dear Leader's bulletproof train, which stopped so the two conductors could discuss the tracks ahead. Rumors spread through the boxcars, a hushed panic at what was about to befall us. People's voices rose, speculating on what was happening to those in other boxcars, whether people would be singled out, so I sang, loud as I could, hoping my mother might hear me above the sounds of anguish.

"Suddenly, the door to our train car opened, and the guards beat a man to his knees. When they told him to bow down, we all followed suit. And there, backlit by the bright light, appeared the Dear Leader.

"*Did I hear a songbird?* he asked. *Tell me, who among us is this forlorn bird?*

"No one spoke.

"*Who has taken our national melody and adorned it with such emotion?* the Dear Leader asked us, pacing through our kneeling ranks. *What person can so distill the human heart and pour it into the vessel of patriotic zeal? Please, someone, finish the song. How can it exist without an ending?*

"From my knees, tears falling, I started to sing:

"*Arirang, Arirang, ah-rah-ree-yoh, I am crossing Arirang Hill.*
I believed you when you told me
We were going to Arirang Hill for a spring picnic.
Arirang, your feet will fail you before you take ten steps
  from me.

"The Dear Leader closed his eyes and smiled. I didn't know which was worse—to displease him or to please him. All I knew was that my mother would not survive without me.

"*Arirang, Arirang, ah-rah-ree-yoh, Arirang all alone,*
With a bottle of rice wine hidden under my skirt.
I looked for you, my love, in our secret spot, in Odong, Odong
  Forest.
Arirang, Arirang, give me back my love.

"When I was finished, the Dear Leader seemed not to hear the faint song answering back.

"I was taken to his personal train car, where the windows were so thick that the light through them was green and warped. Here, he asked me to recite lines from a story he had typed out. It was called 'Tyrants Asunder.' How could he fail to smell the urine on me, or the stink of hunger that creeps up your throat and infects your breath? I spoke the words, though they had no meaning for me in that state. I could barely finish a sentence without succumbing.

"Then the Dear Leader called out *Bravo* and showered me with applause. *Tell me,* he said. *Tell me you will memorize my lines, say you will accept the role.*

"How could he know that I didn't really understand what a movie was, that I'd only heard broadcasts of revolutionary operas? How could I know that on the Dear Leader's train there were other cars whose construction was for propositions much less noble than auditions?

"Here, the Dear Leader gestured large, as if we were now in a theater. *Of course, such is the subtlety of this art form,* he added, *that my lines will become yours. The people will see you fill the screen and remember only the emotion of your voice bringing the words to life.*

"The train beneath me started moving.

"*Please!* I called out, it was almost a scream. *My mother must be safe.*

"*Certainly,* he said. *I'll have someone check on her.*

"I don't know what came over me. I raised my eyes to his. *Safe forever,* I said.

"He smiled with the surprise of new appreciation. *Safe, forever,* he agreed.

"I saw that he responded to conditions. He spoke the language of rules.

"*Then I'll do it,* I told him. *I'll perform your story.*

"This is the moment I was 'discovered.' How fondly the Dear Leader recalls it, as if through his keen insight and wisdom, I was saved from some destructive natural force, such as a landslide. It was a story he loved to recount over the years, when we were alone in his opera box or sailing through the sky on his personal gondola, this story of fortune bringing our two trains together. He never meant it as a threat to me, to remind me of how far I had to fall. Rather, it was a reminder of the forever of us.

"Through the green of the window, I watched the train bearing my mother recede.

I knew you'd agree, the Dear Leader said. *I had a feeling. I'll cancel the other actress right away. In the meantime, let's get you some proper clothes. And that ear of yours could use some attention.*"

In the dark, Commander Ga said the word "cancel."

"Cancel," Sun Moon repeated. "How many times have I thought of that other girl? How could the Dear Leader know that my arms still go cold for her?"

"What happened to her?" Ga asked.

"You know what happened to her," she said.

They were quiet a moment.

"There is another thing the Dear Leader doesn't know about me," she said. "But it's something he'll soon find out."

"What's that?"

"I'm going to re-create one of my grandmother's songs. In America, I will discover the missing words, and this song, it will be about him. It will contain everything of this place that I could never utter, every last bit of it, and I'm going to sing it on the state channel of America's central broadcasting division and everyone in the world will know the truth of him."

"The rest of the world knows the truth of him," he said.

"No, they don't," she said. "They won't know it until they hear it in my voice. It's a song I thought I'd never get to sing." Sun Moon struck a match. In the flash of it, she said, "And then you came along. Do you see that the Dear Leader has no idea that I'm the purest actress, that it's not just when I speak his lines, but every single moment? It is also the actress that I have shown you. But that's not who I am. Though I must act all the time—inside I'm simply a woman."

He blew out the match and took her arm, rolling her to him. It was the arm he'd grabbed before. This time she didn't pull back. His face was near hers and he could feel her breath as it came.

She reached out and gripped his shirt.

"Show it to me," she said.

"But it's dark. You won't be able to see it."

"I want to feel it," she told him.

He pulled his shirt over his head and leaned to her, so that his tattoo was at her fingertips.

She traced his muscles, felt the flare of his ribs.

"Maybe I should get one," she said.

"One what, a tattoo?" he asked. "What would you get a tattoo of?"

"Who do you suggest?"

"It depends. Where on your body would this tattoo be inked?"

She pulled the shift over her head and took his hand, placing it with both of hers over her heart. "What do you think of here?"

He felt the delicacy of her skin, the suggestion of her breasts. Most of all, he felt against his palm the heat of her blood and how her heart pumped it through her body, down her arms and into the hands that clasped the back of his so that the sensation was of being engulfed by her.

"This is an easy one," he said. "The tattoo to place over your heart is the image of what's inside your heart."

Leaning close, he kissed her. It was long and singular and his eyes closed with the parting of their lips. After, she was silent, and he became afraid, not knowing what she was thinking.

"Sun Moon, are you there?"

"I'm here," she said. "A song just ran through my head."

"A good one or a bad one?"

"There's only one kind."

"Is it true, have you really never sung for pleasure?"

"What song would you have me sing?" she asked him. "One about spilling blood, celebrating martyrdom, glorifying lies?"

"Is there no song at all? What about a love song?"

"Name one that hasn't been twisted into being about our love for the Dear Leader."

In the dark, he let his hand roam over her, the hollow above her collarbone, that taut cord in her neck, the fine point of her shoulder.

"There's one song I know," he told her.

"How does it go?"

"I only know the opening. I heard it in America."

"Tell me."

"She's the yellow rose of Texas," he said.

"*She's the yellow rose of Texas,*" she sang.

The English words were thick in her mouth, but the sound, her voice, it was lovely. He delicately touched her lips so he could feel her sing the words.

"I'm going for to see."

"*I'm going for to see.*"

"When I finally find her, I'll have her marry me."

"What do the words mean?"

"They're about a woman whose beauty is like a rare flower. There is a man who has a great love for her, a love he's been saving up for his entire life, and it doesn't matter that he must make a great journey to her, and it doesn't matter if their time together is brief, that afterward he might lose her, for she is the flower of his heart and nothing will keep him from her."

"The man in the song," she said. "Is he you?"

"You know I'm him."

"I'm not the woman in the song," she said. "I'm not an actress or a singer or a flower. I'm just a woman. Do you want to know this woman? Do you want to be the only man in the world who knows the real Sun Moon?"

"You know I do."

Here she raised her body some to allow him to pull free her last garment.

"Do you know what happens to men who fall in love with me?" she asked.

Ga took a moment to think about it.

"They get locked in your tunnel and fed nothing but broth for two weeks?"

Playfully, she said, "No."

"Hmm," Ga said. "Your neighbor tries to give them botulism and then they get punched in the nose by the Dear Leader's driver?"

"No."

"Okay, I give up. What happens to men who fall for you?"

She shimmied her body so that her hips were under his.

"They fall forever," she said.

AFTER the loss of Jujack and Q-Kee's defection to the Pubyok, I stayed away from Division 42. I know I roamed the city, but for how long, a week? And where did I go? Did I wander the People's Footpath, watching birds hopelessly hover above the snares that held their feet? Did I inhabit the Kumsusan mausoleum, where I endlessly stared into the chrome-and-glass coffin of Kim Il Sung, his body glowing red under preservation lamps? Or did I study the Urchin Master as he used his truck, disguised as an ice-cream van, to rid Pyongyang's alleys of beggar boys? Did I at any time recall recruiting Jujack at Kim Il Sung University's career day, where I wore a suit and a tie as I showed the boy our color brochures and explained to him that interrogation wasn't about violence anymore, that it was about the highest order of intellectual gamesmanship, where the tools were creative thinking and the stakes were national security? Perhaps I sat in Mansu Park watching virgins soak their uniforms with sweat as they chopped firewood. Wouldn't I have, here, pondered the notion that I was alone, that my team was gone, that my interns were gone, that my successes were gone, that my chances at love and friendship and family seemed all but gone? Maybe my mind was empty as I stood in line for buses I didn't intend to take, and maybe I thought nothing as I was rounded up for a sandbag brigade. Or perhaps I was reclined the whole time on the blue vinyl of an autopilot chair, imagining such things? And what was wrong with my memory? How come I didn't recollect how I spent these painful days, and why was I okay with the fact that I couldn't recall them? I preferred it this way, didn't I? Compared to forgetting, did living really stand a chance?

*

I was nervous when I finally returned to Division 42. Descending the final staircase, I wasn't sure what I'd find. But all seemed active and normal.

There were new cases on the big board and red lights glowed above the holding tanks. Q-Kee walked past, new intern in tow.

"Good to see you, sir," she said.

Sarge was particularly jovial. "There's our interrogator," he said. "Good to have you back." He said it in a way that suggested he was talking about more than my recent absence.

He had a large metal object on the workbench.

"Hey, Sarge," I said.

"Sarge?" he asked. "Who's that?"

"I mean Comrade, sorry," I said.

"There's the spirit," Sarge said.

Just then, Commander Park walked by, limping, his arm in a sling. He had something in his hand—I couldn't make it out, but it was pink and wet and raw. Let me tell you, Commander Park, with his scarified face, was one sinister figure. The way he looked at you with those dead eyes in their marred sockets, it was like he belonged in some kind of spooky movie about evil dictators in Africa or something. He wrapped the item in newspaper, then sent it via vacuum tube deep into the bunker under us. He wiped his hand on his pants and left.

Sarge snapped his fingers in my face. "Comrade," he said.

"Sorry," I said. "I haven't seen Commander Park up here before."

"He's the Commander," Sarge said.

"He's the Commander," I echoed.

"Look," Sarge said. "I know you got caught up in the harvest, and your apartment is on the twenty-second floor. I know you don't get priority seating on the subway." Here he reached in his pocket. "So I got you a little something," he said. "Something to dispense with all of life's little problems."

I was sure it would be the next-generation sedative I'd heard rumors of.

Instead, he produced a shiny new Pubyok badge. "There's no such thing as a team of one," he said, offering it to me. "You're a smart guy. We need a smart guy. Q-Kee learned a lot from you. Come on, be smart. You can keep working with her."

"Ga's still my case," I said. "I need to see it through."

"That's something I can respect," Sarge said. "I wouldn't have it any other way. Finish your work, by all means, then join the team."

When I took the badge, he said, "I'll have the boys schedule your hair-cutting party."

I turned the badge in my hand. There was no name on it, just a number.

Sarge took me by the shoulder. "Come, check this out," he said.

At the workbench, he handed me the metal object. It weighed a tremendous amount. I could barely wield it. It had a solid handle that connected to a strip of writing cast from forged metal.

"What language is that?" I asked. "English?"

Sarge nodded. "But even if you did know English," he said, "you wouldn't be able to read it. The writing is backward." He took it from me, so that he could indicate the script. "It's called a brand. Pure iron, custom smelted. You use it to make a mark of possession, which you can then read forward. I can't remember if it says Property of the Democratic People's Republic of Korea or if it says Property of the Dear Leader Kim Jong Il."

Sarge studied my face to see if I would make a smart remark like *What's the difference?*

When I didn't, he smiled and nodded in approval.

I looked for a power cord on the device but saw nothing. "How's it work?"

"Easy," he said. "It's old American technology. You put it in a bed of coals until it's red hot. Then you burn the message in."

"Into what?" I asked.

"Commander Ga," he said. "They're going to brand him at dawn in the soccer stadium."

The ghouls, I thought, though I tried hard to show no emotion.

"Is that what Commander Park was doing here?"

"No," Sarge said. "The Dear Leader sent Commander Park here on a personal errand. It seems the Dear Leader misses Sun Moon and wanted a last image to remember her by."

I stared at Sarge, trying to comprehend what he was saying, but as a sly smile crossed his face, I turned and ran, ran as fast as I could to Commander Ga. I found him in one of the soundproof holding tanks.

"They're going to do it in the morning," Ga said when I entered his room. He was lying on an interrogation table, shirtless, his hands in restraints. "They're going to take me to the soccer stadium and brand me in front of everyone." But I couldn't hear his words. I only stared at his chest. I neared, slowly, my eyes fixated on the raw red square where his tattoo of Sun Moon used to be. There had been much blood—the table was dripping with it—but now only a clear fluid wept from the wound, leaving pinkish ribbons trailing down his ribs.

"I could use a bandage," he said.

I looked around the room, but there was nothing.

I watched a chill run across his body. This was followed by a couple of deep breaths, which caused him great pain. A strange laugh came out of him, filled with agony.

"They didn't even ask me about the actress," he said.

"I guess that means you beat them."

His jaw seized with the pain, so he could only nod.

He snatched a couple of quick breaths, then said, "If you ever get a choice between Commander Park with a box cutter—" Here he clenched his teeth a moment. "And a shark . . ."

I put my hand on his forehead, which was running with sweat.

"Take the shark, right? Look," I said. "Don't talk, there's no need to be funny. Don't try to be Comrade Buc."

The name, I could tell, caused him the greatest pain of all.

"It wasn't supposed to work like that," Ga said. "Buc wasn't supposed to get hurt."

"You just worry about yourself," I said.

Sweat was pooling in Ga's eyes, which were burning with worry.

"Is this what happened to Buc?" he asked.

I used my shirttail to dry his eyes.

"No," I said. "Buc went on his own terms."

Ga nodded, his lower jaw shuddering.

Sarge came in, grinning. "What do you think of the great Commander Ga now?" he asked. "He's the most dangerous man in our nation, you know."

"That's not the real Commander Ga," I reminded Sarge. "This is just a man."

Sarge came astride Commander Ga's table.

Wincing, Commander Ga tried to roll his head as far from Sarge as possible.

Yet Sarge neared, leaning over Commander Ga as if to inspect the wound up close. Sarge looked back at me, smiling. "Oh, yes," he said. "The good Commander here has had pain training." Then Sarge took a breath and blew into Ga's wound.

The scream that followed made my ears sing.

"He's ready to talk now," Sarge said. "And you're going to get his confession."

I looked to Commander Ga, who took shallow, trembling breaths.

"But what about his biography?" I asked Sarge.

"You understand this is the last biography, right?" he told me. "That age is over. But you can do anything you like as long as we have his confession in hand when they take him to the stadium at first light."

When I nodded, Sarge left.

I leaned close to Commander Ga. His skin would frost with goose pimples, then go slack. He wasn't a hero. He was just a man, pushed farther than any man should be pushed. Looking at him now, I understood the fairy tale he'd told us about the little orphan boy who'd licked honey from the Dear Leader's claws. The night Ga told us that story, I realized, was the last time my team was whole and together.

"I'm not going to let the bear get you," I told him. "I'm not going to let them do what they're planning to do."

There were tears in Ga's eyes. "Bandage," is all he could say.

"I have an errand to run," I told him. "Then I'll be back to save you."

*

At the Glory of Mount Paektu Housing Block, I didn't bound up the twenty-one flights to my parents. I took the stairs slowly for once, feeling the labor of each step. I couldn't get that brand out of my mind. I saw it scalding red and bubbly across Commander Ga, I imagined its scars, ancient and discolored, running down the thick backs of all the old Pubyok, I saw Q-Kee's perfect body disfigured by it, a burn from neck to navel, splitting the breasts toward the sternum, the belly, and below. I didn't use my Pubyok badge to board the subway's priority seating car. I sat with the average citizens, and on all their bodies, I couldn't help but see "Property of" in raised pink letters. The mark was on everyone, only now could I finally see it. It was the ultimate perversion of the communist dream I'd been taught since childhood. I felt like retching the turnips in my stomach.

I was almost never home in the middle of the day. I took the opportunity to remove my shoes in the hall and ever so silently slip my key in the lock. Opening the door, I lifted up on the knob, so the door's hinges wouldn't squeak. Inside, the loudspeaker was blaring, and my parents were at the table with some of my files open and spread before them. They were whispering to one another as they ran their fingers across the pages, feeling the file labels and paper clips, the embossed stamps and raised department seals.

I knew better than to leave important files at home anymore. These were just requisition forms.

I pushed the door shut behind me. It squealed in its arc until the lock clicked tight.

The two of them froze.

"Who is it?" my father asked. "Who's there?"

"Are you a thief?" my mother asked. "I assure you we have nothing to steal."

They were both looking right at me, though they seemed not to see me.

Across the table, their hands sought one another and joined.

"Go away," my father said. "Leave us alone, or we'll tell our son."

My mother felt around the table until she located a spoon. She grabbed the handle and held it out like a knife. "You don't want my son to find out about this," she said. "He's a torturer."

"Mother, Father," I said. "No need to worry, it is I, your son."

"But it's the middle of the day," my father said. "Is everything okay?"

"Everything's fine," I told him.

I walked to the table and closed the files.

"You're barefoot," my mother said.

"I am."

I could see the marks on them. I could see that they'd been branded.

"But I don't understand," my father said.

"I'm going to have a long night," I told them. "And some long tomorrows to follow. I won't be here to cook your dinner or help you down the hall to the bathroom."

"Don't worry about us," my mother said. "We can manage. If you have to go, go."

"I do have to go," I said.

I walked to the kitchen. From a drawer, I removed the can opener. I paused there at the window. Spending my days underground, I wasn't used to the midday brightness. I observed the spoon and pan and hot plate my mother cooked with. I stared at the drying rack, where two glass bowls caught the light. I decided against bowls.

"I think you're afraid of me," I said to them. "Because I'm a mystery to you. Because you don't really know me."

I thought they'd protest, but they were silent. I reached to the top shelf and found the can of peaches. I blew on the lid, but it hadn't been there long enough to gather much dust. At the table, I took the spoon from my mother's hand and sat, the items before me.

"Well, you won't have to worry ever again," I told them. "Because today you're going to meet the real me."

I sank the opener into the can and began to cut a slow circle.

My father sniffed the air. "Peaches?" he asked.

"That's right," I said. "Peaches in their own sweet liquor."

"From the night market?" Mother asked.

"Actually, I stole them from the evidence locker."

My father inhaled deeply. "I can just see them, plain as day, the thick juice they're in, the way they glow in the light."

"It's been so long since I've tasted a peach," my mother said. "We used to get a coupon for a can every month in our ration book."

My father said, "Oh, that was years ago."

"I suppose you're right," my mother answered. "I'm just saying that we used to love peaches, and then one day you couldn't get them anymore."

"Well, allow me, then," I told them. "Open."

Like children, they opened their mouths. In anticipation, my father closed his milky eyes.

I stirred the peaches in their can, then selected a slice. Passing the bottom of the spoon across the edge of the can, I caught the dripping syrup. Then I reached and slipped the slice into my mother's mouth.

"Mmm," she said.

I fed my father next.

"That, son," he said, "was a peach."

There was silence, except for the blaring loudspeaker, as they savored the moment.

In unison, they said, "Thank you, Dear Leader Kim Jong Il."

"Yes," I said. "You have him to thank."

I stirred the can again, hunted down the next slice.

"I have a new friend," I said.

"A friend from work?" my father asked.

"Yes, a friend from work," I said. "The two of us have become quite intimate. He's given me hope that love is out there for me. He's a man who has true love. I've studied his case very closely, and I think the secret to love is sacrifice. He himself has made the ultimate sacrifice for the woman he loves."

"He gave his life for her?" my father asked.

"Actually, he took her life," I told him and popped a peach in his mouth.

There was a quake in my mother's voice. "We're happy for you," she said. "As the Dear Leader says, *Love makes the world go 'round.* So don't hesitate. Go find that true love. Don't worry about us. We'll be fine. We can take care of ourselves."

I spooned a slice into her mouth. It caught her by surprise and she coughed.

"Perhaps, from time to time," I said, "you have seen me writing in my journal. It's actually not a journal—it's a personal biography. As you know, that's what I do for a living, write people's biographies, which we keep in what you might call a private library. A guy I work with, I'll call him Sarge, says the problem with my biographies is that no one ever reads them. This brings me to my new friend, who told me that the only people in the world who would want to read his biography were gone."

I dished out new slices with ample syrup.

"*People,*" my father said, "meaning the lady that your friend loves."

"Yes," I said.

"The lady that your friend killed," Mother said.

"And her kids," I said. "There is a tragic aspect to the story, there's no denying it."

I nodded my head at the truth of that. It would have made a good subtitle for his biography—*Commander Ga: A Tragedy.* Or whatever his name was.

The peaches were half gone. I stirred them in their can, selecting a new slice.

"Save some for yourself," my father said.

"Yes, that's enough," my mother said. "I haven't tasted sweet in so long, my stomach cannot handle it."

I shook my head no. "This is a rare can of peaches," I said. "I was going to keep them for myself, but taking the easy way, that's not the answer to life's problems."

My mother's lip started to quiver. She covered it with her hand.

"But back to my problem," I said. "My biography, and the difficulty I've had writing it. This biographer's block I've been suffering from—I see it so clearly now—came from the fact that deep down, I knew no one wanted to hear my story. Then my friend, he had the insight that his tattoo wasn't public, but personal. Though it was there for the world to see, it was truly for no one but himself. Losing that, he lost everything, really."

"How can a person lose a tattoo?" my father asked.

"Unfortunately, it's easier than you'd think," I told them. "It got me thinking, though, and I realized I wasn't composing for posterity or the Dear Leader or for the good of the citizenry. No, the people who needed to hear my story were the people I loved, the people right in front of me who'd started to think of me as a stranger, who were scared of me because they no longer knew the real me."

"But your friend, he killed the people he loved, right?"

"It's unfortunate, I know," I said. "There's no forgiving him for it, he hasn't even asked. But let me get started with my biography. I was born in Pyongyang," I began, "to parents who were factory workers. My mother and father were older, but they were good parents. They survived every worker purge and avoided denunciation and reeducation."

"But we already know these things," my father said.

"Shh," I told him. "You can't talk back to a book. You don't get to rewrite a biography as you're reading it. Now, back to my story." As they finished the peaches, I relayed to them how normal my childhood was, how I played the accordion and recorder at school, and while in the choir, I sang high alto in performances of *Our Quotas Lift Us Higher*. I memorized all the speeches of Kim Il Sung and got the highest marks in Juche Theory. Then I began with the things they didn't know. "One day a man from the Party came to our school," I said. "He loyalty-tested all the boys, one at a time, in the maintenance shed. The test itself only lasted a couple of minutes, but it was quite difficult. I suppose that's the point of a test. I'm happy to say I passed the test, all of us did, but none of us ever spoke of it."

It felt very liberating to finally speak of this, a topic I could never commit to paper. I knew suddenly that I would share everything with them, that we'd be closer than ever—I'd tell them of the humiliations I suffered in mandatory military service, of my one sexual encounter with a woman, of the cruel hazing I'd received as an intern of the Pubyok.

"I don't mean to dwell on the subject of this loyalty test, but it changed how I saw things. Behind a chest of medals might be a hero or a man with an eager index finger. I became a suspicious boy who knew there was always something more beneath the surface, if you were willing to probe. It perhaps sent me down my career path, a trajectory that has confirmed that there is no such thing as the right-minded, self-sacrificing citizen the government tells us we all are. I'm not complaining, mind you, merely explaining. I didn't have it half as rough as some. I didn't grow up in an orphanage like my friend Commander Ga."

"Commander Ga?" my father asked. "Is that your new friend?"

I nodded.

"Answer me," my father said. "Is Commander Ga your new friend?"

"Yes," I said.

"But you can't trust Commander Ga," my mother said. "He's a coward and a criminal."

"Yes," my father added. "He's an imposter."

"You don't know Commander Ga," I told them. "Have you been reading my files?"

"We don't need to read any files," my father said. "We have it on the highest authority. Commander Ga's an enemy of the state."

"Not to mention his weaselly friend Comrade Buc," my mother added.

"Don't even say that name," my father cautioned.

"How do you know all this?" I asked. "Tell me about this authority."

They both pointed toward the loudspeaker.

"Every day they tell some of his story," my mother said. "Of him and Sun Moon."

"Yes," my father said. "Yesterday was episode five. In it, Commander Ga drives to the Opera House with Sun Moon, but it's not really Commander Ga, you see—"

"Stop it," I said. "That's impossible. I've made very little progress on his biography. It doesn't even have an ending."

"Listen for yourself," my mother said. "The loudspeaker doesn't lie. The next installment is this afternoon."

I dragged a chair to the kitchen, where I used it to reach the loudspeaker. Even after I tore it from the wall, it was connected to a cable that kept it squawking. Only with a meat knife was I able to shut it up.

"What's happening?" my mother asked. "What are you doing?"

My father was hysterical.

"What if the Americans sneak-attack?" he asked. "How will we receive the warning?"

"You won't have to worry about sneak attacks anymore," I told them.

My father moved to protest, but a stream of saliva ran from his mouth. He reached for his mouth and felt his lips, as if they had gone numb. And one of my mother's hands was showing a tremor. She stilled it with her other hand. The botulism toxin was beginning to bloom inside them. The time for suspicions and arguments was over.

I remembered that horrible picture of Comrade Buc's family, crumpled beneath the table. I was resolved that my parents wouldn't suffer such indignities. I gave them each a tall glass of water and placed them on their cots to await the fall of night. All afternoon and into the twilight, I gave them the gift of my story, every bit of it, and I left nothing out. I stared out the window as I spoke, and I concluded only when they'd begun to writhe on their cots. I couldn't act until darkness arrived, and when it finally did, the city of Pyongyang was like that black cricket in the fairy tale—it was everywhere and nowhere, its chirp annoying only those who ignored the final call to slumber. The moon shimmered off the river, and after the eagle owls had struck, you could hear nothing of the sheep and goats but the clicking of their teeth as they chewed grass in the dark. When darkness was total, and my parents had lost their faculties, I kissed them good-bye, for I could not bear to witness the inevitable. A sure sign of botulism is a loss of vision, so I only hoped they'd never know what had struck them. I looked around the room a last time, at our family photograph, my father's harmonica, their wedding rings. But I left it all. I could take nothing where I was going.

*

There was no way Commander Ga could attempt the arduous journey ahead with an open wound. At the night market, I bartered my Pubyok badge for some iodine and a large compress. Crossing the city in the dark, headed for Division 42, I felt the stillness of the big machine at rest. There was no thrum of electricity in the wires overhead or gurgle of water in the pipes. Pyongyang was coiling in the dark to pounce upon the next day. And how I loved the capital springing to life, morning wood smoke in the air, the smell of frying radishes, the hot burn of trolley brakes. I was a city boy. I would miss the metropolis, its hubbub and vitality. If only there were a place here for a person who gathered human stories and wrote them down. But Pyongyang is already filled with obituary writers. And I can't stand propaganda. You'd think a person would get used to cruel fates.

When I appeared in Commander Ga's room, he asked, "Is it morning already?"

"Not yet," I told him. "There's still time."

I tried to minister to Commander Ga as best I could. The iodine turned my fingers red, making it look as if I were the one who'd brutalized the man before me. But when I placed the bandage on Commander Ga, the wound disappeared. I used the whole roll of tape to secure it.

"I'm getting out of here," I told him. "Would you like me to bring you along?"

He nodded.

"Do you care where you're going, or about the obstacles ahead?"

He shook his head. "No," he said.

"Are you ready? Do you need to do anything to prepare?"

"No," he told me. "I'm ready."

I helped him up, then sailor-carried him across Division 42 to an interrogation bay, where I rolled him into a baby-blue chair.

"This is where you gave me an aspirin when I first came," he said. "It seems like so long ago."

"It won't be a bad journey," I told him. "On the other side, there won't be Pubyok or cattle prods or branding irons. Hopefully, you'll get sent to a rural farm collective. Not an easy life, but you can start a new family and serve your nation in the true spirit of communism—through labor and devotion."

"I had my life," Commander Ga said. "I'll pass on the rest."

I grabbed two sedatives. When Commander Ga declined one, I took them both.

From the supply cabinet, I flipped through the diapers until I found a medium.

"Would you like one?" I asked. "We keep some on hand for when VIPs come through. It can save some embarrassment. I have a large right here."

"No thanks," he said.

I dropped my trousers and secured mine, using the adhesive tabs.

"You know, I respect you," I said. "You were the only guy who came through that never talked. You were smart—if you'd told us where the actress was, they'd have killed you right away."

"Are you going to hook me up to this machine?"

I nodded.

He looked at the autopilot's wires and energy meters. "There's no mystery," he said. "The actress simply defected."

"You never stop, do you? You're about to lose everything you own but your heartbeat, and still you're trying to throw us off the trail."

"It's true," he said. "She got on an airplane and flew away."

"Impossible," I told him. "Sure, a few peasants risk life and limb to cross an icy river. But our national actress, under the nose of the Dear Leader? You insult me."

I handed him a pair of paper booties. He sat on his baby-blue chair, and I sat on mine, and together we removed our shoes and socks to put them on.

"Not to insult you," he said, "but whose pictures do you think are on my phone? My wife and children vanish, but then, from far away, photos of a woman and her children appear. Is that such a mystery?"

"It's a conundrum, I'll admit. I pondered it much. But I know that you killed the people you loved. There's no other way." I pulled his phone from my pocket and used its buttons to erase the pictures. "If an interrogator starts questioning the only thing he knows for sure, then . . . but please, I am not that person anymore. I no longer take biographies. Only my own story concerns me now." I dropped the phone into a stainless-steel basin, along with a few coins and my ID badge, which said only "Interrogator."

He indicated the leather restraints. "You're not going to put these on me, are you?"

"I have to, I'm sorry. I'll need people to know that I did this to you, and not the other way around."

I reclined his chair, then strapped down his legs and arms. I did him the favor of leaving the buckles pretty loose.

"I'm sorry I didn't manage to finish your biography," I told him. "If I hadn't failed, I could have sent your biography with you, so when you reached the other side, you could read who you were and become you again."

"Don't worry," he told me. "She'll be on the other side. She'll recognize me and tell me who I am."

"I can offer you this," I said, holding up a pen. "If you like, you can write your name someplace on your body, a place they won't notice—on your *umkyoung*, or between your toes. That way, later, you might discover who you were. I'm not trying to trick you to learn your identity, I assure you."

"Are you going to do it?"

"I don't want to know who I was," I said.

"I don't even know what name I'd write," he told me.

I knelt to connect all the electrodes to his cranium. "You know they're telling your story over the loudspeakers," I said.

"Why?" he asked.

"I don't know, but since you're not going to be repenting in the soccer stadium tomorrow, I figure they'll have to come up with a new ending for your story."

"An ending to my story," he said. "My story's ended ten times already, and yet it never stops. The end keeps coming for me, and yet it takes everyone else. Orphans, friends, commanding officers, I outlast them all."

He was clearly confusing himself and his story, which is the natural result of certain tribulations. "This isn't the end of you," I told him. "It's a new beginning. And you haven't outlasted all your friends. We're friends, aren't we?"

He stared at the ceiling as though a parade of people he'd once known were passing there.

"I know why I'm in this blue chair," he said. "What about you?"

Aligning all the red-and-white wires leading from his skull was like braiding hair.

"This used to be a place," I told him, "where meaningful work was done. Here, a citizen was separated from his story. That was my job. Of the two, it was the story that was kept, while the person was disposed of. I was okay with that. In this way, many deviants and counterrevolutionaries were discovered. True, sometimes the innocent fell with the guilty, but there was no other way to discover the truth, and unfortunately, once a person has his story taken, by the roots if you will, it can't be given back. But now . . ."

Ga craned his neck to look at me. "Yes?"

"Now the person is lost along with his life. Both die."

I adjusted the output dial of his autopilot. Ga had a strong mind, so I set it at eight.

"Tell me again how intimacy works?" I asked.

"It turned out to be easy," Ga said. "You tell someone everything, the good, the bad, what makes you look strong and what's shameful as well. If you killed your wife's husband, you must tell her. If someone tried to man-attack you, you must tell that, too. I told you everything, as best as I was able. I may not know who I am. But the actress is free. I'm not sure I understand freedom, but I've felt it and she now has it too."

I nodded. It was satisfying to hear again. It restored my inner calm. With my parents, I had finally been intimate. And Commander Ga was my friend, despite the lie about the actress being alive. He'd so fully digested it that it had somehow become true to him. By his twisted logic, he was telling me, his friend, the absolute truth.

"See you on the other side," I said.

He fixed his eyes at some point that didn't exist.

"My mother was a singer," he said.

When he closed his eyes, I flipped the switch.

He made the usual involuntary motions, eye flashing, arm levitation, gulping for air like a carp at the surface of a meditation pond. *My mother was a singer* were his last words, as if they were the only ones he could trust to describe who he'd been.

I climbed into the next blue chair, but didn't bother with the restraints. I wanted the Pubyok to know that I'd chosen my own path, that I'd rejected their ways. I hooked up my own wiring harness and turned my attention to the autopilot's output dial. I never wanted to remember a thing about this place, so I set it at eight and a half. But then again, I didn't want a lobotomy, either. I adjusted it to seven and a half. And if I was being intimate with myself, I could also admit I was afraid of the pain. I settled for six and a half.

Trembling with hope and, strangely, regret, my finger flipped the switch.

My arms rose before me. They looked like someone else's arms. I heard moaning and realized it was me. A tongue of electricity licked deep inside my brain, probing, as molars are inspected after a meal. I'd imagined the experience would be one of numbness, but my thinking was hyper, thoughts flying. Everything was singular—the gleam of a metal armature, the violent green of a fly's eye. There was only the thing itself, without connection or context, as if everything in your mind had become unlinked to everything else. Blue and leather and chair, I couldn't put them together. The scent of ozone was without precedent, the incandescence of a lightbulb lacked all antecedent. The fine hairs in my nose stiffened. My erection stood abominable and alone. I saw no icy peak or white flower. I scanned the room for them, but saw only elements: shine, slick, coarse, shade.

I became aware of Commander Ga moving beside me. Arms aloft, it was all I could do to roll my head slightly to observe him. He had an arm free from its restraint, and he was reaching for the dial. I saw him turn it to maximum, a lethal dose. But I could worry about him no longer. I was on my own voyage. Soon I would be in a rural village, green and peaceful, where people swung their scythes in silence. There would be a widow there, and we would waste no time on courtship. I would approach her and tell her I was her new husband. We would enter the bed from opposite sides at first. For a while, she would have rules. But eventually, our genitals would intercourse in a way that was correct and satisfying. At night, after I had made my emission, we would lie there, listening to the sounds of our children running in the dark, catching summer frogs. My wife would have the use of both her eyes, so she would know when I blew out the candle. In this village, I would have a name, and people would call me by it. When the candle went out, she would speak to me, telling me to sleep very, very deeply, and as the electricity stropped itself sharper in my mind, I listened for her voice, calling a name that would soon be mine.

IN THE MORNING, Commander Ga woke to the roaring engines of an American military cargo jet. The children were already awake, staring at the ceiling. They knew this wasn't the once-a-week flight to Beijing or the twice-monthly grasshopper to Vladivostok. The children had never even heard an airplane over Pyongyang, which was restricted airspace. Not once since the American firebombing raids of 1951 had a plane been spotted over the nation's capital.

He roused Sun Moon and together they listened to it head north, as if it had originated in Seoul, a direction from which nothing was allowed to come. He checked his watch—the Americans were three hours early. The Dear Leader would be furious.

"They're flying low to announce their arrival," he said. "Very American."

Sun Moon turned to him. "So it's time."

He looked into her eyes to see what remained of their lovemaking last night, but she was looking forward and not back.

"It's time," he said.

"Children," Sun Moon called, "we're going on an adventure today. Go put together some food for us." When they were gone, she pulled on her robe and lit a cigarette at the window, watching the American Goliath lower its landing gear over the Taedong and descend toward the airport. She turned to Ga. "There's something you need to understand," she said. "Where the Dear Leader is concerned, there's only one of me. He has many girls, an entire *kippumjo* of them, but only I matter. He thinks that I reveal all to him, that emotions cross my face without my control, making me incapable of conspiring against him. I'm the only person in the world he thinks he can trust."

"Then today, he will feel the sting."

"I'm not talking about him," she said. "This is about you. Understand that if I slip from the Dear Leader's grasp, someone is going to pay, and that price will be unimaginable. You can't stay, you can't be the one who pays."

"I don't know where you got these notions about me," he said. "But—"

"You're the one with the notions," she went on. "I think you saw that movie and got it in your head that a noble man stays behind."

"You're tattooed on my heart," he said. "You'll always be with me."

"I'm talking about you being with me."

"We'll make it work," he said. "I promise. It will all work out. You've got to trust me."

"It's that kind of talk that scares me," she said, and exhaled smoke. "This whole thing feels like some kind of loyalty test. One so sick not even my husband could've thought it up."

How different it was to have warning that your life was about to change, Ga thought, let alone know the moment it would happen. Didn't Sun Moon understand that? And they had a say in it. He had to smile at the notion that things might, for one morning, bend to their influence.

"That look on your face," she said. "Even that makes me nervous."

She came close to him, and he stood to be near her.

"You're coming with me," she said. "Understand? I can't do it without you."

"I'll never leave your side."

He tried to touch her, but she pulled away.

"Why won't you just say you're coming?"

"Why won't you hear what I'm saying? Of course I am."

She gave him a look of doubt. "My sister, my father, my sister, my mother. Even that cruel husband of mine. One by one, they were stripped from me. Don't make it happen again. That's not how it's supposed to work, not when you have a choice. Just look me in the eyes and say it."

He did it, he looked her in the eyes. "You said forever, and that's me, forever. Soon, you'll never be able to get rid of me."

*

After Sun Moon donned her white *choson-ot,* she hung the red one and the blue one in the back of the Mustang. Ga pulled on his cowboy boots, tucked the can of peaches in his rucksack, and then patted his pocket to make sure he had his camera. The girl chased the dog with a rope to leash it.

The boy came running. "My bird snare's gone," he said.

"We weren't going to bring it anyway," Sun Moon said.

"Bring it where?" the boy asked.

"We'll make another sometime," Ga told him.

"I bet it caught a giant bird," the boy said. "One with wings so strong that it flew away with my snare."

Sun Moon stood before the shrine to her husband's Golden Belt. Ga joined her in contemplating the jewels and golden scrollwork, the way the overall flash of it was bright enough to allow its owner to take any woman in the land.

"Good-bye, my husband," she said, and turned off the lightbulb that illuminated it. Then she turned to consider for a moment her *gayageum* case, tall and regal in the corner. So it was pure tragedy on her face when she grabbed instead the simpleton instrument called a *guitar*.

Outside, he took a photo in front of the bean trellis, its white blossoms open, the tendrils of the girl's prize melon plant tangling through the white slats. The girl held the dog, the boy a laptop, and Sun Moon the dreaded American instrument. The light was soft, though, and he wished the picture wasn't Wanda's, but his.

In his best military uniform, Commander Ga drove slowly away, Sun Moon beside him in the front seat. It was a beautiful morning, the light golden as swallows circled the hothouses of the botanical gardens, their beaks popping like chopsticks at the clouds of insects there. Sun Moon leaned her head against the window and stared with melancholy as they passed the zoo and the Revolutionary Martyrs' Cemetery. He knew now that she had no great-uncle buried there, that she was just a zinc miner's daughter from Huchang, but in the morning glow, he saw how the rows of bronze busts seemed to ignite in unison. He noted how the mica in the marble pedestals sparkled, and he, too, understood he would never again see such a thing. If he was lucky, he'd get returned to a prison mine. Most likely, he'd be sent down into one of the Dear Leader's interrogation bunkers. Either way, he'd never again taste spruce sap on the wind or smell the brine of sorghum distilling in roadside crockery. Suddenly, he savored the dust the Mustang kicked up and the pound of the tires when they crossed the Yanggakdo Bridge. He saw the emerald flash of every armored plate defending the roof of the Self-Criticism Pavilion, and he took delight in the red glow of the digital baby counter atop the Pyongyang Maternity Hospital.

To the north, they could see the great American jet steadily circling the airport, looking as if it were on an endless bombing run. He knew he should be teaching the boy and the girl a few words of English. He knew he should be teaching them how to denounce him, should anything go wrong. Yet a sorrow was settling over Sun Moon, and he could attend to nothing but that.

"Have you made friends with your *guitar*?" he asked her.

She twanged a single, off note.

He held out his cigarettes. "Can I light you one?"

"Not before I sing," she said. "I'll smoke when we're safely in the sky. On that American airplane, I'll smoke a hundred of them."

"We're going on an airplane?" the boy asked.

Sun Moon ignored him.

"So you're going to sing the Rower Girl's farewell?" Ga asked her.

"I suppose I must," Sun Moon said.

"What is the song about?"

"I haven't written it yet," she said. "When I start to play, the words will come. Mostly I'm filled with questions." She took up her *guitar* and strummed it once. "*How long have I known you?*" she sang.

"*How long have I known you,*" the girl responded, singing the line as a lament.

"*Seven seas you have rowed through,*" Sun Moon sang.

"*Seven oceans you have known,*" her daughter sang.

Sun Moon strummed. "*But now you're in the eighth sea.*"

"*The one we call home,*" the boy sang, his voice higher than his sister's.

A contentment settled over Ga as he listened to them sing, as if something long-ago was finally being fulfilled.

"*Take wing, Girl Rower,*" Sun Moon sang, "*and leave the sea alone.*"

The girl answered her. "*Fly away, Rower Girl, and leave the eighth one be.*"

"That's good," Sun Moon said. "Let's try it together."

The girl asked, "Who's the Rower Girl?"

"We're driving to bid her farewell," Sun Moon said. "Now all together."

Then the family sang as one, "*Fly away, Rower Girl, and leave the eighth sea be.*"

The boy's voice was clear and trusting, the girl's was graveled with a growing awareness. Combined with Sun Moon's longing, a harmony arose that was nourishing to Ga. No other family in the world could create such a sound, and here he was, in the glow of it. Not even the sight of the soccer stadium could diminish the feeling.

*

At the airport, Ga's uniform allowed him to drive around the terminal to the hangars, where, to welcome the Americans, throngs of people were assembled, all of them conscripted from the streets of Pyongyang, citizens still holding their briefcases, toolboxes, and slide rules.

The Wangjaesan Light Music Band was playing "Speed Battle Haircut" to commemorate the Dear Leader's military achievements, while a legion of children in green-and-yellow gymnastics costumes practiced logrolling large white plastic barrels. Through a haze of barbecue smoke, Ga could see scientists, soldiers, and the Minister of Mass Mobilization's men in yellow armbands arranging a large crowd into rows by height.

The Americans finally decided it was safe to land. They heaved the gray beast around, wings broader than the runway, and brought it down through the gauntlet of Antonov and Tupolev fuselages abandoned along the greenways.

Ga parked near the hangar where he and Dr. Song had been debriefed after his return from Texas. He left the keys in the ignition. The girl carried her mother's dresses, while the boy led the dog by its rope. Sun Moon took her *guitar*, and Commander Ga carried the *guitar* case. He could see in the late morning sun several crows idling in the distance.

The Dear Leader was conferring with Commander Park as they approached.

At the sight of Sun Moon, the Dear Leader gestured for her to raise her arms so he could behold the dress. Nearing him, she spun once, flaring the shimmering white hem of her *chima*. Then she bowed. The Dear Leader took her hand and kissed it. He produced two silver keys and swept his hand to indicate Sun Moon's changing station, a miniature replica of the Pohyon Temple, with its red columns and its swaying, scrolled eaves.

Though no bigger than a travel-document control booth, it was exquisite in every detail. The Dear Leader handed her one key, then pocketed the other. He said something to Sun Moon that Ga couldn't hear, and Sun Moon laughed for the first time that day.

The Dear Leader then noticed Commander Ga.

"And here is the taekwondo champion of Korea!" the Dear Leader announced.

A cheer went up from the crowd, making Brando's tail wag.

Commander Park added, "And he brings with him the most vicious dog known."

When the Dear Leader laughed, everyone laughed.

If the Dear Leader was furious, Ga thought, this was how he showed it.

The jet lumbered toward them, slowly negotiating access strips designed for much smaller aircraft. The Dear Leader turned to Commander Ga, so they could speak in relative privacy.

"It's not every day that the Americans visit," he said.

"I have a feeling today will be quite rare," Ga responded.

"Indeed," the Dear Leader said, "I have a feeling that after this, everything will be different, for all of us. I love those opportunities, don't you? New beginnings, a fresh start." The Dear Leader regarded Ga with a look of wonder. "You never did tell me, there's one thing I've always been curious about—just how did you get out of that prison?"

Ga thought about reminding the Dear Leader that they lived in a land where people had been trained to accept any reality presented to them. He considered sharing how there was only one penalty, the ultimate one, for questioning reality, how a citizen could fall into great jeopardy for simply noticing that realities had changed. Even a warden wouldn't risk that.

But Ga said, "I put on the Commander's uniform and spoke as the Commander spoke. The Warden carried on his shoulders a heavy stone. That's what he was concerned with, getting permission to set it down."

"Yes, but how did you force him to do what you wanted, to turn the key in the lock and open the prison gates? You had no power over him. He knew you were the lowliest of prisoners, a nameless nobody. Yet you got him to set you free."

Commander Ga shrugged. "I think the Warden looked into my eyes and saw that I'd just gotten the better of the most dangerous man alive."

The Dear Leader laughed. "Now I know you're lying," he said. "Because that man is me."

Ga laughed, too. "Indeed."

The tremendous aircraft taxied near the terminal. Drawing closer, however, its engines simmered and the plane came to a halt. The crowd stared up at the dark cockpit windows, waiting for the pilot to advance toward two airport workers who were beckoning it with orange batons. Instead, the craft ramped its starboard engines and, pivoting, turned back toward the runway.

"Are they leaving?" Sun Moon asked.

"The Americans are insufferable," the Dear Leader said. "Is there no trick too petty? Is nothing beneath them?"

The jet taxied all the way back to the runway, turned to position itself for takeoff, then shut down its engines. Slowly the great nose of the beast opened and a hydraulic cargo ramp lowered.

The plane was nearly a kilometer away. Commander Park began berating the assembled citizens, to get them moving. In the sun, the scar tissue on his face shined translucent pink. Scores of children began rolling their barrels toward the runway, while masses of beleaguered citizens fell in behind. Ghosting among the people was a small fleet of forklifts and the Dear Leader's personal car. Left behind were the bands, the barbecue pits, and the exhibition of DPRK farm equipment. Commander Ga saw Comrade Buc on his yellow forklift try to move the temple where Sun Moon was to change, but it proved too unwieldy to raise. But there was no looking backward with Commander Park bringing up the rear.

"Can nothing inspire the Americans?" the Dear Leader asked as they shuffled along. "Uplift, I tell you, is unknown to them." He indicated the terminal. "Look at the grand edifice of Kim Il Sung, supreme patriot, founder of this nation, my father. Look at the crimson-and-gold mosaic of Juche flame—does it not seem truly ablaze in the morning light? And yet the Americans—where do they park? Near the stewardesses' outhouse and the pond where the planes dump their waste."

Sun Moon began to perspire. She and Ga exchanged a glance.

"Will the American girl be joining us?" Ga asked the Dear Leader.

"Interesting you should bring her up," the Dear Leader said. "It's fortunate that I find myself in the company of the most Korean couple in the land, the champion of our national martial art and his wife, the actress of an entire people. May I seek your opinion on a matter?"

"We are all yours," Ga said.

"Recently," the Dear Leader said, "I have discovered there is an operation by which a Korean eye can be made to look Western."

"For what purpose?" Sun Moon asked.

"Yes, for what purpose," the Dear Leader echoed. "Unknown, but the operation exists, I've been assured of it."

Ga felt this conversation veering into a territory where wrong moves could unknowingly be made. "Ah, the miracles of modern medicine," he said in a general way. "Too bad they should be applied for cosmetic purposes when so many are born lame and cleft in South Korea."

"Well spoken," the Dear Leader said. "Still, these medical advances might have a social application. This very dawn, I assembled the surgeons of Pyongyang and posed to them the question of whether a Western eye could be turned Korean."

"And the answer?" Sun Moon asked.

"Unanimous," the Dear Leader said. "Through a series of procedures, any woman could be made Korean. *Head to toe,* they said. When the doctors were done, she would be as Korean as the handmaids in King Tangun's tomb." He addressed Sun Moon as they walked. "Tell me," he said. "Do you think this woman, this new Korean—would she be considered a virgin?"

Ga began to speak, but Sun Moon cut him off. "A woman, by the love of the right man, can be made more pure than the womb that produced her," she answered.

The Dear Leader regarded her. "I can always count on you for the thoughtful response," he said. "But seriously, if the procedures were successful, if she was restored, through and through, would you use the term "modest" to describe her? Could you call her *Korean?*"

Sun Moon didn't hesitate. "Absolutely not," she said. "This woman would be nothing but an imposter. 'Korean,' this is a word written in blood on the walls of the heart. No American could ever use it. So she has paddled her little boat, so some sun has beat down on her. Have the people she loved faced death so that she might live? Is sorrow the only thing that connects her to all who came before? Has her nation been occupied by Mongolian, Chinese, and Japanese oppressors for ten thousand years?"

"Spoken as only a true Korean could," the Dear Leader responded. "But you have such venom for this word 'imposter.' It's so ugly when you say it." He turned to Ga. "Tell me, Commander, what is your opinion of imposters? Do you think that, over time, a replacement could become the real thing?"

"The substitute becomes genuine," Ga said, "when you declare it so."

The Dear Leader raised his eyebrows at the truth of this.

Sun Moon shot her husband a vicious look. "No," she said, then turned to the Dear Leader. "No one can have feelings for an imposter. An imposter will always be a lesser thing, it will always leave the heart hungry."

People emerged from the bow of the aircraft. Ga saw the Senator, as well as Tommy and Wanda and a few others, all accompanied by a contingent of security personnel in blue suits. Right away, they were assaulted by flies from the lavatory lagoon.

Petulance crossed the Dear Leader's face. To Sun Moon, he said, "And yet last night you pleaded for the safety of this man—an orphan, a kidnapper, a tunnel assassin."

Sun Moon turned and stared at Commander Ga.

The Dear Leader took her attention back with his voice. "Last night, I had a roster of gifts and delights prepared for you, I canceled an opera for you, and you thanked me by begging on his behalf? No, do not pretend a dislike of imposters."

The Dear Leader looked away from her, and Sun Moon followed his face, desperate to get him to lock eyes with her. "It is you who made him my husband," she said. "It is because of you that I treat him so." When he finally looked at her, she said, "And it is you who can unmake it."

"No, I never gave you away. You were taken from me," the Dear Leader said. "In my own opera house, Commander Ga refused to bow. Then he named you as his prize. In front of everyone, he called your name."

"That was years ago," Sun Moon said.

"He called for you and you answered, you stood and you went with him."

Sun Moon said, "The man you speak of is dead now. He's gone."

"And yet you don't return to me."

The Dear Leader stared at Sun Moon to let that sink in.

"Why do we play these games?" she asked. "I'm right here, the only breath-drawing woman on earth worthy of you. You know that. You make my story a happy one. You were there at the start of it. And you are the end of it."

The Dear Leader turned to her, ready to listen more, doubt still in his eyes.

"And of the Girl Rower?" he asked. "What do you propose for her?"

"Hand me a knife," Sun Moon said. "And let me prove my loyalty."

The Dear Leader's eyes went wide with delight.

"Withdraw your fangs, my mountain tiger!" he declared. He stared into her eyes. More quietly, he said, "My beautiful mountain tiger." Then he turned to Commander Ga. "That's quite a wife you have," he said. "Outside, peaceful as the snows of Mount Paektu. Inside, she's coiled like a rock mamushi, sensing the imperial heel."

The Senator with his entourage presented himself. Bowing slightly to the Dear Leader, he said, "Mr. General Secretary of the Central Committee of the Workers' Party of Korea."

The Dear Leader responded in kind: "The Honorable Senator of the democratic state of Texas."

Here, Commander Park came forward, shuttling several young gymnasts before him. Each child carried a tray bearing a glass of water.

"Come, it is a warm day," the Dear Leader said. "You must refresh yourselves. Nothing invigorates like the restorative waters of the sweet Taedong."

"The most medicinal river in the world," Park said.

One of the children raised a glass to the Senator, who had been staring at the sight of Commander Park, at the way the sweat beaded on his face, then ran diagonally along the ridges of his scars. The Senator took the glass. The water had a cloudy, jade tint.

"I'm sorry for the location," the Senator said, taking a tiny sip before returning the glass. "The pilot feared the plane was too heavy for the tarmac near the terminal. Apologies, too, for circling so long. We kept calling the control tower for landing instructions, but we couldn't raise them on the radio."

"Early, late, here, there," the Dear Leader said. "These words have no meaning among friends."

Commander Ga translated for the Dear Leader, adding his own words at the end: "Were Dr. Song here, he would remind us that it is the American airports that impose control, while all are at liberty to land in North Korea. He would ask if that wasn't the more democratic transportation system."

The Senator smiled at this. "If it isn't our old acquaintance Commander Ga, Minister of Prison Mines, master of taekwondo."

A wry smile crossed the Dear Leader's face.

To Ga, he said, "You and the Americans look like old friends."

"Tell me," Wanda said. "Where is our friend Dr. Song?"

Ga turned to the Dear Leader. "They ask after Dr. Song."

In broken English, the Dear Leader said, "*Song-ssi have become no longer.*"

The Americans nodded with respect that the Dear Leader would respond personally with the sad news and that he would do so in the language of his guests. The Senator and the Dear Leader began speaking quickly of national relations and the importance of diplomacy and bright futures, and it was difficult for Ga to translate fast enough. He could see Wanda staring at Sun Moon, at her perfect skin in a perfectly white *choson-ot*, the *jeogori* of which was so fine it seemed to glow from within, all while Wanda herself wore the woolen suit of a man.

When all were smiles, Tommy intervened and addressed the Dear Leader in Korean. "From the people of the United States," he said, "we offer a gift—a pen of peace."

The Senator presented the pen to the Dear Leader, adding his hopes that a lasting accord would soon be signed with it. The Dear Leader accepted the pen with great fanfare, then clapped his hands for Commander Park.

"We offer a gift as well," the Dear Leader said.

"We, too, have a gift of peace," Ga translated.

Commander Park advanced with a pair of rhinoceros-horn bookends, and Ga understood that the Dear Leader wasn't here to toy with the Americans today. He meant to inflict pain.

Tommy advanced to intercept the gift while the Senator himself pretended not to see it.

"Perhaps," the Senator said, "it is time to discuss the matter at hand."

"Nonsense," the Dear Leader said. "Come, let us rejuvenate our relations over music and food. Many surprises lie ahead."

"We're here for Allison Jensen," the Senator said.

The Dear Leader bristled at the name. "You've been flying for sixteen hours. A lifting of the spirits is in order. What person has too little time for children's accordions?"

"We met with Allison's parents before we left," Tommy said in Korean. "They're quite worried for her. Before we proceed, we'll need assurances, we'll need to speak to our citizen."

"Your citizen?" the Dear Leader snapped. "First you will return what was stolen from me. Then we will discuss the girl."

Tommy translated. The Senator shook his head no.

"Our nation rescued her from certain death in our waters," the Dear Leader said. "Your nation trespassed into our waters, illegally boarded our ship, and stole from me. I get back what you thieved before you get back what I saved." He waved his hand. "Now for entertainment."

A troupe of child accordion stars raced forward, and with expert precision, began playing "Our Father Is the Marshal." Their smiles were uniform, and the crowd knew the moments to clap and shout "Eternal is the Marshal's flame."

Sun Moon, her own children behind her, was glued to the little accordionists, all working in perfect unison, their whole being contorted to project glee. Silently, she began to weep.

The Dear Leader took note of her tears, and the fact that she was once again vulnerable. He signaled to Commander Ga that it was time to prepare for Sun Moon's song.

Ga led her past the crowds to the edge of the runway, where there was nothing but grass, strewn with rusted airplane parts, all the way to the electric fence that surrounded the airfield.

Slowly, Sun Moon turned, taking in the nothingness around them.

"What have you gotten us into?" she asked. "How are we going to get out of this alive?"

"Calm," he said. "Deep breaths."

"What if he hands me a knife, what if it's some kind of loyalty test?" Then her eyes went wide. "What if I'm given a knife and it's not a test?"

"The Dear Leader's not going to ask you to kill an American, in front of a senator."

"You still don't know him," she said. "I've seen him do things, before my eyes, at parties, to friends, to enemies. It doesn't matter. He can do anything, anything he wants."

"Not today. Today, we're the ones who can do anything."

She laughed a scared, nervous laugh. "It sounds good when you say things like that. I really want to believe them."

"Then why don't you?"

"Did you really do those things?" she asked. "Did you really hurt people, kidnap them?"

Commander Ga smiled. "Hey, I'm the good guy in this story."

She laughed in disbelief. "You're the good guy?"

Ga nodded. "Believe it or not, the hero is me."

And here they saw, nearing them at only a couple of kilometers an hour, Comrade Buc atop a low-belly hoist made for lifting aircraft engines. Suspended from its chains was Sun Moon's changing station.

"I needed a bigger machine," Buc called to them. "We spent all night building this thing. No way I was leaving it behind."

When the temple was dropped, the wood shuddered and groaned, but Sun Moon's silver key turned in the lock. The three of them stepped inside, and Buc showed them how the back wall of the changing station opened on a hinge, like a corral gate, big enough to allow the blades of a forklift to enter.

Sun Moon reached to Comrade Buc. With her fingertips, she touched his face and stared into his eyes. It was her way of saying thanks. Or maybe it was good-bye. Buc held her gaze as long as he could, then turned and ran toward his forklift.

Sun Moon changed before her husband without shame, and while she was tying her *goreum,* she asked him, "You really have no one?" When he didn't answer, she asked, "No father for guidance, no mother to sing to you? No sisters at all?"

He adjusted the tail of her bow.

"Please," he said. "You must perform now. Give the Dear Leader exactly what he wants."

"I can't control what I sing," she said.

Soon, in blue, she was with her husband at the Dear Leader's side. It was the climax of the accordion number, which found the boys stacked on each other's shoulders three high. Ga saw that Kim Jong Il's eyes were lowered, that children's songs—bouncy, boundless of enthusiasm—truly spoke to him. When the song was finished, the Americans made a clapping motion from which no sound came.

"We must have another song," the Dear Leader announced.

"No," the Senator said. "First our citizen."

"My property," the Dear Leader said.

"Assurances," Tommy said.

"Assurances, assurances," the Dear Leader said. He turned to Commander Ga. "Might I borrow your camera?" he asked.

The smile on the Dear Leader's face scared Ga anew. Ga took the camera from his pocket and handed it to the Dear Leader, who moved through the crowd toward his car.

"Where's he going?" Wanda asked. "Is he leaving?"

The Dear Leader climbed into the back of the black Mercedes, but the car didn't move.

Then the phone in Wanda's pocket beeped. When she examined its screen, she shook her head in disbelief. She showed it to the Senator and Tommy. Ga motioned for the little red phone. Wanda handed it to him, and there was a picture of Allison Jensen, the Girl Rower, in the backseat of a car. Ga nodded at Wanda, and right in front of her, slipped the phone in his pocket.

The Dear Leader returned, thanking Ga for the use of his camera. "Assured?" he asked.

The Senator made a signal, and a pair of forklifts backed out of the plane's cargo bay. In tandem, they carried the Japanese background radiation detector housed in a custom crate.

"You know it won't work," the Senator said. "The Japanese built it to discover cosmic radiation, not uranium isotopes."

"All my top scientists would beg to differ," the Dear Leader told him. "In fact, they're unanimous in their opinion."

"One hundred percent," Commander Park said.

The Dear Leader waved his hand. "But let's speak of our shared status as nuclear nations another time. Now let's have some blues."

"But where's the Girl Rower?" Sun Moon asked him. "I must sing the song to her. She's who you told me to write it for."

A cross look appeared on the Dear Leader's face. "Your songs are mine," he told her. "I'm the only one you sing for."

The Dear Leader addressed the Americans. "I've been assured the blues will speak to your collective American conscience," he said. "Blues is how people lament racism and religion and the injustices of capitalism. Blues is for those who know hunger."

"One in six," Commander Park said.

"One in six Americans goes hungry each day," the Dear Leader echoed. "The blues is for violence, too. Commander Park, when did a citizen of Pyongyang last commit a violent crime?"

"Seven years ago," Commander Park said.

"Seven long years," the Dear Leader said. "Yet in America's capital, five thousand black men languish in prison due to violence. Mind you, Senator, your prison system is the envy of the world—state-of-the-art confinement, total surveillance, three million inmates strong! Yet you use it for no social good. The imprisoned citizen in no way motivates the free. And the labor of the condemned does not power the machine of national need."

The Senator cleared his throat. "As Dr. Song would say, *This is most enlightening.*"

"You tire of social theory?" The Dear Leader nodded, as if he'd expected more from his American visitor. "Then I give you Sun Moon."

Sun Moon kneeled down upon the cement runway and placed the *guitar* on its back before her. In the shade of those who closed the circle around her, she stared silently down at her *guitar,* as if awaiting some far-off inspiration.

"Sing," Commander Park whispered. With the toe of his boot, he tapped her in the small of the back. From Sun Moon came a gasp of fear. "Sing," he said.

Brando growled at the end of his rope.

Sun Moon began playing the neck of the *guitar,* fretting with the tips of her fingers and plucking with the quill of an eagle-owl feather. Each note sounded discordant from the next, eerie and alone. Finally, in the plaintive rasp of a *sanjo* nomad, she began to sing of a boy who wandered too far for his parents to find him.

Many citizens leaned in, trying to place the tune.

Sun Moon sang, "A cold wind rose and said, *Come, orphan, sleep in my billowing white sheets.*"

From this line, the citizens began to recognize the song and the fairy tale it came from, yet none sang the response, "No, orphan child, do not let yourself freeze." It was a song taught to all the children in the capital, one designed to make some merriment of all the befuddled orphans who scurried through Pyongyang's streets. Sun Moon sang on, with the crowd clearly unhappy that such a gay song, a children's song, one that was ultimately about finding the fatherly love of the Dear Leader, should be so gleelessly sung.

Sun Moon sang, "Then a mineshaft called to the child, *Come shelter in my depths.*"

In his mind, Ga heard the response, "Avoid the darkness, orphan child. Seek the light."

Sun Moon sang, "Next a ghost whispered, *Let me inside, orphan child, and I'll warm you from within.*"

Fight the fever, orphan child, Ga thought. *Do not die tonight.*

"Sing it properly," Commander Park demanded.

But Sun Moon carried on, singing in her melancholy way of the arrival of the Great Bear, of the Bear's special language, of how he took up the orphan child and with his claws cracked the honeybees' comb. Her voice was edged with the things the song had left out, like the sharpness of those claws, of the stinging swarm of bees. In the sonor of her singing could be heard the insatiability of the Bear, of its unrelenting, omnivorous appetite.

The men in the crowd didn't shout, "Partake of the Great Bear's honey!"

The women didn't chorus, "Share the sweetness of his deeds!"

A shudder of great emotion ran through Commander Ga, but he could not tell why. Was it the song, the singer, that it was sung now and here, or was it the orphan at its center? He knew only that this was her honey, this was what she had to feed him.

By the time the song concluded, the Dear Leader's demeanor had greatly changed. Gone was his breezy surface and his gestures of delight. His eyes had flattened, his cheeks gone slack.

His scientists reported that, after inspecting the radiation detector, they'd found it intact.

He motioned for Park to fetch the Girl Rower.

"Let's get this over with, Senator," the Dear Leader said. "The people of our nation wish to donate some food aid to the hungry citizens of yours. When that's complete, you may repatriate your citizen and fly off to your more important business."

When Ga had translated this, the Senator said, "Agreed."

To Ga, the Dear Leader said only, "Tell your wife to get into red."

If only the Dear Leader still had Dr. Song, Ga thought. Dr. Song, who moved so fluidly in such situations, for whom such scenes became simply ruffles, so easily smoothed over.

Wanda brushed past him, amazement on her face.

"What the fuck was that song about?" she asked.

"Me," he told her, but he was off with the boy and the girl and his wife and his dog.

The Pohyon Temple, when they entered it, seemed worthy of prayer, for inside, Comrade Buc had placed a pallet decked with four empty barrels. "Don't ask anything," Sun Moon told her children as she tore off the barrels' white lids. Commander Ga opened his *guitar* case and from it withdrew Sun Moon's silver dress. "Leave on your own terms," he told her, then he swept the girl up and into a barrel. Opening her palm, he placed into her hand the seeds from last night's melon. The boy was next, and for him, Ga had the whittled trigger sticks, the thread, and the deadweight stone of the bird snare they'd made together.

He stared at the two of them, their heads poking up, forbidden any questions, not that they'd know the right ones to ask, not for a long time, anyway. Ga took a moment to marvel at them, at this rare, pure thing that was coming into being. It was suddenly so clear, everything. There was no such thing as abandonment, there were only people in impossible positions, people who had a best hope, or maybe only a sole hope. When the graver danger awaited, it wasn't abandoning, it was saving. He'd been saved, he now saw. A beauty, his mother, a singer. Because of that, a terrible fate awaited—she hadn't left him behind, she'd saved him from what was ahead. And this pallet, with its four white barrels, he saw it suddenly as the life raft they'd long dreamed of aboard the *Junma*, the thing that meant they wouldn't go down with the ship. They'd once had to let it sail away empty, and here it had made its way back. Here it was for the most essential cargo. He reached out and ruffled the hair of these two confused kids who didn't even know they were being rescued, let alone what from.

When Sun Moon was clad in silver, he spent no time in admiring her. He lifted her high, and once in place, he handed her the laptop.

"This is your letter of transit," he told her.

"Like in our movie," she said, and smiled in disbelief.

"That's right," he told her. "The golden thing that gets you to America."

"Listen to me," she said. "There are four barrels here, one for each of us. I know what's going through your head, but don't be stupid. You heard my song, you saw the look on his face."

"Aren't you coming with us?" the girl asked.

"Hush," Sun Moon told her.

"What about Brando?" the boy asked.

"He's coming," Ga told them. "The Dear Leader's going to give him back to the Senator, saying that his nature is too vicious for the peace-loving citizens of our nation."

The kids didn't smile at this.

"Will we ever see you again?" the girl asked.

"I'm going to see you," Ga said, and handed her the camera. "When you take a picture, it shows up on my phone, here."

"What should we take pictures of?" the boy asked.

"Anything you want to show me," he said. "Whatever makes you smile."

"Enough of this," Sun Moon said. "I did what you asked, I put you in my heart. It's the only thing I know, not to separate, for everyone to stay together, no matter what."

"You're in my heart, too," Ga said, and at the sound of Comrade Buc's forklift, he pounded the lids onto the barrels.

The dog found this development quite distressing. Whimpering, Brando circled the barrels, looking for a way in.

Into the fourth barrel, Commander Ga shook out the remaining contents of the *guitar* case. Photographs fluttered inside, thousands of them, all the lost souls of Prison 33, each with names, dates of entry, dates of death.

Ga swung open the back wall of the temple, then guided Buc in with hand signals.

The color was gone from Buc's face. "Are we really doing this?" he asked.

"Swing wide around the crowd," Ga told him. "Make it look like you're coming from the other direction."

Buc lifted the pallet and shifted into reverse, but he held the forklift there.

"You're going to confess, right?" Buc asked. "The Dear Leader's going to know this is your doing?"

"Trust me, he'll know," Ga said.

When Buc backed into the light, Ga was horrified to see how clear it was that people were in the barrels, at least the outlines of them, like willow worms shifting in their white cocoons.

"I think we forgot air holes," Buc said.

"Just go," Ga told him.

Out on the runway, Ga found the Dear Leader and Commander Park orchestrating teams of children rolling barrels onto forklift pallets. The children's motions were choreographed, but without the music of a band behind them, the pantomime resembled the tractor-assembly robot on display at the Museum of Socialist Progress.

With them was the Girl Rower in her golden dress. She stood silently by Wanda's side, wearing heavy sunglasses behind which her eyes could not be seen. It gave her the effect of looking deeply drugged. Or maybe, Ga thought, that surgery had been done to her eyes.

The Dear Leader came near, and Ga could see that his smile had returned.

"Where is our Sun Moon?" he asked.

"You know her," Ga said. "She must look perfect. She'll fuss until perfection is found."

The Dear Leader nodded at the truth of that. "At least the Americans will soon see her undeniable beauty as she bids farewell to our gruff visitor. Side by side, there will be no question of who is superior. At least I will have that satisfaction."

"When do I return the dog?" Ga asked.

"That, Commander Ga, will be the final insult."

Several forklifts raced past Tommy and the Senator, heading off toward the ramp of the plane. The two took an interest in the strange cargo going by—one barrel glowed the vinalon blue of labor-brigade jumpsuits, while another was the nightmare maroon of barbecue beef. When a forklift went past bearing fertilizer toilets, Tommy asked, "Just what kind of aid is this?"

"What does the American say?" the Dear Leader asked Ga.

Ga said, "They're curious about the variety of aid to be found in our shipment."

The Dear Leader spoke to the Senator. "I assure you, the only items included are ones that might be needed by a nation plagued with social ills. Do you wish an inspection?"

Tommy turned to the Senator. "You wanna inspect a forklift?" he asked.

When the Senator hesitated, the Dear Leader called for Commander Park to stop one of the forklifts. Ga could see Comrade Buc approaching from the far side of the loitering crowds, but luckily, Park hailed a different forklift—yet this driver, terror on his face, pretended not to hear and drove on. Park hailed another one, and again, the driver feigned utter concentration on the path to the airplane. "Dak-Ho," Park yelled after him. "I know that's you. I know you heard me."

The Dear Leader laughed. He called to Park, "Try using some sweet talk."

It was hard to tell the emotion on Commander Park's face, but when he hailed Comrade Buc, it was with authority, and Ga knew that Buc was the man who would stop.

Not ten meters away, pallet hoisted high, Comrade Buc halted his forklift, and it would be clear to anyone who bothered to look upward that human shapes shifted inside.

Commander Ga moved to the Senator, clapping a hand stiff on his back.

The Senator gave him a hard look.

Ga pointed at Buc's forklift. "This will be an excellent batch of aid to examine, no?" he asked the Senator. "Much better than the contents of that forklift over there, yes?"

It took the Senator a moment to process this. He pointed to the other forklift and asked the Dear Leader, "Is there some reason you don't want us to inspect that one?"

The Dear Leader smiled. "Examine any one you like."

As people began moving toward the forklift the Senator had selected, Brando lifted his nose in the air, and tail wagging, started barking at Comrade Buc's forklift.

"Never mind," Ga called to Comrade Buc. "We don't need you anymore."

Commander Park cocked his head at the barking dog.

"No, hold on," Park called to Buc, who stared away in an effort not to be recognized.

Park kneeled down beside the dog and studied it. To Ga, he said, "These animals are supposedly good at detecting things. It's said their noses have great strength." He studied the dog's posture, then Park looked between the dog's ears and down the length of its nose, where he saw, as if in a gun sight, the barrels on Buc's forklift. "Hmm," Commander Park said.

"Commander Park, get over here," the Dear Leader called. "You're going to love this."

Park took another moment to contemplate the situation, then called to Buc, "Don't you go anywhere."

The Dear Leader called again. He was laughing.

"Come on, Park," he said. "We have need of a skill only you can provide."

Park and Ga walked toward the Dear Leader, Brando bounding at the end of his leash in the other direction.

"They say that canines are particularly vicious animals," Park said. "What do you think?"

Ga answered, "I think they're only as dangerous as their owners."

They approached the forklift where the Dear Leader stood with the Senator and Tommy, Wanda and the Girl Rower now joining them. On the forklift's pallet were two barrels and a stack of boxes, shrink-wrapped.

"How can I be of service?" Park asked.

"This is perfect," the Dear Leader laughed. "This is too good to be true. It seems we have a box that needs to be opened."

Commander Park pulled a box cutter from his pocket.

"What's so funny?" Tommy asked.

Commander Park ran his razor down the box's seam.

Park said, "Because I've never actually used this thing on a box before."

The Dear Leader laughed all over again.

Inside the box were bound volumes of the complete works of Kim Jong Il.

The Dear Leader grabbed one, bent its spine open, then breathed deeply of the ink inside.

The Girl Rower removed her sunglasses, her eyes looking deeply sedated. Squinting, she regarded the books, and it was with sudden horror that she recognized them. "No," she said, looking as if she might be sick.

Tommy pulled the lid off a barrel and scooped up a handful of rice.

"This is short grain," Tommy said. "Isn't it Japan that grows short-grain rice, while Korea grows long?"

Wanda adopted Dr. Song's voice. "North Korean grains are the tallest-statured grains in the world."

The Dear Leader could tell from her tone that an insult was being done, but he didn't know what kind. "Just where is Sun Moon?" he asked Ga. "Go see what could be taking her so long."

To buy some time, Ga spoke to the Senator. "Did Dr. Song not promise you in Texas that if you ever visited our great nation, the Dear Leader would inscribe his work to you?"

The Senator smiled. "This might be an opportunity to test out that pen of peace."

"I've never signed one of my books before," the Dear Leader said, both flattered and suspicious. "I suppose this is a special occasion."

"And Wanda," Ga said. "You wanted one for your father, yes? And Tommy, weren't you clamoring for a signed copy?"

"I thought I'd never get the honor," Tommy said.

Commander Park turned toward Comrade Buc's forklift.

Brando was lunging on his rope.

"Commander Park," Ga called. "Come with me, let's make sure everything's okay with Sun Moon."

Park didn't look back. "In a minute," he said as he neared the forklift.

Commander Ga saw how Buc's hands were fear-gripped on the wheel, how the figures in those barrels were turning in the heat and worn-out air. Ga got low beside Brando. He slipped the rope from the dog's neck and held him by a fold of skin.

"But Commander Park," Ga said.

Park paused and looked back.

Commander Ga said to him, "Hunt."

"Hunt?" Park asked.

But it was too late, the dog was already upon him, seizing an arm in its jaws.

The Senator turned in horror to see one of his prized Catahoula dogs tearing through the tendons of a man's forearm. The Senator then passed an appraising gaze upon his hosts, the look of dark discovery on his face suggesting that he now understood there was nothing that North Korea wouldn't eventually make maniacal and vicious.

The Girl Rower screamed, and at the sight of Commander Park slashing the dog, at the great gouts of dog blood that began to fly, she ran hysterically toward the plane. Arms pumping, her drugged athlete's body, dormant underground an entire year, answered the call.

Soon, the dog's pelt was black with blood. When Commander Park slashed again, the dog shifted its bite to Park's ankle, where you could tell the teeth had gotten to bone.

"Shoot it," Park shouted. "Shoot the damn thing."

MPSS agents in the crowd drew their Tokarev pistols. That's when citizens began running in all directions. Comrade Buc sped away, weaving through the U.S. security agents who were racing to secure the Senator and his delegation.

The Dear Leader stood alone, confused. He'd been halfway through a long book inscription. Even though he stared at the bloody spectacle, he seemed not to recognize an event that occurred without his authorization.

"What is it, Ga?" the Dear Leader asked. "What's happening?"

"It's an episode of violence, sir," Ga told him.

The Dear Leader dropped the peace pen. "Sun Moon," he said. He turned to look at the pavilion, then dug the silver key from his pocket. He began trotting as fast as he could toward it, tummy bouncing inside his gray jumpsuit. Several of Commander Park's men followed behind, and Ga fell in with them.

Behind them a protracted attack, now gone to the ground, a dog that wouldn't relinquish.

At the changing station, the Dear Leader paused, uncertain, as if he had approached the real Temple of Pohyon, bastion against the Japanese during the Imjin Wars, home of the great warrior monk Sosan, resting place of the Annals of the Yi Dynasty.

"Sun Moon," he called. He knocked on the door. "Sun Moon."

He slid his key into the lock, seeming not to hear pistol shots behind him and a dog's final death howl. Inside, the little room was empty. Hanging from the wall were three *choson-ots*—white and blue and red. On the floor was her *guitar* case. The Dear Leader bent to open it. Inside was a *guitar*. He thumbed a string.

The Dear Leader turned to Ga. "Where is she?" he asked. "Where did she go?"

Ga said, "And what about her children?"

"That's right," he said. "Her children are also missing. But where could she be with none of her clothes?"

The Dear Leader touched all three dresses, as if verifying that they were genuine. Then he sniffed a sleeve. "Yes," he said. "These are hers." On the cement, he noticed something. When he picked it up, he saw it was two photographs, clipped back to back. The first showed a young man, dark uncertainty on his face. When the Dear Leader flipped to the other picture, he saw a broken human figure on the ground, dusted over with dirt, mouth open and spilling with dirt.

The Dear Leader recoiled, tossing the pictures aside.

He stepped outside, where you could hear the jet's engines ramping, its hydraulic cargo bay closing. The Dear Leader looked once around the building. Inexplicably, he glanced upward to the clouds.

"But her clothes are here," he said. "Her red dress is right here."

Comrade Buc arrived and dismounted his forklift. "I heard gunfire," he said.

"Sun Moon's missing," Ga informed him.

"But that's impossible," Buc said. "Where could she be?"

The Dear Leader turned to Ga. "She didn't say anything, did she, about going someplace?"

"She said nothing, nothing at all," Ga said.

Commander Park joined them. He was limping. "That dog," he said and took a big breath. He'd lost a lot of blood.

The Dear Leader said, "Sun Moon's missing."

Park leaned over, breathing heavily. He placed his good hand on his good knee. "Detain all the citizens," he told his men. "Confirm their IDs. Canvass the grounds, sweep all the abandoned aircraft, and get someone dredging that shit pond."

The American jet began to accelerate down the runway, the noise of its engines making it impossible to be heard. For a minute, they stood there, waiting until they could speak. By the time the plane had lifted and begun to bank, Park had figured things out.

"Let me go get you a bandage," Buc said to Commander Park.

"No," Park said, looking at the ground. "No one's going anywhere." To the Dear Leader, he said, "We must assume that Commander Ga had a hand in this."

"Commander Ga?" the Dear Leader asked. He pointed. "Him?"

"He was friends with the Americans," Park said. "Now the Americans are gone. And Sun Moon is gone."

The Dear Leader looked up in an effort to locate the American plane, his eyes slowly panning the sky for it. Then he turned to Ga. On the Dear

Leader's face was a look of disbelief. His eyes roamed over all the options, all the impossible things that might have happened to Sun Moon. For a moment, the Dear Leader's gaze went completely blank, and Ga knew the expression well. This was the face that Ga had shown the world, that of a boy who had swallowed the things that had happened to him, but who wouldn't understand what they meant for a long, long time.

"Is this true?" the Dear Leader asked. "Out with the truth."

They were in the quiet now, where the sound of the plane used to be.

"Now you know something about me," Ga told the Dear Leader. "I've given you a piece of me, and now you know who I really am. And I know something of you."

"What are you talking about?" the Dear Leader asked. "Tell me where Sun Moon is."

"I've taken the ultimate from you," Ga told him. "I've pulled the thread that will unravel you."

Commander Park stood upright, looking only partly renewed. He lifted his bloody box cutter.

With a finger, the Dear Leader halted him.

"You must speak the truth to me, son," the Dear Leader told Ga in a voice that was slow and stern. "Did you do something with her?"

"I've given you the scar that's on my heart," Ga told him. "I will never see Sun Moon again. And neither will you. From now on, we'll be like brothers that way."

Commander Park gave a signal, and two of his men took hold of Ga, their thumbs sinking deep into his biceps.

"My boys in Division 42 will get this straightened out," Park told the Dear Leader. "Can I give him to the Pubyok?"

But the Dear Leader didn't answer. He turned to look again at the changing station, at the simple little temple with the dresses inside.

Commander Park took charge. "Take Ga to the Pubyok," he told his men. "And you might as well grab the other drivers, too."

"Wait," Ga said. "Buc didn't have anything to do with this."

"That's right," Comrade Buc said. "I didn't do anything."

"Sorry," Commander Park told Buc. "But the amount of pain that will come of this, it'll be too much for a single man to bear. Even when we spread it around to the rest of you, it might be too much."

"Dear Leader," Buc said. "It's me, your closest comrade. Who gets your cognac from France and your sea urchin from Hokkaido? Who has pro-cured for you every brand of cigarette in the world? I'm loyal. I have a family." Here Buc stepped close. "I don't defect," he said. "I never defected."

But the Dear Leader wasn't listening. He stared instead at Com-mander Ga.

"I don't understand who you are," the Dear Leader said to him. "You killed my nemesis. You escaped Prison 33. You could have gotten away for good. But you came here. What kind of person would do that? Who would make their way to me, who would throw away his own life, just to spoil mine?"

Ga looked up to the jet trail overhead and followed it toward the hori-zon. A wave of satisfaction ran through him. A day wasn't just a match you struck after all the others had gone out. In a day, Sun Moon would be in America. Tomorrow would find her in a place where she could perform a song she'd waited a lifetime to sing. From now on, it would no longer be about survival and endurance. And this new day, they were embarking on it together.

Returning the Dear Leader's gaze, Ga felt no fear looking into the eyes of the man who would get the last word. In fact, Ga was oddly carefree. *I'd have felt this my whole life,* Ga thought, *if you had never existed.* Ga felt his own sense of purpose, he was under his own command now. What a strange, new feeling it was. Perhaps this was what Wanda had in mind when she stood before that expanse of Texas sky and asked if he felt free. It could be *felt,* he now knew. His fingers were buzzing with it, it rattled his breathing, it allowed him to suddenly see all the lives he might have lived, and that feeling didn't go away when Commander Park's men knocked him to the ground and dragged him by his heels toward a waiting crow.

CITIZENS, gather 'round your loudspeakers! It is time for the final installment of this year's Best North Korean Story, though it might as well be titled the Greatest North Korean Story of All Time! Still, in this last episode, ugliness makes its inevitable appearance, citizens, so we recommend you not listen alone. Seek the comfort of fellow factory workers. Embrace the stranger in your subway car. We also suggest you protect our youngest comrades from today's content, as they are unaware of the existence of human injustice. Yes, today the Americans let loose the hounds. So sweep sawdust from the mill-house floors, gather cotton from the machine-loom motors—use anything you can find to pack the tender ears of the innocent.

At last, the moment had arrived to return the poor American Rower Girl, rescued from dangerous seas by our brave fishing fleet. You remember well the American's pitiful appearance before Sun Moon beautified her. This day the Girl Rower wore her hair braided long by Sun Moon herself. True, no *choson-ot,* however golden, could hide those slouching shoulders and ungainly breasts, but the Girl Rower at least looked more fit since her diet had been balanced by healthy portions of flavorful and nutritious sorghum. And after the Dear Leader delivered her a stiff lecture on chastity, she appeared instantly more womanly, her face sobered, her posture erect.

Still, her departure was a sad one, as she was returning to America and a life of illiteracy, canines, and multicolored condoms. At least she had her notebooks, copied full of the Dear Leader's wisdoms and witticisms, to show her the way. And we must admit: she belonged with her people, even in a land where nothing is free—not seaweed, not suntanning, not even a basic blood transfusion.

Imagine the fanfare with which our Most Reverend General Kim Jong

Il received the Americans who flew to Pyongyang to retrieve their young Rower Girl. In the spirit of good cooperation, the Dear Leader was willing to set aside for a day memories of the American napalming of Pyongyang, the American bombing of the Haesang Dam, the American machine-gunning of civilians at No Gun Ri. For the good of mutual friendship, the Dear Leader decided not to bring up what American collaborators did at the Daejeon Prison or during the Jeju uprising, let alone the atrocities at Ganghwa and Dae Won Valley. He wasn't even going to mention the Bodo League Massacre or the press-ganging of our prisoners at the Pusan Perimeter.

No, better to set the past aside and think only of dancing boys, animated accordion play, and the joys of generosity, for this day was about more than the vim of good-natured cultural exchange: the Dear Leader's agenda included a humanitarian mission of delivering food aid to the one in six Americans who goes hungry each day.

At first, the visiting Americans pretended to be pleasant enough, but they sure did bring along a lot of dogs! Remember that in America, canines get regular lessons in obedience, while the people, regular citizens like you and your neighbor, receive none. Should it be a surprise then that after the Americans had what they wanted—the return of their homely compatriot, and enough food to feed their poor—they showed their appreciation through cowardly aggression?

Yes, citizens, it was a sneak attack!

At the uttering of a coded word, the dogs all bared their teeth and set upon their Korean hosts. Then hot lead began blazing from American pistols toward their noble Korean counterparts. And that's when a team of American commandos grabbed Sun Moon, and roughly handling her, dragged her toward their Yankee jet plane! Did the Americans elaborately plan to steal the greatest actress in the world from our humble nation? Or did the sudden sight of her, transcendently beautiful in a red *choson-ot*, compel them to take her on the spot? But where was Comrade Buc? the astute citizen must be asking. Wasn't Comrade Buc near Sun Moon's side to defend her? The answer, citizens, is that Buc is no longer your comrade. He never was.

Steel yourselves for what happens next, citizens, and do not self-combust from your need of vengeance. Channel your outrage into effort, citizens, by doubling your output quotas! Let the fire of your anger stoke the furnaces of productivity!

When the Americans seized our national actress, the despicable Buc, fearing for his own safety, simply handed her over. Then he turned and ran.

"Shoot me," Sun Moon shouted as she was hauled away. "Shoot me now, comrades, for I do not wish to live without the benevolent guidance of the greatest of all leaders, Kim Jong Il."

Marshaling his military training, the Dear Leader sprinted into action, chasing the cowards who had stolen our national treasure. Into the onslaught of gunfire, the Dear Leader ran. Dove after dove flew into the path of the bullets, each bursting with the downy glow of patriotic sacrifice!

And here we have the coward Commander Ga—imposter, orphan, practitioner of poor citizenship—standing idly by. But witnessing the Dear Leader fend off dogs and dodge bullets, a spirit rose in this simple man, a revolutionary zeal he had never quite known. By viewing firsthand an act of supreme bravery, Ga, the lowest member of society, was moved to similarly serve the highest of socialist ideals.

When an American GI shouted "Free adoptions!" and scooped up an armload of young gymnasts, Commander Ga sprang into action. Despite lacking the Dear Leader's powers of dog defense, he did know taekwondo. "*Charyeot!*" he yelled to the Americans. That got their attention. "*Junbi,*" he then said. "*Sijak!*" he shouted. That's when the kicks and punches began. Fists flying, he raced after the retreating Americans, fighting his way through jet wash, copper-jacket bullets, and ivory incisors to the accelerating aircraft.

Though the jet's engines screamed with takeoff power, Commander Ga summoned his Korean fortitude, and using Juche strength, he chased the plane down and leaped up to its wing. As the jet rose from the runway, rising over Pyongyang, Ga pulled himself up and fought the harsh winds to the windows, where through the glass, he saw the Girl Rower laugh as the Americans in celebration blared South Korean pop music and, garment by garment, stripped Sun Moon of her modesty.

Dipping his finger in a bloody wound, Commander Ga wrote inspirational slogans on the plane's windows, and to give Sun Moon some measure of resolve, he wrote in red, backward, a reminder of the Dear Leader's eternal love for her, nay, of his love for every citizen of the Democratic People's Republic of Korea! Through the windows, the Americans made angry gestures at Commander Ga, but none had the guts to climb out on the wing and fight him like a man. Instead, they accelerated the plane to astounding speeds, executing emergency maneuvers and aerial acrobatics to shake loose their tenacious guest, but no barrel roll was going to stop a determined Commander Ga! He dropped low and gripped the wing's leading edge as the plane rose over the blessed mountains of Myo-hyang and over sacred Lake Chon, nestled in the frozen peaks of Mount Paektu, but finally he lost consciousness over the garden city of Chongjin.

Only the powerful reach of North Korean radar allows us to tell the rest of the story.

In the cold, thin air, Commander Ga's frozen fingers kept a firm grip, yet the canines had taken their toll. Our comrade was fading. That's when Sun Moon, hair disheveled, face bruised, came to the window and with the power of her patriotic voice sang to him, repeating verses of "Our Father Is the Marshal" over and over until, at just the right moment in the song, Commander Ga muttered, "Eternal is the Marshal's flame." Wind pulled freezing strings of blood from his lips, but the good Commander roused, repeating "Eternal is the Marshal's flame" as he stood.

Braving the great winds, he made his way to the window, where Sun Moon pointed to the sea below. There, he saw what she saw: an American aircraft carrier aggressively patrolling our sovereign waters. He also saw a chance to finally evade the ghosts of past acts of cowardice. Commander Ga gave Sun Moon a crisp, final salute, then dove off the wing, making a missile of himself as he barreled downward, sailing toward the conning towers of capitalism, where, in the bridge, an American captain was surely plotting the next illegal sneak attack.

Do not imagine Ga falling forever, citizens. Picture Ga in a cloud of white. See him in a perfect light, glowing like an icy mountain flower. Yes, picture a flower towering white, so tall that it reaches down to pick you. Yes, here is Commander Ga, picked in his prime and lifted high. And there emerge—all is shining, all is bright—the clasping arms of Kim Il Sung himself.

When one Glorious Leader hands you to the next, citizens, you truly live forever. This is how an average man becomes a hero, a martyr, an inspiration to all. So do not weep, citizens, for look: a bronze bust of Commander Ga is already being placed in the Revolutionary Martyrs' Cemetery! Dry your eyes, comrades, for generations of orphans to come will now be blessed with the name of both a hero and a martyr. Forever, Commander Ga Chol Chun. In this way, you'll live forever.

ACKNOWLEDGMENTS

Support for this book was provided by the National Endowment for the Arts, the Whiting Foundation, and the Stanford Creative Writing Program. Portions of this book first appeared in the following publications: *Barcelona Review, Electric Literature, Faultline, Fourteen Hills Review, Granta, Hayden's Ferry Review, Playboy, Southern Indiana Review, Yalobusha Review,* and *ZYZZYVA.* The author is also indebted to the UCSF Kalmanovitz Medical Library, where much of this book was written.

Thanks to my traveling companions in North Korea: Dr. Patrick Xiaoping Wang, Willard Chi, and the esteemed Dr. Joseph Man-Kyung Ha. Kyungmi Chun, Stanford's Korean Studies Librarian, proved especially helpful, as was Cheryl McGrath of Harvard's Widener Library. The support of the Stanford writing faculty has been invaluable to me, particularly Eavan Boland, Elizabeth Tallent, and Tobias Wolff. I'm grateful for Scott Hutchins, Ed Schwarzschild, Todd Pierce, Skip Horack, and Neil Connelly, all of whom read versions of this book and responded with sage advice.

This novel could have no finer editor and champion than David Ebershoff. Warren Frazier, as always, is the prince of literary agents. Special thanks go to Phil Knight, who made a student of his teacher. Special thanks also to Dr. Patricia Johnson, Dr. James Harrell, and the Honorable Gayle Harrell. My wife lends my work inspiration and my children its purpose, so thank you Stephanie, and thank you Jupiter, James Geronimo, and Justice Everlasting.

ABOUT THE AUTHOR

ADAM JOHNSON teaches creative writing at Stanford University. His fiction has appeared in *Esquire, The Paris Review, Harper's, Tin House, Granta,* and *Playboy,* as well as in *The Best American Short Stories.* His other works include *Emporium,* a short-story collection, and the novel *Parasites Like Us.* He lives in San Francisco.

ABOUT THE TYPE

This book was set in Minion, a 1990 Adobe Originals typeface by Robert Slimbach. Minion is inspired by classical, old-style typefaces of the late Renaissance, a period of elegant, beautiful, and highly readable type designs. Created primarily for text setting, Minion combines the aesthetic and functional qualities that make text type highly readable with the versatility of digital technology.